W9-CUQ-378

LEGALLY DEAD

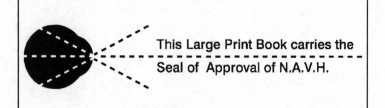

This Large Print Book carries the
Seal of Approval of N.A.V.H.

LEGALLY DEAD

EDNA BUCHANAN

THORNDIKE PRESS

A part of Gale, Cengage Learning

GALE
CENGAGE Learning™

Detroit • New York • San Francisco • New Haven, Conn • Waterville, Maine • London

GALE
CENGAGE Learning™

LIBRARY OF CONGRESS CATALOGING-IN-PUBLICATION DATA

Buchanan, Edna.
  Legally dead / by Edna Buchanan.
    p. cm. — (Thorndike Press large print mystery)
  ISBN-13: 978-1-4104-1065-8 (alk. paper)
  ISBN-10: 1-4104-1065-X (alk. paper)
  1. Witnesses—Protection—Fiction. 2. Miami (Fla.)—Fiction. 3.
Large type books. I. Title.
PS3552.U324L44 2008b
813'.54—dc22   2008032997

Published in 2008 by arrangement with Simon & Schuster, Inc.

Printed in the United States of America
1 2 3 4 5 6 7 12 11 10 09 08

*For the warriors,
the heroes who protect our flag,
our shores, and us, every day*

. . . You know that we live in an important time. It is now time for you to wake up from your sleep. Our salvation is nearer now than when we first believed. The night is almost finished.

— Romans 13:11–12

The world is a world of lies. Raise a cup to the dead already — and hurrah for the next who dies!

— Anonymous

PROLOGUE

She was all he desired but everything forbidden.

Her appeal was lethal. Her spirited steps, her laughter, each reckless toss of her shiny blond hair struck him like bullets to the heart. She had a way about her. And the body type that never failed to excite him.

By daylight she haunted him, materializing like an apparition in the supermarket, at the community center, or walking her dog. As he collected his mail or plucked his paper off the grass, he'd glimpse her face in a passing car. Wherever he went, she was there.

He thought of her the most when he was alone in the dark.

Fate was giving him the finger. That he knew. Led into temptation, he resisted. Why complicate his existence in this community of six thousand souls in neat frame houses with maple and pine trees standing like sentinels along streets that all led to nowhere? A bowling ball rolling down Main Street at 11 p.m. would not strike anyone. If he hungered for a late-night steak or burger he had a choice: stay hungry or learn to cook.

The huge flocks of Canada geese migrating overhead were another frequent frustration. Honking and flying, flying and honking, until all he wanted was to shotgun them out of the goddamn sky. The profound silence when they neither honked nor flew was even worse. He'd wake up alone in the night convinced he'd gone deaf in the dark.

His passion went unrequited, but he and the object of his attention did share rare moments: they nearly collided one Saturday morning as he browsed hangover remedies in an aisle at the Rite Aid Drugstore. Her megawatt smile deepened her killer dimples and crinkled her mischievous blue eyes. She obviously recognized him.

He whistled softly through his teeth as he watched her go. "You know what you just did to me," he whispered.

They always knew.

He fought his basic instincts, kept his profile low, and stuck to the rules — some of them. He had a secret plan about to spin into play. Who could blame him? Bored to distraction, he missed the money, the sex, the power. Nightlife here revolved around a pizza joint that closed early and monthly church suppers at which participants prayed, no doubt to survive the inedibly gummy spaghetti dinner.

Sleepless, he paced his modest middle-class home like a caged and moody lion yearning for his natural habitat, a concrete jungle astir with the wild life and high-risk encounters among the creatures of the night.

During a routine physical his new doctor suggested that he smoke less and exercise more. They won't be satisfied, he thought bitterly, until I am stripped of every comfort and simple pleasure. Nonetheless, he began a regimen of brisk daily walks. Fresh air and exercise would keep him too busy for un-healthy obsessions. But soon her house became a major landmark on his route. She lived on the far side of a small park sur-rounding an imposing stone sculpture, a horseman wielding a raised sword.

He paused to read the plaque at its base. The inscription identified the rider: he was General John Stark, who led the New Hampshire Minutemen to battle in the Revolutionary War and coined the state's motto, Live Free or Die. He studied the horseman's face and his sword, then checked his watch and quickly moved on. His walks were synchronized with her schedule so he could see what she wore — and didn't. How much more smooth, milky skin would she bare as the long, dreary days of winter began to yield to blindingly bright yellow daffodils? Unlike the stone-faced general, she exuded life and energy. He obsessed over the impatient jut of her hip, her merry laughter, and the graceful curve of her neck, exposed when she pinned her glowing hair back. They all fueled his fantasies.

Spontaneous and typically female, she was not always predictable, or inclement weather would intervene. Often he was disappointed, but when she was on her front porch, in the driveway, or her yard, it was worth the wait. Eventually, she began to acknowledge him with a look of recognition, then a smile, and most recently, a friendly wave.

He responded with a neighborly nod, nothing more.

He had been told to make friends. How do you do that in middle age, when all your previous friendships were forged and flourished in childhood? Friends grow up together, cover each other's backs, and build alliances through a lifetime of history shared back in the day.

An outsider here, he was as disoriented as an alien from a distant planet. He and his new neighbors shared nothing in common. Many seemed short on teeth but still spoke in uppity tones. The women appalled him. Where did they grow these heifers? Yet the gaggles of runny-nosed kids who trailed behind them were proof that men actually slept with them. Disgusting. So he kept to himself, kept control, held his demons at bay.

He did wrestle the devil on occasion. He emerged from the exercise room at the community center one sunny afternoon, sweaty and exhausted, and she was there at the pool, hair wet, skin glistening, a thirsty towel draped around her neck. She giggled with a friend, hunched her slim shoulders, and hugged her arms against a chilly breeze. Teeth chattering, she turned away.

He licked his lips and swallowed, close enough to see the gooseflesh rise on the inside of her pale thighs and how the clingy fabric of her wet bikini bottom rode up her crotch.

He positioned his exercise bag in front of him to conceal his excitement, catching his breath at the sight of her daintily extended bare leg as she slid gracefully into the car for the ride home.

The moment was defining. She saw him watching, he thought, and flaunted herself. Deliberately. Tried to turn him on and succeeded. Females are born knowing how to drive a man crazy.

Still, he never would have touched her but destiny intervened. Late one afternoon, as he nodded off in his underwear and socks watching a Yankees game taped over the weekend, the doorbell launched him to his feet, totally awake.

Instinctively, he dove for the small silver-colored automatic pistol concealed beneath a sofa cushion. He pressed his thick back to the wall and released the safety.

There was a growing chill outside the window and the feel of rain in the air. The streetlights were still dark. Cautiously, from behind the curtains, he squinted into the deepening dusk.

When he saw the figure alone in the lengthening shadows, persistently pushing his doorbell, he gasped. Quickly, he scanned the street. Perfect. No traffic in sight. No one watching.

"Hold on! I'll be right there!" He snatched his trousers off the back of a chair.

He zipped up, fingers fumbling as he fastened his belt, afraid she might leave.

He checked the window again before

unlocking the door. Nothing had changed. She still stood there alone. He could scarcely believe his good fortune. What she wore electrified him: a badge, and her crisp, neatly starched uniform. *His wildest fantasy come true!*

He threw the door open and laughed aloud when he saw what had brought her, delivered her, to his door.

She was selling Girl Scout cookies.

CHAPTER ONE

Michael Venturi hit the airport late. His own fault, exacerbated by traffic. The security line stretched across the building, a slow-moving, mind-numbing hell presided over by morons. At last, he sprinted down the concourse to the gate where his flight should have been boarding. It wasn't.

"*De*-layed," chirped the pretty girl behind the counter. She smiled flirtatiously and batted her big blues. Her obvious interest failed to diminish the cloud that hovered over him. Flying was no longer fun. Neither is my job, Venturi thought, or my life.

His head pounded; his fault as well. Not enough sleep and too much to drink. He needed to find hot coffee, which he hoped, with a few aspirins, might provide relief.

At the end of the concourse, he found a Starbucks, picked up some newspapers, and returned to the gate. He sipped the coffee, which was good, as he skimmed the news,

19

which was not: car bombs in Baghdad, celebs in rehab, the globe warming, a new cold war looming, corrupt politicians, crisis in Cuba, same old, same old.

A headline below the fold on page five caught his eye as he searched for sports.

Small Town Mystery
Little Girls Lost

The Flemington, New Hampshire, dateline jumped out at him. He read the first paragraph, blinked, then reread it.

An eight-year-old schoolgirl had vanished from that rural township in broad daylight. Weeks earlier another girl, age nine, had disappeared from the same neighborhood. Last seen selling Girl Scout cookies she, too, remained missing.

Both gone without a trace, despite Amber Alerts, tearful appeals from anguished parents, and intense searches by police and volunteers on foot, on horseback, and in the air. The coffee he'd swallowed rose in his throat.

The PA system kicked in. Pretty girl behind the counter made eye contact, smiling again as she announced that his flight was now ready to board. But he was not. Michael Venturi would not fly today. He snatched up his duffel bag, left his half-empty coffee cup, and retreated.

"Am I responsible?" Venturi wondered. "Is it my fault?" Full of dread, sick at heart, he knew the answer was yes, and that his life had changed forever.

"What the hell you doing here?" Tom Mc-Mullen, the Chief U.S. Marshal for the Southern District of New York, looked startled and checked his watch with an exaggerated gesture. "Shouldn't you be halfway to Chicago?"

Venturi, who had interrupted a meeting, dropped the newspaper onto his boss's desk. "Have you seen this?" He pointed out the New Hampshire story. "Check the dateline. What the hell did we do?"

The chief gave the paper a cursory glance, scowled, and looked up too quickly. "So?" He shrugged. "Heard something about it. Whadaya, jumping to conclusions?"

"We put him there."

"Sure, and it doesn't mean a thing," said Rich Archbold, an assistant U.S. Attorney, from his chair in front of the chief's desk.

April Howard, a deputy U.S. Marshal like Venturi, sat next to Archbold. She nodded repeatedly, like a bobble-headed doll.

That they all knew about the story before

he did agitated Venturi more.

"We were aware of that sick son of a bitch's sexual preference. We knew what his ex-wives confided off the record. I knew it was a mistake, I argued against it, but no," he turned and paced the room, "we did it anyway."

"Gino Salvi's a terrific witness," Archbold said, "and we still need him for Schoenberg, the biggest union corruption case in the history of our office."

"He's a murderer!"

"Those were mob hits on other hoodlums, not children or innocent bystanders," Archbold said, hitching his shoulders and gesturing, palms up, as if to grant Salvi absolution for bad-boy pranks.

"Somebody has to go to New Hampshire," Venturi said, "and get to the bottom of this."

"What are you? Nuts?" Archbold's body language registered alarm. "You'd sabotage the case on a hunch? Schoenberg goes to trial next month."

"Forget the trial." Venturi's voice rose. "Children are missing. I'll go." He looked around. "Who's going with me?"

"Nobody." Chief McMullen's voice dropped ominously. "*Nobody* goes to New Hampshire, especially you. Sit down, Michael. You're getting on my nerves."

Venturi reluctantly took a seat near the others.

"There is no evidence against Salvi," Archbold said. "Only your suspicion. We've worked years to make this case. The trial's a go this time. We're in it to win it!"

"It's no game," Venturi argued. "We can't play with children's lives."

"They could be runaways," April Howard offered, her high-pitched voice thin, her eyes averted. "You know how kids can be."

"They're not teenagers, they're eight and nine."

Even Archbold didn't buy the runaway theory. "If they were stranger abductions," he said quietly, "they're probably dead. Not much we can do."

"We can stop him."

"What *him?*" McMullen demanded plaintively. He raked his thick fingers across his receding crew cut, signaling an impending rant. "Hundreds of perverts are trolling this country for victims as we speak."

"Sex offenders *are* everywhere." April's slim, well-manicured fingers twirled a lock of her shiny dark hair. "Dirty uncles, nasty stepfathers, lecherous grandpas. Happens all the time." She sounded breezy.

Archbold snatched up the newspaper, scowled briefly at the headline, then slapped it back onto the chief's desk in disgust. "Our man isn't dumb enough to pull that in his own backyard."

"We've had no negative feedback on Salvi," Chief McMullen said, "not a word. The man's innocent till proven guilty."

"So let's go up there and prove it. We can polygraph him," Venturi suggested, keeping his voice steady.

They stared in unanimous dismay.

"At least we should give the local cops a heads-up," he continued. "They're beating their brains out searching for the missing girls."

"Not our job!" The chief's face reddened. "It's a local issue. Let the locals solve their problems."

Archbold, the prosecutor, agreed. "We all know the pressure they're under. It's a high-profile case and they've got nothing. They'd pile on our guy like dogs fighting for a bone. If his name surfaces, if he's even routinely interviewed, his credibility is shot, we've lost our star witness, and our case is down the crapper. We can't afford it."

"We can't afford not to," Venturi insisted. "No small-town police department is equipped to solve a thing like this."

"Stay out of it," the boss growled, focusing his venomous stare on Venturi. "Got that? Let them do their jobs. That is a god-damn order!"

He lowered his voice. "You know how small-town police departments work, they leak like sieves. No hick cop can keep a secret. They've got no reason to. They don't care about our case, our reputation. They'd like nothing better than to stick it up our federal asses."

"There is no cause," Archbold said firmly, "to believe our star witness is involved. You sound paranoid, Venturi."

They ganged up on him.

"He's right, Michael," April cooed re-assuringly. "You've been under too much stress. You're not yourself." She crossed her legs, smoothed her pencil-slim suit skirt, leaned forward, and wagged her finger at him. "I always said, you should have taken more time off after the accident. You should see someone. Really." Her tone was conde-scending.

He studied each face — his boss, a federal prosecutor, and a fellow agent, and came to a conclusion that sickened him: not a conscience in the room. Aware the girls were missing, they never mentioned it. Why? Was it the reason for his sudden weeklong assignment in Chicago? Or was he paranoid?

They continued to berate him.

"She's right." The chief shook his head. "We all saw this coming. I urged you to take more time, offered all the compassionate leave you needed. But no, Mr. Macho here came right back to work, to tough it out. It took its toll. Look at you." His face puckered in distaste. "Alcohol has affected your brain, clouded your judgment."

Enough was enough. "What the hell are you talking about?" Venturi said angrily. "My work hasn't suffered. My evaluations are all excellent."

"You know more than anybody how much manpower and hard work we've invested in this case, this witness," Archbold said reasonably. "The office has a lot at stake here."

"It's only fair to give the local cops a clue," Venturi said stubbornly.

The sigh was collective.

The chief's stubby index finger stabbed the air between them. "Don't go there, Venturi. I'm warning you. Stay out of it! Keep your mouth shut. Got that?"

"Yes, sir."

Archbold broke the silence that followed. "You know how local police resent our interference in their investigations," he said ingratiatingly. "Our job is justice, to win a conviction. Derailing us at this point would be unacceptable."

Venturi nodded and got to his feet.

"Forget Chicago," the chief said offhandedly. "I'll send Wolfson instead. Take the week off. Chill out. And quit reading the newspapers!"

Even Ruth Ann, the motherly middle-aged office manager and trusted friend, offered no comfort.

"Take the time off," she whispered persuasively as he removed some personal items from his desk. "Give yourself a break. It will all work out. You'll see."

"I don't see how," he said bleakly.

"Bad things happen everywhere," she said cheerfully. "We've got no shortage of psychos on the loose. He wouldn't be that stupid."

The more they denied the possibility, the more Venturi believed that he and the program had unleashed a monster on unsuspecting, law-abiding, small-town America.

The chief had issued his orders, loud and clear. Venturi had always followed orders like the elite Force Recon U.S. Marine he had been. The first thing a Marine learns is to follow orders. Once a Marine, always a Marine.

He sighed.

His cell rang a short time later as he drove over the Triboro Bridge. Caller ID revealed that they were already checking up on him.

"You okay, hon?" April asked sweetly.

"Sure. Before he changes his mind, tell the chief I'm taking him up on his offer. Driving down the shore to chill."

"Great! Wish I could, too," she said, way too enthusiastically. "Atlantic City?"

In his mind's eye, he saw her thumbs-up to whomever was listening. Are they right? he wondered. *Am* I paranoid?

"Nah," he said casually. "Farther south, maybe Wildwood, Cape May."

"Cool. Have a blast. But stay in touch. You know I worry about you. Once you're back, all rested and relaxed, why not talk things out with a professional? Give it some thought, Michael. Couldn't hurt. Our insurance pays."

He promised to consider it.

"Call me when you get home, hon, and we can do dinner."

"Sounds good," he said, and snapped the phone shut.

He picked up what he'd need from his apartment, swapped his car and his cell phone for loaners from Iggy, his mechanic, who always wore a baseball cap and big shades and spent every weekend with a

28

girlfriend in Cape May. Then he drove northeast and picked up I-95 north.

He'd be in New Hampshire soon enough.

Chapter Two

Venturi punched the button to hear what Iggy had left in his CD player. Chris Rea's ominous *Road to Hell* seemed a fitting soundtrack to his dark and painful thoughts during the more than five-hour drive.

Eventually pastoral fields and shaggy hillsides dotted with spotted cows diminished his anger. Dread and loneliness took its place.

He had been alone for the past few years and missed the Marines, the camaraderie of teamwork with those who shared goals and whose lives were often in each other's hands. His specialized Force Recon unit carried out small, high-risk operations in volatile hot spots all over the globe.

He had joined the U.S. Marshals Service eager to become part of a team again. But the job, by comparison, seemed disappointing, boring, and often absurd.

He and Madison, a fashion writer for a

New York magazine, were newlyweds then. Soon they were expecting a child. Their personal lives were blissfully anticipatory. Her contagious effervescence always buoyed his spirits. He had no time to dwell on his growing doubts about his assignment to the Federal Witness Protection Program, better known as WITSEC. She was a sure cure for the blues. She had a talent for happiness. It went with her to her grave.

After losing Madison and the baby, he focused on his job, saw more problems, asked more questions, and experienced profound doubts. Government lawyers, eager for convictions at any cost, agreed to grant dangerous criminals their freedom and new identities in exchange for testimony against former criminal associates. Many of the deals seemed more risky to others than raids or rescue missions in Somalia, or the Gulf War, or the jungles of Colombia. He suspected that some protected witnesses were more degenerate than the defendants they helped to convict. Many reverted to their former criminal behavior after being relocated.

War was simpler.

The dialogue in his boss's office that morning replayed on an endless loop as the miles swept by and traffic thinned out.

His colleagues had no clue. Work, action was what he needed most, not free time to think, to relive his loss. He needed to keep his mind and body too occupied to remember the images that haunted him. His pace was furious. He frequented the gym, pounded the hell out of the speed bag, lifted weights, kickboxed, and jogged the dark city streets to exhaustion. When not running, he was shooting, spending hours at the firing range. The empty hours between midnight and dawn were the most difficult. Sleep was elusive. He drank as a result. He didn't realize it was so obvious to others.

Work was all that sustained him. Now that had turned to crap. No, that was what it had always been. Without a cause to believe in, without making a difference, without her, he had nothing.

Three years ago, they had a future and a family in progress. New Hampshire's rolling hills and little villages with yellow school buses and playing children evoked bittersweet memories.

He made good time. Ten miles from his destination he saw a homemade sign nailed to a tree.

PUPPIES FOR SALE.

He turned into a long gravel driveway that

led back to a farmhouse, a barn, and some outbuildings, then tooted the horn.

Several small children came running. They surrounded his car, along with half a dozen shepherd-mix pups that roughhoused about, yelping and yapping.

"Hi, guys," he greeted them, and stepped out to stretch his legs.

The children simultaneously stepped back. None answered.

"These must be the puppies," he said, smiling.

"We can't talk to strangers no more," a little girl sang out.

A screen door slammed and a slim, light-haired woman in her thirties appeared on the front porch of what looked to be a hundred-year-old farmhouse.

She looked harried, eyes wary.

He understood and said he'd seen the sign.

"Take your pick," she offered with relief. "Twenty dollars."

"Do you have something a little older?"

She looked confused.

He said he worked and had no time to train a pup.

Her pale, disappointed eyes roamed the farmyard and the several dogs on the property.

A sad-faced black and brown mutt of uncertain ancestry lay in the shade beside the barn, his muzzle resting between his paws.

"He's been neutered," the woman said, following Venturi's eyes. "Somebody took off his collar and pushed him out of a car up on the highway last year. He sat and waited by the side of the road for two days, then limped on down here. He must be smart. He knew which house to come to," she said good-naturedly.

He was perfect: the universal nondescript, medium-size, floppy-eared dog everyone has known at least once in their life.

"Ain't much of a watchdog. He don't bark much."

The animal seemed to know he was being discussed, his melancholy brown eyes rolling back and forth between them as they spoke.

"How much?"

She thought for a moment.

"The kids really love him. He's their favorite," she said slyly. "Twenty dollars?" She gnawed at her lower lip, eyes speculative, expecting him to bargain.

He didn't want to disappoint her. "How about fifteen?"

She countered with eighteen and looked

pleased as he counted out the bills.

"What's his name?" Venturi asked, as she tied an old piece of rope, a makeshift collar and leash, around the dog's shaggy neck.

She turned to the children. "What do you kids call him?"

They looked bewildered.

"What's his name?" she demanded, eyes warning that the sale might depend on their answer.

"Lassie?" the oldest boy finally piped up.

This dog was no Lassie.

Even the child's mother looked dubious as she handed Venturi the rope.

"How old do you think he is?" he asked.

"Five. Maybe six." She lifted her narrow shoulders. "No way to tell."

He looked older to Venturi but that made the animal even more perfect.

"He's a good dog," she said quickly. "Not a bit a' trouble."

The animal favored a front foot as he limped to the car beside his new owner and climbed obediently into the passenger seat. He looked back only once, at the children who ran after the car, shouting and waving.

"Don't worry, partner," Venturi assured him. "We'll get along fine. Just you and me for a while."

He stopped at a hardware store in the next

town and paid cash for a brown leather collar, a matching six-foot leash, and two stainless-steel dishes, for food and water. At a Wal-Mart he bought jeans, work pants, shirts, and several caps similar to those worn by the locals.

Pictures of the two missing girls were everywhere, on posters in store windows and on telephone poles.

He studied the faces of Samantha, the petite, blond Girl Scout, and Holly, a winsome freckle-faced third-grader with a gap-toothed grin.

"You don't fool me with that alias," Venturi told his passenger as they drove back to the highway. "You're no Lassie. What's your real name?"

The dog turned his back, then curled up on the front seat, head between his paws, bored, sad, or about to barf.

"Sport? Pal? Lucky?"

No reaction.

"Rocky? Blackie?" They stopped at a traffic light, next to a pole with Samantha's poster. "Scout?" The dog's ears perked up and he lifted his head.

"So you're Scout. Perfect. I'm Mike."

He lowered the passenger window. Moments later, Scout got to his feet and stuck out his face, tongue lolling, as though enjoying the ride.

Venturi imagined the sensory thrill that rush of air must bring to the sensitive nose of a dog. No wonder they look so ecstatic in convertibles and cars with open windows.

Talking to his new friend violated no security agreement, so Venturi explained how he'd been recruited to join the world's best personal protection service, one with a reputation for never losing a client. He believed them then. But they lied.

He told Scout it had been destined to end like this. It was only a matter of time.

He turned up the volume when the missing girls were mentioned on the radio.

"Samantha would never go off with a stranger," her mother said, her voice trembling. "She's only nine but bright for her age."

The reporter asked the question they always do when a loved one is missing. "What would you like to say to Samantha in case she's listening?"

"Sam, sweetheart . . ." The woman choked back a sob. "We love you very much. We miss you and want you home."

The child's father roughly cleared his throat. "Be brave, honey. We're coming to bring you home. Just be brave."

Venturi clenched the steering wheel in a

viselike grip as the newsman said there were no new leads and asked anyone with information to call a special police phone line.

At dusk, they drove down Main Street in Flemington, the picturesque little New Hampshire town where bad things were happening to good people.

Main Street's solitary traffic light blinked red. Few cars were on the road.

He found the innocent-looking neighborhood where the Brownie scout, age nine, had disappeared like melted snow, at precisely this time of day. He watched the foot and vehicular traffic around him for joggers, delivery trucks, or motorists routinely arriving home. Anyone who might have seen something suspicious during that window in time.

He drove slowly past Gino Salvi's small neat house. There was a light in the kitchen. The living room pulsed with flickering shadows from a television screen. He parked several doors down the street and watched the rearview mirror.

Shortly after 8 p.m. Salvi emerged and stood for several moments. The big man looked up and down the street as though sniffing the air like a wild animal before climbing into the Ford in his driveway. He backed out and drove to a neighborhood tavern a mile away.

Venturi followed. Salvi had demanded a Cadillac, claimed he always drove one, and had exploded in a red-faced rage when Venturi explained that it was exactly why he must not drive one now. In his new life, his image, his habits had to change.

His baseball cap pulled down, Venturi strolled by the tavern with Scout on his leash. Salvi sat alone, an amber-filled shot glass and a sweaty beer on the bar in front of him. Thirsty, Venturi went back to the car, ate a chocolate bar, and drank bottled water from a small cooler.

Twenty minutes later Salvi emerged alone, carrying a large cardboard pizza box.

When Venturi parked near the house minutes later, he saw through binoculars that Salvi appeared to be settled in front of a computer screen with his pizza and a six-pack.

While Salvi ate, he found a fast-food drive-through. He and the dog ate burgers in the car, then explored nearly empty streets, enjoying the cool night air.

A strange, unearthly sound, a high-pitched howling, rose in the distance. The dog's ears pricked up and he whined, tugging at the leash. The sound grew louder, coming closer on the evening breeze. Chills rippled up and down Venturi's arms. He'd heard something like it before, in Africa, the high-pitched keening sound of women wailing as his unit came upon a burned-out village in the aftermath of a massacre.

What he'd seen there flashed back in a shock of memory that nearly staggered him. The dog paused and gazed up at him, eyes unflinching, as though he understood.

They forged toward the sounds, turned a corner, and saw them. Hundreds of flickering lights, men, women, and children marching slowly toward a small park.

Their singing or chanting carried like a funeral dirge on the night air. Soon, he could make out the words.

". . . once was lost but now am found. 'Tis grace hath brought me safe thus far, and grace will lead me home."

The two couples in front had to be the parents — supported by friends, relatives, and neighbors. Some wore T-shirts with pictures of the lost girls.

A little boy held a handmade posterboard: WE MISS YOU, SAMANTHA AND HOLLY.

Half a dozen marchers carried a long banner bearing a painted plea: BRING THEM HOME.

Venturi, the dog, and several other pedestrians fell in behind them, following into the shadowy park. Flashlights aglow, candles flickering, they assembled at the base of a statue, a swordsman on horseback.

"Come home, come home . . . ," they implored. As the voices soared, Venturi searched faces in the crowd for a man out of place, someone nervous or excited. He wanted to be dead wrong about Salvi. But other than a few obvious undercover cops, all he saw were earnest, troubled small-town Americans gathered in crisis to comfort one another, to hold a candlelight vigil, and to pray for help.

The hymn ended and a middle-aged preacher stepped forward to lead prayers for the girls' safe return. First he read from the Bible, Jeremiah 31:15. Lamentations. Rachel weeping for her children . . . hoping for their return . . .

Venturi watched a wide-eyed, curly-haired tot nestled in her mother's arms, her profile a tiny replica of the teary-eyed young woman who held her.

His own eyes stung and blurred for a moment, then he left. He knew what he had to do.

CHAPTER THREE

Gino Salvi was a dangerous, admitted killer.

Venturi had been ordered to keep away from him and this small, tense community, which was already on edge and wary of strangers.

He was accustomed to conducting missions on forbidden turf, but this time he was stateside, alone, with no chain of command.

Officially, he was at the Jersey Shore. He couldn't risk a traffic stop by some sharp-eyed cop who would run his ID through the system.

He blended in as best he could and wondered why the FBI hadn't entered the case. Had the people he worked for asked them to hold off?

He used Iggy's credit card to check into a small guest cottage, one of six clustered near a trailer park a mile away from Salvi's place. The arthritic desk clerk asked what had brought him to Flemington.

He and his wife hoped to relocate to a slower paced rural community, Venturi said, and he was scouting the area on his way home from a business meeting in Burlington.

"Children?" the old man asked.

Venturi nodded. "One, she'll be three soon."

He always knew precisely how old their daughter would be — had she been born. Madison's name was constantly at the tip of his tongue, her laughter an echo, her touch a memory just out of reach. His ghost family was always with him.

"Have to pay people to live here if they don't bring those little girls home soon," the clerk grumbled. "Born and raised here, I've never seen the town in such an uproar."

"Saw all the posters," Venturi said. "A parent's worst nightmare. What do you think happened to the girls?"

"Whatever it was," the old man said, wagging his head, "they better solve it quick, before it happens again." His swollen, misshapen fingers trembled as he handed over the key.

Venturi took what he needed into his room from the car, set up his laptop, made coffee, and took the dog for a long walk.

They passed Salvi's house. The computer screen in the dining room had gone dark. A light was on in the bedroom. They returned to the motel and waited.

He was solo. Salvi knew him, and he had to keep moving so no fearful neighbor called the cops to report a stranger or an unfamiliar car. A perfect surveillance requires three teams who switch off frequently. Venturi had three strikes against him, so he did what he had to do. At 2 a.m., he pulled on a dark color sweat suit and running shoes, left Scout in the room, and set out on foot through a wooded area bordering the road between the motel and Salvi's neighborhood.

He emerged a block from the house and jogged by. Everything quiet, the bedroom was now dark. He jogged by again, dropped to the ground, and slid beneath Salvi's Ford in search of a metal surface. He found a perfect spot next to the gas tank. Penlight clenched between his teeth, he attached a magnetized device half the size of a small cell phone. The job took less than fifteen seconds.

He was ready to go, but suddenly the entire driveway was bathed in a light so brilliant that it hurt his eyes.

A policeman on patrol? Or Salvi with a

powerful flashlight? He froze.

Then he heard the engine. An SUV swept around the corner, its white high-intensity beams ablaze. The driver braked, almost to a stop, just feet away.

A tiger-striped cat dashed for cover under Salvi's Ford, detoured when he saw the space occupied, and streaked across the street.

Did the stray give him away? He didn't dare look. He expected to see a pair of patrolman's boots next. But the lights began to ease away as the vehicle rolled slowly into the driveway next door.

He heard the engine die. The slam of a car door. A high-pitched beep as the driver locked it with his remote. Then footsteps, the jangle of keys, and finally, a front door closing. He lay motionless, breathing deeply.

He waited in case the driver came back for something in the car or to check his mailbox. He wondered if the neighbor's late arrival woke Salvi, who, among his myriad of complaints, had once bitched and moaned that he hadn't slept well since his arrival in Flemington.

Salvi's place stayed dark. Eventually the lights went out next door.

Venturi slid cautiously out from beneath the car, jogged to the end of the street, then disappeared into the woods.

Scout wagged his tail furiously. "What's wrong?" Venturi asked him. "Did you think I wouldn't come back?"

He went straight to the laptop, tapped into the program, and smiled. The signal from the GPS tracking device was strong and bouncing off the satellite. He set the timer on his watch, so he could check the monitor every two hours.

The display on the screen was Salvi's address. The Ford never moved.

At 6:30 a.m. Venturi took the dog for a short walk, put the laptop in the car, and took Scout out for a fast-food breakfast.

He swung by Salvi's house on the way and was startled. Salvi was no morning person, but there he was, big as life, the man himself, wearing sneakers and a red and white sweat suit, up and out at 7 a.m. He plucked the newspaper off his lawn, tucked it under his beefy arm, and climbed into his car.

Venturi followed from a distance, the map on his computer screen showing Salvi's position and each change of direction. Was he bound for a rural jogging path or hiking slope? No. The man parked at a Denny's just off the interstate.

Salvi took a rear booth, near a window overlooking the parking lot. He was joined minutes later by a muscular dark-haired man in his late thirties. Everything about the newcomer, his ramrod posture, his haircut, the way he carried himself, screamed military. Venturi recognized the face but couldn't quite match it to a name. Salvi had to be violating the rules by associating with him. He watched from a distance through powerful lenses as the men attacked their breakfasts like wolfish animals. Venturi wished he could monitor the animated conversation between them as Salvi speared bacon strips and drowned his pancakes in butter and maple syrup. The discussion grew more intense over coffee but they stopped speaking whenever anyone passed near their table.

Salvi picked up the check, then they lingered beside his car talking. Venturi copied the New York tag number on the other man's vehicle, a black Escalade, then loosely tailed Salvi back to his house. He reemerged shortly, swinging a gym bag. He worked out at the community center gym for nearly an hour, then drove to the Krispy Kreme for doughnuts and coffee. Afterward he bought a few groceries at Hannaford's and drove home. Salvi never did go to work.

Venturi wondered what had become of the job that had been arranged for him.

Iggy called later to report that Deputy U.S. Marshal April Howard had left a message on Venturi's cell. Said she wanted to touch base and say hello.

He had Iggy reply with a text message. "Hvng a blst. c u sn." Her caller ID would display his number. Anyone who checked would confirm that the signal bounced off the cellular tower in Cape May, New Jersey.

Salvi's morning schedule remained identical for two more days, except that the breakfast boys chose a different booth each time. Worried they might be bugged?

The breakfast club grew by a third the following morning. Short, stocky, and middle-aged, with a thick shock of wavy salt-and-pepper hair. The three pored over papers brought by Salvi and the new man. Through military-grade binoculars from the far end of the parking lot at least one appeared to be a road map. Were they planning a trip?

The trio's body language as they left the restaurant set off alarms. Puffed up, purposeful, energized, and acting in concert — they were ready to rumble.

Yet, Salvi, again, drove home alone. Would he stick to the community center routine?

He did. Or did he? His demeanor was furtive as he left the house. No gym bag. Instead, he gingerly placed two heavy military-style duffel bags in the trunk, scanning the landscape as he did.

Did a sixth sense warn that he was being watched? Or was he edgy because of what he was about to do?

Venturi wanted to follow but felt a strong sense of urgency. If Salvi did go to the gym, he'd have a one-hour window. He had to hit the house in what little time he had left.

He had already checked the frequency and timing of local police patrols, which he found alarmingly predictable considering the crisis in the community.

He pulled on latex gloves and took his digital camera. What if a once-a-week housekeeper arrived and let herself in with a key? He had to risk it.

He rang the doorbell first — several times — then skirted the side of the house. The kitchen door was the easiest target, hidden from the street and shielded from neighbors by a six-foot fence. The lock was a simple deadbolt, commonly sold at hardware stores. Venturi opened a small leather case and selected a tiny wrench from a dozen delicate metal tools, some of which resembled miniature dental instruments.

He chose a lock pick, inserted it, and simultaneously manipulated both the wrench and the pick. The welcome click came on his fourth try. He slipped into the kitchen.

His actions had now escalated from an unauthorized surveillance to an illegal search. He did not hesitate. He had to know the truth.

No need to worry about a housekeeper. Salvi obviously didn't have one on the payroll. Dirty dishes filled the sink. Stale-smelling beer cans and empty pizza boxes were scattered everywhere, along with half-empty Scotch bottles. Venturi moved swiftly from room to room. He found a gun, a small-caliber automatic pistol, fully loaded, beneath a sofa pillow. The bed unmade. Dirty clothes on the floor.

Scribbled notes inside Salvi's nightstand were a puzzling series of initials and times. Phone numbers with no matching names were scribbled in the margin of a newspaper on the floor beside his bed.

A New Hampshire road map lay open on the dining room table, a short stretch of interstate highlighted in yellow.

Child porn on Salvi's laptop. The son of a bitch, Venturi muttered to himself.

Back to the kitchen for another look at a

wall calendar. Today's date circled in red. No other dates had been circled since Salvi arrived in Flemington. What was so special about today? It wasn't his birthday. He knew Salvi's real date of birth as well as the new one he had been given.

Advertising magnets posted on the doors of the big side-by-side refrigerator/freezer came from a local pizzeria, a pharmacy, and an auto repair shop. Venturi opened the freezer, stared through the icy cloud that emerged, then closed his eyes.

He opened them and cursed out loud. She was still there, her pale, naked body twisted, long eyelashes frosty, shiny blond hair matted. Her eyes were blue. A small amount of blood had pooled beneath her head, which rested on the bottom shelf. Lividity had purpled the skin on her face. Her feet were wedged up toward the top.

He had been right from the start.

His need to retch was quickly overcome by something stronger, the need to kill Gino Salvi. Who deserved it more? Rage shortened his breath.

She was the missing Girl Scout. Where was the other girl? He thought he knew.

He shut the freezer gently, as though closing a coffin, took a long ragged breath, and reached for the refrigerator door.

51

Footsteps stopped him dead. Up the front stairs, across the porch, to the door. He had dreaded coming face to face with Salvi. Now he couldn't wait. He drew his gun and moved swiftly to the front of the house, extraordinarily light on his feet for a man his height. Poised, he waited for the metallic turn of Salvi's key in the lock.

Instead, the jarring sound of the doorbell raised the hair on the back of his neck.

He stood motionless, like a deer in the gun sights just before the rifle crack. He could hear his heart beat in the silence. The doorbell rang again, a loud, impatient chime. Expected, but still unsettling.

He'd been seen. A neighbor must be checking. Were police en route? Or were they already here? Venturi calculated his options. How many were out there?

He heard voices, two of them, but could not make out their words. Then a scrabbly sound on the other side of the door. The knob shook. Then nothing.

He moved in closer, scarcely breathing, gun in hand, and put his eye to the peephole. A middle-aged man in a suit and a younger woman in a modest print dress were leaving. Down the stairs, across the front walk. Each carried a book and some papers.

He watched them cross the street.

They had left something. He cracked Salvi's door open and it fluttered to the floor.

DEATH, IS IT REALLY THE END? the headline asked.

The publication they left was *Awake.*

They were Jehovah's Witnesses.

He sighed and put his gun away.

CHAPTER FOUR

Steeled for the worst, Venturi took a deep breath, wrenched open the refrigerator door, then blinked.

Well-stocked shelves: orange juice, bacon, eggs, two quarts of milk, fruits and vegetables, cold cuts, a cheese cake, coffee creamer, three six-packs of Bud, and a fifth of Grey Goose vodka.

Where was Holly, the missing third-grader? He'd already scrutinized the yard. No fresh-turned earth, no newly poured cement. No suspicious odors.

He shot photos of what was in the freezer, then descended a narrow flight of stairs to the musty basement. There he found a stained mattress along with discarded ropes and duct tape, indicating that someone had been tied up. He wondered how long she'd been alive here, while the world searched.

He was careful not to disturb a thing. The scene was a forensic gold mine, blond hairs on the duct tape, blood and body fluids on the mattress. Crime-scene investigators would have a field day if Salvi didn't clean it up first.

He took more pictures. The beauty of a camera's eye and of good science is that they never blink and do not lie.

Nothing suspicious in the attic. The dust and undisturbed cobwebs indicated that Salvi was never up there.

How simple it would be to dial 911 like any good citizen reporting a crime. But his illegal search could prove fatal to a prosecution.

He checked his watch. He still needed to know why this day was different. Salvi was not at the gym. His hand weights and gym bag sat near the front door. Left behind. What was in the heavy duffel bags that he did take?

Venturi revisited the road map on the dining room table and studied the highlighted stretch of highway about twenty miles east of Flemington. He returned to the bedroom and the scribbled papers and penciled notations in Salvi's nightstand.

PU had to represent pickups listed at WaMu, clearly Washington Mutual, at the supermarket, the Rite Aid Drugstore, and other local establishments along with the times the PUs took place. Who picks up at those stops?

Armored cars, Brinks trucks.

A handwritten notation next to the target area on the road map was "bwt 10:45 a.m. and 11:05 a.m." It was now 10:47.

If an attack on an armored car was what made this day special, it was happening now.

He locked the back door behind him, peeled off the gloves, and stuffed them in his pocket.

Scout, waiting in the car down the street, stood up, wagging his tail hopefully. He wanted out.

"Sorry." Venturi slid into the driver's seat. "No time."

He checked the computer screen. Salvi's car was parked at the community center, had been for more than an hour. He probably changed cars there. Venturi couldn't call the police, but maybe he could thwart the robbery and end the nightmare now — if he wasn't too late. He snatched a custom-made brass catcher from the glove box and attached it to his gun. The device would collect his ejected casings. He wished he had lights, a siren, or a chopper; instead, he stuck to the posted speed limit until he reached the on-ramp.

"Hang on!"

The dog whimpered and hunkered down on the floorboard as though he understood.

Mere minutes from the highlighted stretch of highway, he slammed on the brakes.

DANGER — ROCKSLIDE
ROAD CLOSED

The sign, dead center in the road ahead, looked official. Black block lettering on international orange. So did the Detour sign directing all traffic to an off-ramp.

The robbers had planted it to detour potential witnesses after the armored truck passed. As he maneuvered his car around it, he heard an explosion. A plume of black smoke curled into the sky around the next curve about a mile ahead.

He floored it, then heard a second blast. The car rocketed forward. He braked to a stop just off the road before the curve.

Gun in hand, several clips in his pockets, he sprinted through the trees and under-growth that bordered the roadway. Then he saw it. The still-smoking Brink's truck, its skin ripped and crumpled like aluminum foil. The armored car listed toward the driver's side, its windshield shattered.

What did they use? It looked like a road-side bomb. The robbers had converged. A dark blue Oldsmobile blocked the path of the armored vehicle. A moving van stood at the rear.

A robber in camouflage and a black ski mask and armed with an AK-47 assault rifle paced between the vehicles. He covered two accomplices working in tandem, unloading canvas money bags from the back of the truck. A man inside lobbed sacks of cash out to the other, who heaved them into the back of the van.

The armored-car driver was slumped, motionless, over the wheel. But as Venturi watched, the damaged passenger-side door slowly creaked open, spitting broken glass onto the pavement. The second guard stumbled coughing from the smoking truck. Dazed, face bloody, he fumbled for his gun.

The lookout advanced, brandishing the assault rifle. The guard staggered, reeled on his feet, saw what was coming, and lurched clumsily for cover behind the door of his smoking truck. He hesitated at the last moment, apparently fearing fire or an explosion. He turned, helpless, to face the gunman. The masked man showed no mercy. He lifted his weapon for the kill, as Venturi opened fire from the trees.

The robber spun and hit the ground hard. But moments later, as Venturi watched in disbelief, he slowly climbed to all fours, then got to his feet. They were wearing body armor. The lookout shouted to the others, who looked wildly around them for the source of the gunfire.

The shots and shouts brought them scrambling from the back of the truck. Both drew handguns. The one Venturi recognized as Salvi, despite his mask, stopped to snatch a long gun from inside the moving van.

He heard their curses, saw their confusion, as all three brandished their weapons, backed up, spun around, and scanned the brush along the road.

"Who's out there?"

"How many?"

"You see 'em?"

"Where'd it come from?"

Hyperaware, experiencing the crystal clarity that always came when engaging the enemy, Venturi fired rapid bursts as he scuttled swiftly through the cover of dense foliage along the road. Lucky it was spring, he thought, and not the starkly bleak and leafless winter.

His goal was to keep them confused and unaware that he was outmanned, outgunned, and alone. He regretted not coming prepared with at least a second weapon. Who knew? He never expected this.

Crouched behind a boulder, he fired a volley of six shots, scrambled to another position yards away and opened fire. He had to make them believe they were under attack by several shooters.

As their shots went wild, he broke into a dead run, then fired from a stand of trees. Again, he brought down the lookout, the gunman who had tried to execute the bleeding Brinks guard. This time he stayed down.

Salvi and the third robber panicked and retreated toward the moving van. Venturi rolled into a better position and fired repeatedly. His slugs kicked up dust, shattered the pavement in front of them, and cut them off from the van.

He moved again, sat on the ground behind a thick tree trunk, slammed in a new clip and got off six more rounds as they fled toward the Olds. One stumbled. The stocky man he'd seen with Salvi that morning screamed and tore off his ski mask, blood streaming from the side of his head. Salvi cursed and ran hard for the Olds. The wounded robber staggered after him. He was only halfway in the car when Salvi burned rubber back toward Flemington.

The injured man hung on and managed to close the car door behind him. The wound did not appear fatal, but he'd need medical attention.

Venturi trotted back to his car unaware of his half smile, more in his comfort zone than he had been in years. He hadn't even worked up a sweat. But it wasn't over. Not yet.

The dog stood on the seat, staring as Venturi drove his car up the ramp into the moving van, running over some of the scattered money-stuffed bank bags.

He used the van's dashboard controls to lift the ramp, closed the truck's doors, then went out to check the Brinks crew.

The driver, unconscious or dead, had not moved. His partner was down on all fours on the pavement, bleeding profusely from the nose.

"You'll be okay, pal," Venturi told him. "Stay down. Don't move. Help is on the way."

He saw how they'd blasted the armored car off the road. Rocket-propelled grenades. They left the launcher behind when they fled. Shoulder mounted, with a scope. Venturi hadn't seen one up close lately. Where the hell did they get that? he wondered.

The robber he'd shot lay on the pavement, sprawled in the dust. He crouched beside him, lifted the ski mask, and saw the man who had looked familiar at Denny's. Now he placed the face. Salvi's nephew, a veteran of the war in Afghanistan and Iraq. Despite his protective vest, a slug had struck him under the armpit — a vulnerable spot, exposed when he raised his weapon to fire — and penetrated his chest cavity.

Venturi didn't bother to check his vitals.

He climbed into the moving van, unaware of how much, or how little, time he had left. Was the Detour sign still in place? Had the guards been able to activate an alarm?

He drove steadily at the speed limit for ten minutes without hearing sirens, then took an off-ramp and turned onto a side road. A small wooden church, its parking lot empty, was the only structure in sight. He quickly loaded as many money bags as he could fit into his car, lowered the ramp, and backed it down out of the van. He left the truck behind the church, keys in the ignition.

Before driving away he exited the car to be sure he had left no tire tracks in the dry ground. As he did, Scout jumped out the open door and ran into the woods. *Damn,* Venturi thought. *He's gone.*

Would the dog find his way back to the farmhouse? Would the police find him wandering and link him to the van? Would the woman who sold him step forward to describe the buyer to the police? Did that woman, wary from the start, take down his tag number?

He called. No sign of the dog. Time was running out. He had to leave before he was seen. But as he drove back toward the main road, something burst out of the woods and charged after the car.

"Come on!" He threw open the passenger-side door. "Atta boy!" The panting dog scrambled headlong into the car, claws scrabbling, his attitude indignant at nearly being left behind, again!

"Thought you ran away. Guess you just made a pit stop."

Venturi called Flemington City Hall, using an untraceable, prepaid cell, and asked for the mayor's office. "This is an emergency," he told a secretary who answered. "An armored car was robbed and people were shot. Dispatch an ambulance and the police. Now!" He repeated the location twice.

She asked for his name. He ignored the question.

"The man responsible is a mobster, a killer with a long rap sheet. He lives at 1410 Belmont Street, in Flemington, using the name Louis Sabatino. His real name is

Salvi. S-A-L-V-I. He's armed and dangerous. Got that?"

She did and asked, "Did you dial 911?"

"No. It's up to you. Do it now!" He hung
up.

He clenched a pencil between his teeth
and affected a Spanish accent when he
spoke to the assignment editor at the nearest TV station and again to an editor at *The
Flemington Times Register,* a weekly.

He gave both the same information, then
hung up without leaving a name. He wished
he could call the police himself but couldn't
risk leaving his voice on tape.

He drove back toward New York City.

At rush hour in the bleakest Bronx neighborhood he could find, he stopped, slit the
canvas money bags with his knife, then flung
them one by one off an overpass thirty feet
above the surface street. Brisk breezes
caught the free-flying bills that twirled and
spun as they fluttered down in every direction.

Seconds later he heard shouts, brakes
squealing, horns blowing. He saw pedestrians running, drivers bailing, homeless
people with outstretched arms. He wanted
to watch, but didn't. He kept moving.

Hell, he thought as he drove away, it's all
insured, insured by the government, the

same government he blamed for all that had happened.

He did it for all those who had lived routine, small-town lives until recently. Head pounding, he wished he could somehow make the government pay more.

They would, he thought. Only he and Salvi knew what police would find in his freezer and his basement. He hoped they'd hurry. He wanted the world to know.

CHAPTER FIVE

Michael Venturi arrived home from the "Jersey Shore" that night, after switching cars and credit cards with Iggy and retrieving his cell phone. While Scout explored the apartment, Venturi checked his hotline, used only for protected witness emergencies.

One message, a few hours old.

A familiar voice, hoarse and stressed.

"It's Gino. Where are ya? Pick up the phone, will ya? Call me at this number, right away," he said. "I ran into a situation here. You gotta run some interference for me. It's important. They wanna serve a search warrant on my house."

Venturi laughed. He didn't return the call.

He watched the late news instead. Local stations all led with the same story: the happy chaos and pandemonium as cash rained down on a blighted urban neighborhood.

An armored-car robbery in New Hampshire rated a brief mention late in the broadcast. No one had connected the dots. Yet. With luck, the search warrant had already been served on 1410 Belmont Street. He visualized Salvi in handcuffs, the house roped off and surrounded by crime-scene trucks.

Venturi went into his kitchen, reached for the half-empty bottle of Jack Daniel's black, paused, then closed the cupboard instead.

At midnight he called April Howard, said he just got home, and apologized for the hour.

"You sound terrific," she bubbled enthusiastically. "How was the beach?"

"Cool. I need to get away more often."

He said he'd see her soon, then checked the cable news.

Nothing yet. He relaxed in his chair, Scout curled up at his feet, and waited without regret for everything to hit the fan.

During the night Salvi left another, more desperate, message. Venturi neither picked up nor returned the call. He slept soundly for the first time in months.

In the morning, he applied a bronze coat of spray-on tan, then took Scout for a walk. The mutt was a magnet. Never had so many people, including total strangers, engaged him in friendly conversation.

He said he rescued the stray on the Jersey Shore.

"So that's where you were. I thought you were out of town," said his neighbor, a middle-aged librarian, as they passed on the stairs. "I had a dog who looked a lot like him when I was little," she said, baby-talking and petting the animal, who basked in the attention.

"So did I," Venturi said. "He looked so hungry I couldn't resist feeding him. Then he followed me to my car. He didn't have a collar and looked so sad. I was afraid he'd wind up at the local pound."

"Scout," she said sweetly, causing the dog's ears to perk up. "How'd you come up with that?"

He shrugged, backing into his apartment.

"Nice tan," she said with a smile.

"Thanks. It was a good couple of days," he said truthfully.

He cooked himself and the dog a hearty breakfast. Scout liked bacon, eggs over easy, fried potatoes, and even a cinnamon muffin. They watched the morning news as they ate.

The story didn't take long to break. CNN and Fox News reported that New Hampshire police and the FBI were investigating a possible link between the armored-car heist and the big bills spilled over the Bronx.

A CNN anchor wondered aloud why robbers who pulled off a high-risk holdup would toss away the loot.

"Can this be the case of a modern-day Robin Hood?" another newscaster asked.

Not likely. The armored-car driver's condition was guarded after brain surgery. The second guard was expected to fully recover, but had suffered temporary hearing damage and was unable to remember the crime due to head injuries.

The media jumped to the conclusion that he had bravely tried to fight off the gang, killing one who was left behind by his accomplices as they fled with an estimated $1.6 million.

No wonder those bags were so heavy, Venturi thought.

Fox News was first to report that two persons of interest, one injured, were being interviewed.

Investigators stonewalled, saying they were still piecing the facts together.

That the guard's weapon had never been fired, much less drawn, or that the persons of interest were identified by an anonymous tip went unmentioned.

Little, if any, cash had been recovered from the chaotic scene in the Bronx, making it difficult to positively link it to the robbery.

Even police and other city employees dispatched to a dozen minor accidents, a major traffic snarl, and free-for-all fights in the street had reportedly succumbed, abandoning their own cars to pursue, scoop up, and snatch fistfuls of wind-borne bills from the air.

Residents had run to fill pots, pails, and garbage bags. Eyewitness accounts described two women stuffing a baby carriage with cash. Now, however, all denied knowledge of the windfall. Those who would talk to police and reporters claimed they were in the bathroom, asleep, or somewhere else when bedlam broke out.

Hundreds of people were involved. Only one had returned any money. A small boy who handed a $50 bill to a policeman because it didn't belong to him was now an instant celebrity, slated to appear on *The Tonight Show.*

The sole official complaint came from an irate motorist who reported that a hail of quarters pelted his car and damaged the finish.

Venturi sipped his coffee and acknowl-

70

edged that in his enthusiasm, he had gone too far. He never should have dumped that sack of loose change off the overpass.

To kill time while waiting, he went out to stock up on dog food and Milk Bones, among other things.

When he returned an hour later, his home phone, the hotline, and the cell phone in its charger were all ringing. He checked Caller ID but didn't pick them up.

The Flemington, New Hampshire, police department was on the hotline. Salvi had obviously given them the number. The office was calling his home phone and April Howard was speed-dialing his cell. She finally gave up. It rang again minutes later. Ruth Ann.

The news was out.

He poured another cup of coffee, took a deep breath, then called the office.

His call was directed to Rich Archbold, the prosecutor, who happened to be there.

"Chief McMullen wants you in here right now," he said tersely.

"What's up?" Venturi asked innocently. "I'll be in Wednesday."

"Get your ass in here, ASAP."

"Sounds important."

"Damn right. I'll tell him you're on the way."

Before leaving the apartment, he played an old telephone message again. The last message that Madison, his wife, had left him. She sounded young, vibrant, and alive — all the things she was and ceased to be that day.

He had never erased it. It was all he had left. Listening to it was not as acutely painful as it had been when it was new; now it felt more like the ache from a severed limb.

"Be home in a little bit. Love you, Mikey. We're boarding now. Wait till you see our loot!" Her spontaneous, happy laughter followed, joined by a familiar chuckle.

His pregnant wife and her mother. Listening to their voices together still made him smile. He held on to that smile as he walked into the storm.

CHAPTER SIX

Normally the genial security guard greeted Venturi by name and waved him through. Today he asked for identification, frowned as he scrutinized it, then picked up the phone.

Not a good sign. He'd been gone less than a week.

Venturi stepped off the elevator. Archbold was waiting, in shirtsleeves, his tie loosened.

The office appeared to be in crisis mode. Clearly agitated prosecutors who had used Salvi to win convictions or were prepared to have him testify in the upcoming Schoenberg trial huddled in a glass-walled conference room. "How the *hell* could this happen?" one loudly demanded, apoplectic and red-faced.

Another muttered something Venturi didn't hear and they all turned to stare at him.

April Howard did not even look up from

her desk when he greeted her. Ruth Ann watched from her cubicle, her brow furrowed in an expression of concern.

"This way. Let's go." Like a cop, Archbold steered Venturi away from his own desk toward the chief's office.

"What the hell's going on?" Venturi asked. "Who died?"

"You tell us," Archbold said.

The chief slammed down his phone when he saw them.

"What do you know about Flemington?" he demanded.

"It's in New Hampshire," Venturi said. "Nice to see you, too."

"Salvi's under arrest," he snapped.

"Why am I not surprised?" Venturi took a seat in front of the man's desk. "What for?"

"He said he tried all night to reach you on your hotline. Where have you been?"

"The Jersey Shore. Got home late last night."

"You haven't seen the news? Read the papers?"

"I quit reading them and chilled at the beach. Your suggestion, remember?" He turned to Archbold as if for confirmation.

Fury gathered in the chief's eyes.

"He's charged with armed robbery," Archbold said, "of an armored car, and three

74

homicides, among other major felonies. He's through. *We're* through. Schoenberg walks. Without Salvi we have no case. And the convictions already won will be back to bite us on appeal based on his lack of credibility."

"An armored car?" Venturi feigned surprise.

"Salvi, his nephew, and an ex-con named Joe Russo used military ordnance to take out an armored truck," Archbold explained. "The FBI thinks it was procured from an illegal arms dealer they've been investigating in Virginia."

"Somebody apparently broke up the robbery, then dropped a dime on Salvi." McMullen's pale eyes glittered malevolently.

"Three murders?" Venturi asked.

"The little girls you were so worked up about and his own nephew, killed in the armored car caper. They're not sure who shot him, but they charged Salvi and the other surviving robber under the felony murder rule."

Venturi nodded. "Makes sense." When someone is killed during a crime, the perpetrator can be charged with homicide even if he did not pull the trigger.

"So they found the little girls?" he asked solemnly.

"One in his house, on ice, last night." The chief's voice was cold. "The other one an hour ago."

"Where?"

"At a nearby house for sale," Archbold said, "unoccupied for some time. In the septic tank, in the backyard."

"Jesus." Venturi shook his head in disbelief.

"Why do I think you know more than we do?" The chief looked grim. "Were you there, Venturi?"

"Flemington?"

"You were hot to trot right up there last time we spoke."

"You ordered me not to," Venturi reminded him. "And before you try to accuse me of anything, take a look in the mirror. I always said Salvi was not a good candidate for WITSEC. Remember? He's a sick son of a bitch. Always has been, admitted to participating in nine mob hits, yet we relocate him to a small town so the government can fry a bigger fish. Would you want him next door to your wife and kids?"

"Whoever broke up the armored-car robbery may have stolen the money," Archbold said.

"All I know is that what you're telling me," Venturi said, "sounds like a double cross among thieves. One of them turns on his accomplices, shoots one, steals the loot, and throws the others under the bus."

"Possible," the chief said, "except that the loot fell out of the sky over the Bronx."

"Is that confirmed?" Venturi frowned.

"Not yet."

"How do they know that Salvi and Russo didn't kill the nephew, then stash the money before their arrests?"

"Then who was the tipster?" Archbold asked.

"Tipster?" Venturi shrugged. "You got me. But they must have his voice on tape. The FBI works wonders with audio."

"So you'll take a polygraph?" The chief spat out the words.

"Hell, no," Venturi said. "Salvi's the criminal, not me. What's the plan for damage control?"

"Too late for that now." Archbold paced the room like a grieving mourner.

"News is already breaking about the girls' bodies being found," McMullen said. "The media's descending on Flemington. The next big revelation will out Salvi and connect him to WITSEC. When certain politicians in Washington hear this, we're screwed. The future of the fucking program is totally screwed."

He looked like a man about to stroke out. Venturi hoped he didn't. He'd hate like hell to have to give him CPR.

"Sorry," he said. "This all stinks. One in four protected witnesses go back to their old bad habits or invent new ones. Look at Salvi, Sammy the Bull, and the others like them. Animals don't change their stripes. They find new prey and become somebody else's problem, while you slap each other on the back and celebrate conviction rates."

Venturi sighed and shook his head. "I can't do this any more." He reached for his badge case.

"Damn right you can't," the chief blurted. "The only way you ever work in law enforcement again is over my dead body. I want your badge and gun. Now."

Venturi handed over his government-issued weapon, which he had never used, and the badge with the silver star, then suffered the humiliation of being escorted from the building by security. Other agents, lawyers, and the office staff watched. He half-expected them to applaud.

He stepped out onto the sunlit street, no longer a deputy U.S. Marshal who helped create new lives and identities, mostly for people who deserved them the least.

He knew he'd be the scapegoat. Two days

later, as the national story grew into a firestorm, the U.S. Marshals Service issued a press release announcing that the individual responsible for relocating Gino Salvi to Flemington had been fired.

Venturi made plans to leave town. They accelerated when a too-chatty woman, who identified herself as Judy Grimes, an investigative reporter at *The Washington Post,* called his unlisted home number. He said he'd get back to her, then visited his financial adviser.

An FBI agent with a degree in accounting, Jim Dance had retired from the bureau and parlayed his expertise into a successful Manhattan practice. He and Venturi had worked together on a number of cases in the past and were friends.

Dance's office was impressive, plush carpets, dark leather and mahogany furniture, and floor-to-ceiling windows overlooking the East River. Framed degrees and awards were displayed on the walls. And his blond, younger second wife and baby smiled from a silver picture frame on his desk.

"Michael, Michael. How are you?" His greeting was heartfelt, his handshake strong.

"You've heard, I'm sure."

Dance nodded.

"It's not about to get better. I'm out of here. Probably won't be back."

"Sorry." Dance shook his head somberly. "Their loss. You were their best and brightest."

"Couldn't be happier to be unemployed," Venturi said. "The job was a mistake from the start."

"How can I help you?"

"All I want now is distance between me, this city, and that agency."

Dance nodded. "Can't say I blame you for that."

"I'll let you know when and where I decide to settle."

"I guess you'll want to transfer your portfolio." Dance picked up his fountain pen.

"Why? You've done a great job."

Dance looked pleased, then chuckled. "So you *have* been checking your statements. I hear from you so rarely, I often wonder if you even open them. Need to cash out some investments now?"

Venturi shook his head. "You know how I feel, Jim."

He had never touched a dime of his $19 million wrongful-death settlement for the loss of his wife and their unborn child. He considered it blood money and put it out of his mind after investing it.

"I have some savings. I'm all right for now. I'll find something to do."

Dance looked troubled. "You haven't been active in trading, or taken advantage of any of your assets."

"I'm not comfortable doing that."

"What about charity?" Dance asked thoughtfully. "Overnight I can put together a list of worthy causes you might support in Madison's name."

"I'll give it some thought later, sometime in the future. I have too many other things to think about right now."

"Well, keep it in mind. Call me any time, day or night, if you need anything. And for God's sake, stay in touch. Let me know where you land, so I can forward your statements. Here, take my cell phone number." He scrawled it on his business card and pushed it across the desk. "I can always transfer the money to you or your new financial adviser."

"I know you take good care of everything," Venturi said, getting to his feet. "I'll be seeing you."

"I wish you well, my friend." The two men embraced.

"Take care of yourself, Michael." Dance stepped back and gazed like a concerned

81

father into his eyes. "Remember. You're still young, only thirty-eight. Despite the past, your future still lies ahead. It's just up to you to find it, enjoy it, and be happy again."

Dance saw him out of the office and watched him walk away.

Venturi's steps felt light. He was happy as hell to be free of his job and on his way out of town. If a Senate investigating committee began issuing subpoenas, he wouldn't make it easy for them. He'd simply get lost, no forwarding address.

He'd arranged too many fresh starts for undeserving people. Considering his own role in the New Hampshire tragedy, he probably didn't deserve a new life, either. But he thought about what Jim Dance said and decided he'd do the best he could.

Chapter Seven

He had to say good-bye, could not leave without seeing her.

They met for lunch. She arrived first, as always, and waved to catch his eye. Her smile lit up the room. She looked terrific, blond hair cut in a sleek, swingy style, a feminine eyelet blouse under her stylish linen suit.

He planted an affectionate kiss on her cheek, inhaled her sweetly familiar scent, and realized again how much he loved this woman. Their lives were forever linked by joy and pain.

"How are you, sweetheart?"

"Good," he lied. "Couldn't be better."

"Something's up. You sounded so serious on the phone."

He was glad the waiter interrupted.

She ordered iced tea, lifting an eyebrow in approval when he told the waiter to make it two.

He asked about her work. She taught seminars on protocol to newly appointed ambassadors, political figures, and business executives who traveled abroad. Her business had taken off and lately, she said, she'd branched out.

"I'm doing jail time." She revealed over Caesar salads that she was now teaching classes in table manners, etiquette — and life, to youthful offenders in jails, prisons, and detention centers.

As they dined on tiny, light-as-a-feather ravioli, she told stories, including one about "a baby-faced fifteen-year-old, so bright and funny that I wanted to take him home and adopt him." Later, she'd asked why he was there. "Homicide," she whispered. "He actually killed someone."

"Bad people never look like the monsters they really are, Victoria. That's how they get away with so much. You're never left alone with them, are you?" he asked with alarm. "Tell me guards are always present. Please?"

She laughed, a light and airy sound that could wring his heart and hang it out to dry.

"I worry," he said gruffly.

"I worry about you, too, sweetheart. I think of you every single day."

"Vicki, I need to tell you something."

She put down her dessert spoon, her expression grave.

He told her how he'd left the job, without mentioning New Hampshire.

She nodded solemnly. "When I read about that awful case in Flemington, I thought that terrible man might be one of your witnesses."

"He was. I couldn't stay on the job after what he did. But in the end I had no choice. They fired me."

"Their loss," she said. "Like they say, 'It's dangerous to be right when the established authorities are wrong.'

"The U.S. Marshals Service isn't what it used to be." She stirred her tea. "Wyatt Earp must be spinning in his grave.

"I did wonder how that monster happened to be caught, and how all that stolen money . . ." She paused expectantly, her look sly and knowing.

He smiled and averted his eyes.

"Just thought I'd ask," she said lightly. "I take it I'm not alone in asking."

Their eyes held for a long and meaningful moment and, for him, it felt like the old days — almost.

"So, I'm about to ride the wind blowing out of this burg. I'm taking off."

"To where?" She looked alarmed.

"Not sure yet. A place where I can go fishing, read, and decide how to live the rest of my life."

"You could have told me after I finished my tiramisu." She pouted, eyes shiny. "I've lost my appetite. You're saying good-bye."

He nodded.

"Forever?" she asked softly.

"Hell, no!" The idea startled him. "I'll be in touch as soon as I settle somewhere."

She sighed. "Promise?"

"We'll always be there for each other," he swore. "Always."

"Wherever you go, I'll visit." She dabbed at her eyes with a lacy handkerchief and tried to smile. "You can't hide from me, you know."

They both knew he could, of course.

"How's Sidney?" he asked.

She sighed. "Same old. Same bad. You know what he's like. Trouble and nothing but. I shouldn't say it, but I swear that boy was a bad seed."

"Myself? I'm convinced they handed you the wrong baby at the hospital. Want me to talk to him before I go? I'm leaving tonight." Venturi frowned. "Is he around?"

She wagged her head forlornly. "Haven't heard from him in weeks. Doesn't answer his cell. I hope he's not in trouble. I'm sure

I'd hear if he was. Bad news travels fast. No news is good news with him."

"Speaking of that," he said. "No matter who asks, you don't know where I am, haven't heard from me, and don't expect to."

"Absolutely. That first part will even be true, won't it?"

Her limp was scarcely noticeable as they left the restaurant. The handsome carved wooden cane she still carried seemed more an accessory than a necessity these days.

They hugged on the sidewalk. "Love you, Mikey."

"Ditto." He kissed her forehead. "Love you, too."

No one who saw her climb into the cab would suspect she'd lost a leg in the Staten Island Ferry crash that killed eleven passengers, including his wife and unborn child, and injured 165 others. Doctors had doubted she would live. When she did, they predicted she'd be confined to a wheelchair.

He smiled and waved back at his mother-in-law, as her cab merged into traffic. Moments later she was gone.

That night as his neighbors slept, he loaded the car with what little he was taking with him.

He took Scout's food and water dishes but

left the twenty-pound sack of dog food behind. He'd stocked up on pet food too late. Scout was already hooked on people food. He preferred pasta to Purina.

At 1 a.m. he took Scout for a brisk walk and a last look at the old neighborhood. Venturi left a note and a check for the landlord, filled a thermos with coffee, picked up a sack of roast beef sandwiches from Arby's, and drove into the night. Neither he nor the dog looked back.

CHAPTER EIGHT

His internal compass drew him south like a magnet. Was it the fishing, the boating, or the possibility that he might find the only other human being he knew he could trust? Maybe the latter, if the return address on an old Christmas card was still good. But that seemed unlikely, given Danny Trado's lifestyle.

Not at all sleepy, Venturi felt energy charged and expectant, escaping the past by speeding into an unknown future. Traffic was light except for big eighteen-wheelers on all-night interstate runs. He made a pit stop near Baltimore for gas and a brief jog with the dog.

As they raced south through the night, he listened to the radio, switching from volatile talk shows, to news, to music, and back, signals fading as he drove out of range.

Eventually he switched it off and listened to the sound of his tires on the road. They outran thunderclaps and lightning, encountered a few light rains but no serious storms.

After a misty dawn, he paid cash for breakfast, careful to use no credit cards along the way.

Later, caught in a crush of commuters headed home, he stopped at the South of the Border motel for dinner. He intended to rent a room and sleep until traffic thinned out, but still on an adrenaline high, he kept moving, through heat waves rising off the pavement as the temperature soared, through traffic slowed by mishaps and accidents, both major and minor. Scout, weary of the scenery, curled up on the passenger seat and slept soundly.

"We're in Florida!" Venturi told Scout at last. When night fell around them, Venturi realized that Florida was one long, long peninsula. Pink mist rose to meet a sun-scorched dawn along the turnpike. The closer they came to Miami, the more congested traffic became.

Bumper to bumper in a new rush hour, he consulted his GPS and was relieved to find the address he sought was only thirty miles away. He stopped for gas, jogged with the dog, washed his face, brushed his teeth, and combed his hair. He wanted to shave but the restroom was too dirty and had no hot water.

When he found the ranch-style suburban house, he drove by slowly. A black SUV and a Harley sat in the driveway; a little yellow tricycle was parked on the porch.

He stopped halfway down the block and tried the old number using a new prepaid cell phone.

"Hola?" She sounded young.

"Is Danny there?"

She switched seamlessly to English. "Hold on, I'll call him."

He heard a radio or TV, and the high-pitched laughter of children.

Someone finally picked up. "Danny here."

"Trado?"

"Who's this?"

"The guy next to you when we jumped out of a Blackhawk into shark-infested waters in full scuba gear."

"Mike! Venturi? That you? How the hell are you? Where are you? What are you doing?"

"Hoping to visit you. Sometime soon."

"The sooner the better, bro. *Mi casa es su casa.* Can't wait to see you."

Venturi hung up and swung into a U-turn. It was too hot and sticky to leave Scout in the car so they walked to the front door together. He rang the bell.

Danny threw the door open and let out a whoop.

"Mike! It's you! You sneaky SOB!" Danny hadn't changed since they last saw each other. As robust and muscular as ever, he caught his visitor in a fierce bear hug as a number of small children darted out from behind him.

"Look! A dog! A dog!"

"Doggie!" piped the youngest, a diapered toddler still unsteady on his feet. There were only three of them, but their energy levels made it seem like more.

"Does he bite?" demanded a sturdy, crew-cut boy about five years old.

"No," Venturi assured them, hoping, as the children rushed Scout, that he hadn't spoken too soon.

"Yes! Yes, he does! He bites!" yelped the woman who answered the phone. Her white-flowered sundress showed off her glistening tan and long, shiny black hair. "That dog has teeth like a shark. He *will* bite you — if you bite him first. You hear me, Julee? He bites back. He'll bite off your nose, your toes, or your ears."

The little girl closed her mouth abruptly, pursed her rosebud lips, and paused to weigh the warning. About three, and bare-foot, she had dark curly ringlets and big, black olive eyes.

"A little biting situation we've been dealing with," Danny muttered in an aside. "They say it's just a stage."

He turned to the woman, exposing his white teeth in a wide grin. "Luz, guess who this is?"

She gazed up at Venturi, who, like Danny, at six feet four, towered over her. "He called you Mike." Her lively eyes darted from one to the other. "*The* Mike? *Michael* Venturi?"

"The one and only," Danny said. "My wife, Luz. She's the mother," he said, nodding toward the children.

She hugged him warmly. "Danny talks about you all the time. He says you're like brothers." Inside, she snatched up the toddler who protested noisily.

"Does he know?" Luz asked, face bright with anticipation.

"How could he?" Danny said, taking the boy from her arms. "Michael Venturi, meet Michael Trado."

The curious, big-eyed toddler gazed up at the stranger.

"Is he named for . . . ?" Venturi's words trailed off as the child waved tiny fists.

"Damn straight," Danny said. "You can't say we weren't thinking about you."

"Let's take the dog for a drink of water."

Luz herded Scout and the children toward the kitchen.

Bright yellow cereal bowls and a small TV tuned to news and traffic reports sat on the table of a nearby breakfast nook.

Danny switched off the TV. "Coffee?"

"Too much caffeine aboard now. I just drove straight through from New York."

"A beer?"

"Wouldn't hurt."

Danny disappeared and returned with a six-pack of ice-cold Coors. "A little early." He shrugged. "But you don't show up every day."

"And it's happy hour somewhere," Venturi said.

"Look! He likes Fruit Loops!" a child shouted in the kitchen.

The boy stuck his head out the kitchen door. "Can we keep him?"

"I don't think so," Danny said. "He's your uncle Michael's dog. But maybe he'll let you play with him."

"We have no dog food," Luz said from behind the boy.

"That's all right. He doesn't like dog food," Venturi said apologetically. "But he's fine, he ate on the road."

They popped two beers and went to Danny's study. As he locked the door behind them, he lost the smile and his expression changed. "You okay, bro? Any problems? Do we need to circle the wagons?"

"Nope," Venturi said. "Except I'm out of a job. Kicked to the curb before I could quit."

"Sorry, bro."

"Don't be. I'm not. I never felt better."

"Heard the rumors. The grapevine was all abuzz. Can't wait to hear the real story," Danny said. "What's said in this room stays in this room." He pulled a punch at Venturi's shoulder. "You don't know how great it is to see you, man. You stayed in shape."

"You, too. It's been way too long. Knew you were married, didn't know you had three kids."

"Time flies. Just found out another one's on the way. Should be here next March." His smile faded. "Heard about your wife. Sorry, amigo."

"Me, too," Venturi said reflectively. "A tough time. How you doing?"

"I didn't re-up." Danny looked wistful. "They're offering big bonuses to reenlist. A hundred and fifty thousand to stay on. I taught recruits for a while." His boyish face grew serious. "I'd rather be in combat. Training is too damn stressful. You know their lives depend on what you're teaching 'em, and some won't survive. I'll take action anytime. You know how it is."

"Tell me about it."

"But when you have a family, life is different."

Venturi nodded and leaned back in the comfortable chair, his eyes roving the room. Danny had a large-screen TV. Above it and set in a horizontal wall panel were four smaller screens. Three of the small ones were tuned to local network affiliates, the fourth was on CNN, and the big screen was broadcasting Fox News. They were all on with the sound on mute. Danny always did have a need to know what was going on in the world.

Marine memorabilia decorated the walls and shelves, and his old guitar stood in a corner, next to a locked gun cabinet. There were a leather couch, several chairs and a desk, a computer, a printer, and a fax.

"I was a security specialist for a while," Danny was saying, "an independent contractor. The sky's the limit. Some people will pay anything for security. But Luz wanted to live in Miami. She's Cuban, has family here.

"Miami," he said fondly, "is not like living stateside. It's not your USA, bro. It's high octane, a foreign capital alive with rumors

96

of war, plots, schemes, international intrigue, alien smuggling, and drug trafficking. This town is full of thieves, liars, con men, and killers all caught up in superstition, greed, lust, and espionage. It is *so* damn cool. I love it, man.

"And my Spanish is good." He winked. "You know I can pass for Cuban, Colombian, whatever."

Both men were multilingual and with a talent for dialects that had served them well in Force Recon.

Danny took a long swallow from his beer. "This whole damn state's a disaster theme park. People like you and me fit right in here. Being trained to kill gives us an edge. And I still see action, occasional missions to the old familiar places and a few new ones. The rest of the time I stay busy as hell here."

Venturi looked puzzled. "Doing what, Danny?"

"Spy catching mostly, foreign agents operating clandestinely in South Florida. Miami's crawling with them."

"You with the FBI?"

"No, not the fat boys in suits." He leaned happily back in his chair, knees apart, grin widening. "The company, man. The boys with big toys."

"CIA?"

97

He nodded.

Made sense to Venturi. Danny's innate street smarts and love of action generated a freewheeling charm that made him the best at what he did. Men and women were attracted to him. He could walk into a crowded bar in a strange city, or country, and in fifteen minutes know everything that was going on — and he'd be the new best friend of everybody there. People gravitated to him.

"Your cover?"

"I manage a funeral home in Little Havana. Don't laugh. It's perfect. The customers never talk back and you wouldn't believe the intel you pick up from the bereaved. They're surprisingly talkative, bro. Of course I had to learn a lot of new skills that could come in handy some day. Like embalming."

The two friends picked up where they'd left off, as though they had never been apart. For the first time, Venturi told the full story of his trip to New Hampshire: the surveillance, the house, the freezer, the armored car, and what followed.

"Salvi's nephew, the damn lookout, was wearing military camouflage, body armor, and firing a silver AK-47."

"Kidding me! Wish I'd been there." Danny

paced the room, indignant at missing the action.

"Wished you were. Surveillance is damn hard alone, to say nothing of engaging the enemy when you're outnumbered and out-gunned."

Danny shrugged nonchalantly. "Not the first time."

"First time on American soil. That felt strange as hell."

"A preview of what's to come," Danny said darkly. "The world is shrinking into a smaller, scarier place, bro."

"Ever notice how training kicks back in when you need it?" Venturi said. Relaxed, he was beginning to feel the fatigue. "Amazing how that happens."

"Oh, yeah." Danny grinned and popped another beer. "A great high, if it doesn't kill you. Had a messy little mission to Colombia recently. Illegal paramilitary group with close links to a U.S. company was executing the local union leaders.

"Was down in Cancún six weeks ago, where five people who smuggled Cubans into the U.S. through Mexico were shot in the head and dumped in a sinkhole. The shooters painted red arrows pointing to the bodies, wanted to be sure everybody got the message.

"And in Miami, everybody who's anybody has an assault weapon. Had four cops shot with one a month ago. Homeless guy killed a detective the other day. Used to be that every street punk had a Saturday night special, now it's an AK-47." Danny checked his watch. "What are your plans now?"

Venturi blinked at his own watch, eyes gritty. "Find a place to stay, then go fishing."

"Saltwater? I know a guy with a deep-sea fishing boat."

"Nah, nothing elaborate. I just want to go into the Everglades and fish for bass."

"Okay, but we'll have to fight off the mosquitoes this time of year. By the way, forget finding a place to stay. We've got a little guesthouse out back, behind the pool. Nothing fancy," he said, "but it's off the radar. Crash as long as you want. Looks like you could use some shut-eye right now."

The shaded cottage surrounded by palms and banana trees was small, clean, and comfortable. Venturi backed his car up the driveway beside the house so the tag couldn't be seen from the street, brought in his bag, then walked Scout around the block with Danny's two oldest children, Javi and Julee. He let the boy hold the leash. He held the little girl's hand.

"Are you really our uncle?" the boy asked dubiously.

"Sure," Venturi answered. "That's what your dad said. Friends are the family you choose."

"Then why didn't you come before?" he protested, his brow furrowed.

"I was working far away."

"Very, very far away?" Julee asked.

"Very far," he said, then changed the subject. "So what's the best thing about a big brother?"

"Kisses!" She giggled.

He turned to the boy. "And the best thing about a little sister?"

"Nothing." He grimaced. "I don't like her."

By the time he returned to the cottage, the room was cool, and the water hot. Luz had turned on both the room air-conditioner and the water heater. The linens were fresh, the towels fluffy, and she had turned down the bed. There was even a cold bottle of water and a bowl of fresh fruit on the dresser.

He shaved, showered, drank some of the bottled water, drew the blackout drapes, pulled back the crisp cool sheets, and sighed contentedly. Though the semitropical sun blazed outside, the room was totally dark.

He was asleep before his head hit the pillow.

He awoke rested but disoriented. For a moment, in a strange bed in the dark, he didn't know where he was. The last time he had slept was twelve hundred miles away in his own apartment, which he would likely never see again. He sat up bewildered then heard a sound in the dark, a dog's claws clicking across the tile floor.

"Scout?"

The dog panted patiently at his bedside.

Venturi fumbled for the night table lamp and turned it on. He saw the fruit bowl and water bottle on the dresser and his familiar suitcase open on a chair. It wasn't a dream, he was really in Miami, with Danny and his family.

He'd slept for seven hours. He dressed quickly, in khakis and a white shirt, and stepped outside. The air was fragrant and overheated. Pink clouds etched in gold drifted across an azure sky. The turquoise surface of the pool shimmered in the late afternoon light, as a fiery orange sun dipped behind the trees.

"Uncle Mike's awake!" little Javi shouted as Venturi approached the screened-in back patio. "He's awake!"

Mouthwatering aromas wafted from the

102

kitchen. He hadn't realized he was so hungry.

The kids were playing with Gil the gerbil, who was driving his Critter Cruiser, a bright red toy car with a racing stripe, at breakneck speed through the house. The furry creature, with a pink nose and a tail as long as his body, propelled the car by running on an exercise wheel in the passenger compartment. The faster he ran, the faster the car sped, straight ahead.

Adults laughed, the kids loved it, and so did Scout, who watched, fascinated.

Danny wore jeans and a black T-shirt that read: TO ERR IS HUMAN, TO FORGIVE IS DIVINE. NEITHER IS MARINE POLICY. He captured the children and carried them off to bed despite their protests.

Luz was in the kitchen when he returned. "Don't be surprised," Danny warned Venturi, "if some woman, or women, show up."

"Women?"

"Luz asked if you were single. She cried when I told her what happened, then she wanted to know which one of her girlfriends is your type.

"Don't panic," he said, seeing Venturi's expression. "The woman is Miami's matchmaking queen. It's in her blood, and her friends are hot. I mean *smoking*."

"I'm sure they are," Venturi said. "But right now, all I want to do is go fishing."

"I told her that," Danny said. "But she won't be happy until everybody is married and making babies."

"I tried that once," Venturi said.

"It's been, what, more than three years?" Danny asked.

Venturi nodded. "She was the best thing that ever happened to me. I was the worst that could happen to her."

"How so? I only met her once, but you seemed great together."

"But if we hadn't met, she wouldn't have been pregnant or on that ferry when it smashed into the pier. She'd be alive."

"Bullshit," Danny said.

"No, it's not. I blew it. I was so damn careful. Wouldn't let her breathe the fumes when I painted the nursery, but I let her and her mother take that ferry to Manhattan for the baby shower her coworkers gave."

"Don't beat yourself up, man. She would have been on that same damn ferry, or hit by lightning or a goddamn taxi cab whether she knew you or not. You know my theory: There's a big blackboard up in the sky. If your name is on it, you're gonna die that day. If it ain't, you ain't — no matter what."

Danny's Blackboard Theory was older

than their friendship.

It neatly explained fatal bolts from the blue on sunny days, and stray bullets that fall from the sky on New Year's Eve and find their mark.

"How else do you explain a guy who uses the same electric drill for twenty years and all of a sudden one day it electrocutes him?" Danny asked. "Or the motorist who drives under a familiar overpass just as a giant concrete slab falls off a crane? How do you explain that?"

"Shit happens?" Venturi asked.

"Nope. Danny's Blackboard Theory. Here's a new one. Look at this." He fumbled among the newspapers on his desk and found the story about a snorkler attacked by an alligator. The gator ripped the man's arm off at the shoulder. Bleeding profusely, with minutes to live, he staggered out of the remote lake and collapsed — in front of five strangers on a picnic.

"And who were the strangers?" Danny asked triumphantly. "Five registered nurses with a cooler full of ice."

Their fast action saved the man's life. Doctors called it a miracle. Danny's explanation? "His name wasn't on the damn blackboard."

Dinner was *boliche* — Cuban pot roast,

slow-cooked in light gravy, thick slices that melted succulently in their mouths, *moros* — black beans and rice — and fat, sweet, moist plantains.

"Now you know why I married her," Danny said fondly, "and why I work out every day and run six miles every night."

The doorbell rang as they ate *tres leches,* a sweet and spongy milk-soaked cake, and drank Cuban coffee.

Danny lifted an eyebrow at Mike.

Tanya, a leggy, brown-eyed blond aerobics instructor, had dropped by and was invited to join them for dessert. Then Luz insisted that Danny go with her to see something in the garage.

Tanya and Venturi made small talk. As their hosts returned he heard Luz ask, "Why is an organized garage an impossible dream?"

Venturi smiled. Tanya smiled back. She smiled a lot, he thought. She was friendly, had a hard, lithe body, and offered to show him around Miami, but his heart wasn't in it. Somehow he and Danny wound up watching the news in his study, while Luz and Tanya talked in the kitchen.

Danny assured him in the days that followed that the Miami media focused only on

Castro, Cuban and Haitian issues, and the city's constant public corruption scandals. And he was right. The distance between Venturi and the headlines the Salvi case still generated in New York, middle America, and Washington, D.C., was a relief.

Luz persisted in her efforts to find him a mate. She and Danny invited Venturi on family outings to parks with pony rides, to the Children's Museum, and to an ocean-side picnic where Mirta, another of her friends, demonstrated a tracker's skill by finding them on a crowded beach. She wore a black thong bikini, a thin gold chain around her waist, and a demure gold cross on a chain that dangled deep into her decolletage.

She and Luz greeted each other with glad cries.

"Oh, man," Danny muttered, nudging Venturi, "she's the one I was telling you about. Boobs out to her elbows."

Luz gave them a look then pretended to ignore them.

When Venturi mentioned fishing, Mirta wrinkled her nose.

"Please," she said, "do me a favor. Do not kiss them on the mouth."

"Excuse me?" What was Luz telling her friends about him?

"You didn't see the show?" Her long red fingernails slowly brushed sand from her inner thighs.

"The show?" Where did Luz find these women? He found it difficult to focus on her face and not her skimpy bikini top. When she suddenly darted off to help Luz chase down Javi, who had plunged headlong into the surf, he and every other man on the beach could not help but gape at her even skimpier string bottom.

"Don't fight it, amigo," Danny said. "Miami's Matchmaking Queen never fails."

Mirta returned out of breath, chest heaving, water dripping, breasts struggling to escape the confines of her bikini top.

"Where were we?" She tossed her long thick hair and smiled, her teeth flashing.

"The show?" He licked his lips.

It was a national cable television series starring sportsmen devoted to wildlife and the environment, she explained. As cameras zoomed in for close-ups, the TV anglers would kiss the fish they caught on the mouth, then release them.

That symbolic signature gesture caught on and was emulated by viewers and sportsmen. Advertising writers seized upon it. Resort and tourism ads urged vacationers to "kiss a fish," among other idyllic experiences.

Nationwide warnings were issued after an unfortunate rash of incidents received much less coverage. Yet the shows still aired, and the ads were still being published.

"Snook and leatherjackets have teeth," Mirta explained. "The bites are very nasty."

Only yesterday, she said, another angler had been rushed to surgery, *"Plastic surgery,"* she said, on his upper lip and right nostril. Mirta was an emergency-room nurse.

"Never kiss them."

Venturi vowed he wouldn't. He had never thought about kissing a fish. Now, like a child warned not to lick a frozen pump handle, he wondered what it would be like. Bemused, he went as far as asking Mirta for her phone number but never called.

He felt most at home — at peace — in the Everglades, where time slows and ancient instincts awaken. He loved to see the congestion of the city give way to vast open spaces at the end of the road. He liked it so much that he leased a house with an option to buy. It had once been a remote fishing camp deep in the Glades. Through the years, as Miami's urban sprawl crept west, it had been improved and added on to and was now a rambling one-story four-bedroom house in a relatively isolated area now on the fringe of the great swamp. The property backed onto a wide canal with a wooden dock. It was fenced in, too, with room for Scout to run and roam.

He bought an eighteen-foot bass boat with a shallow draft hull that could float in eight inches of water. It had a small windshield, a seventy-five-horsepower engine, and locked compartments with deck hatches to store equipment. He and the dog took daily trips into the wild. No danger he'd become lost. As a boy he'd hike as far as he could into the woods, then find his way back. As a Force Recon Marine he aced courses in land navigation, and Survival Evasion Resistance and Escape (SERE) Training. He was a scout sniper. What he enjoyed most now was being out on the boat among the tree islands, surrounded by birds, sky, and water. Nothing else interested Michael Venturi. He felt stalled in a holding pattern, and he hated feeling aimless. At early ages, he and Danny had become part of something larger than themselves, had learned the value of teamwork, discipline, and tradition.

Now, he felt part of nothing except this ancient sea of grass. He was waiting, watching for a signal that would point the way to a new direction in life.

The day it happened, he took sandwiches, water, and the dog to an area he wanted to explore further.

He anchored near a placid lake and listened to the wind and the birds, mesmerized by low-hanging clouds and his vast surroundings. He baited a hook but paid little attention to the line.

He thought they were alone. The low moan he heard first could have been the wind astir in the saw grass. The louder anguished human groan caught him off guard. He stood to get a read on the direction. The dog got to his feet, as well, stiff-legged in the small wooden boat, whimpering under his breath. Another groan was followed by an almost inhuman cry of despair, then a gunshot.

Scout leaped from the boat and splashed barking in the direction of the sounds.

Venturi cursed. It was too dangerous for the dog. There were pythons and alligators out here — and somebody with a gun.

He called the dog again, then picked up his own gun and went after him.

CHAPTER NINE

Venturi found the dog at a small campsite, barking furiously at something in the serene woodland lake. A man floated facedown in the water, his unbuttoned white shirt billowing around him as he drifted farther from shore.

There was no one else in sight.

Venturi cursed, stripped off his own shirt, yanked off his boots, and waded into the tea-colored lake. When his footing dropped off into deep water, he swam out to the man, trying to avoid the reeds, vines, and aquatic grasses reaching like tentacles to entangle an unwary swimmer.

The man never moved as Venturi came up behind him. He turned him over in the water, wrapped one arm around his neck and under the armpit, then saw blood on his arm, swirling in the water, everywhere. The man's throat was cut.

Gators roamed the lake. Venturi knew the

creatures normally fed at night but were hungry now. The drought had shrunk their hunting habitat during mating season, forcing them to forage farther and hunt longer for food and sex. He had seen them here before. He saw one now.

An alligator at least twelve feet long had been sunning itself on the muddy shore just a moment ago. Now it slid swiftly into the water about a hundred feet away.

Scout was also in the lake, gamely dog-paddling behind him. Venturi tightened his grip on the man and shouted at Scout to get out of the water: "Go! Go! Go!" He swam as hard as he could, using a side-stroke, hip pressed against the man's back to keep him above the surface so he could breathe, if he had any breath left in him.

Behind him, a muffled splash signaled the entrance of a second, slightly smaller gator that came from nowhere, gliding smoothly toward them at a thirty-degree angle.

"Go!" he shouted, desperation in his voice. The dog, a few feet away, was swimming toward him. Suddenly obedient, Scout turned, and began paddling back toward shore with Venturi right behind him.

As his feet touched the mucky shallows he caught the stranger under the arms to drag him toward solid ground. Scout was already ashore, at the water's edge, barking fiercely at the gators.

Making it out of the lake didn't mean they were safe. Surprisingly fast on dry land, gators often attack, then drag their prey into the water. They kill pets, wildlife, and people who venture too close to lakes and canal banks.

He knew he couldn't outrun them. Struggling to gain purchase on dry land, he slipped in the mud. The man, a dead weight, nearly fell from his arms. The gators were just a few feet behind. Venturi saw their flat reptilian eyes and their upper teeth. The stranger might be dead already. Should he save him, or the dog? If the man was still alive, he had made his own choice, put himself in this position. At least Scout was alive. So far. A barking thirty-five-pound mutt would have no chance at all against a hungry four-hundred-and-fifty-pound alligator.

He rolled the man up and out of the water, then ran for his gun, tucked into one of his boots twenty-five feet away. Then he saw something better. A heavy piece of wood, a four-foot-long branch from an Australian pine. Venturi disliked shooting an animal. He hated to kill these prehistoric-looking reptiles unless he had no choice —

114

humans were the intruders here after all. And gunshots might attract a forest ranger or a deputy on patrol. He did not feel comfortable identifying himself to law enforcement at the moment.

The first, bigger gator splashed out of the water and paused for a millisecond, as though deciding whether to go for the motionless body on the ground or the furiously barking dog, an annoying moving target. He went for the dog.

Venturi advanced, swung with all his might, smashed the clublike weapon across the gator's snout, and let it go. The startled creature hissed, then splintered the thick branch between his teeth with a loud crunch.

The second gator paused, giving Venturi time to drag the stranger to his boat. "Let's go! Let's go!" he called to the still-barking dog. Scout scrambled into the boat with them, shaking water off his coat, panting, and glancing indignantly over his shoulder.

If the dog didn't realize it before, he knew it now — he wasn't in New Hampshire anymore.

The man sprawled in the bottom of the boat coughed, then snorted. He was bleeding but still alive. Venturi checked his airway, found it clear, then turned his head to one side. A surprising amount of water gushed from his nose and mouth.

He appeared to be in his forties, medium height, and slender, at about 145 pounds. His hands, though bruised and scratched, were soft and pale, not those of a laborer. He looked like someone who worked indoors at a sedentary job.

Venturi had no doubt that he had interrupted a suicide attempt. The man's wrists were slashed, as well. The cuts were not hesitation marks, but he had done it wrong and the wounds were superficial. He had also stabbed himself in the chest, but his breastbone had apparently deflected the knife thrust. The throat wound was bloody, but if the blade had penetrated his carotid artery he'd already be dead. The head wound bled freely, as head wounds do, but the bullet had only grazed his scalp. Venturi decided this was the most inept suicide attempt he'd ever seen. Yet it was no cry for help or bid for attention. The man was serious. Dead serious. He never intended to be found.

Who is he? Venturi wondered. Few suicides travel deep into the wilds to dispose of their own bodies, which was exactly what this man had done. Bleeding from self-inflicted injuries, he had plunged into an alligator-infested lake. He clearly intended to disappear without a trace and would have succeeded, had Venturi not stumbled upon the scene.

Keeping an eye on the gators just offshore, Venturi checked the campsite. There had been a small fire at the center. Papers had been burned, and the fire stirred until all had been incinerated and reduced to ash. Even the FBI lab would find it impossible to resurrect evidence from it.

The clues were few. He was a Marlboro man. He'd left a Bic lighter and two of the brand's flip-top boxes, one empty, the other half full. He was neat. The empty pack held a small pen knife and a pair of fingernail clippers.

It appeared as though he had been there for hours, maybe days, trying to find the strength to complete his plan.

He had left two untouched sandwiches, both American cheese on white bread wrapped in plastic, and a half pint of blended whiskey. The bottle was empty, the final toast consumed.

It must have been to bolster his courage. It was not enough to anesthetize him.

Venturi found the man's shoes, a bent steak knife, and the gun, a small-caliber two-shot Derringer in the shallows at the lake's edge. The gun was empty. No trace of anyone else.

He went back to the boat.

The moaning stranger struggled to sit up, making his wounds bleed more. His hair was dark brown, his eyes light brown. He looked oddly familiar.

Venturi opened his first-aid kit and began to check the man's injuries. The first shot was probably a test to see if the gun worked. When he fired the second, his hand must have been shaking.

Venturi wrapped a Curlex compression dressing around the man's left wrist, tight enough to stop the bleeding but not enough to cut off circulation. The patient tried to jerk his arm away.

"No! Don't do that. Let me die," he pleaded in English.

"You'll be all right," Venturi assured him. "I'll take you to the hospital. They'll fix you up, then you can talk to a shrink."

"No way!" Tears mingled with the water glistening on his face and dripping from his hair.

"Way," Venturi said firmly. "What's your problem?"

"I'm having a bad day."

"Better than no day at all. You just came damn close to being gator food. Not a good way to go, man. Life can always get better. Suicide is a permanent solution to a temporary situation."

The man seemed about to laugh but winced instead, as Venturi cleaned his scalp wound with a Betadine-soaked swab. "My life is over," he blurted, "dead in the water. The way I should be. No hospital. I can't go there. Word will get out. The vultures will be all over me."

Venturi gazed at him curiously. "You mean the press?"

The man nodded, gasping. "Please," he said, despair in his voice, "just go away. Leave me here."

"That's not an option."

He struggled feebly to hurl himself out of the boat. Venturi easily restrained him, held him down with one hand, and warned him to stop or he'd be handcuffed.

"You're a cop?"

"Nope. But that doesn't mean I don't have handcuffs."

The man maintained a defeated silence nearly all the way back to Venturi's place. He sat hunched over across from Scout, who watched him, his expression grave.

"I had a dog like that once," the man mumbled, his voice breaking.

Venturi nodded. "You were lucky."

"He's all wet. Did he pull me out of the water?"

"No. He's not Lassie." Venturi smiled at the private joke. "He was too busy barking at the gators that were about to drag you under."

"You should have let 'em." His voice sounded hollow. "My life is broken and can't be fixed."

"Anything can be fixed," Venturi lied, acutely aware of so many things that never can be fixed, like the lost girls in New Hampshire. "You wanted by the law?"

"No." The man reacted with umbrage at the suggestion. "I've never been arrested. I wish it was that simple. Then I could surrender, do time, and it would end."

"What's your name?" Venturi couldn't shake the nagging feeling that he'd seen this man before.

"When this gets out . . ." The thin voice trailed off. "A lot of people would be happy to hear I was dead," he said after a moment. "I didn't want to give them the satisfaction."

Venturi had planned to drop the man off at a hospital emergency room without becoming involved. But if he did, what would stop the guy from boarding an elevator to the roof and jumping?

He couldn't let that happen after all the

trouble he'd gone to to keep him alive. And he was curious.

The man seemed lucid and was in no danger of dying, but they were both in sticky, dirty, unpleasantly wet clothes. He docked the boat, helped the man up the bank, and took him into the house instead.

The man's shirt and jeans were way too big, not even close to his correct size. His shoes were also too big by several sizes. Yet he did not appear to be homeless. He sounded educated, had good teeth, and seemed to be healthy.

The man showered. He had no tattoos or old scars that Venturi could see, but scores of mosquito, spider, and red ant bites had increased his torment. Venturi gave him some of his clean clothes that were also too long and too large on the smaller man.

Venturi checked the pockets of the man's oversized garments, found nothing, and tossed them into the washing machine. He'd gone into the Glades to think, hoping to sort out his future. Quiet time close to nature had always comforted him. Instead, he'd encountered gunshots, blood in the water, and jeopardy.

What the hell is this? Venturi wondered. The man could be a serial killer who couldn't live with himself and decided to disappear, leaving his fate an unsolved mystery. Half a dozen possible scenarios crossed his mind. He wanted the real story.

He poured the man a shot of bourbon and heated some of the bright yellow homemade chicken soup from a quart bottle Luz had sent home with him the night before. Danny swore the rich broth cured colds and hangovers faster than aspirin or Advil.

They sat across from each other at the rough-hewn wooden table.

"Okay," Venturi said calmly, as the man scratched his multiple mosquito bites between sips of soup. "What's up?"

"I used to work for NASA," he said, resigned. He paused as though expecting a response. When none came, he continued. "When I was four years old I told everybody I was going to be an astronaut when I grew up. By high school I knew it was impossible. I could never pass the physical — a heart murmur, allergies, and so on — so I focused on the next best thing. I studied computer sciences and electrical, mechanical, and aeronautical engineering and actually wound up working for NASA. The next best thing to that childhood dream was to support the astronauts and their missions."

In a sudden flash of revelation, Venturi knew exactly who the man was and where he had seen him: on television, and in newspapers and magazines.

The man caught his look of recognition.

"That's right." He nodded. "It was me. I'm the one who killed the astronauts. That's what they say. The whole world believes it. Even my wife believed it. My kids, too. I lost my job, my reputation, my family and friends.

"The press convicted me in the court of public opinion and will never stop hounding me. Ever."

Venturi remembered the two veteran astronauts killed in a freak accident and the man blamed and accused of trying to cover up his mistake, or worse. The two, part of the crew on a mission to the space station, died during a routine repair procedure.

A 125-foot mechanical arm, attached to the shuttle and stored along the hinge line of the payload bay doors, malfunctioned and swung wildly, severing the tether of the astronaut working on it. Then it slammed into the second spacewalker, knocking off his helmet, splitting his space suit, killing him instantly.

The first man floated free in space, his radio still operational. "That wasn't supposed to happen," he blurted. The shuttle crew, Houston, and the entire world heard his last words: "Damn it, Lyle!"

He never uttered another word, although he apparently remained alive and conscious for some time. A rescue attempt failed. Plans for a recovery mission were still under way.

Lyle was the engineer who designed a virtual-reality simulation used to train astronauts in such repairs. He had taken them through the procedures in a wind tunnel, in space suits, over and over.

Now that man, Lyle Gates, a lifelong NASA employee, sat in Venturi's kitchen and explained how he had become a scapegoat, damned by a hero's last words, and blamed by coworkers and superiors for a freak accident that was not his fault.

During the chaotic press coverage that followed the accident, coworkers pointed fingers, made accusations. The national media anticipated an indictment. But it never happened. Gates was forced off the job, his reputation ruined. Divorced by his wife, shunned by family and friends, the press continued to hound him.

The goal of every major news organization was to land "the get," the interview in which Gates finally confessed to acts of carelessness, incompetence, or downright malice against the heroes he saw soar to heights that he could never achieve.

He explained it all to Venturi.

While he was training the lost astronaut, he had carefully demonstrated the proper technique and warned repeatedly against overtightening a mechanism, that if stripped, would loosen and cause the arm to swing the other way.

"He made a mistake," Gates said. "When he said my name, he remembered our sessions and realized what he'd done wrong. He knew he'd been properly instructed. I don't believe he intended to damn me with his last words, but that's how it sounded. He knew he screwed up but didn't want to admit it to the world. So he never spoke again. That wasn't the legacy he wanted to leave."

Gates said he had urged more training sessions before the mission. But none of his memos were found.

"My mistake was that I devoted too much time and energy to the job. I neglected my family and pissed off coworkers who were unwilling to make the same sacrifices.

"But to me it wasn't a job, it was a mission, it was my identity," he said softly. "I loved working for the program. The men and women who venture into space were my heroes. I would have died to protect them."

His words had the ring of truth.

"I think the best way to waste your life," he said, "is to go to work for a government agency."

"You're preaching to the choir," Venturi said. "If what you say is true, it's a damn shame the spacewalker didn't man up to his mistake. But surely, with your background, there are other lines of work you could pursue outside the space program."

"There are. I could design video games, software, virtual-reality tours. I'm interested in biochemistry as well, specifically the field of nutrition. But they won't let me."

Every time he found a new job, word leaked out and the media pack invaded, disrupting business until he was fired.

"I'm more hated than O. J. Simpson, who is still treated like a hero by some people. The only person I ever hurt was myself.

"I was investigated by everybody from a grand jury right up to a U.S. Senate committee. But I was never indicted. There was nothing to indict me for, not a single shred of evidence. But some things you never live down. Life isn't long enough." He finished his soup and swallowed a small, tentative sip of the whiskey.

His expression made it clear that he didn't even like the taste.

"What's with your clothes?" Venturi asked. "Why are they all too big?"

Gates smiled ruefully. "When I ran out of money I told my landlady I was moving to Chicago. I didn't want to be reported missing. Then I traded my clothes and shoes with some homeless men who live under the MacArthur Causeway bridge. I remembered reading that police can often identify human remains by the labels and the sizes of their clothes, belts, and shoes. They release the information to the public and hope someone will recognize it. If my remains were found, I wanted the information they released to be all wrong."

Damn, Venturi thought again, he seriously wanted to disappear.

"How did you get way out there? I didn't see a car."

"A small, flat-bottomed boat. I scuttled it in another lake about two miles east, then slogged over to where you found me. It took a couple hours. Didn't see another soul. I thought it would work," he said, voice flat.

"It almost did."

"Sorry to be so much trouble." He gingerly fingered the scalp wound, then studied his bandaged wrists.

"I won't apologize for ruining your plans."

They talked till dark. Gates, still queasy from his near-death experience, wasn't hungry but didn't refuse more soup. Venturi heated it for him and, because he didn't want to stay up all night to protect the man from himself, dissolved two Ambien in the bubbling broth.

He showed him to a guest bedroom with an adjoining bath after removing anything Gates could use to hurt himself.

"I have personal issues of my own to work out," he said, "and I've also had run-ins with the press, so do me a favor, Lyle. Don't do anything crazy in my house tonight. Get some rest. Things always look better in the morning."

Lyle promised. But, as a precaution, Venturi offered him a pill for pain. It was actually another sleeping pill. Lyle gratefully washed it down with water.

Then Venturi hid the pill bottle.

He checked an hour later to be sure the man was still breathing. Lyle Gates looked younger in sleep, the stress lines not etched as deeply in his face. Venturi locked the bedroom door from the outside so his houseguest would not escape.

He'd learned long ago: Never trust a man who is not afraid to die.

He drank coffee, ate a sandwich, booted up his laptop, and Googled Lyle Gates. Hundreds and hundreds of hits came up: vitriolic editorials, politicians launching investigations, citizens demanding justice, and zealous reporters' interviews with relatives, teachers, and childhood friends who described Gates' lifelong passion and his disappointment when he failed to make the grade.

Gates had offered to undergo a polygraph test. When he did, the press reported he had passed, then listed all the methods that cheaters use to beat lie detectors, along with quotes from experts explaining that sociopaths and psychopaths can often pass polygraphs despite their obvious guilt.

So much for the unbiased mainstream press, Venturi thought. He began to believe that through no fault of his own, Gates' life had been short-circuited by events totally out of his control. He would go down in history as The Man Who Killed The Astronauts, probably out of jealousy, or to sabotage the space program that rejected him. No way to salvage that future.

Or was there? Wide awake at 4 a.m. Venturi paced the shadowy room, mind racing, recalling the fiery crash of a commuter train in London.

The estimated toll was high — more than one hundred rush-hour passengers missing and presumed dead. But workers who cut apart the molten metal once the wreckage cooled were shocked. All the victims they expected were not there. Dozens of waiting body bags went unused. And for months after the crash numerous sightings of people who'd been presumed dead were reported. Many survivors had embraced unexpected disaster as an opportunity to escape, hoping to shed their identities as snakes do their skins.

The news accounts had fascinated him. He had realized then that winning the lottery was no longer the world's most popular fantasy. Caught in frustrating and stress-filled lives in a world of traffic jams, voice mail, e-mail, and marital malaise, people now dreamed of a chance to start over, free from the baggage of the past.

Who wouldn't want a fresh start, a new life? he thought.

He and the dog strolled in the bright moonlight along the canal bank behind the house. He had spent the last several years creating new identities and new lives for people who didn't deserve them.

Why couldn't I, he wondered, *give a new start to someone who actually deserved it?*

He laughed aloud at the idea, wishing that Maddy was there to share it. She would have loved it.

Could Lyle Gates, the would-be suicide, thrive again and fulfill some other dream? The possibility intrigued him.

Such a fascinating experiment would be a huge challenge. Lyle Gates could not simply be whisked away and relocated by federal agents. He'd have to be declared legally dead. There had to be proof, a corpse, eyewitnesses, or irrefutable forensics.

He never slept. At dawn his mind was still racing.

He had to find a way to kill Lyle Gates.

CHAPTER TEN

He woke up the only person he trusted.

"Bad night at the funeral home," Danny mumbled into the phone, his voice groggy. "An all-night viewing for a member of Brigade 2506."

"Didn't know many were still alive."

"One less now. Fought to the last bullet during the Bay of Pigs invasion, was shot and captured. Some of his Santero friends showed up last night for a ritual to raise the dead. I was cool with the drums, but then they brought in the goat and the chickens. Some mourners objected. Others didn't. When I laid down the law that no animals would be sacrificed on the premises, all hell broke loose. A Brigade vet pulled a gun. Half a dozen others drew down on 'im. Everybody else ran out the door. Think they were running away? Hell, no! They were running to get guns from their cars. Had a situation on my hands."

"Damn. What'd you do?"

"Locked half out, the other half in, got it under control, and barely managed to keep the cops out of it. Convinced 'em that all the shots fired had nothing to do with us, that it was a brawl that spilled out of a bar around the corner."

He yawned. "Had a few bad moments. We almost wound up with more corpses than caskets. Made sure that the wounded and maimed all went to hospitals in different jurisdictions.

"A dozen detectives from Miami to Coral Gables to Hialeah and the Beach must be scratching their heads, trying to figure out what the hell went down. They never tell the truth, you know."

He paused, then raised his voice. "It's these damn Cubans! They lie for the hell of it even when they don't need to! Every last one is crazy! Especially the women!"

Venturi heard Luz attack as she called him a son of a dog in Spanish.

He heard squeals, pleas for help, screams of laughter, and bedsprings bouncing. Tickling sounded like the weapon of choice.

"Should I call back?" Venturi asked.

"No, no, buddy," Danny finally gasped. "I've got the crazy Cuban woman pinned down and under control. Hey, we thought

133

you were coming by last night."

"Had a coupla bad moments, myself — with somebody I want you to meet."

"A woman?"

"Michael found a woman?" Luz sounded crushed that he might have done so without her help.

"No, a guy. Not one I'd introduce to your wife and kids right now."

"Gotcha."

"Can you stop by here for breakfast? I want you to meet him and then brainstorm with me about an idea I had last night."

Venturi was frying bacon and eggs over easy when Danny arrived on his Harley. Lyle Gates was still asleep.

"You and Luz sounded like you were having fun this morning," Venturi said wistfully as he poured orange juice and coffee. "Reminded me of Maddy." He smiled. "I thought about her a lot last night. You two are so lucky."

Danny dug into his eggs. "It's not all bliss, you know. Kids screaming, baby crying, no sleep. Luz wanting me to stay home and organize the garage while I'm out trying to save the world. And now another baby's on the way."

"She thrives on it," he said. "If she has

134

her way, we'll have eleven kids — like Bobby Kennedy. He could afford them. I'm thinking we should stop at four. But she wants a damn platoon.

"Of course," he said reflectively, "I wouldn't trade a minute with that woman for anything in the world."

"I know."

"And the upside," he said with a grin, "is the cleavage she develops when she's pregnant. I'm looking forward to that.

"So who is the guy?" he asked, mopping up egg yolk with his toast. "Where is he?"

"Still asleep when I unlocked his door."

Danny stopped chewing, raised eyebrows questioning.

"Had to lock him in last night."

"Afraid he'd murder you in your sleep? Or escape your hospitality?"

Venturi filled him in.

Danny gave a long, low whistle after Mike finished his description of the slashing, the stabbing, the shooting, and the alligators. Then he smiled.

"Know why he's alive?" he said, picking up his coffee mug.

"I know," Venturi said. "His name wasn't on the goddamn blackboard in the sky. By the way, you might recognize that name." He finished the story.

"I remember him." Danny looked impressed. "Everybody was after his ass. If he was guilty of a damn thing, even negligence, he'da been nailed for sure."

"Thank you. Here's what I'm thinking."

Danny cocked his head as he absorbed the details. "You sure you want to get that involved?"

"I'm not saying it'd be easy. But it might make up for some of the shit I did for the Marshals Service — for Salvi specifically." He shrugged. "Maybe the right word is atonement."

"You don't owe penance or apologies to anybody, Mike. You didn't write the rules."

"No excuse. I should have tried to change them, fought harder, and refused to follow them. I could have quit, blown the whistle, and gone to the press. But no, I was too wrapped up in my own personal problems."

"Which you had at the time, bro."

"But look at the cost. Two children dead. Two Brinks guards hurt, almost killed. And who knows what other crimes Salvi did while we were 'protecting him' and not the public? Maybe I can make up for it a little by helping somebody. And think of what an interesting experiment it would be, given what we know about human behavior. My question to you is, do you think we can pull it off?"

"Sure," Danny said without hesitation. "We can pull off anything we set our minds to, man. Us being alive proves that. Remember Somalia, Afghanistan, Cali? Think about it, bro.

"But it's not just us. What's up with Alligator Man? Is he stand up or screw up? The real question is, can *he* pull it off?"

"Lyle was not exactly at the top of his game when we met yesterday," Venturi replied. "But he's smart and might want it bad enough. He'd have to work like hell. We would too. It's tricky. We'd need proof of death: a body, evidence, or eyewitnesses so damn convincing that he's declared legally dead, no questions asked."

Danny bit into a muffin slathered with strawberry preserves, took a bite, half closed his eyes as he swallowed, and gave a satisfied sigh before answering.

"Oh, it's doable, definitely doable." He patted his mouth with a napkin. "In Miami, man, *anything* is possible."

Scout stopped slurping and looked up from the bacon and eggs in his bowl, ears cocked and alert. Then they, too, heard the shuffling sound in the hall.

Lyle Gates appeared in the doorway.

Despite being middle-aged and unshaven, he looked like a boy dressed up in his father's clothes.

"I smelled coffee and bacon," he said apologetically. Blinking, he looked around the kitchen, his expression dazed, as though he had not seen it before.

"Good morning," Venturi said. "Lyle, this is Danny. Sit down and I'll get you a plate."

Lyle reached out to shake Danny's hand, but jerked his back, embarrassed by the bandages on his wrist.

"Sorry." He turned to Venturi. "That pain pill really knocked me out. When I woke up I didn't remember where I was at first."

"Used to happen to me all the time," Danny said. "Then I got married."

Lyle's appetite had returned. He ate heartily and his color looked better. "Never thought I'd taste one of these again," he said, buttering a muffin. After his second cup of coffee he seemed alert, though quiet.

He fingered the stubble on his chin. "I was going to shave," he said, "but I couldn't find a razor in the bathroom."

Venturi promised to find him one.

Then Gates answered any and all questions:

No, he had never been treated for depression or any other form of mental illness. He was not on medication. Yes, his overall health, physically and mentally, was good, until recently.

"I'm depressed, but not a victim of depression," he explained. "I have good reasons for my state of mind. Depression didn't cause my problems; my problems caused my depression."

"Most suicide attempts are once-in-a-lifetime events," Venturi said. "Most who are saved don't try again." He asked Gates if he thought it was true in his case.

"Yesterday I saw no other way out," Gates said matter-of-factly. "Nothing's changed. Don't get me wrong, I loved my life. If I could still contribute and live like a normal person, it would never happen again.

"But right now, I'm living in the moment, enjoying an excellent meal in good company. I thank you for both. But at the end of the day I'm still me, with the same past and no future."

"What if that could change?" Venturi asked, arms folded.

"It can't." He shook his head sadly.

"Maybe it could." Venturi shrugged.

"You can die," he offered. "Not alone and anonymous in a swamp, but publicly. Officially. Legally dead. A vital statistic. And soon after, somewhere else in the world, you could surface, with a different look, a brand-new name, a different date of birth, and a new occupation."

Gates looked bewildered for a moment. He licked his lips and sat up straighter in his chair, a fleeting look of hope in his eyes. "Is that possible? Could that actually happen?"

"The federal government does it all the time for witnesses in their protection program. Many are career criminals. Why not somebody like you?"

"Is it legal?" He looked confused.

"Hell, no," Venturi conceded. "But technically, neither is suicide. Why not try something less lethal?"

"The government . . . ?"

"Wouldn't be involved, at all," Venturi said. "I just used it as an example."

"It sounds like reincarnation," Gates said.

"Exactly," Danny said, "except you don't have to die or go through puberty again."

"I've heard about people who fake their own deaths for insurance money or to escape arrest. They get caught. They find them in Australia or . . ."

"Most do little or no planning," Venturi said. "They seize the moment, like the people who tried to disappear in the aftermath of 9/11, at the World Trade Center.

The trouble was they remained the same people, kept the same habits — they just changed their names. That's sloppy. The FBI was on them like white on rice.

"We, mostly you, would have to do it right or not at all. It would mean hard work, study, and determination on your part. It takes a superhuman effort to change a lifetime of habits and become somebody else. You'd have to leave everything behind. All your personal possessions, your personality, all your likes, dislikes, and quirks, and every other human being you ever knew. No exceptions. You smoke Marlboros, right?"

Gates nodded uncertainly.

"Not anymore. Commit to this and you can never smoke another Marlboro. You'd change brands permanently, or better yet, quit smoking forever. You'd be an entirely new person, with new traits, tastes, and habits.

"People fail because they remain the same person despite changing their names and maybe even their appearances."

Danny sipped his coffee, his eyes on Gates' face.

"The key to identifying you lies in your past," Venturi said. "A good investigator would study your background, learn all about your childhood, the schools you attended, your jobs, your friends and associates. He'd want to know your voice and speech patterns, gestures and mannerisms, eccentricities and secrets, the clothes you wear, the cars you like to drive, your hobbies and special interests. Armed with that, a sharp detective would know where you'd most likely go, what you'd do when you got there, even the people you would gravitate to and associate with.

"All those bits and pieces create a picture of you that normally remains unchanged no matter what you call yourself or whatever color you dye your hair.

"So, for this to work, you'd have to permanently break old habits, create new ones, and really become someone else. It's not simple," Venturi said. "Anything to add, Danny?"

"Nope," Danny said. "Except that it's permanent. No coming back."

"Stay here," Venturi said. "Rest, think about it for a few days, then let us know if you're interested. Whatever you decide, you can never repeat this conversation to anyone."

"Right." Danny drew his index finger across his neck, a somewhat empty threat since the man had tried to cut his own throat less than twenty-four hours earlier.

Gates stared at one, then the other, and leaned forward.

"Gentlemen, I don't need thirty seconds to think about it. If the slightest possibility exists that it could happen, that you could help me do it, I want to go for it." His eyes were eager. His voice rose. "I want it more than anything. I'd do whatever it takes."

Venturi cut his eyes at Danny. "What do you think?"

Danny nodded. "I'm down with it. I'm in."

"My cousin Billy died young, up in New Jersey," Gates offered. "A handsome, athletic, daredevil kid, only sixteen. School was out for the summer when he raced down a steep hill on his bike, lost it, and slammed into a pole in Paterson. Smashed his skull. Maybe I could use his identity. We could get a copy of his birth certificate. We were almost the same age. His last name was Raneletti."

Venturi shook his head. "Let dead friends and relatives stay buried. That's the kind of fact a good investigator would unearth right away. Don't worry, let us come up with a name."

Gates' brow furrowed. "I know I can do it," he said. "But obviously there are costs involved. Expenses. I don't have any money. My wife and kids got everything. But I can pay you back over time, once I'm established and situated."

"Negative," Venturi said. "You're to have absolutely no contact with anyone you ever knew, including me. That's shit waiting to happen. You won't Google old high school sweethearts and start exchanging e-mails. You won't subscribe to your hometown newspaper. Zero. Nothing. *Nada.* Like Lot's wife, no looking back. You will have no past. Everything will be brand-new, like being born again."

"He doesn't mean that in the religious sense," Danny said. "He means for real."

"I can do that," Gates swore. "Absolutely. But how do I pay you?"

"You don't."

Gates stared. "What do we do first?"

"Find you some clothes that fit," Venturi said. "What's your favorite color, Lyle?"

"Blue."

"Enjoy it now, because it won't be in the future. Think about things you never did before but might want to take up now. Think about where you want to live for the rest of your life. I suggest it be out of the United States, since you're so high profile here."

"You speak anything other than English?" Danny asked.

Lyle shook his head. "Just enough Spanglish to live in Florida, and a little high school French."

"So we're looking at an English-speaking country."

They plugged in a coffee pot in the big L-shaped Florida room facing the canal at the back of the house. That became their war room, with maps, reference books, chairs, a table, a desk, and a computer.

"Whataya do for fun, Lyle? You have a pilot's license, ski, sail, sky, or scuba dive?" Danny asked.

"Mostly, I worked," he said ruefully, "but I did get my scuba certification ten years ago before a family vacation. I love to spearfish, but haven't done much boating or diving lately."

"Bingo." Danny snapped his fingers. "Time to get back in the water."

Venturi agreed. "Any friends or relatives here in Miami?" he asked.

"No. My wife and the kids moved back to her hometown in Connecticut. I've kept pretty much to myself since my marriage broke up."

"Loner. Okay, that's part of your profile. It's vital that the circumstances of your death fit your prior behavior patterns."

"Right." Danny paced the long room. "But we need somebody who can substantiate a call or contact with you to satisfy the cops who will want to know exactly what you were doing prior to the fatal event."

"I met a girl," Gates said, "a woman actually. Divorced. Didn't seem to care about my notoriety. We ate lunch once, had a little picnic at Lummus Park."

"Think she'd be receptive if you called?"

He nodded. "She seemed lonely, too. We had no big spark, but it was nice having somebody to talk to. We went to a movie once and talked about diving. She asked me to teach her. But I couldn't afford to take her out so I didn't call her again."

"So we have her." Danny bit his lip, still pacing. Suddenly he stopped. "I think I've got it!"

He grinned at Lyle. "Here's how you can die."

Lyle Gates blinked as Danny spun the scenario he envisioned. Venturi interrupted, improvised, and filled in details.

"God, we're good!" Danny finally said.

"I love it!" Venturi said. "It's great!"

They shared a high five.

Venturi turned to Gates. "What do you think?"

"When?" the doomed man demanded. "When can we do it?"

CHAPTER ELEVEN

"Hi, darlin'," Venturi said. "Told you I'd call."

"It's about time, sweetheart. Are you all right?"

"Yes, I am," he said enthusiastically. "Anybody ask about me?"

"A few. None too serious. Nobody's given me the third degree under hot lights. So far."

"You'd never crack if they did."

She laughed. "All they'd get is my name, rank, and serial number. No black helicopters hovering yet."

"FYI, they're dark green, not black. Any chance you might have some vacation time?"

"I'm the boss, remember? I create the schedule."

"I'd love to see you, and I'd also like your help and expertise on a new project."

"Work with you? Sounds like fun. Where

are you? When should I be there?"

"Miami. Yesterday."

"How's tomorrow?"

"I'll pick you up at the airport. By the way, this is a non-call. Didn't happen. You just decided to cruise to Mexico."

"Can't wait to see your face."

"Ditto."

His next call was to the Manhattan office of his financial adviser, Jim Dance.

"Glad to hear your voice, Michael. So you finally decided to light somewhere and get in touch."

"I also decided to take your advice, Jim, and use some of the money."

"Good for you! It's about time. Madison would be pleased."

"I think so, too." He instructed Dance to wire $100,000 to his bank in Miami.

Dance took down the account number. "I can have it there tomorrow. Sure that's all you need?"

"I think so. If not I'll be in touch."

"What? You investing in real estate? Buying a boat?"

"More of a local charitable project."

"Don't forget to retain all your receipts for tax purposes."

"Sure." Venturi hung up smiling, wondering how anyone could sell this to the IRS.

He winced when he spotted her. Why didn't she ask for a wheelchair? She had navigated the long concourse on her prosthesis, toting a heavy bag slung over her shoulder and dragging a wheeled carry-on bag. So like her, he thought.

He hugged her hard, took the bags, had her wait while he brought up the car. Back at his place Scout greeted her as though she were an old friend.

"Who is this? Who is this handsome boy?" she asked, scratching his head as his tail wagged furiously.

Venturi showed her to the bedroom closest to the war room.

"A little rustic," he apologized.

"I noticed." She still cuddled the dog.

"I'll put you up in a beachfront hotel," he offered. "I thought this might be more convenient. We may work long hours."

"I don't mind roughing it," she said warmly. "Where do I plug in my laptop?"

He showed her, as she surveyed the surroundings. "Mind if I do a little decorating in my spare time?"

"Have at it," he said. "Just make sure I get all the bills."

She rolled her eyes.

While Venturi took his mother-in-law to lunch and explained the project, Lyle Gates rented an efficiency in a comfortable but aging building near Dinner Key Marina in Coconut Grove. The landlady offered it month to month, but he insisted on a one-year lease. She resisted. High-rise developers had long been interested in the property. Hoping for bigger offers as values rocketed out of control, she had held out, for too long. The bubble had burst. Due to over-building and a glut of empty condos, she now had no potential buyers but hoped for a rebound and wanted to keep her options open.

Wheeling and dealing over coffee, they finally negotiated a six-month lease. He paid first and last month, along with a security deposit.

Single, with no pets, he promised to be a model tenant. He said he planned to go into business and added that he liked the apartment because he could walk to the marina, where he had rented a berth for his boat. He liked to dive, he said.

Later that afternoon, the signed lease in his pocket, he strolled shady streets to the sun-drenched marina, his healing wounds concealed beneath a blue turtleneck, a baseball cap, and athletic wristbands like those worn by tennis players.

He brought diving gear and a speargun for his boat, a twenty-five-foot open fisherman, and chatted with several dock hands and a middle-aged couple returning to the berth next to his after a day of fishing.

"You don't plan to dive alone, do you?"

He was asked the question three different times. The sport's number one safety rule is to always dive with a buddy. It's basic common sense.

He laughed and waved off their concerns.

"I know, I know. Never dive alone. But I know what I'm doing. I maintain my own equipment and I like the tranquillity, the peace and quiet, when I'm alone down there. I don't like the responsibility of having to watch out for somebody else."

He showed up the next day at the same time, wearing an orange and black buoyancy compensator, similar to a life vest. He had also added a DPV, a diver's propulsion vehicle — an underwater scooter — to his gear. Like a miniature outboard motor, it can propel a diver along faster than he can swim.

Gates became a creature of habit. His daily late-afternoon routine was to pilot his boat out to the reefs off Haulover Beach, and occasionally as far north as Fort Lauderdale, to dive and spearfish.

His mornings were spent at Venturi's place, where he crammed intensely with him, Danny, or Victoria. They studied maps, books, and articles about England, Ireland, Scotland, and Australia.

Gates had never visited Ireland but became fascinated upon learning that it is now one of the world's top computer technology and pharmaceutical centers.

Once one of Europe's poorest countries, the Irish are fast becoming Europe's wealthiest people. The economy boomed in the early 1990s, when the country became home to more than eleven hundred multinational companies focused on science, technology, and engineering. Income from technology exports was further boosted by a huge rise in property prices and high savings rates.

Ireland became Lyle's destination, and Victoria immersed him in its long, rich history — its myths, poetry and literature, politics, and people.

His enthusiasm grew for the ancient castles dating back to the fifth century; the prehistoric, volcanic landscape in the north; dramatic coastal scenery, tranquil beaches, and the colorful rolling countryside in the south of Ireland. They all spoke to him.

He played tapes of the speech, the accents, and the local vernacular.

Much later in the day, alone on the boat beneath a wide blue sky, drifting clouds, and a setting sun, he would practice aloud as though rehearsing the lead role in an important play or film. He wanted his performance to be Oscar caliber, the most important role of his life.

He soon knew more about Dublin, Ireland, than he remembered about his own hometown.

Everyone at the marina soon knew he was an avid spear fisherman who dived alone. Some realized who he was but, to his immense relief, there were no ugly confrontations or accusations. He hoped he'd be gone before his presence was leaked to the press, before pushy reporters invaded.

Heads turned the first time he showed up with Fran. Not because she was strikingly beautiful, curvaceous, or vivacious. She was none of those. It was because he was normally alone.

He took her out on the boat several times. She'd asked him to teach her to dive, but she was a poor swimmer, prone to sea sickness, sunburn, and migraine headaches when out on the water in the summer sun's white-hot glare.

So they established their own routine. On Tuesday evenings she'd cook his catch of the day, and after dining at her place, they'd go to a movie or out for drinks.

Weekends, he studied for his real estate license. Once he passed the test, he indicated they might spend more time together.

Too bad Lyle Gates would not live long enough to take the test.

CHAPTER TWELVE

On the day Lyle Gates died the dawn was clear and superhot beneath a brittle cobalt sky. Early in the afternoon a line of fast-moving thunderstorms slammed through Miami, released a fatal lightning bolt that killed a golfer, and briefly cooled the air. The humidity remained dense.

Lyle Gates appeared on the dock at Dinner Key Marina at 4 p.m. He waved to the regulars, boarded his boat, and took it out to the reefs for his usual late-afternoon dive.

He anchored about a mile off the beach in thirty to forty feet of water. He hoisted his red and white dive flag, a safety precaution that alerts other boaters to a diver in the water, then slipped into the shimmering turquoise sea with his speargun. He caught several grouper and yellowtail and put them in the cooler.

The underwater scenery seemed extraordinarily vivid on this day, its colors brighter and more intense. He absorbed the beauty of it all with a keen sense of nostalgia, almost mournfully, aware that he would never see it again.

He worried about his memorial service, if there was one. He hoped his ex-wife, or his older only sister in Wisconsin, would arrange something, if only for the sake of appearances, and for the children, who had refused his calls for more than a year. He wondered who, if anyone, would attend, what they might say, and whether tears would be shed. He abruptly thrust such thoughts from his mind. None of it mattered where he was going. He was too busy to dwell on it now, or ever. He had too much to do. The adventure of a lifetime lay before him. The future beckoned. The excitement was almost sexual.

A brilliant vermilion snapper flashed by in the water, good to eat but too beautiful to kill on this day. He didn't even try to spear it.

He took a few more pompano and amberjack and changed his air tanks several times, leaving the empties on deck.

Finally it was time, as the sun dropped toward the horizon.

He strapped on a new tank, checked his watch, and picked up his cell phone. Fran answered on the first ring, cheerful and expectant.

"The reef is teeming with fish today," he said. "I'm gonna make one more dive, then call it a day."

She was slightly put out. There was a movie she wanted to see, some chick flick about a princess. "I guess that means we'll have to go to the midnight show, instead of the ten o'clock," she said, her words frosty. "I already tossed the salad. Call me when you leave the marina, so I know when to put the rice on."

"I'll pay a kid on the dock to help clean my catch," he said. "That'll speed things up. I'll be there as quick as I can."

She sounded pacified by the time they said good-bye. "I made a surprise for dessert," she said coyly.

He tried to persuade her to reveal what it was, but she refused.

"Then it wouldn't be a surprise. Don't forget to call when you leave the dock."

"I won't. See you shortly." He felt guilty, but their relationship was casual. He had neither taken advantage of her nor led her on. His death would leave no permanent scars.

She'd barely remember him.

And he really didn't want to see that movie.

He opened the cooler again and took out the blood drawn from his forearm and refrigerated by Venturi. Carefully, as they had rehearsed, he left a trailing, bloody handprint, drag marks, and more blood at the boat's transom, as though someone had tried desperately to climb out of the water as something dragged him back.

Everybody knows that spearing fish attracts sharks.

He checked everything, left the dive flag flying, submerged on the diver propulsion vehicle and rode it north, parallel to the shoreline.

His pulse quickened at the sight of Danny's boat approaching right on schedule.

He surfaced. When he heard Venturi shout — "There he is!" — he popped out the batteries, sank the scooter, and swam toward them.

"Look who's here. It's Richard Lynch! Welcome aboard, Richard," Venturi said, as they pulled him into the boat.

The diver removed his air tank, still attached to his buoyancy vest. Danny wanted to drag them through a shark tank at the Miami Seaquarium, where he knew somebody on the night shift. But Venturi prevailed, insisting it would be safer and simpler to use a set of shark jaws sold everywhere as souvenirs.

They used the razor-sharp teeth from the jaws of a huge, long-deceased bull shark to shred the vest.

"Too bad about Lyle." Danny slid the damaged vest over the side.

"Everybody warned him not to dive alone," Venturi said, watching it float away.

"I'm glad the dumb son of a bitch is gone," said the newly named Richard Lynch.

"Richard, I'm shocked!" Danny said. "Never speak ill of the dead."

"Sorry," Lynch said. "But I was so sick and tired of that man and all his problems."

"Let's go home and have a beer," Venturi said.

CHAPTER THIRTEEN

The nightly TV news at eleven o'clock reported a missing diver. The man's worried girlfriend had called the Coast Guard after he did not return on schedule. His unoccupied boat was found anchored a mile offshore.

Bloodstains indicated the diver had been injured and a damaged flotation vest found nearby bore evidence of a shark attack, according to the next morning's *Miami Herald.*

The missing man's name was withheld until next of kin could be notified. The story ended with a cautionary quote from a Coast Guard spokesman who warned that no one should dive alone.

"Europeans think Americans are rude," Victoria said, as she coached Richard Lynch on Irish customs and international awareness, "because we're too quick to use their first names and invade their personal space by standing too close. They won't use a coworker's first name, even after working side by side for years. It's still Mister Jones, and Missus Smith. So keep your distance, learn to be more formal and respectful."

They glanced up as Venturi appeared in the doorway.

"I'm looking at him," he told his cell phone. "He's right in front of me."

"That was Danny," he said, ending the call. "Channel Seven just reported a body, apparently the missing diver, floating near Government Cut."

Danny roared into the driveway on his big black and orange Harley for lunch. They watched the news at noon.

The dead man had been pulled from the water wearing a dark blue suit, a silk tie, and brand-new shoes. Doctors at the medical examiner's office also noted that he was embalmed.

The well-dressed corpse was apparently the victim of a botched burial at sea.

"Not one of mine," Danny said, chortling. "Happens all the time. The people in charge screw up, the damn coffin breaks open, and the dead return to haunt the funeral director."

"To say nothing of his family," Victoria said. "How sad."

Another body bobbed to the surface a short time later, this one off Key Biscayne. Competitive TV reporters again speculated that it must be the missing diver. After all, how many corpses could be out there?

The second dead man was later identified as a hard-drinking college student who jumped or fell off a rented boat during an all-night cruise with friends who did not miss him for hours.

Richard, who now referred to Lyle in the third person, became agitated.

"What if they don't straighten it all out?" he said. "What if they send a stranger's body to Lyle's ex-wife and kids?"

Danny's face brightened. "Not a bad idea." He put his sandwich down, swallowed, and began to think aloud. "No open casket in these cases. With a buried body or, better yet, a cremation, there'd be even less chance of future questions."

"Forget it," Venturi said. "If you bury or cremate a stranger, his family's left in limbo. They'd never know what happened to him."

"You don't want to know how many people spend eternity in somebody else's cemetery plot," Danny said. "Or how many families don't know they've got a stranger's ashes on the mantel. People are human. They make mistakes. Shit happens between the hospital, the morgue, the funeral home, and the cemetery. You saw the story last week. Guy dies twenty years ago. His widow arranges to be buried in the same plot. She dies last week, but guess who's not there when they open the grave? Must have planted him in the wrong place back in the day. Which one? Who knows? The children go to court and a judge orders the cemetery staff to break out the shovels and find him. I told Luz to quit complaining. Here's a woman who didn't know where her husband was for twenty years. And he was dead!

"And that veteran named McCoy? Dies in the VA Hospital but when his widow tries to bury him in a military grave, they find that his death benefits were paid out eight years ago and his burial site is already occupied. The name, rank, and serial number, and dates of service were identical. The guy in the ground was obviously not the real McCoy."

"Life is so complicated. Death should be simpler," Lynch said. "The press . . ."

"Don't worry. Nothing will hit the fan," Venturi assured him, "until the lost diver is officially identified as Lyle Gates. Then the news media will be all over it. But you'll be gone."

■ ■ ■ ■

Two nights later, Richard Lynch boarded an American Airlines flight to New York with a connecting flight to Dublin. He hadn't shaved since his fatal fishing trip and wore spectacles he didn't need, with plain plastic lenses. Victoria had salt-and-peppered his hair, giving him an older, more distinguished appearance.

"My passport looks so real." He studied it again as they drove to the airport.

"It is," Venturi said. He gave Lynch an account number at a Dublin bank where enough cash had been deposited to last him a year. The future was up to him.

"This is it." Venturi shook his hand. "Remember everything you've learned. Don't get involved in local politics or anything newsworthy or controversial."

"Don't pose for pictures. Try to avoid cameras," Victoria reminded him, "as difficult as that can be in today's world."

"I know, I know," Lynch said impatiently.

"You better know," Danny warned. "Slip back into any old habit and it will bite you on the ass. Richard Lynch, Irish citizen, never heard of Lyle Gates. Neither did we."

"How can I thank you?"

"Have a nice life," Venturi said.

CHAPTER FOURTEEN

It took the press almost a day to confirm that lost diver Lyle Gates was *the* Lyle Gates. Then the story exploded.

Police released his name after a detective searched Gates' apartment, found Bridgeport, Connecticut, telephone numbers for his ex-wife and children, and notified the family.

News organizations nationwide dispatched investigative reporters to Miami in a race to uncover the real story behind Gates' death.

The bloody fingerprints left by the diver as he tried to climb back into his boat matched those in Gates' NASA personnel records.

DNA tests confirmed that the blood was his.

Shark experts studied the damage and identified the deep-sea predator that left teeth marks on Gates' vest and air tank as a giant bull shark.

Fran, now identifying herself as Gates' fiancée, wept copiously in front of news cameras as she described their last, loving conversation and plans for the future.

No suicide note was found, and experts who conducted a psychological autopsy ruled out the possibility based on the following factors:

- Gates' apparently untroubled relationship with a loving fiancée with whom he had plans that evening.
- He had argued for a longer lease and talked optimistically about the future.
- Books and papers in his apartment confirmed that he had been actively studying for his Florida real estate license.
- The dive flag and the fish in his cooler confirmed that he'd been spearfishing. So did witnesses at the marina.
  And everybody knows that spearfishing attracts sharks.
- Evidence showed that he had struggled to return to the safety of his boat but had apparently suffered injuries so grave that he could not.
- The Coast Guard reported that their search had yielded "no sign of survivability."

"The truth will never be known about Gates' real role, if any, in the astronauts' deaths," a network anchor somberly concluded. "He took his secrets with him to a watery grave."

A cable talk show host called it "a fitting finale to a dark chapter in the history of America's space program."

Several editorial writers smugly noted that Gates now faced a higher justice.

Gates' death certificate was issued. Cause: accidental.

Venturi was elated. So was Danny. Mission accomplished, a high-five moment. Venturi slept well and agonized less about New Hampshire.

Victoria rarely asked questions but was puzzled by the news coverage. "So you're actually still on the job?" she asked him.

"No, this was volunteer work."

"The government didn't sponsor it?"

He shook his head.

"Nice work. A mitzvah."

"You could call it that," he said. "But we won't. Because we never met him. None of us will ever speak his name again. To anyone."

"Got it," she said affably. "He was a nice fellow, too bad we never met." She kissed his cheek. "Maddy always said you were full of surprises."

Danny threw a barbecue to celebrate. But a redheaded stranger answered the door. Petite, bubbly, and blue-eyed, she wore green surgical scrubs and seemed to be on a high of her own.

Venturi rolled his eyes.

The redhead vanished into Luz's kitchen while Danny crushed spearmint leaves for mojitos. His T-shirt read: TIME FLIES WHEN YOU'RE HAVING RUM. He mixed ice, fine sugar, club soda, and rum, then garnished the drinks with lime wedges. He left the rum out of Luz's glass and fired up the grill.

The kids romped with Scout. Gil the gerbil drove his car. Salsa music came from the kitchen, and the TV news aired, as usual, in Danny's study.

"Do not look at her," Luz warned Venturi, drawing him into the kitchen. "She is not for you."

The redhead was chatting with Victoria in the next room. "She is no fix-up." Luz wagged her finger. "Not for you."

Reverse psychology, Venturi thought. A crafty change of tactics. "Why not?" he asked.

"That woman is married — to her profession. On call twenty-four seven. She has no

170

time for you."

"So, what's the four-one-one on her? Is she another nurse?"

"No." Luz sliced a ripe avocado that had come from a tree in the backyard and deftly scooped out the pit. "A physician, too busy for you."

He sipped his drink and tried to look disappointed. "I guess I'll have to live with that. Breaks my heart."

"I am not joking with you." Luz's dark eyes flashed. The knife glinted in her hand. "Call Tanya, Mirta, or Ana. They like you."

"I like them, too. But I'm not looking. I'm busy too."

"Fishing, boating, playing?" She rapidly diced two tomatoes.

"Somebody has to do it."

He trailed after her as she carried the salad bowl out to the patio. The redhead held out her hand. "I'm Keri Spangler. Nice to meet you, Michael. Your mother-in-law is a delight. She obviously loves you like a son."

"Thanks. Vicki is a trip."

Keri had a fresh-faced look, no makeup except for a pale pink gloss on her lips. *Or was that natural, too?* he wondered. Her only jewelry was a pair of tiny gold earrings.

"Didn't mean to crash your party," she

said. "But I was on my way home from the hospital and stopped to see Luz."

Sure, he thought.

"She invited me to stay and I couldn't resist. In part because I don't spend enough time with them and the kids, but," her voice dropped to a whisper, "mostly because I'm starved. I haven't eaten all day and Danny's secret barbecue sauce is spectacular."

"He never does anything halfway," Venturi said. "Luz said you're a doctor. What's your specialty?"

"The best one," she said proudly. She cocked her head and smiled. "I deliver new lives."

The irony was not lost on him, having just accomplished something similar.

"I'm still on a high," she confessed, her words breathless. "It happens every time. Nothing else is like it." She drew herself up, her posture as straight as a soldier's. "This afternoon, I delivered a beautiful seven-pound, five-ounce boy. And unlike most, he was thoughtful enough to arrive at two p.m. instead of two a.m. I'm Luz's obstetrician."

He blinked. "You delivered their children?"

"All three." Her eyes fondly followed them as they tore around the backyard screaming. "They're playing Kissy Monster," she

172

said, laughing. "It's like playing tag but with kisses.

"That's how we became friends," she said. "I'm Julee's godmother. And you're the Michael for whom they named their youngest?"

He nodded.

"So you and Danny were special ops?"

"U.S. Marine Corps Force Reconnaissance, better known as Force Recon. We go in before the special ops."

"Right." Danny joined them. "Small-scale, high-risk operations our specialty. Our motto: *Celer, Silens, Mortalis.*" He grinned at Venturi.

" 'Swift, silent, deadly,' " Keri said. "I'm impressed. Which one of you is silent?" She watched Danny return to the grill. "I know it's not him."

They both laughed.

"Is your wife here?" Her blue eyes roved the patio as though Maddy might materialize at any moment.

Luz hadn't told her. Maybe this was no fix-up. The woman was friendly but not flirty.

"No, she isn't," he said evenly.

The barbecue was great.

The table was cleared, dishes stacked in

173

the washer. Danny brooded over the TV news in the kitchen, and the children were up too late.

"Let's round them up," Luz said, as Javi, Julee, and Scout stampeded out the patio door into the yard, trailed by little Michael.

A bloodcurdling scream brought the women to their feet. The children had screamed all evening, but this one was different. Danny burst out of the kitchen.

"Is the pool alarm on?" Luz said, fear on her face.

He was already out the back door. But Keri made it to the pool first.

The others followed and saw it on the bottom. A little red car. The children were screaming, Scout barking, the baby howling.

Keri slipped out of her shoes and dove into the water.

"Oh, shit," Danny said. He turned off the alarm and kicked off his shoes.

But Keri had already surfaced. She handed the little car up to him. Water gushed from its windows. The driver was still inside.

"Get back, get back. Give him air," Luz said, restraining the children.

Javi streamed tears. Julee wailed. The little one wasn't sure what had happened but howled anyway, red faced and exhausted.

"Is he all right?" Javi demanded. "Will Gil be all right?"

Danny opened the car door and extricated the limp, sodden body, the size of his thumb.

"I don't think so," he said.

The children shrieked louder.

"Let's try!" Keri said. Venturi gave her a hand up out of the pool, her scrubs dripping, hair soaked. He couldn't help noticing how her wet clothes clung to her body, accentuating the small waist and rounded breasts.

"Aw," Danny objected. "Mouth to mouth on a gerbil?"

Keri counted, using her pinky to compress the tiny chest.

Danny blew gently into the gerbil's mouth, a finger over its nostrils.

Victoria held Julee's hand as she wept.

"The sliding-glass door to the pool was open," Luz said softly. "He could drive, but he never learned to steer."

Gil had raced his car straight out the open door and into the deep end of the pool.

The children seemed inconsolable when efforts to revive Gil failed.

Their father tried to comfort them. "If you promise to take better care of it, maybe we

175

can find you a new gerbil who doesn't drive."

"Can we have a dog instead?" Javi choked between sobs.

"No," Danny said. "Your mom has too much to take care of now. Maybe when you're older."

The children continued to weep.

"He wouldn't want you to cry," Danny said, morphing into funeral-director mode. "Gil had a wonderful life and a family who loved him."

"Why did this happen, Daddy?" Julee whimpered, clinging to his leg.

He picked her up and pointed to the stars. "See, Julee, there's a big blackboard in the sky. Gil's name was on it today."

Luz rolled her eyes. "Somebody left the sliding-glass door open. That's why it happened," she told the children. "We were all supposed to keep that door closed. Remember?" She kissed Julee. "Calm down now. We need to plan Gil's funeral."

"Funeral?" The two older ones blinked away their tears and looked curious. Baby Michael, eyes swollen, followed their lead.

"Yes," she said. "We can bury him under the avocado tree in the backyard." She glanced at Danny. "Your father is going right now to find us a nice box. We will bury him in it, with his favorite toys and his car."

Danny went to his study and returned with a Cuban cigar box.

"Perfect." Luz turned back to the children. "We'll say our prayers and you can sing the songs you learned in Sunday school."

"Can we put flowers in, too?" Tears still sparkled on Julee's long eyelashes.

"Yes, lots of flowers. We'll pick some that Gil would really like."

Keri changed into dry clothes borrowed from Luz, and the children were put to bed, exhausted, but no longer crying.

"Hell," Danny told Venturi in the study. "The kids are so in love with the funeral plans that if the poor little bugger came back to life right now, they'd probably kill him."

"How nice to see them following in your footsteps," Venturi said. "I nearly lost it when you were explaining your Blackboard Theory to the kids."

They laughed, until bad news broke on CNN.

A congressman killed by a bomb blast outside the Philippine House of Representatives. The victim had supported U.S.-backed military operations against al Qaeda–linked rebels.

"Goddammit!" Danny punched a fist into

his palm. "We're getting hammered! The whole damn planet's a dangerous neighborhood and here I am, bringing all these kids into the world. What the hell am I doing?" He paced the room, generating a coiled, frustrated intensity, then dropped into a chair across from Venturi. "I feel so helpless. Remember when we felt we were accomplishing something? Making America safer, the world better? Hell, what's happened to us, man? We once were warrior kings."

"I remember," Venturi said. "We accomplished something the other day."

"What? Oh yeah. I loved that. But he's only one man in a world full of trouble."

"You can't save every starfish in the sea, Danny. But we saved one."

"I'll never get used to it, or get it right. Civilian life is a goddamn challenge, bro."

"Tell me about it. It's the hardest thing I've ever tried to do."

The three women were drinking decaf in the kitchen. Keri looked fetching in white shorts and a halter top, her clothes in the dryer.

"Don't forget to take your blood-pressure pill," she told Luz before changing back into her dry scrubs. "And get some rest. I want you to come in no later than Wednesday for those tests."

Danny was cleaning the grill, so Venturi walked Keri out to her car.

She gently touched his arm before sliding into the driver's seat. "I didn't know about your wife," she said softly. "I had no idea. I am so sorry."

"Thank you," he said, and watched her drive off into the night.

CHAPTER FIFTEEN

"Damn," Danny said. "We've got plans."

Venturi had called to invite them to dinner with him and his mother-in-law.

"Why don't you two come with us?" Danny suggested.

He consulted Luz. "She says it's a great idea!"

He sounded almost too happy.

"Sure, but where we going?"

Danny sighed. "They call it a gallery walk. I call it the Miami Death March through hell. We walk in groups between several Design District art galleries, drink wine, eat cheese, and eyeball what passes for art these days. I'm so thrilled I can hardly spit. First chance we get we bail and find a decent restaurant."

The babysitter answered the door — it was Keri, in blue jeans and a T-shirt, her hair pulled back.

She and Vicki greeted each other like long-lost relatives. Danny had been preoccupied all day by a mysterious plane crash off Venezuela.

"Why don't *I* babysit while you four take the gallery walk?" Vicki suggested, as they were about to leave.

Bait and switch, cooked up by whom? Venturi studied the suspects.

"I'm not dressed." Keri's cheeks reddened.

"You look fine, dear," Vicki insisted. "Miami casual. Throw a jacket over your jeans, put on some heels. Borrow something from Luz."

Venturi protested. "But you'll be going home soon, Vicki, and you haven't seen much of Miami."

"Nonsense. I may never go home." She winked.

"Is that a promise?"

"No, a threat."

"But I invited you tonight."

"I'm not up to a lot of walking." She patted her right leg, the artificial one.

"There really isn't much walking," Luz said quickly. "The galleries are all within a block or two."

"Is there a problem?" Venturi leaned close to his mother-in-law. She never played the invalid card. Ever.

"Can't I be in the mood to read bedtime stories to little people?"

"What's wrong?" he persisted.

"As much as I love you, sweetheart," she muttered in his ear, drawing him aside, "I am *not* about to double-date with my son-in-law."

He looked startled.

"Plus," she hissed, "the woman is a doctor."

He saw she was determined.

"Okay," he said aloud, surprising himself. "Good idea. But you haven't eaten."

"I left some salmon, rice, and vegetables for Keri." Luz sounded resigned.

"Sounds wonderful, though much too healthy," Vicki said. "At my age I need preservatives, lots of them . . ."

The local elite greeted Danny and Luz with hugs, high fives, and handshakes. Photographers snapped pictures as he and Venturi discreetly dodged the cameras.

When it became unbearably noisy, they stepped outside. The hot Miami night was sultry and sticky. Neither normally smoked, but Danny pulled out a pack of Camels. "Wish I was back in boots," he said, lighting up. "See some of the guys in there?

They're carrying purses, for Christ's sake. The men we were never would have wound up here," he said wistfully.

"This was your idea," Venturi said, accepting a proffered cigarette.

"Hell, no, it wasn't."

"Don't knock it," Venturi said. "The men we were are lucky to be anywhere. Was it Luz's idea to bring Keri?"

"Hell, no. She's pissed. She loves Keri, and she loves you, but not necessarily in the same room. Beats me. I think she's jealous. Scared that you might monopolize her doctor's time and attention. Being pregnant, she wants it all for herself."

"Makes sense," Venturi said. "Can't blame her for that."

Keri took his arm as they strolled to the next gallery. She was chatting about an upcoming expedition into the Everglades hoping to find and photograph the rare and elusive ghost orchid.

"Is its name Casper?" Danny asked.

She laughed, a nice sound. "Most people never see one. It's on my list of things to see before I die. If none of my patients go into labor I'll try this weekend. But with the full moon on Saturday, it probably won't happen."

183

"What does the moon have to do with it?" Venturi asked.

"Everything," she said. "I'm sure you've heard that emergency rooms, psychiatrists, and the police are busier then. Same for maternity wards. We set up extra beds forty-eight hours before the full moon rises."

"It's true," Luz said. "Remember? I went into labor with Javi and the baby just before full moons."

"Has to do with gravity and the high tides," Danny said.

"The human body *is* seventy-two percent water," Keri pointed out.

"And the rest is contamination." Danny laughed. "Seriously, when you see that moon hang over Miami, so low in the sky you can almost touch it, you know all hell's about to break loose."

Artists were competing for a major prize at the next gallery. One had spread sand and seashells across the floor.

Mike and Danny explored a curtained cubicle in which the recorded voices of fifty terminally ill AIDS patients simultaneously discussed their symptoms.

"Oh, this is uplifting," Danny said.

"Look at this," Venturi said, as they emerged near *Two Couches Creating Closeness.* The artist had pushed two battered brown sofas together.

"What the . . . ?" Danny said aloud.

"The artist," a young gallery spokesperson chirped brightly, "is noted for his exploration of the commonality of working-class life through the use of everyday objects."

Danny was becoming increasingly restless.

"Javi's fingerpaintings show more talent," he muttered, regarding a collage of baseball cards, beer ads, snapshots, duct tape, and balloons. "Only five, and he can draw a tree that looks like a tree. What the hell is that?" He stared at another display, bags of dust its creator had collected from various places.

Luz elbowed him in the ribs and said she was hungry.

"Hallelujah!" Danny said. "Let's go. I have to feed this woman or she gets cranky."

He and Venturi went for the car, in a parking garage several blocks away.

"Let's cut down Second Avenue," Danny said. "It's quicker."

The sidewalks were dark and nearly deserted, with most of the street lights burned out.

"Nine o'clock," Danny muttered, as they became aware that they had company.

"I see 'im. Two more behind us."

A tall black man planted himself in their path, then brandished a wicked-looking carving knife at Venturi's midsection.

"I'd just as soon cut you," he said, spitting out a stream of curses.

Two shorter Hispanics came up behind them and swiftly sliced off their trouser pockets with box cutters.

Danny and Venturi exchanged "Do you believe this?" looks.

"Sorry, man. The money's gone." Danny slurred his words. "Got paid today, hit that little club down the street. The girls were all over us. We bought 'em drinks all night. But when the money and the whiskey ran out, so did they. Left us broke."

"Those bitches!" snarled the knife-wielding man. "Those goddamn whores! They do it every time!"

Danny swayed, continuing to act drunk. He was playing with them.

Venturi didn't want to play. He objected when strangers waved sharp blades so close to his crotch.

He and Danny acted simultaneously.

Venturi gripped a hand clutching a box cutter, spun it around, and slammed his fist into the back of the man's forearm, snapping the elbow. The bone broke with a loud crack.

Danny dropped the second man with a straight kick that split his right kneecap backward. The man writhed on the pavement.

Both dropped their box cutters. Their screams echoed down the dark street.

The man with the knife lunged forward. Danny caught his arm, twisted it behind him, and slammed the back of his shoulder, dislocating it.

He went down screaming.

All three struggled to their feet and fled whimpering, limping, and stumbling. One dragged a leg that no longer worked. The man with the dislocated shoulder howled as he loped away, listing to one side like the Hunchback of Notre Dame in an old black-and-white movie.

"Let's go before somebody calls the cops," Danny said.

"They should thank us." Venturi scooped up the belongings from their slashed pockets.

"Maybe. But there's all that paperwork and Luz is hungry."

"Look what he did to my pants." Venturi squinted in the poor light. "Sliced the pockets off clean. Didn't even damage the fabric."

"Mine, too," Danny said. "Those guys were good."

"Maybe there is something to that full-moon stuff," Venturi said, as they reached the parking garage.

"Could be," Danny agreed. "The emergency room is about to get busier, just as Keri predicted."

"It's always amazing, how training kicks in."

Venturi was referring to MCMAP, the Marine Corps Martial Arts Program, which teaches how to disarm and disable the enemy.

"Can't tell you how happy I am you're in town, buddy," Danny said. "I'm finally having fun."

"What took you so long?" Luz asked, as Danny helped her into the back seat.

"We ran into some guys."

Keri, already in the car, blinked as Venturi slid behind the wheel. "What happened to your trousers, Michael? Where is the pocket?"

"Right here." He handed it to her.

"Where do we eat?" Danny asked.

Two Miami fire rescue units raced by in the opposite direction, lights flashing, sirens wailing.

Luz made the sign of the cross. "I hope no one was killed," she whispered.

"See, I told you about the full moon,"

Keri said. She studied Venturi's profile thoughtfully.

Focused on traffic, he didn't seem to notice.

CHAPTER SIXTEEN

Victoria was oddly quiet after they left Danny's.

Venturi hoped she was just tired. But the next morning, she clearly hadn't slept well. "We need to talk," she said.

He saw the look in her eyes and his heart sank. *She's leaving,* he thought. She'd already stayed longer than anticipated. He'd grown accustomed to her company, her warmth and humor. She and Danny were his only family.

But she had friends, a business, a life in New York. When she left he didn't know when he would see her again.

"Shoot." He braced for the bullet.

"Something's been on my mind." Her brow furrowed. "It kept me awake last night. I can't stop thinking about it."

"You're the one who insisted that Keri take your place. It wasn't my idea," he protested.

She laughed out loud. "I wasn't referring to that, but since you brought it up, did you two hit it off?"

"I don't know her." He shrugged. "I met her when you did."

"I think she's exactly your type, Mikey. Smart, talented, in love with life and what she does. Reminds me of Madison."

He disagreed. "They're nothing alike."

"I'm not saying they look alike, sweetheart. I'm talking about women of character. I'm glad you might be seeing her. You know what they say — it's not good for a man to be alone."

"You're about to bail out on me, aren't you?" He pushed his coffee cup away and leaned back in his chair, his expression disconsolate.

"What on earth are you talking about?"

"You're not leaving?"

"Only if I've overstayed my welcome. What is this, Mikey? We usually communicate so well."

"Okay, let's start again. What's troubling you, bunky?"

"Remember the Barretts?"

He frowned. "Should I?"

"Laura and Casey Barrett were the young couple at the center of the Devonbrook Day

191

Care scandal in New England some years ago."

Venturi vaguely remembered. They'd gone to prison. He'd been a Marine at the time.

Victoria refreshed his memory. Day care was among the amenities offered to buyers at Devonbrook, a sprawling single-family housing development in a Boston suburb.

After eleven months, a police detective noticed that her little girl's panties were inside out after picking her up from day care. The child, age two and a half, couldn't tell her about anything unusual that had occurred. But after being questioned over several days, the little girl began to talk about bad things that had happened at day care. The story grew and grew as other parents panicked and began to question their own children.

After the initial accusation, police and prosecutors brought in psychologists, psychiatrists, and pediatricians to interview and examine the children.

All denied that anything improper had happened, but after repeated interrogating by persuasive adults, terrible stories began to emerge.

First one accusation, then several, then a flood. Horrific child-sex-abuse charges were filed against the Barretts, who operated the center. The couple was arrested and jailed without bond until trial.

By the time it ended, nearly two dozen children, age five and under, told tales of grotesque sex rituals, adults and children naked, group sex, small animals slaughtered, and threats of physical violence.

It was one of the nation's first high-profile, nationally televised child-molestation trials. A jury convicted Laura and Casey Barrett on multiple counts. They were sentenced to life terms.

"I watched the entire trial," Vicki said. "The psychologists used anatomically correct dolls so the children could demonstrate where and how they were touched. They played taped interviews between them and those little children.

"I always had doubts. Children that age are always so eager to please. They want to help. And how many places can you point to on an anatomically correct doll before you satisfy the adult you're trying to please?

"The questions were leading, the questioners so persuasive, the children so young.

"To me it seemed like the mass hysteria that led to the Salem witchcraft trials centuries earlier. The only difference was that Laura and Casey Barrett weren't burned at the stake, though they might as well have been." Vicki hugged her thin cotton housecoat around her as though cold, despite the Florida heat.

"From the beginning," she said, "I wondered how all that perversion and naked dancing, those sex games and the animal slaughter went on without ever being interrupted, or even suspected by parents and all the other adults who constantly came and went, picking up children, dropping them off. No one ever saw a thing.

"The doctors who examined those poor little children found no evidence of penetration. All they said was that one or two of them had a rash. And some began wetting their pants after being hysterically questioned by panicky parents.

"What child doesn't have a rash somewhere, sometime, or wet their pants when scared? They were kids.

"The Barretts had no prior record of any sort. Yet outrage against them spread like wildfire. I always suspected some of it might have been fueled by the deep pockets of the developers who were now targets for civil suits.

"And were there ever civil suits!

"The news stories never stopped. Even after the criminal convictions, the civil cases proceeded. The developers' insurance company eventually settled. Hundreds of thousands of dollars went to the parents of each victim.

"And of course," she said sadly, "none of it ever really happened. The Barretts, the most hated people in New England or perhaps the entire country at the time, were innocent."

"Ugly," Venturi said, "but I remember reading something about a happy ending not long ago. Weren't they released?"

"Yes. Their verdicts were reversed," Victoria said indignantly, "but not until after they'd spent eight years in prison! Where . . . where . . ." She grew red in the face.

". . . child molesters are targeted by other inmates and corrections officers." He finished her sentence.

"So what's the bottom line?" he asked.

"The bottom line is that they walked out of prison with two hundred dollars and the clothes on their backs. A judge ruled that there was probable cause for their arrests, so no one is held liable.

"There's still so much anger and outrage against them that they couldn't stay in New England. So they tried to resettle in Florida, near Orlando. They found menial, low-level jobs and tried to start over. Then somebody recognized them.

"They lost the jobs. He was badly beaten by a gang of thugs, with the promise of worse if they didn't leave town. Their apartment was vandalized, their few belongings stolen.

"The story was reported on the TV news at the beauty salon the other day. Everybody talked about it, Mikey." She leaned forward, a look of disbelief in her soft eyes. "They supported the thugs! Those women, having their fingernails and toenails painted, all said: 'I'd do the same thing.' 'I wouldn't want them living next door to me, in my neighborhood, or my town.' 'Guilty people get out of jail all the time.' 'Where there's smoke, there's fire.' 'They weren't sent to prison for no reason.'

"Of course I had to put my two cents in, told them they should be ashamed and show some compassion. Unfortunately, the only result of my efforts is this haircut," she said ruefully.

"I wondered about that but didn't want to say anything."

She slapped his hand. "I'm serious."

"We'll find you a new hairdresser," he promised. "But try to keep your mouth shut. Although I know from experience that's impossible."

She slapped his hand again.

"You know where I'm headed with this," she said meaningfully.

He knew, but asked anyway. "Where?"

"When you helped 'he who shall go nameless' solve his problem, you were happier and more involved than I've seen you for a long time. Why not do it again?"

His pulse quickened, but he resisted. "That was a onetime experiment. I wanted to see if it was possible, if it could work. And I felt responsible for the man. You know when I stumbled upon him he was trying to commit suicide."

"I thought it was something like that," she said. "I wonder how it ends for this couple? How can they live down their notoriety, the pain and trauma of their trial, the prison time they served? They lost everything."

"It's risky." He kneaded the back of his neck as though it felt stiff.

"Since when did that ever stop you?"

He didn't respond, just sat there, thinking.

"You did it for criminals, bad people. I know how much you regret that."

"We don't even know if they'd want to do it."

"Why on earth would they refuse?"

"You'd have to stay, to help transform them into other people."

"Certainly. I never thought otherwise."

"First we have to find them, see if they're still together, and if they're willing."

Forty-eight hours later, they were driving the two hundred miles north to Orlando to find the low-income neighborhood and two-story rooming house where the Barretts shared a bathroom with seven other tenants.

Vicki, who looked less threatening, knocked at their door. Laura Barrett had been twenty-one and her husband twenty-five when they went to prison. She'd be twenty-nine now.

The face that peered furtively from behind a chain on the door appeared older.

"I'd like to talk to you, dear," Vicki said warmly. "My son is here with me. We may be able to help you."

"Are you lawyers?" The woman's voice sounded flat and emotionless. "I'm sorry. We can't afford a lawyer."

"We're not lawyers. May we come in?" Vicki turned as a door opened at the other end of the cluttered, foul-smelling hallway. A bearded man, shirtless and unkempt, leered out at her. Venturi stepped out of the shadow of the landing and stared back. The man shut his door.

Another door opened and a wild-haired obese woman in a shapeless nightgown stepped out.

"Are you the social worker?" she bellowed.

"No, dear," Vicki answered. "We're not social workers."

Her friendly tone apparently encouraged the woman, who began to pad barefoot down the hall toward them, mumbling to herself as she came.

Venturi stepped out again, made eye contact, and without a word, pointed back toward her room. She wilted for a moment, then turned, plodded back inside, and closed her door.

"Mrs. Barrett, we'd like to talk to you privately, for just a moment. Please?" Vicki said.

Alone and apprehensive, Laura Barrett took the risk.

She shut the door, removed the chain, and let Vicki in.

"This is Michael," Vicki said. "We're here to help you."

Laura's sidelong glance was edgy and narrow-eyed, but she admitted him as well, locked the door behind them, then kept her distance.

Her husband was out looking for work, she told Vicki. They were trying to raise enough money to leave town and find another place.

"This is all wrong," Venturi said, taking in the sad, shabby, grim room.

Embarrassed, Laura Barrett avoided his eyes but held her head high. "It's not so bad," she said, "compared to our next address, which will be a homeless shelter, if they accept us. People don't — they won't forget," she explained.

Thin and angular, about five feet six inches tall, with brown eyes and hair, she looked a good ten years older than her age. She was not sure when Casey would be back.

Venturi had hoped to talk to them both.

"Do you two plan to stay together?" Vicki asked sympathetically.

Laura nearly laughed. "Because I was young and female they promised I'd get off lightly if I confessed and testified against my husband." Her voice grew brittle. "There was *nothing* to confess to or testify about. Nothing happened. They wanted me to lie. They said if I didn't cooperate I'd be in prison until I was an old lady. We loved that day-care center. We loved the children. We'd only been married a year. We were planning our own family. How could I lie and testify against him?"

She perched tentatively on the edge of the bed, like a wary bird poised to take flight. Victoria sat in the only chair. Venturi stood near a window where he could watch the street.

"We didn't see each other for eight years. We weren't allowed to write or call each other. So if none of that drove us apart, nothing, not even this" — Laura glanced bleakly around her — "will now. For better or for worse . . ." Her smile was sardonic.

"We're here to talk about better," Venturi said briskly. "Here's what I propose."

Casey Barrett came home ninety minutes later. Laura rushed to unlock the door. Victoria gasped. Barrett's black eye was much more than a black eye — it covered the entire left side of his face, in shades ranging from black, to purple, to green. The cuts on his forehead had just begun to heal. He wore a cast on his right hand.

"Did they arrest anybody?" Venturi asked angrily.

Startled by the strangers in their room, Casey shook his head. He, too, looked older than his true age.

"The police said they couldn't do anything and don't have enough manpower to protect us," Laura said. "They said it would save us a lot of trouble if we just moved on."

201

"Laura? Who . . . ?" Casey began.

She stood up, her posture resolute.

"I hoped you'd be back soon," she said softly. "Any luck?"

When he shook his head, she motioned to two battered suitcases, packed, and standing near the door.

"Pick them up," she said. "We're going to Miami."

They hugged in the backseat of Venturi's car, not sure exactly where they were headed, or with whom. All they knew as they raced south was that their future could not be worse than the past. And maybe, just maybe, it might be better.

Chapter Seventeen

The couple slept like exhausted children during the drive.

Venturi woke them when he stopped at a restaurant off the turnpike. The Barretts exchanged nervous glances after studying the menu.

"Order whatever you like," Venturi said. "It's on me."

They ordered comfort food: meatloaf with smashed potatoes and gravy, mac and cheese with vegetables and salad. They ate ravenously.

Like inmates, they averted their eyes when people passed or a waitress approached, hesitated to smile back at a stranger.

"These two need a lot of work," Venturi warned Vicki as he paid the check.

He took Casey and Laura home, to the room where Lyle Gates had slept. Vicki had brightened it up since then, adding a colorful rug, a fluffy comforter, cheerful curtains, and thick, thirsty, pastel towels.

It was far from luxurious, but Laura loved it. "We have our own bathroom!" she gleefully told her husband.

Venturi called Danny while they got settled.

"I have a couple of guests you should meet," Venturi said. "We need to brainstorm."

"You kidding me?"

"No. You have a problem with it?"

"Hell, no. I had a feeling you weren't going to Orlando to see the mouse. I'm down with saving a few more starfish. See you tomorrow."

The more he, Laura, and Casey talked that night, the more Venturi believed that Vicki was right.

Who more deserved a second chance? Somebody owed them something for their lost years. If he could provide it, why not?

They were perfect candidates. They had no problem, they said, permanently cutting off contact with everyone they knew. Warned about no good-byes, they agreed without hesitation.

"Once we get situated," Casey said, "we can pay you back."

"No." Venturi frowned and shook his

head. "What did I just say about no contact with your past? That includes me."

"So why are you doing this?" Laura demanded skeptically.

"I know it sounds corny," Venturi said, "but because it seems like the right thing to do. So don't let me down."

Speechless, Laura reached for her husband's hand. "It's like we won the lottery," she finally whispered. "Only better. Because if we won the lottery, we'd still be us. And the people who hate us would despise us even more."

Danny arrived early the next morning with Scout, who had stayed at his place while they were gone. The dog ran from room to room, excited to be home, then stopped, ears alert, outside the Barretts' bedroom.

"I think they're still in love," Vicki said, pouring coffee. "Did you hear them last night?"

Venturi nodded wearily.

"No wonder they're still asleep," she said. "They were at it all night."

"Remind me to fix that headboard," he said, "so the next time that bed sees action it doesn't bang against the wall."

"Action? What action?" Danny asked eagerly.

They filled him in.

"What's their mental condition?" he demanded, pacing the room. "What if they're too institutionalized, too screwed up from bad times behind bars to pull it off? They have major decisions to make, serious information to absorb. It's hard work. And being a couple is a negative. They're easier to recognize together. That doubles the chance of a slipup."

"You're right," Venturi agreed. "I want to polygraph them first." He saw Vicki's expression. "I have to be sure we're not making a mistake."

She nodded.

"I know a guy," Danny said. "He's the best."

"I'm sure they'll have no problem with it," Vicki said. She began to think out loud. "Their appearances shouldn't be difficult to change. She needs a good haircut. She'd look good as a blonde. Both need dental work. Put her in the hands of a stylist, a good makeup artist, dress her in the right clothes, and nobody would ever recognize her. Most of her published photos are from the arrest or the trial. She was hardly more than a teenager. She grew up and became a woman behind bars. She won't look like the waif she was back then. He can grow a little facial hair and buff up in the gym. We can change his hairline. She needs to add some weight and muscle tone. Their walks, their posture, and their body language all need major work. I'm excited," she said, elated. "What a wonderful project!"

"Mission," Danny said. "It's a mission. Let's go wake them up."

Laura and Casey agreed to be polygraphed. They sat in the war room holding hands as everyone brainstormed and ultimately pieced together a plan. Casey especially liked the fact that they'd have the last word.

Danny's friend, Clay Ramsey, the polygraph expert, agreed to test them immediately. People never said no to Danny. He led them up a back staircase at Ramsey's small downtown office so the Barretts would not be seen in the building. No one else was present. Ramsey had sent his secretary on an errand that would take hours. No names were used. The questions focused on a single issue. Did either of them ever commit a crime against a child?

They aced the tests. Clay destroyed the graphs.

That same day Vicki found the couple a tiny third-floor efficiency in North Miami. The apartment wasn't much but had its own bathroom. There was a Murphy bed, a tiny two-burner stove, a room air conditioner, and a window view of treetops and open sky. They signed a year's lease.

The manager, from Honduras, did not appear to recognize their names or faces.

At the driver's license bureau, the line of Haitian, Spanish-speaking, and other applicants wound around the block. Casey and Laura studied the Florida handbook while waiting, applied for licenses, took their driving and written tests and passed.

Laura lamented her driver's license photo.

"It's horrible," she told Venturi over the telephone.

"Great," he said. "That's exactly what we want."

Later that afternoon at Metro Ford, a new dealership in the north end of town, they bought a trade-in, a ten-year-old Ford Taurus, off the used-car lot. They told the salesman, who tried diligently to interest them in newer models, that it was all they could afford. They paid cash.

They shopped for clothes at Kmart that night.

Each day Casey and Laura Barrett left their tiny apartment early and drove to Venturi's place to work on themselves. Their choice of countries was limited since they were fluent only in English. They chose the last great frontier, Australia, a nation built by prisoners and criminals sent to colonize the country. They loved the irony.

"Aussies are gregarious, fun-loving people with a frontier spirit and a big pub culture," Victoria told them. "Go to a pub, start talking to people. Observe, and do as the locals do. Their football will take a while to get used to; it's a mix of rugby and a few other things."

The couple hoped to work together, perhaps in the hotel industry or restaurant business. Both loved animals and dreamed of owning horses.

Venturi called Jim Dance again, to tap into his ever growing portfolio.

Laura and Casey applied for jobs almost every day. Neither ever had an offer, not even from Burger King. The eight-year blank in their résumés was too wide a gap. When asked, they were truthful. They had been in prison. The next query, of course, was, why?

The sordid answer was enough to turn off any would-be employer, even when the couple presented paperwork confirming their ultimate exoneration.

Casey even applied to the Miami Police Department and filled out all the forms. He was never contacted.

They kept careful records of their job search.

One morning at Venturi's, Laura bolted to the bathroom at the first smell of coffee.

"She's nauseous, a little under the weather," Casey mumbled.

"And how long has this been going on?" Vicki asked.

He looked concerned. "About a week." He paused, then confessed. "We took a drugstore pregnancy test last night. It said positive. But sometimes they're wrong."

Venturi got up from his desk.

"Will this spoil it?" Casey asked, his expression stricken. "Does it ruin every-thing?"

Venturi considered the question.

"Has she seen a doctor?"

"No, not yet."

"Good. Don't. Make sure she doesn't. We'll find her a doctor. If she is pregnant we don't want records."

Laura emerged from the bathroom, red faced, wet eyed, and clearly uncomfortable.

"I told them," Casey said.

"Is it a problem?" she asked, blowing her nose.

"I don't think so," Venturi said. "We may have to speed things up, but it could be a good thing, a very good thing."

Venturi intended to keep Keri on a strict need-to-know basis. The less she knew the better.

He took her to North One 10, a cozy and intimate restaurant, and over oysters topped with spinach and brie, asked for her help.

To his relief, she readily agreed to examine and treat a possibly pregnant young woman.

Over porcini-dusted sea bass, he mentioned that there could be no official medical records.

She began to fire questions at him.

"Why isn't normal doctor/patient confidentiality good enough in this case?"

He hesitated to answer.

"Was she the victim of a sexual assault?"

"Negative."

"Is she a fugitive? A celebrity? An illegal alien?"

He shook his head.

She drained her wineglass before her final question.

"Are you the father?"

A woman at the next table turned to stare.

"No, no, no. Absolutely not." He dropped his voice. "She's just a girl, a young married woman . . ."

He saw the skepticism in her eyes.

"Look, it is what I do," she said quietly,

"but I value my license to practice. I have to know what I'm becoming involved in. All I know about you, Michael, is that you're Danny's best friend and he and Luz love you. You and he were Marine commandos. You went into law enforcement and Danny sometimes disappears for days or weeks. Luz doesn't talk about it, but I know she worries. I assume," she said, hitching her shoulders, "that he's involved in something clandestine, undercover, or confidential. Miami has more than its share of such people. But do you actually think you can buy me a fabulous dinner and talk me into doing whatever you ask without questions."

Dismayed, he said nothing.

"I mean, what was that thing?" She gestured impatiently with both hands.

He had no idea what she meant.

"That thing! When you and Danny went for the car. Instead of coming back with your hands in your pockets, you had your pockets in your hands! What the hell was that?"

"Calm down," he said, uncomfortably aware of the diners around them. "A couple, three guys with a knife and box cutters tried to rob us," he whispered sheepishly. He quietly described the scene. "We only did what we had to do. Self-defense."

212

"Okay," she said stoically. "Now, who's pregnant? What's her story? Is the baby available for adoption? Who's the daddy? Is he in the picture?"

He sighed. "I thought the Hippocratic Oath meant that you administer to patients, not interrogate them."

"You have no respect for me as a professional."

"I do," he whispered. "That's why I asked for your help."

She was unrelenting.

"Swear this conversation goes no further, whether you help or not?" he finally asked.

She nodded, dangly earrings bouncing. "I won't do anything unethical, professionally or personally, which also means I won't break a confidence."

"Did you ever hear of Laura and Casey Barrett?"

She processed the names for a long moment, then gave a sharp little nod. "The married couple who went to prison? I interned in Boston. I read that they were released, that they were innocent all along."

"Would you like to meet them?"

She blinked. "Sure," she said, her expression cocky, as if to call his bluff.

He called for the check.

■ ■ ■ ■

Laura and Casey were working late. Laura in the war room with Vicki, studying Australian history, politics, newsmakers, lifestyle, and TV and radio personalities.

In another room, converted into a gymnasium, Casey was taking martial arts, learning from Danny how to handle himself in a fight, protect his wife, and never again take a beating like the one he had suffered in Orlando.

Their cars were parked out of sight, behind the shed.

If Keri was startled to walk in on Danny and Casey, shirtless and sweaty, raiding the refrigerator for Gatorade, she didn't show it.

"Hello, Danny. Does your wife know where you are?"

"Hi, doc." He grinned and nudged Casey. "Meet the baby doctor."

They all joined Vicki and Laura in the war room.

"It *is* them," Keri whispered, as Casey planted a kiss on Laura's forehead.

"Would I lie to you?"

Venturi introduced her to the Barretts, using her first name only. "Consider her a friend," he said. "You can tell her anything."

"We'll make an after-hours appointment at my office," Keri told Laura. "But if you're comfortable with it, I can take a history right now, in private, and answer any questions you may have."

"Now." Laura nodded with a look of relief.

Keri took a notebook from her handbag and everyone else cleared out. Danny watched the late-night news in the kitchen. Vicki and Michael drilled Casey on lesson material at the table.

After nearly an hour, Keri emerged from the war room, notebook in her hand, tears in her eyes.

Danny left. So did the Barretts. Venturi drove Keri home. "This wasn't exactly the evening I expected," she said softly, as he parked outside her Coral Gables town house.

"What did you expect?"

"I thought you would kiss me."

He turned off the headlights and ignition. "Like this?"

The kiss was long, slow, and warm.

"No," she finally gasped, "not quite like that."

She closed her eyes and lifted her mouth. He tried again.

"Can I come in?" he finally asked.

"It's already late and I'm due in the office early. But this evening has been an experience. Promise me something?"

"If I can."

"No more secrets?"

"No secrets," he said, and sealed it with a kiss.

CHAPTER EIGHTEEN

Delighted to have the last word, Laura and Casey enjoyed collaborating on their suicide note.

Many such notes are cruelly calculated to leave a legacy of guilt to the living. In their case it was appropriate.

Venturi encouraged them to keep it short and simple — and to leave their fingerprints all over it. Literally.

It didn't take long to produce a final, so to speak, draft.

To whom it may concern,
By the time you read this we will be dead.

It seemed like a dream come true, that justice had finally triumphed when we were released and the world knew what we knew from the start, that we were innocent, always innocent. But our dream of justice became a nightmare. We have been repeatedly threatened, physically attacked, and denied employment. We can no longer survive and with nowhere to turn, we choose this way out. Perhaps God will forgive you all for refusing to accept the fact of our innocence and driving us into this downward spiral of hopelessness and despair.

Good-bye.

Casey handwrote two copies which they both signed.

They mailed one to *The Miami Herald* and the other to the Miami-Dade Police Department early on the day they died.

The Barretts left their apartment at the usual time that morning, but on the way to Venturi's they made stops at four service stations. They filled a five-gallon gasoline can at each one.

They stayed at the house, while Venturi carefully drove their car west on the Tamiami Trail and turned down a remote dirt road into the Everglades.

Danny followed in his SUV.

They left Laura's purse and Casey's wallet containing their driver's licenses, ID, and all the money they had left — two $1 bills and some small change — on a tree stump near the turnoff to the dirt road.

"Sure this will be hot enough?" Venturi asked.

"Who knows more about cremation than me?" Danny confidently removed two cardboard boxes from his car.

Each was marked with a label from a Florida medical examiner's office.

April 9, 1995, Jane Doe, unidentified Caucasian female, age thirties.

Dec. 17, 1998, John Doe, unidentified Caucasian male, age thirty to forty.

"Intact skeletons like this," Danny proudly explained the night before, "are rare and hard to come by. You never find them out in the open. Wildlife scatters them, wild dogs run away with big bones, land crabs carry away the small bones like fingers and toes.

"We're damn lucky. Whoever wrapped Jane in plastic rolled her up in a heavy rug and buried her deep. If some farmer didn't decide to dig a well, she never would have been found.

"And Johnny here came out of the closet in an abandoned house. A demolition crew found him when they were about to knock it down. He might have been homeless, crashed there and died of natural causes or a drug overdose, or he was killed and dumped there. Nobody knows.

"No cause of death established on either one. No bullet holes, no knife nicks. Pristine condition," he said proudly.

"So how did you happen to . . ."

"You'd never get them in Miami-Dade. Here, the medical examiner's office boils 'em in meat tenderizer, strips the bones, and stores 'em indefinitely, hoping to identify them someday. But smaller ME offices around the state don't have that kind of storage space. These were kept for at least ten years. Eventually they're released to a funeral home for cremation or burial. Need I say more?"

"I already heard more than I want to," Venturi said.

He and Danny had originally discussed cleaning out the nagangas of several Santería priests he knew. The large metal cauldrons usually contain a human skull and long leg bones along with other ritualistic items.

"Where do they get the bones they use in ceremonies?"

"Don't ask," Danny said. "Some from Africa and Haiti. They busted a woman at the airport here just recently. Came in from Haiti with a human skull in her purse. Couldn't understand why it was a problem. But most are harvested locally. More graves are robbed here than in anywhere in

America.

"Even the dead aren't safe in Miami."

They arranged the man's bones on the seat behind the steering wheel of the Taurus and the female's in the passenger seat. From counties in different parts of the state, they almost surely never met in life, but John and Jane Doe were about to be linked forever.

Wearing work gloves and masks to protect themselves from the fumes, Venturi and Danny drenched the bones, the seats, the dashboard, and the carpet with gasoline. The fuel tank was a quarter full, a volatile mix of fumes, gasoline and air.

"Got a cigarette?" Danny asked as, choking on fumes, they used the last of the gasoline to soak the inside of the trunk.

They left the car windows open just a hair, allowing in enough air for the fire to breathe, and hung a gasoline-soaked rag out the driver's-side window.

Venturi attached a road flare to the end of a fifteen-foot-long painter's pole, pulled off the cap, and slid it across the flare's pyrotechnic bubble as though scratching a match.

The flare ignited. Backing away, he touched it to the gasoline-soaked rag.

Danny was already behind the wheel of the SUV.

Venturi extinguished the flare in the dirt, telescoped the pole and tossed it, the flare, and the cap into the backseat, and scrambled into the SUV.

"Sure you got the cap?" Danny said.

"Yeah, yeah. Let's go, let's go!"

Danny swung back onto the Trail and turned east. Venturi called 911 on a prepaid cell to report a raging brush fire thirty miles from the real flames roaring in the rearview mirror.

"Look at that sucker burn!" Danny whistled through his teeth as he watched the rearview mirror. "Wait till that gas-soaked trunk burns cherry red and the fuel tank blows.

"So long, Laura and Casey."

"Ashes to ashes," Venturi said. "May they rest in peace."

CHAPTER NINETEEN

"Hullo, Audra and Aiden Faircloth!" Danny said.

Audra hugged Aiden's neck, as Mike and Danny walked in.

"It's over? Is it really over?"

"It's over. They're gone," Mike said.

Their Kmart clothes and the rest of Laura and Casey Barretts' meager belongings remained in the tiny efficiency with the window view of treetops and sky. A third copy of the signed suicide note was found on the kitchen table, with a postscript apologizing to the landlord for any inconvenience regarding the lease. Homicide detectives found it along with stacks of want ads, job applications, and letter after letter of rejection. The landlord later showed camera crews and reporters around the modest single room and bath.

The deaths of the couple at the heart of the sex scandal at Devonbrook Day Care made national news as did the untimely death, the same week, at age forty-four, of Richard Jewell, the security guard hero who was hounded, hunted, and ruined when the media falsely accused him of being the Olympic bomber.

The difference was that Richard Jewell was really dead.

Their transformation was so effective that Audra and Aiden already considered Laura and Casey sad strangers they had left behind.

Audra, now blond, walked like a high-stepping model, her shoulders and hips in motion, and spoke like an Aussie. Once brown-eyed, she now wore green contact lenses. Her pregnancy, confirmed at Keri's office the night after they met, didn't show yet. Aiden was a jock, head shaved, beard short, mustache well groomed. He even looked taller due to lifts in his shoes and his improved posture, which appeared almost military. Neither resembled the sad-sack photos on Laura's and Casey's driver's licenses.

Their new birth certificates and passports would pass scrutiny anywhere in the world.

Venturi had again called upon a friend who in a prior career had provided similar documents for protected witnesses. Nelson

Drumheller now owned a company with lucrative government contracts to control access to federal buildings, computer systems, and sensitive areas with a new high-tech generation of badges and ID cards. His were encrypted with biometric data including fingerprints, facial recognition, and license and passport information.

And Danny had reached out to a former CIA contact, now a travel agent expert at moving people all over the globe without leaving trails. Enough money to see them through the first year was waiting in an Australian bank.

As Venturi drove them to the airport for their long, first journey home, he reinforced their training: how to spot a tail, how to lose one, and how to cheat the omnipresent security and television cameras.

"Never sit bareheaded in the stands at sports events. TV cameras often pan the fans. Always wear hats and shades. You have long lives ahead," he said earnestly. "As you raise your family, you'll fall into the rhythm of life in your community. But break no laws, however minor. Draw no attention to yourselves. No letters to the editor, no man-on-the-street television interviews. Live quietly, under the radar. Even in intimate situations when you're alone together, never use your old names. You never knew those people."

Audra and Aidan had been drilled relentlessly on their new dates of birth, mothers' maiden names, fathers' occupations, their new wedding anniversary, until everyone was sure that no momentary slip of the tongue would betray them.

"If someone on the street shouts out the name Laura or Casey, don't react, don't turn around. Walk away normally. Someone who thought they recognized you will assume they were mistaken."

They said their good-byes in a parking garage at Miami International Airport.

"It's such a long, long flight," Keri fretted. "I want you both, especially you, Audra, to get up and walk around. Don't sit in a cramped position for long periods. Drink lots of fluids, nonalcoholic, of course. Take your vitamins and find a good ob-gyn from the list I gave you as soon as you arrive."

"Okay, okay," Audra said, rosy cheeked and excited. "We get it, we got it the first time. You're starting to sound like you're our parents!"

She threw her arms around Venturi's neck from the backseat, catching him off guard.

"You are our parents," she said emotionally, and hugged him hard. "The family we never had. You're our gift from God."

Her chin trembled, her eyes filled. "We'll live up to your expectations, I promise."

"From now on, you are the family," Venturi said. "Congratulations! Australia! What an adventure." He sounded almost envious. "Be happy."

"We will," she promised tearfully. "We'll never forget you."

Danny pumped Aiden's hand. "Watch out for the crocs, mate."

After a round of hugs and kisses, the couple hurried into the terminal.

The others followed slowly, from a distance, watching until they cleared security.

Audra looked back at one point and waved. No one waved back. They were history now. But they kept watching until the couple, caught up in a tidal wave of humanity, disappeared.

The Miami-Dade County medical examiner's office announced weeks later that tests had been unable to confirm through DNA the identification of the remains in the Barretts' car.

The chief medical examiner explained that the fire's heat had been so intense that the victims' teeth had exploded and that even the large leg bones, usually a reliable source of DNA, had been incinerated to the extent that only splinters remained.

"They were literally cremated," he said.

However, experts had authenticated the handwriting on the suicide notes as that of Laura and Casey Barrett.

The burned remains of a couple their age had been found in a car registered to them, and their identification was located nearby.

A psychological autopsy of the victims revealed histories of despondency, depression, and incarceration. The experts concluded that the Barretts were indeed deceased at their own hands. Their death certificates were signed.

Case closed.

CHAPTER TWENTY

Pounding on his bedroom door jolted Venturi awake late that night. Scout responded from his rug on the floor with only a single startled woof.

"Mikey? It's me, I need to talk to you."

He rolled out of bed naked, focused on the stress in Victoria's voice. The digital face on his bedside clock read 3:10 a.m. He slipped on a pair of shorts, unlocked the door, and edged it open.

"Vicki? Is everything all right?"

"Here, yes. In the rest of the world, no." Her hair tousled, she wore a pink cotton robe and slippers. She looked pale but was alone.

"You know I always leave my cell phone on. The New York City police just called. It's Sidney."

"Is he all right?"

"No. All wrong, as usual."

"I'll be right out."

When he stepped back from the door she saw the .45-caliber automatic in his right hand.

He pulled on blue jeans and a shirt, then joined her in the kitchen.

He knew she'd seen the gun. "Old habits," he explained.

"I know. Madison told me," she said softly.

"Did it bother her?" he asked, his interest piqued. "Did she complain?"

"Oh, no, she always said she never felt safer than when she was with you."

He swallowed and nodded. "It's pretty remote out here. You can never be too careful."

She gazed fondly into his eyes and smiled. "I see the things you do. It reminds me of the two of you together. You know there's an old love song with lyrics about how little things remind me of you. A cigarette with lipstick traces, a ticket to romantic places, and so on.

"Of course with you it's little things, like always refilling your gas tank before going home, even if it's already three quarters full. And then there's the parachute cord, compass, ropes, papers, and maps in the car, to say nothing of a handgun under the pillow and a shotgun in the pantry."

She laughed, as though she found them

all endearing.

He poured them each a glass of milk and sat across from her in the dimly lit kitchen, illuminated only by the clock on the microwave.

"So what's with Sidney?"

She blinked back tears and covered her eyes with her hand.

"If he's still alive and isn't quadriplegic or comatose, it's not that bad," he said gently. "What's the kid stepped in now?"

She lifted her chin and met his eyes. "My apartment actually. He broke in. Stacked everything he could steal at the front door and was busy vandalizing the rest when the police arrived. The doorman called them. He knew I was out of town.

"Sidney struggled with the police, severely bit a female officer on the chin and forearm, and resisted until they shocked him with a Taser. Three times. It scarcely affected him. They said it was most likely because he was high. He was also in possession of cocaine and marijuana.

"How could two children be so different?" she murmured forlornly.

He shook his head. Sidney, the youngest by three years, had always been trouble. His father's first and fatal coronary had occurred at a Suffern, New York, police station, where he'd gone after Sidney, then fourteen, took his car without permission. He led police on a wild high-speed chase that ended in a three-car collision, which seriously injured three people, one of them a child.

"We tried everything." Her voice sounded thin. "Love, therapy, rehab, tough love, juvenile boot camp. The only thing we didn't do was a lobotomy. I wish we had. He's not a kid anymore. He's an angry twenty-eight-year-old man who hates the world. Especially me."

She had stopped giving him money because it went for drugs, gambling, or lap dances. He was furious when she did not share the settlement she received for the grave injuries that cost her her daughter and unborn grandchild, her leg, and nearly her life.

"He said Madison was his sister and demanded his share. I said no. If he'd been going to school, working, or buying a house, it would be different, of course. But I won't support his bad behavior. He and his sister were never close. He always resented her, too.

"I'm actually afraid of him, Mikey." She reacted as though startled by the thought. "How can you be afraid of a child you brought into the world?"

He took her hands. "With Sidney, it's easy. He's more than troubled. I wish I knew what it would take to straighten him out."

She sighed. "You know, I grew so fond of those young people we just sent on their way. Wished I could disown Sidney and adopt them. That sounds terribly disloyal, doesn't it?"

"You don't have a disloyal bone in your body, Victoria. You've done everything you can do. Sidney chose his own path for whatever reasons. He must be a throwback to some evil ancestor, a pirate, Ali Baba, or one of the forty thieves."

"I prefer the 'mix-up in the maternity ward' theory," she said. "I'm going to New York tomorrow to sort things out. The police say it's up to me if I want to prosecute my son for breaking and entering, vandalism, and destruction of property. They are prosecuting him for assault on a police officer, resisting arrest with violence, and drug possession."

Her gaze was steady. "I want to prosecute, Mikey. God knows, nothing else has worked. Maybe jail time will. If not, at least he'll be in a cage and not hurting anyone for a while. What do you think?"

"It's your decision. He's your son. I wish

I'd been more helpful. I tried, too. I saw Madison cry over her little brother more than once. Personally, I think you're right to do it, but either way, I'll back you a hundred percent."

"I started packing but wanted to let you know that I'm going tomorrow."

"I should go with you," he said.

She shook her head. "We both know you should stay out of New York for a time. And Sidney would be even angrier if you were involved. He's always been jealous of you. I'll handle it."

On the way to Miami International Airport the next morning, Venturi said, "The last three people I dropped off at the airport won't be back. Promise that's not the case with you."

She smiled. "Be careful what you wish for."

He took her as far as security allowed.

He'd been elated to see the others fly out of his life. This departure was painful.

Her last words to him were, "Please see more of Keri. She's a wonderful girl. Do me a favor, take her out to lunch, or a romantic dinner."

He called Keri later. Harried, with pregnant women lined up in her waiting room, she was too busy for lunch. She'd love dinner.

She wore blue, with high heels and sparkly earrings. But her pager sounded shortly after they ordered. She rolled her eyes and made the call.

"How far apart are the contractions?" he heard her ask. "You're sure? Okay, take her to the hospital now. I'll meet you there. Don't worry. I'm on the way.

"I'm so sorry," she told Venturi.

He hailed their waiter. "Can you wrap that to go?" He nodded toward Keri. "A doctor. She just got paged. It's an emergency."

"That's not necessary," she whispered, as the people at the next table stared, engrossed by the drama.

"Sure it is. Sooner or later you will be hungry. If all goes well, you'll be ravenous."

In ten minutes, they were in his car with their carefully wrapped meals. He drove directly to the hospital and insisted they would dine together no matter how late.

"It could be an hour or two, or twelve or twenty, we don't know."

"That's all right. You promised to have dinner with me and I'm holding you to it, even if we wind up eating shrimp scampi for breakfast."

She laughed. "You're a stubborn man, Mikey."

He did a double take. "Mikey?"

"Sorry. I've heard Victoria call you that and thought it was all right."

Only two people had ever used that name. She was the third.

As they parked near the emergency room, a familiar sound, a low-flying helicopter pounding the air overhead, sent him back in time. It was about to land at the trauma center.

"Reminds me of the military," he said.

"Tell me about it," she said. "The trauma center's full of military personnel, surgeons, registered nurses, and medics, training to go to Iraq and Afghanistan. We have more than four thousand major traumas a year, gunshot and knife wounds, burns, blunt trauma, and the sort of chaos they'll see on the battlefield. Miami's the perfect place to train for war."

Inside the ER, the anxious father-to-be, a short, middle-aged man wearing a guayabera, rushed toward them.

He saw Venturi and how Keri was dressed. "Sorry to ruin your evening, Doctor."

"Not at all." She turned to introduce them, but Venturi simply signaled her to call him and faded into the background as the flustered man directed her to a curtained cubicle.

For the second consecutive night a woman woke him in the wee hours.

"A girl," she said softly. "A little early, a little jaundiced, but beautiful. Mother and baby are fine. The father fainted in the delivery room, but he'll be okay, too."

"The guy actually passed out?"

"Not unusual," she said. "It's relatively common."

She sounded happy and excited. So did he.

"I'll pick you up in twenty." He rolled out of bed naked, this time without a gun.

"Are you sure? It's so late. Maybe we should take a rain check. I can take a taxi home."

"No way."

"Okay, I just have to check the baby's footprint and sign the birth certificate. I'll meet you outside."

"No," he said quickly. "Things get crazy outside an emergency room after midnight. If I can't find you, I'll have you paged."

He warmed up their meals, nestled a bottle of Veuve Clicquot in an ice-filled cooler, and drove to the hospital.

She was waiting. "Come on," she said eagerly. "I want you to see her."

She took him to the third-floor nursery.

"There she is. Right down in front."

Asleep, tiny fists clenched, her mouth puckered, she wore a pink ribbon in her soft downy hair. A pink knitted skull cap kept the back of her head warm.

"Isn't she precious?"

"Nice work," he said approvingly.

"Well, I'm not a hundred percent responsible," she conceded. "Mom and Dad had something to do with it."

She seemed giddy in the car. He'd never heard her talk so much.

"I was so elated for the couple we will never mention. Now this." Her long sigh was contented. "It's the same feeling. A fresh start. Delivering new life."

"Life," he said, "is what it's all about." He turned toward the marina. He had borrowed the keys to Danny's boat, docked downtown.

"I'm starved, Michael. Where's my dinner?"

He wondered if she'd ever call him Mikey again.

She did. Under the stars, out on the water, then again on a blanket on the sandy beach of an offshore island in the bay. From a distance came the sound of drums, gut-quivering rhythms, and the African soul of

Cuban rumba. Voices calling and responding, hypnotic sounds heard in secret Santería ceremonies. The moon sailed across a velvet sky; the lights of the city begin to dim. The music did not fade until the first soft blush of dawn in the east.

"I have to be at the office in a few hours," she said sleepily.

She was awake and alert, her hand resting lightly on his thigh, as he drove her home. "I have just enough time to shower and dress but I'm not even tired. I'm still high on the last forty-eight hours. I feel great."

"Tell me that about four o'clock this afternoon." He kissed her. "You'll be cursing my name."

"I don't think so," she sang sweetly.

At home, he listened to several messages from the other woman in his life.

She was neither content nor happy.

CHAPTER TWENTY-ONE

"The damage is far worse than I expected," Vicki said later. "I can't even sleep in my own apartment. Sidney jammed the toilets, turned on all the faucets full blast, and flooded the entire place.

"I went to see him at Riker's Island this morning. It was awful."

Venturi winced. "I'm sorry."

"I wanted to hear his explanation or apology. He had no intention of offering either. He was delighted to see me, thought I'd post his bond and hire him an attorney. You can't say the boy doesn't have chutzpah. He asked, then demanded, then threatened, then pleaded and threatened some more. I made it clear he's an adult and owns the pink slip on his life. He can go on driving, but I'm not buying the gas, changing the oil, or paying for repairs."

"Good for you, Vicki. What's next?"

"I intend to prosecute. I'm meeting with

the assistant district attorney tomorrow."

He gave his mother-in-law a silent thumbs-up.

"In the meantime, I'm considering a rather drastic life change." She paused.

"Don't tell you're eloping with that jazz musician you were seeing last fall."

She laughed, despite the pain in her voice. "You know I like to stay too busy to dwell on the past. The business is my baby. I built it, worked hard, and it's been fun. But I'm tired of it now. At this point in life, I find projects such as the ones we recently tackled far more fulfilling.

"I'm mulling over a few ideas, but set nothing into motion, of course, until speaking to you."

"What kind of ideas?"

She took a deep breath. "I hope you don't think me irrational." The words tumbled out. "But after twenty-four hours back in this city, I'm seriously considering relocating, putting my apartment on the market. I'd sell the business, of course. I've had a number of nibbles, inquiries and offers in the past, when I wasn't ready."

"Relocate to where?"

"Where would you suggest?"

It wasn't like her to answer a question with a question.

"Here, where else?"

Her sigh of relief was audible. "I'd find a place of my own," she said quickly, "a condo or a town house. I don't want you stuck with a crazy mother-in-law on your hands."

Yes! he thought. "Listen to me, woman," he said emphatically. "Go see the DA, call a good Realtor, get references. See who might be interested in the business, then get yourself on the next flight home."

"Home?"

"I'll pick you up at the airport."

"Okay, Mikey. Love you."

"Ditto."

"By the way," she added, "I called you very late. Your cell was off and you weren't home."

"I followed your advice and took a doctor to dinner."

"It took all night?"

"We can talk about that later."

He divulged no details, but she heard the smile in his voice.

He was napping when Keri called that afternoon at four o'clock. She was not cursing his name.

Then Danny called, sounding serious. "What's up, bro? You asleep?"

"Trying."

"It's five in the afternoon, man. That

means you scored big last night! I want every detail."

"Like crap."

"Had to be hot."

"Yeah. We went to the hospital and she delivered a baby girl."

"You know, man," Danny said, clearly disappointed, "you've been alone too long. You forgot how to have a hot time, if you ever knew."

"You ever pass out in the delivery room, Danny?"

"Hell, no. I cut the umbilical cord myself every time — with my teeth."

"Thanks for use of the boat, you sick bastard, and for telling me about that island beach."

"You're welcome. Listen, I called for a reason. It's important. We've got a new client."

Venturi sat up in bed. "What the hell you talking about?"

"Can't discuss it on the *teléfono.*"

"Damn straight. Where are you?"

"Pulling into your driveway."

They took a few beers to the war room.

"If we don't take this new client, she's dead. For real," Danny said.

"She?"

"You remember Judge Solange Dupree?"

"Read about her, sure, the Louisiana judge whose family was murdered last year."

"Not murdered. Executed. Slaughtered. Her mother, her husband, and her little twin boys. They haven't released it to the media yet, but there's been a second attempt to kill her. Yesterday, as she left the courthouse. For obvious reasons she now has a car and a driver. The driver, an off-duty cop, was on a break when she was ready to leave her chambers. Normally, he escorts her to her car, but she was in a hurry and said she'd meet him in the parking garage.

"He heads for the car on foot, sees her step off the elevator, then spots something under the car.

"He gets her out of the garage fast and calls for help."

"A bomb?"

"You got it. The bomb squad successfully defused it, after a few hairy moments. All the media knows is a bomb scare at the courthouse. But the truth is bound to leak out soon. It was the real deal.

"Sophisticated, radio-controlled, enough C-4 plastique explosives to take out the car, the street under it, and God knows how many passing pedestrians."

"Close call."

"Third time will probably be the charm."

"Her security must be supertight now," Venturi said.

"A lotta good that'll do. The people who want her dead are in it for the long haul. You know how our people drop their guard as time goes by. The bad guys have long memories. Ours are short. Too short. She'll be protected for a while, but if we don't step in, she's dead."

Venturi remembered the case well. Dupree had presided over the trial of a major Colombian drug kingpin. The defendant didn't want a jury. He chose to have the judge decide his fate. She proceeded with the highly publicized trial, convicted him on all counts, and sentenced him to consecutive life terms with no prospect of parole.

After death threats, police posted a manned patrol car outside her home. But after several months and budget cuts, the car was gone and Judge Dupree's protection was reduced to a patrol car passing her house at least once a shift, if not too busy with other calls.

One Saturday shortly after dawn, Judge Dupree broke from her usual weekend routine and left the house alone for an early-morning jog. She enjoyed the spring weather, the rare sense of freedom, and the chance to stretch her legs, she said later.

She'd be back in time for breakfast with her still-sleeping family.

When she returned, emergency vehicles ringed her home. Police were restraining the press and stringing yellow crime-scene tape.

Homicide detectives were surprised to see her alive.

Her mother, her college-professor husband, and their children, three-year-old boys, had all been shot in the head execution-style. Her husband was slumped at the kitchen table in his bathrobe, an untouched cup of coffee and the morning newspaper in front of him. Her mother was killed in her own bed. The children's bodies were found in an upstairs hallway as though they'd been caught scampering from their room after hearing noises.

Police had not yet searched the entire scene but assumed that the judge was also dead, or abducted. Solange Dupree was the sole survivor. All she loved was lost, all but her work.

After the funeral, she returned to the bench, stoic and dedicated, and under heavy guard. The murder investigation stalled. Only one thing was clear. Her days were numbered.

"She's not safe anywhere in the world."

Danny paced the room, cracking his knuckles. He seemed unusually agitated about a stranger's fate.

"I get the impression that this won't be your first hello if we get involved with the judge," Venturi said.

Danny glanced over his shoulder as though fearing he'd be overheard. "Yeah. I know her." His expression, body language, and tone of voice gave his words a singular significance.

"How?"

"Your ears only?"

Venturi nodded.

"I infiltrated an outfit that was running drugs, money, and guns out of Uruguay. They moved the money to buy the guns, which provided protection for the drugs.

"For reasons I won't bore you with, the case wound up in federal court in Louisiana. I couldn't testify in open court, because officially I was never there. I didn't exist. The government filed a sealed document requesting an in-camera proceeding that excluded the defense attorneys. Judge Solange Dupree presided."

"That's all?"

Danny turned to stare out a window at the sun-dappled canal behind the house. "She wasn't married yet, although I think she was seeing that college professor. I wasn't married, either."

"Oh, don't tell me . . ."

Danny quickly took the seat opposite him. "There's something about her, Mike. She's beautiful, sensitive, smart as hell, loves the law, the flag, justice, all that shit. She's like us.

"First time I saw her I wondered, fantasized, about what she had going on under that black robe. When I found out, it totally outdid my imagination. She has a tattoo. Believe it? Probably the only U.S. District Court judge with a tattoo around her ankle, a chain with a little red heart dangling from it.

"I swear, it was pure animal magnetism. Nothing else was possible. Me, a CIA spook, for God's sake. With a damn federal court judge."

He read Venturi's expression.

"So we had a little thing. Very brief. Very hot. Okay, okay. Dangerous, totally unethical, conduct unbecoming. Might have messed up the entire case. But we weren't stupid. We made sure nobody knew, just us.

"They'll kill her, Mike. She doesn't deserve it."

Danny's words did not make Venturi as uncomfortable as did their intensity.

"She sounds stand-up, like she's toughing it out, sending the bad guys a message. She might not be interested." He fervently hoped she wouldn't be.

Danny shook his head adamantly. "We're her only chance."

"With somebody that high profile and federal government connected, it would be next to impossible to pull off without a body."

"You want a body, we'll get a body!" Danny said hotly. His energy filled the room as, back on his feet, he began to pace again, unable to contain his anger and anxiety.

"The reason we've succeeded so far is because we had no links, no emotional connections to the clients," Venturi said calmly. "Emotions create problems."

"You're worried about me?" Danny jabbed his chest savagely with his thumb. "Nobody's more professional. Besides," he said, voice raised, "I'm married. With kids. How do you think I feel when I look at them and think about what happened to hers?" He sighed. "Look, I don't even have to see her. I'll work under the radar. You can handle it."

"How do we reach out to her, without her bodyguards, the FBI, and the U.S. Attorney's Office recording the conversation?

She must be superinsulated. How do you penetrate that? She's not picking up her own phone, answering her door, or shopping at the mall."

"She has a private number, a safe line, in her office."

"How do you know, after all this time? And if so, how do you know she's not sharing it with the FBI?"

Danny took a deep breath and gave it up. "Because she picked it up when I called. We talked. She's the strongest woman I've ever met, yet she heard my voice and started to cry. She's so ready to be out of there, Mike. Her brave facade is crumbling. She has nothing left. She won't look back.

"The wannabe judges, the lawyers who practice in front of her, are circling like vultures," he said bitterly. "They openly joke about not scheduling any long trials in her courtroom. They're taking bets, have a pool, on the date she buys it, and another one on which of them will be appointed to fill the vacancy."

"You spoke to her at the courthouse?" Venturi frowned. "You'll probably find the FBI waiting at your front door when you get home. How do you know she still trusts you?"

"She trusts me." Danny's gaze was level.

250

He clearly believed it.

"Did you discuss the possibility with her?"

"Hell no, not on the *teléfono*, but she's coming to Miami, using an alias, for a monthlong vacation while the bomb attempt is investigated and new security precautions put in place. I may have hinted, but not in so many words, that there's a way out."

"She knows you're married?"

Danny averted his eyes. "What does that matter?"

"Christ! Do I have to spell it out? What if she misinterpreted your offer, thinks you're inviting her to Miami for a romantic reunion, and that the two of you are going to walk off into the sunset?"

Danny closed his eyes and kneaded the back of his neck, as though his head hurt. His voice dropped. "She knows about Luz and the kids."

"She'll bring bodyguards, right?"

"She doesn't want to. But if she does, she's smart enough to give them the slip."

Venturi rolled his eyes and sighed. The whole idea gave him a bad feeling. "There's a helluva lot more to deal with here than a hostile or accusing press. She's part of the federal government. The feds . . . the Colombians. Jesus, I don't need to tell you how careful we'd have to be."

"We're always careful," Danny said. "Always have been, always will. That's how we survive."

"Any ideas?"

"The possibilities are endless. People think of judges as bookish, nerdy types who wouldn't know how to open a window. Not her. She's aggressive, athletic, a sports-car driver, snow skier. Swims like a fish, dives, sails, hang glides. Like I said, lots of possibilities."

"The feds have more efficient, organized ways to protect her," Venturi pleaded. "She'd be safer with them. If she was a witness, not a judge, she'd be in the protection program in a heartbeat."

"And how good is that?" Danny demanded. "They still deny that they've ever lost a protected witness. We know that's a joke. I can name three off the top of my head and I never even worked for them. They still claim that no protected witness who followed their rules was ever killed. What a laugh."

Venturi nodded wearily. He didn't like arguing with Danny.

"I don't want to pick up a newspaper and read that the bastards killed her because some bureaucrat screwed up or let her have her way. Like I said, she's a strong woman.

This has to be done right," Danny said, "by people who understand her and won't screw up."

"You know this could go bad, very bad," Venturi said.

Now he was the one who didn't want to look his friend in the eye.

"Whenever you need me, Mike, I'm here."

"I know."

"We always had each other's backs, bro."

"We still do." How could he refuse? "When do you think this Florida vacation of hers will happen?"

"She's traveling under the name Marilyn Moya. She'll be here in forty-eight hours."

CHAPTER
TWENTY-TWO

Venturi and the dog had returned from an early morning fishing trip, and he was out on the dock cleaning his catch when he heard a car at the gate.

He slipped into the house through the back as Scout raced headlong around the side of the building to confront the visitor.

The car was a sleek silver-green Jaguar convertible. The driver had stepped out and stood at the gate. Long legs, short skirt, young looking. She pulled off a silk scarf and shook out her hair, as dark and shiny as a raven's wing. It lifted like a banner in the brisk winds spawned by storm clouds on the outskirts of a hurricane out in the gulf. He pushed the button to open the gate so she could drive up to the house.

Scout ran alongside the approaching car, barking his brains out.

If it was the judge, Venturi wished Danny had given him a heads-up. Uncomfortably aware of the blood on his jeans and the fish knife in his belt, he opened the door as she approached on foot.

The big sunglasses shielding her eyes didn't hide her disappointment. She tilted her head, peering behind him, as though expecting someone else.

"I'm Marilyn Moya. You're Michael?"

He nodded. Close up, her tawny skin was luminous, her perfect teeth flashed white. She looked younger than her age, which he knew to be thirty-eight. She wore a black cotton eyelet blouse over a slim white skirt. Her high-heeled black sandals exposed bloodred toenails that matched her perfect manicure. Diamond ear studs and a tiny gold cross on a thin chain around her neck were her only jewelry. No wedding ring.

He scanned the road behind her. "Think you were followed?"

"No." She said it with the utter confidence of a woman accustomed to handing down life-changing decisions to others.

She saw his doubtful expression. "I went shopping. Aventura Mall has three levels with a seven-story parking garage, movie theaters, restaurants, and hundreds of stores. I breezed through a dozen, hit the restrooms, the dressing rooms, and exited through different doors every time. I bought a movie ticket, then left the theater through an inside exit. My rental is still in the mall's parking garage. I took a taxi to a dealership and picked up my friend's car, which was being serviced. That's what I'm driving now. Satisfied?"

"Good," he said, but stopped to glance back over his shoulder again as they entered the house.

She took off the dark shades and looked around eagerly. But they were alone. Her dark eyes, sad, bloodshot, and hollow, didn't appear as youthful as the rest of her.

He poured her a cup of coffee.

She stared at it. "Do you have anything stronger?"

"Such as?"

"Vodka."

He brought a bottle of Smirnoff to the table, along with small bottles of orange and tomato juice. She never touched the juice. He asked for her car keys and she tossed them across the table. He caught them and moved her car into the shed — behind it wasn't good enough. He didn't want it visible from the air. A cursory search revealed no obvious tracking device.

She looked hopeful when she heard his footsteps on the porch, but her smile faded when she saw it was only him.

He asked what kind of security had been sent with her.

"No bodyguards," she said. "They wanted them, but I insisted that I had to get away alone. I have a gun and go to the range twice a week. I've been target shooting since I was a kid at camp."

"You're psychologically ready to use it, to shoot to kill if threatened?"

"Oh, yes."

"Good. Keep it loaded and close to you until this is over. Even though you declined protection, we have to assume that the local FBI office and police departments have been told that you're in Miami and have been asked to keep tabs on you."

"True." She looked around again. "Is Danny here?"

"No."

She frowned. "I can't wait to see him." She paused to read his expression. "We're old friends, you know."

He nodded.

Outside the house the wind began to whine, then whistle, as its strength and speed accelerated. Whenever a thunderstorm blew up, something in the design of the old structure magnified the shriek of a strong wind into a howl that sounded like a chorus of screaming women. Punctuated by fierce lightning bolts and thunderclaps, it electrified the room.

Marilyn Moya, chin raised, listened raptly, as though inhaling the storm's energy. "It must be wild out on the water right now." The look in her eyes said she'd like to be out there.

"Not a place to be," he said.

She smiled without comment.

He opened a fresh notebook.

"What's your blood type? Do you have any old fractures or other injuries that would show up on X-rays? What about identifying characteristics? Scars, tattoos, birthmarks?"

"Only fractures of the heart, invisible to the naked eye," she said, slowly pouring more vodka into her glass. She paused. "A-positive blood. No birthmarks. No scars. One tattoo." She lifted her eyes and her glass as though in a toast, then brought it to her lips.

"The tattoo on your ankle, that's it?"

She smiled seductively. "You noticed."

"I need to photograph it."

She abruptly removed her high-heeled sandal and lifted her bare foot onto the rough wooden table, exposing her long shapely right leg to the thigh.

"You're sure this is necessary?" She

sounded almost mocking.

"Absolutely." He picked up the digital camera, wondering if her attitude shielded her fears and uncertainties, or if this was her normal behavior. He could see what attracted Danny to this woman.

She watched, eyes guarded as he shot close-ups from every angle.

A small red heart appeared to dangle from a fine dark chain delicately etched link by link around her ankle.

"It has to go," he said.

She sighed. "Nothing lasts forever. Can we cover it with something darker, denser, more dramatic?"

"No."

"Is the removal process painful?"

"I don't know."

"Fair enough," she said almost absently, dark eyes moving hopefully toward the door.

He had hoped she'd refuse, indignantly announce that the tattoo was a deal breaker and that she would choose to entrust her safety to her less-demanding government protectors.

Her eyes shifted back to his. "Can you shave a few years off my age?"

"That can be arranged, within reason."

She smiled sardonically. "Don't be alarmed, Michael, I won't ask to be eighteen years old. Been there, done that. But I'd like to postpone forty for just a little longer."

The entrance gate bell sounded.

"Is it Danny?" she asked eagerly.

He peered out the front window. Keri's car. She was punching in the gate's security code. She'd be at the front door in seconds.

"No, someone else. You shouldn't be seen."

He showed her to the bedroom used by prior clients.

"Stay here," he said, and firmly closed the door.

He stashed the vodka and other bottles and rinsed out her glass.

Keri dashed through the rain from her car. He swung the front door open as she raised her hand to knock and she almost fell into his arms.

"It's a hurricane out there," she gasped, laughing as she caught her balance.

"I didn't expect you."

She blinked up at him. "Sorry. I should've called." She looked around. "Is Victoria back?"

"No, not until tomorrow."

Keri's smile faded and she took a small step back. "I'm intruding."

"No."

"I smell perfume, Michael."

260

"Perfume?" He smelled it, too.

Tail awag, Scout grinned up at them and, as if on cue, trotted toward the bedroom.

Busted, he thought bitterly, by his so-called best friend.

Keri cut her eyes at Venturi, followed the dog, and opened the door.

Solange was sitting on the bed. "Excuse me," Keri said, then quietly closed the door, walked past Michael and out into the deluge. The rain had not let up at all.

"Wait a minute." He followed her into the rain and caught up with her at her car. Her face was red.

"I should have known better," she muttered, and refused to look at him.

He could let her go, but she knew too much — and irate women can wreak endless havoc. More important, he realized, he didn't want her to go. He leaned against her car door so she couldn't open it.

"The woman's a new client," he said. "You know, like the couple we don't mention. Her situation is complex and dangerous. I didn't want you involved, for your protection, in case things go wrong."

"Shouldn't I decide that?" She squinted up at him as the hard rain pelted her face. "I'm already involved."

The relentless downpour pounded them,

soaked their clothes, and ran down their faces.

"It's wet out here," he finally said.

"I noticed."

"Come back inside," he said.

"Only if you include me. Remember, we said no more secrets."

He nodded.

"Now, what's her story?"

He put his arm around her shoulders and they dashed back to the house, skidding on wet grass and splashing through mud.

She vaguely recalled news reports about the judge and her murdered family.

They were using towels to dry each other's hair when Solange emerged from the bedroom, tired of waiting.

"When will Danny be here?" She spoke in the imperious tone of a no-nonsense judge demanding to know why an attorney is late.

"I'm not sure," Venturi said, his voice edgy. "But he knows you're in good hands."

He introduced Keri. "She's a friend," he said, "who may be able to answer your question." He turned to her. "How painful is it to remove a tattoo?"

Keri rolled her eyes and frowned. "I'm not sure," she said, her voice chilly, "but it's definitely not as uncomfortable as childbirth."

"Thank God for small favors," the woman muttered.

Solange was staying in the empty apartment of a trusted friend, an old college roommate whose car she was driving. Venturi instructed her to return the next day using similar precautions to avoid being followed. He warned her to keep the Jaguar in a locked garage so no tracking device could be planted. "It would help," he said, "if you drove something a little less conspicuous.

"One other thing," he added, almost casually. "We've come up with a tentative plan and need a pint of your blood. Now."

Keri did not look surprised that he had the necessary items ready.

"I don't like needles," Solange complained, as Keri tightened the rubber tubing around her arm.

"Well, you certainly survived quite a few when that tattoo was done," Keri said cheerfully. "This little procedure won't take anywhere near as long." She snapped her finger against the woman's forearm to locate a vein she liked.

Keri seemed to be enjoying herself.

Solange looked the other way to avoid seeing her blood flow into the bag.

"See, that wasn't so bad, was it?" Keri said, when the bag was full. She applied a sterile gauze pad to the site and instructed the patient to hold it there for a few minutes.

"Do you have some orange juice for her, Michael?"

"We may need to do this several times," he said, handing Solange a glass of juice. "Make sure you don't have anything to drink next time you're here. And never, ever, come walking out of that room or any other until I invite you. You had no idea who was here. A mistake like that could risk the whole operation."

Her eyes and body language made it abundantly clear that she was unaccustomed to being spoken to that way, but she nodded.

"I understand that you're a good sailor."

She shrugged. "I've sailed all my life."

"Good. Tomorrow morning go to the nearest busy marina, rent a sailboat, and take it out off the beach for a few hours. The winds we're having should make it interesting. Make sure you ask for and keep the receipts and any other paperwork."

The rain had stopped. He backed her car out of the shed. Then he and Keri watched Solange pick her way in high heels through the muddy yard to the Jag.

"Was that our Danny that she asked about?" Keri inquired.

He nodded and tried a quick diversion, catching her around the waist. "Now, let's get you out of these wet clothes."

"They know each other?" She looked troubled.

"Years ago, before he met Luz. I'm not too crazy about it, either."

Danny called later, after Keri left.

Venturi peered out the front window, phone in hand, to make sure he wasn't in the driveway.

"How does she look? Is she all right? Did she ask about me?" He sounded like a lovesick teenager.

"She looks fine, was disappointed you weren't here. She's sad. Her tattoo has got to go. In fact, I'm thinking we need to change more than just her hair, clothes, and cosmetics. Remember Gordon, that plastic surgeon we met in Somalia? The one from Medecins sans Frontières? Doesn't he practice down here somewhere?"

"Boca, I think. Charging the rich and not-so-beautiful big bucks for facelifts, nose jobs, and tummy tucks," Danny said. "A long way from Doctors without Borders in Africa, when he was sewing burn-and-bomb victims back together and operating on babies with birth defects."

He sighed. "It'd be a damn shame to

change a hair on that woman's head," he lamented.

"In Boca? Think Gordon Howard will be glad to see us?"

"Why not?" Danny said. "We saved his life."

"We took some blood from her today."

"We?"

"Keri took the blood. It's in my refrigerator."

"So Keri's in?"

"She happened to be here."

"Is that good?" Danny didn't sound happy about it. "Sure we can trust her?"

"You tell me, you've known her longer. Afraid she'll tell your wife?"

"The reason Luz doesn't know much about what I do is to protect her and the kids. The less they know, the safer they are. And she has her hands full with the house, the little ones, and another one on the way. I don't want her to worry."

"I agree. Glad to hear you to say that. Make sure you don't give her anything to worry about, Danny. I'm serious."

Venturi picked Victoria up at the airport in the morning. Buoyant and happy to be home, she had lots of news. Sidney remained behind bars, her apartment was on the market, and two interested parties were preparing bids on the business.

Elated about the new project under way, she, the client, and Venturi quickly settled down to business in the war room. Something new had been added. One wall was dominated by a handsome full-color world map framed in leather, with color-coded pins and flags to mark specific locations.

Because Solange already spoke French, she considered both Geneva, Switzerland, and the Loire Valley in France's wine country. She had abandoned her early studies as an art major to pursue the law and was also a wine aficionado.

She soon focused on the French heartland with its sculpted flower gardens, scenic countryside, and le Clos Luce, the final home of Leonardo da Vinci, where many of his drawings and inventions remain on display, only an hour or so away from Paris by train.

"This is no vacation," Victoria warned. "It's the rest of your life."

"And what better place to spend it?" Solange countered. "I'm sure I can acclimate, and find a future there."

Victoria pulled together crash courses in the region's dialect and its vineyards, wines, local laws, history, politics, customs, and cuisine.

Venturi and Danny arrived at the swank office of plastic surgeon Gordon Howard at the end of the business day.

En route to perform surgeries in a remote village, his Doctors Without Borders helicopter lost power and crashed. The pilot and nurse were killed. Howard climbed from the wreckage with minor injuries but was quickly captured and roughed up at gunpoint by heavily armed rebels. A local warlord held him for ransom.

Venturi and Danny, on recon in the area, heard of the doctor's plight and, upon learning he was American, decided on their own to rescue him.

Their nighttime raid deep into enemy territory escalated into a bullet-punctuated skirmish.

When they kicked in the door wearing camouflage and dark face paint, the frightened captive didn't know whose side they were on.

"We're Americans!" Danny said. "Let's go! Let's go!"

"How did you find me?" the astonished doctor asked.

"We happened to be in the neighborhood," Mike said. "Keep your head down and do what we tell you."

They exchanged gunfire with his captors, hurled hand grenades, and escaped into the night.

Now, years later, they browsed the well-appointed outer office of Dr. Gordon Howard.

"I'm sorry," the receptionist said, her voice frosty. "The doctor is extremely busy and sees no one without an appointment. He's about to leave for the day."

"Tell him that Danny and Mike, his friends from Somalia, are here," Danny said.

She did so reluctantly.

Howard burst from his office. "I don't believe it! It's really you! How did you find me?"

"We happened to be in the neighborhood," Venturi said.

The doctor hugged them both. "You don't know how often I think of you guys. I didn't know where you were, or if you were still alive."

He sent the receptionist home, locked the outer doors, and ushered them into his private office.

The interior was even more opulent than his reception area.

"Far cry from a tent with no running water," Danny said, taking in the ambience.

"The competition in Boca is huge," Howard said, taking a seat behind his big desk. "Motorists can have botox injected at any traffic light. I've been lucky. Spent a couple years busting my butt, working long hours, and missing time with my family to build the practice. Then a mentor of mine gave me the best advice I ever got.

"He was a retired plastic surgeon. He told me to double my rates for every procedure. I was shocked, said I'd lose half my patients. 'That's the idea,' he said. 'Half will stay and you'll be working half as hard for the same money.'

"He said certain people only trust the best, and to them that means the most expensive.

"It was a big risk. But I took the chance, and he was right!" Howard beamed at them. "Can I buy you guys dinner? I'd love you to meet my family. My wife's heard me talk about you hundreds of times."

"We'd like that, another time," Venturi said. "But this is a work-related visit."

"At least let me buy you a drink. There's a great little bar right around the corner."

"We'd love a drink," Danny said. "But not in public. We're under the radar."

"We need a favor," Venturi said.

"Anything." The handsome, blue-eyed

doctor unlocked a polished wooden cabinet and opened the door to a small, well-stocked bar.

He poured them each a whiskey, then raised his own glass. "To the Marines, *Semper Fi*," he said emotionally.

"To Medecins sans Frontières," Mike said.

"Who'da thought back then that we'd wind up here and now?" Howard studied them curiously. "What are you doing these days? Still with the Marines?"

"Once a Marine, always a Marine," Danny said. "We just fight closer to home these days. That's what we need to talk to you about." His leather chair creaked as he leaned forward intently.

"We have someone who needs to change her appearance."

"Hey, your wives or girlfriends need anything done, bring 'em in, no charge, professional courtesy. My pleasure," the doctor said.

"It's no wife or girlfriend — it's a woman whose life is at stake through no fault of her own. It's top secret, strictly confidential. No medical records, no witnesses."

The doctor looked more serious.

"We realize it's a lot to ask," Mike said. "If you say no, we understand. No hard feelings."

"You broke rules to save my life," Howard said. "Whatever you need from me," he gestured, palms up, "you've got it. No questions asked."

Mike described the patient as a woman in her late thirties, in good health. She needed a different look and a tattoo removed with as little scarring as possible.

"How many colors in the tattoo?" Howard asked.

Mike showed him a photo.

"No problem." The doctor was relieved to see that the anklet was finely etched and not a thick black band. Black, he said, is the most difficult color to remove. "Laser technique leaves the least scarring. There's a different frequency for each color," he explained, estimating that it would take three or four sessions.

"I'd have to see her before making suggestions on changing her face."

Mike drove Solange to Boca Raton the following night.

Alone in the office, the doctor took digital photos, full face and profile, and displayed them on a computer screen.

"Excellent bone structure," he said, "under a somewhat thin face. Chin and cheek implants would be best. You'd have no external scarring."

"How do you insert implants without incisions?" Solange asked.

"Oh, there are incisions — inside your mouth. I'd insert cheek implants right above your eyeteeth. The sulcus is like a blind cul-de-sac. Soft tissue is dissected from the cheekbones, taking care not to damage the nerves. Silicone implants are cut to fit precisely into the pockets. The size of the pockets controls the implants and keeps them in place. The fit has to be perfect. We don't want them moving around."

He tapped the computer keys, moved the cursor, and the face on the computer screen changed. Same eyes, same mouth. Different face.

"This would be the result."

"That's how I'd look?" Solange's eyes widened as she studied the face.

The doctor nodded.

"I like those cheekbones. It's like the Linda Evans look." Pleased, she glanced at Venturi. "What do you think?"

He agreed.

"What about breast implants?" she asked.

"There would be scarring and you might be left with a loss of sensitivity. If you want them, fine. But all you need for that change of appearance is Victoria's Secret, or any lingerie department." He glanced at Venturi.

"Makes sense," he said.

"You're right," Solange said. "I'm comfortable with them now. The less surgery the better."

"Normally we insert facial implants under general anesthesia, but to reduce the number of people involved we can do it here in the office under a local anesthetic.

"She could leave in four or five hours," he told Venturi, "if you have a place for her to rest and recuperate."

"We do," he said. "How much downtime?"

"Four to six weeks, depending on bruising and swelling."

"That long?" Mike frowned.

"That's to reach her permanent, optimum look. She could probably travel in ten days or so. Even if she still has swelling, her appearance will be different."

"We need to wrap a few things up first," Mike said.

"Just give me twenty-four hours' notice," Howard said. He instructed Solange not to take aspirin or vitamin E prior to surgery, to minimize bruising, then asked, "Where's Danny tonight?"

He and Solange both looked at Venturi expectantly.

"He's tied up, working on other details,

but sent his regards."

Keri stockpiled more blood. She and Victoria both mentioned to Venturi that Solange repeatedly asked to see Danny.

She sailed every morning for two weeks, always renting the same boat, one she felt comfortable with.

Danny called late one afternoon, his voice tight.

"We have to do it tomorrow. It's a must," he told Venturi, "or we lose a huge advantage."

Solange balked. She was ready and eager, but refused to die without seeing Danny first.

"I won't go until I do," she insisted.

Venturi hoped a phone chat would suffice but it wasn't enough for either of them.

Face time was arranged for ten o'clock at Venturi's.

Solange was radiant at the news.

Danny showed up early. "Where is she?"

"In the war room." Safer, Venturi felt, than a room with a bed.

Danny closed the door behind him.

Venturi and Victoria talked in the kitchen. "Should we have gone out to dinner to give them a little privacy?" she asked.

"Absolutely not."

"You're right, sweetheart. I wasn't think-ing."

They heard nothing for a long time after Danny closed the door. Eventually they heard voices, murmurs at first, then quar-reling, then Solange weeping. More silence, then murmurs. Then quiet again. That was the worrisome part.

"My heart breaks for the woman," Vic-toria said. "I'm truly sorry for all she's suf-fered. You can't blame her for her attitude. But between us, I'll be glad when she's gone."

"So will I," Venturi said truthfully.

"This is so complicated," she said sadly. "I love Luz and their children."

"Ditto."

Venturi took Scout for a walk, came back, and checked his watch. They'd been alone for an hour and a half. They all had a big day ahead of them. He felt like the frustrated father of a lust-crazed teenager, worrying and watching the clock. He wished he could have flashed porch lights.

Finally he knocked on the door to the war room.

"Danny, it's late. We have work to do tonight."

No response.

He rapped louder. "Danny!"

"Give us five minutes, bro."

"See you in five." How had he let this happen?

He knocked after ten minutes, then tried the door. Locked from the inside. Danny opened it after several moments, flushed and breathing hard.

Solange was curled up in an oversized armchair near the conference table. She did not look at him.

Both were disheveled but clothed.

"Man," Danny muttered under his breath. "Cut me a break. It's the last time we'll see each other."

"No. Are you crazy? You know what you're risking?"

They glared at each other, then Victoria interrupted. Ignoring the hot glances and supercharged atmosphere, she marched in cheerfully carrying a tray of sandwiches and coffee.

Solange refused to meet their eyes, but she was clearheaded, detail oriented, and alert as they pored over charts, maps, and schedules again and again.

Danny left after the briefing. He turned at the door. Their eyes locked. Solange sighed. She was ready to die.

CHAPTER
TWENTY-THREE

The day Solange Dupree died was beautiful and breezy, a perfect day for sailing.

Danny and Mike took to the water early, to take her off the sailboat.

"Hello, beauty," Danny greeted her. When he helped her into their boat they clung to each other longer than necessary.

"Break it up, you two," Mike said, glad this would all be over soon. "We have serious work to do."

They let the small sailboat dash against the rocks until it was badly damaged, then removed several pints of blood from the cooler on Danny's boat.

"Be careful now. Let's focus," Mike said. "It can't look poured. Blood obeys the laws of physics. The first blow brings it to the surface. The second spatters it. Remember, these bloodstains will be studied, analyzed, and debated by the foremost experts in the field."

They set the crippled boat adrift with enough blood on deck to convince any pathologist that the person who lost it could not possibly have survived.

"Hey, babe, I need your suit," Danny said, as Mike took the helm.

Her eyes on Danny, Solange began to slowly strip off her red swimsuit, right there on deck.

"Get below!" Mike said, exasperated. "You can't be seen! Look up, for God's sake."

A small plane towing a banner had made a pass over the Miami Beach shoreline and was circling for another.

Solange ducked below, then returned in white jeans and a T-shirt, her shiny black hair tucked up under a baseball cap. She tossed her red swimsuit to Danny, who caught it and crumpled it in his hand like a flower.

Mike feared he was about to lift it to his nose, but Danny saw him watching and shoved it under his shirt instead.

They docked near downtown and Mike drove Solange back to his place.

Several hours later, he drove alone to the marina and took the boat out again, his destination an empty waterfront mansion on Miami Beach's North Bay Road. Danny knew the developer who had it slated for demolition.

Mike arrived first. Shortly after, Danny drove a van up the wide circular driveway that branched off to one side leading down to the boathouse and dock, where Mike waited.

"We could have found another way," he said doubtfully.

Danny shot him a dark look. "You're the one who said we needed a body, bro." He opened the back of the van and pulled back a pale pink blanket.

The dead girl had raven hair like Solange. She appeared to be in her late twenties, early thirties. Venturi's heart skipped several beats when he saw the tattoo on her ankle.

"Who the hell did you get to do that? And how?"

"It's not really a tattoo," Danny admitted. "It's permanent Magic Marker."

"Sure it's waterproof?"

"We're about to find out."

The dead girl wore the red bathing suit Solange had worn to go sailing that morning. Solange had bought the distinctive suit with a daring cutout design at Macy's in the Aventura Mall. She paid for it with her own credit card after trying on a dozen suits, all while chatting up and joking with several sales associates. They'd remember her well.

Venturi stared at the dead girl.

"How did you find somebody who fits her description so well? Danny, if I thought for a minute that you —"

"Christ, what do you think I am? Grab her feet. Help me get her onto the boat."

"She's so cold."

"I kept the temperature in the cooler as low as possible."

"Hold it. Is that a bullet hole in her stomach?"

"It's where the trocar, an embalming tool, was inserted. She's been embalmed," Danny said impatiently.

"Where'd you get her?"

Danny sighed. "Funeral homes take turns handling unclaimed, indigent corpses for the county. I've been stopping by the medical examiner's office early every day to see who was up for grabs. When I saw her, I volunteered. Happened to be my turn anyway."

"How old is she? Who is she?" Venturi persisted.

"Twenty-seven. A hooker who worked the Boulevard south of Seventy-ninth Street. She checked into a hot-sheet motel with an unidentified john last week. They were snorting some shit. Her name was on the Big Blackboard in the Sky. She OD'd and he took off and left her. Swell guy. Stole her purse, too. Guess he figured she didn't need it anymore. She was a Jane Doe until they identified her fingerprints. Had a couple of arrests for DUI, soliciting, lewd and lascivious, and one for trespassing naked in the fountain outside the Justice Building. Had family in Ohio. They declined to claim her body."

"Geez," Venturi said.

"Don't feel bad. Think of it as her last chance to do something noble for somebody else."

"What's supposed to happen to her?"

"Every ten days or so a work crew, prisoners from the County Jail, is sent to Potter's Field with a backhoe. They dig a long trench, then stack the cheap wooden coffins in side by side. A sad and sorry way to go, bro. But that's life. Like I said, she's helping somebody who needs it."

They checked the time then headed out to sea, toward the Gulf Stream. What they watched for appeared promptly on the horizon. "There she is," Danny said, watching through binoculars, "right on time."

The Lucky Star, a South Beach–based casino boat, offers five dinner cruises a week. The main course is blackjack and roulette. She was packed, as usual, with tourists and gamblers.

Keeping their distance, Danny pulled on his scuba gear and maneuvered the underwater scooter over the side.

"If you're spotted we're dead," Venturi warned.

"Quit your complaining and stop worrying," Danny said. "You're turning into an old lady, bro." He grinned, took the cold dead girl into his arms, and slid into the water.

Once they were submerged, he adjusted the weights on her body, tied a clear cord into a makeshift harness under her arms, then towed her toward *The Lucky Star* with the underwater scooter.

He descended deeper, then began to release some of the weights.

She slowly rose to the surface, floating gently, facedown, long hair streaming.

Mike used the two-way radio as he watched through high-powered binoculars from a distance.

"Danny, they're cruising right by. Everybody's focused on roulette. Damn. That red suit should be easy to spot. Whoops! Here we go. They see her. Got people crowding to the port side. Good deal, good deal. I see three, no, four cameras and lots of cell phones. Try to maneuver her a little more to the east so they get good looks and clear shots of her ankle. The captain's circling. Careful. He may try to throw a line on her. They're already on the radio to the Coast Guard. I'm monitoring their transmission.

"Reel her in! Reel her in and bring her back."

As *The Lucky Star* came about, the dead girl, arms outstretched, sank beneath the surface and disappeared into the deep.

Danny towed her back to the boat, secured her and the weights in a shrimp fishing net below the waterline, then clambered aboard.

"Let's rock-and-roll, 'fore the Coast Guard gets here."

A cutter had already appeared on the horizon.

Mike started the engine, then cut it off.

"What are you doing?" Danny demanded.

"What the hell is that?"

Danny turned to look. A flash of red in the water about forty yards off the stern.

"Holy shit! She slipped out of the net."

"We have to get out of here," Venturi said tersely, as the Coast Guard cutter approached *The Lucky Star.*

"No way," Danny said.

"Tell me about it!" Mike said. "She can't

284

be found."

"I'd have some 'splaining to do. She's supposed to go in the ground tomorrow."

"Go get her, Danny." He was talking to a splash and a trail of bubbles.

Shortly after Danny submerged, as the Coast Guard boat approached them, lights flashing, the red suit in the water suddenly sank out of sight.

A Coast Guardsman on deck hailed Mike to ask if anyone aboard had seen a woman's body in the water.

Mike replied that he hadn't but he'd be on the lookout.

The cutter headed back toward *The Lucky Star.*

Danny surfaced as the prelude to a savage sunset painted the water blood red and gold all around them.

"Got her?"

He nodded grimly. "Don't want to do that again soon. Spooky as hell. Had to grapple across half the ocean bottom with that woman to wrestle her back into the net. Some of the grommets had come loose and she slid right the hell out like she had a mind of her own."

"They always do," Mike said.

"Think about it," Danny said, at dusk, as

285

they dried her with towels and wrapped her in a blanket behind the empty mansion on North Bay Road. "This girl lived a pretty wild life. Sex, drugs, rock and roll. Brief, but never boring. And unlike most of us, her story didn't end when she did. If she was watching us today, she must have laughed her ass off."

CHAPTER
TWENTY-FOUR

The surgery took place at Dr. Howard's Boca Raton office late that night.

Keri scrubbed in to assist.

Venturi was present. Both he and Solange insisted that Danny stay away. She didn't want him to see her exposed and vulnerable. Mike had reasons of his own.

The patient was sedated, with an endotracheal tube and an intravenous line. The surgeon made incisions inside her mouth and cut away soft tissue, creating pockets to accommodate the surgical-grade silicone implants that would change the shape of her face — and her appearance — permanently.

"Fillers and fat are resorbed and have to be reinjected," the doctor said, in cheerful running commentary, as classical music played softly in the background. "But these midface implants sit on the bony skeleton and stay in place forever."

The incisions were sutured with self-dissolving stitches.

Several hours later, Micheline Lacroix was rolled out to the van in a wheelchair. She wore a compression bandage to reduce swelling and held the ice packs in place herself, despite feeling groggy.

They made her as comfortable as possible in what was now considered the client guest room. Victoria looked in several times during the night to administer pain pills and cold packs.

Venturi let Danny know that the procedure had gone well and that Micheline was doing fine.

The next day, Micheline sipped soup through a plastic straw as Victoria read aloud to her from the morning paper:

Miami, Fla.

Gamblers enjoying blackjack and roulette games on *The Lucky Star,* a party boat off South Beach Saturday, took a moment to enjoy the ocean view and saw a woman in the water.

Her luck had run out.

She was dead, floating facedown. Women screamed, tourists snapped pictures, and the captain called the Coast Guard. In the confusion the corpse, tentatively identified as the victim of an earlier sailboat accident, sank beneath the waves and disappeared.

The Coast Guard and Metro-Dade police say photos shot by the party-boat passengers fit the description of a woman who failed to return after renting a sailboat in Sunny Isles that morning.

The damaged sailboat was found foundering offshore about two hours before the body was sighted. Witnesses said the woman, clad in a lipstick-red bathing suit, showed no signs of life. Before *The Lucky Star* could come about to try to retrieve the corpse, it had vanished.

"It ruined our whole day," grumbled blackjack dealer Linda McGrory. "First we had to wait for the Coast Guard and give statements. After that, nobody felt lucky."

The identity of the missing boater was not released pending notification of next of kin. But receipts from the rental company show that the woman, apparently a tourist, had rented the same boat a number of times over the past two weeks.

"She looked hot and seemed to be a good sailor. You could see she knew what she was doing," said Ronald Booth, an employee of the rental firm. He said she was wearing a bright red bathing suit Saturday morning when she last rented the boat.

A Coast Guard spokesman said the body may have been carried north by the Gulf Stream.

"How'd it go at Potter's Field today?" Venturi asked, when Danny called again to check on the patient.

"It didn't," he said.

"What do you mean?"

"I've had a helluva day, bro. The goddamn family had a change of heart. Decided to bury her up there. They want the body shipped to goddamn Cleveland."

"Christ. You can't ship her anywhere with that thing on her ankle," Venturi said, alarmed.

"Thank you. Tell me about it. The goddamn marker won't come off. I tried paint remover, even Brillo. I'm thinking about painting something over it."

"Like what?"

"A snake. A big black serpent coiled around her ankle, it could go up to her thigh. And the red heart could be enlarged, into an apple. You know, like in the garden of Eden."

"Don't," Venturi said. "Families always request a copy of the ME report. The line for identifying characteristics won't mention her tattoo. You have to get that thing off her. No two ways about it."

"Goddammit," Danny said. "Son of a bitch. You're right. She has to be on a flight tomorrow." He sighed. "I guess the ME report would mention a missing foot, too."

"Don't even think about that," Venturi warned. "Call the marker manufacturer for info on what will take it off. You were right, buddy."

"About what?"

"That dead girl. She's somewhere laughing her ass off again today."

A news story days later reported that the FBI was attempting to digitally enhance the photos taken by passengers and crew members aboard *The Lucky Star* and that U.S. Navy sonar was being used in efforts to recover the woman's body.

The Navy? The FBI? When does the military or a federal agency become involved in a search for a lost boater or accident victim? Alert reporters began to ask questions.

A savvy police reporter coaxed the missing woman's name from an employee of the boat rental firm, but could find no trace of a Marilyn Moya from Louisiana. She didn't exist.

It took more than a week for the FBI to announce the victim's real identity: Solange Dupree, the Louisiana federal court judge who had lost her entire family to killers who had made repeated death threats against her.

The FBI lab had studied the enhanced photos and determined through certain identifying marks that the woman in the water was indeed Judge Dupree.

Her damaged sailboat, confiscated by the FBI, showed signs of an accident. Her DNA was found on board. No foul play suspected.

Members of the press found that conclusion — that she died in a freak accident shortly after escaping a second murder attempt — hard to swallow. Reporters clearly suspected that federal investigators had failed the courageous judge and that their ineptitude resulted in her murder.

FBI spokesmen protested that although Judge Dupree was an avid sailor, she was unfamiliar with South Florida waters.

Federal officials in Louisiana noted that Judge Dupree "was a very strong-minded and independent member of the judiciary, who had refused security during her Florida stay. However, bodyguards would have made little difference since she persisted in sailing a small boat alone. Therefore, the accident and her death most likely could not have been prevented."

Louisiana's legal community lamented its loss at a well-attended memorial service for Judge Dupree, then indulged in rampant speculation about her possible successor.

After four laser treatments, Micheline Lacroix's ankle, now temporarily red and swollen, showed no trace of a tattoo.

Days later, she was ready to return home to her native France. Her hair was now platinum blond in a sleek, swingy, shoulder-length cut. Her cheekbones were classic, her eyes sultry.

Her papers were ready, a morning flight booked.

One obstacle remained. She wanted to see Danny again. Venturi said no. Tensions ran high.

Victoria met him at the door when he returned home from arranging a cash deposit to a bank in Tours, France.

"Danny's here," she said softly, her eyes grave. "He's with her, in her room. I couldn't stop them."

Venturi knocked. No answer. He used the key.

They were naked. The room reeked of sex. Lips swollen, their eyes and skin glistened, their expressions were sated.

"Get the hell out!" he told Danny, then turned to Micheline. "Do you know the risks we've taken for you?"

Danny objected, hopping on one foot as he pulled on his pants. "You don't get it, bro."

"Don't 'bro' me, you son of a bitch."

His fist connected with Danny's chin in a powerful punch that knocked him down. He sprang to his feet, his lower lip bleeding.

"Stop it!" Micheline screamed. "You don't understand! Danny's going with me!"

"I'm not gonna fight you, bro." Danny held up his palm. "I won't hurt you, Mike. You're my brother."

"You couldn't hurt me if you tried. You dumb son of a bitch. You want to try?"

"You don't understand."

"Yeah. That's what your girlfriend just said."

"It's not like that."

"What you mean, it's not like that?" Micheline demanded.

Danny ignored her and focused on his friend.

"She was needy, nervous, and scared, Mike. I said and did whatever it took to save her."

"What are you saying?" She clutched a sheet around her with one hand, gesturing wildly with the other. "Are you saying we're not going to be together?"

He sighed and turned to her. "Maybe we will," he said. "Sometime. We never know what the future will bring. But I have to raise my kids first. Things may be different by the time they're all twenty-one."

She blinked in disbelief. "And how many years will that be?"

He paused. "The youngest is due next year. When he's twenty-one, maybe . . ."

She slapped him, hard.

"I deserve that." He caught her hand, raised for a second blow. "But don't do it again."

She burst into tears.

He reached to comfort her but she resisted, then turned her back on him.

He touched her shoulder. "I want to walk you through all the minefields but I can't. You're smart enough and strong enough to navigate them on your own. Look at you."

He spun her around so that they both faced the full-length mirror. "This woman will live a long and wonderful life." He stroked her hair.

She was weeping.

Both were getting dressed as Venturi left the room.

"Don't share with Danny exactly where she's going," he told Victoria, rubbing his bruised knuckles. "Although I'm sure she's already told him."

"I agree."

Danny emerged, still fastening his belt. "Sorry, man." He pressed a handkerchief to his still-bleeding lip. "See you in the morning."

"Want some ice for that?" Victoria said.

"Nah." He winked. "It was a sucker punch. That's the only way he landed it. I've been hit a helluva lot harder," he glanced at Venturi, "by my wife."

"You probably deserved it then, too," Venturi said mildly. "Will Micheline be trouble tomorrow?"

"No. She's ready to go," Danny said, and stepped out into the sultry night.

Micheline stayed in her room and refused to come out for dinner. She ate yogurt and fruit for breakfast but spoke only in monosyllables.

Danny showed up, his lip swollen. Unlike the prior departures, they rode to the airport in silence. Keri, busy at the hospital, was unable to join them.

In a corner of the parking garage, a subdued Micheline took Venturi's hand. "Thank you for everything," she whispered. "I'm sorry I've been so difficult."

He nodded.

She kissed Victoria's cheek.

She'd been ignoring Danny, who walked her to the gate as the others watched from a distance.

"If he boards that plane, I swear to God I will hunt him down like a rabid dog," Venturi said.

"I'll ride shotgun," Victoria told him.

Danny's kiss glanced off her cheek as Micheline neatly avoided his lips. Then she walked away. He turned to leave, then stopped to look back. She did not. She walked faster, chin up, moving forward into her future.

He stood watching for a long moment, then rejoined the others. No one spoke until they were in the car.

Danny broke the dense silence. "I love my wife," he said, "and my kids. All of us over the age of fifteen have old loves in our pasts.

I did the best I could for them both. She's safe, on her way now, and my life can get back to normal."

"How's your lip?" Venturi asked.

Danny shrugged nonchalantly. "*No problemo,* bro. I've been hit harder by my little girl, and she's three."

"I trusted him," Venturi said later. Keri had joined him and Victoria at the house for a quiet dinner. The earlier transitions, farewells, and departures had been celebratory. Nobody celebrated this one.

"I should have followed my gut," he said. "I knew it was too risky and could turn ugly. Without grossing you both out, I can tell you that my hair stood on end more than once. I regret involving you. I should've quit when we were ahead.

"I can't figure Danny out anymore. He's changed. What happened to trust and honor?"

"Love and lust." Keri took his hand. "When sex or money is involved, trust no one."

"Ain't that the truth. Although what Danny did does seem noble in a romantic sort of way," Victoria said dreamily.

"Luz wouldn't think so, especially in her condition," Keri said earnestly, as she and

Victoria loaded the dishwasher. She turned to Venturi. "Luz can't ever know about this. It would break her heart, and there'd be nobody left to raise the children because she'd kill him."

"No jury would convict her. I'm exhausted." Victoria yawned. "I'm going to turn in early. Good night, you two."

Keri had been quiet all evening. "I know this is not the time to bring it up," she said softly, curled up beside him on the couch, "but it can't wait. I know someone who needs your help, our services."

"Please tell me you're joking," he said.

"Dead serious, Mikey. But I promise you that this time there will be absolutely no romance, no lust, no sex involved."

CHAPTER
TWENTY-FIVE

"No more." Venturi shook his head. "I'm done."

"Just listen. Please," Keri said. "I'm heartsick about it. She's done so much for so many."

"She? Swell, what's this one escaping? Hired killers? Old lovers? Paparazzi?"

"No," Keri said. "Her children."

She chewed her lower lip. "Obviously you have no faith in my judgment."

"Not true." He reached for her. "You're the only sane woman I know, except for Vicki."

She giggled in spite of herself. "How weird is that? Every day I meet fathers-to-be who fear, loathe, and despise their mothers-in-law."

"But you know Vicki. Doesn't that make it less weird?"

"Absolutely. You're right," she conceded.

"So who is this woman who birthed the

children from hell? I hope they're not ten and twelve years old. I refuse to aid and abet in the abandonment of minors, no matter how obnoxious or homicidal they are."

Keri pulled away to look him directly in the eye.

"I wouldn't call them adults. They're childishly greedy, grasping, and unscrupulous middle-aged people. She's an extremely wealthy widow dedicated to philanthropic causes large and small.

"Born to money, she married more. When her husband died relatively young, she took over management of his business affairs, and through astute investing and sound judgment made their assets grow like Topsy. She's been an absolute godsend and guardian angel to countless people, including me. She knew my grandmother. And when I needed help paying my way through med school, she stepped up without being asked. She didn't call it a loan, she called it an investment in the future.

"She founded a neonatal clinic in Brooklyn to save premature babies, supports young artists, especially in music and ballet, and has funded spay/neuter clinics and adoption centers for homeless animals.

"Her late husband established ample trust funds for their children; two sons and a daughter. There was enough to set them up for life, but they squandered the money. Now they're impatient and tired of waiting to inherit hers. They want it now."

"How old is she?"

"A spry, sharp, and funny seventy-six years young."

Venturi scowled. "No woman that age would undertake such a drastic life change."

"Seniors are pretty adventurous these days, in case you haven't noticed," Keri said. "And she has no other option. Her children, along with several organizations that have enjoyed her largess in the past, want her declared incompetent so they can assume power of attorney over her affairs. Their complaint? She's too generous. What she gives to good causes leaves less for them.

"If they succeed, she'll be dumped into an assisted-care facility and forgotten. She's already been embarrassed, harassed, and threatened. Now they're taking legal action, alleging that she's incapable of handling her finances."

Keri leaned forward, her hand on his cheek. "Mikey, she is one of the brightest, most caring and capable women I have ever known. It would kill her."

He shook his head more slowly.

"Stop imitating a metronome and just

302

meet her. Talk to her. See for yourself. Please, Mikey?"

He caved. "Maybe we could invite her here for lunch, just the four of us."

"She lives in Manhattan," Keri said eagerly, "but she's here now, in Palm Beach."

The guest of honor wore sensible shoes, a blue seersucker suit, and a permanent wave in her curly gray hair.

She and Victoria, who fixed her famous shrimp salad, hit it off immediately. They discussed life in Manhattan versus South Florida, drank cappuccino, nibbled on pastries, then settled down to business.

Marian Pomeroy was refreshingly candid about her plight.

"My health is excellent," she said at one point. "My parents enjoyed active lives well into their nineties. With any luck I shall as well. But I don't want it to be as a helpless, captive animal — confined, controlled, and abandoned. There's still so much I'd like to see and do. Does that sound selfish on my part?"

"Not at all," Victoria said. "But how did this happen?"

Marian sighed, looked pained, and folded her hands in her lap.

"Nothing," she confided, "is more heart-breaking than realizing the mediocrity of one's own children.

"My husband provided a five-million-dollar trust for each of them, to be paid out in increments at various ages. He was a generous, well-meaning man and intended to relieve me of the burden, but in retrospect, it was a terrible mistake. Each of the children should have had to finish college and work in the real world long enough to learn the value of money before receiving such large sums. They were still in their teens when their father died. He knew he was ill and wanted to be sure they were well provided for. But the money didn't bring them security, wisdom, or happiness. What it brought instead was a sense of entitlement, and I must say they've grown quite ugly about it.

"Each went through their final payment some time ago. In their late forties and early fifties now, each claims to be broke, as do their children. They've all been divorced more than once — one of them four times. None has ever held a real job.

"They are the barbarians at the gate," she said sadly. "I had to give up inviting them to my home. Each time I did, valuables vanished with them. Artwork, jewelry, cash — even the goddamn Paul Revere silver tea service and an antique clock that is one of just two in the world. The other is in the White House. I kid you not." She sighed and sipped the sherry Victoria had brought to the table.

"How can they be cash strapped after inheriting that kind of money?" Mike asked.

"Joan, the only girl, went shopping and never stopped. There are always newer designer fashions, flashier sports cars, bigger houses, bigger diamonds, and longer, more lavish trips. Why she needs such frequent vacations is a puzzle to me. She's never worked a day in her life.

"Wesley, the oldest, became a self-described entrepreneur and investor, without ever studying business or finance. He's never even balanced a checkbook. He's made so many bad investments that he's become a joke in the business community and the dream target of every sort of scam artist. He knows it all, refuses good advice from experts, and constantly pressures me for large sums to invest in new, increasingly dubious enterprises."

She frowned. "He generates negative energy, is in a constant manic state of desperation. He always has deadlines looming and is frantic to get in on the action before it's too late.

"Victor, the youngest, discovered drink, drugs, and nightclubs early. He spends his time on the party circuit with the so-called beautiful people. He's had drug and drunk-driving arrests and constant rounds of rehab. You know how that is."

Victoria nodded ruefully. "I certainly do."

"Unfortunately, I heeded a lawyer's suggestion that the children be appointed to the board of my foundation, formed to distribute a great deal of money to various charities. The experience was supposed to raise their consciousness about social causes and give them a sense of responsibility.

"Instead they've persuaded the other board members that I donate too much to other charities and individuals. They want me stopped and actually voted to take action against me. Luckily, a loyal employee at the foundation and one of the lawyers I've known for many years warned me. They plan to have the authorities throw some sort of a net over me, so I can be involuntarily committed for an evaluation of my mental faculties while they assume power of attorney over my assets."

Her lips never trembled, her voice did not waver. She never flinched. But the eyes behind her gold-rimmed glasses glistened with unshed tears. She quickly blinked them away.

"The attorneys I've consulted say that with my children and the longtime board members aligned, it would be extremely difficult, and highly unlikely, for me to prevail. Similar cases have recently established a precedent. Out with the old, in with the new."

"It's so common these days," Victoria said sadly, "for the younger generation to turn on older family members whose brains and hard work accumulated the assets and built a fortune."

Venturi wasn't sure how much Keri had told Marian.

"How would you prefer to live the rest of your life?" he asked casually.

"Without greed, constant battles, and betrayals. I have my own silly daydreams."

Eyes alight, she clutched her arms in an endearingly girlish gesture, her voice an ardent whisper. "I would love to live placidly in a tiny, tidy cottage near the English seaside, in a place where I could attend concerts and art shows and volunteer to read to little schoolchildren. That is my retirement wish, my dream and fondest fantasy."

She leaned back, her spine straight. "It

doesn't seem too much to ask, does it?

"And of course," she added slyly, "a part of that fantasy is terribly wicked." She looked at them each, one at a time. "Before departing, I would like to anonymously donate the bulk of my assets to the needy, then pay the required fee to whoever might help me accomplish my transition. Whatever is left would finance my new, somewhat spartan lifestyle.

"Once I'm gone, the vultures will be shocked to learn that the money is, too. They will investigate, litigate, and spend years accusing each other. What great fun to leave them doing to one another what they've been trying to do to me."

She laughed heartily.

"That, dear friends, is my fantasy." She smiled warmly at Keri. "I shared it with my dear Keri after visiting Florida to say good-bye. My tipsters report that action is imminent, the inevitable net about to be hurled over this old gray head. My lawyer stands alert, but he's not optimistic."

Scout scratched at the door, then gazed meaningfully at Venturi.

"Excuse me." He left the table. "I'll be right back, just have to take the dog out."

His guests watched him walk across the yard, Scout beside him, wagging his tail.

"You can judge the condition of a man's soul by the way he treats animals," Marian said.

The yard was fenced, Venturi had no real reason to accompany the dog. But he wanted a moment to think. He sucked in a deep breath of humid air, took out his cell phone, and made a brief call. As he reentered the house Vicki was carrying plates to the kitchen. She winked, silently mouthing the words, "I love her."

"Can you stay awhile longer?" he asked the guest of honor.

She could.

"Good," Venturi said. "I'd like you to meet a friend of mine. He'll be here shortly."

CHAPTER
TWENTY-SIX

Danny's Harley rumbled through the gate as Scout romped to greet it. Venturi followed.

"We have a client," he said, as Danny took off his helmet. "Another woman in distress."

The two stared at each other.

"How's your lip?" Venturi finally asked, focusing on Danny's split lip and bruised mouth.

"No problemo," Danny said. "I've been hit harder by Gil the gerbil, and he's dead."

"I hesitated to call you," Venturi said. "She's here now. I haven't checked for tattoos yet. We could use your help, but if you can't be trusted to keep your pants zipped, as difficult as that might be, then you're out."

"Can't make any promises until I see her." Danny grinned.

"And, oh yeah," Venturi added, as they approached the door. "Keri is in."

"Ouch," Danny muttered. "Why me?"

They and the dog went inside.

"This," Venturi said, "is Marian Pomeroy."

Danny cut his eyes at him, gave the woman a friendly grin and a warm handshake, then pulled up a chair.

They eventually discussed lifestyle and habits. Marian Pomeroy favored gardening, art museums, concerts, cruises, and red wine with dinner. She had a great affinity for photography and all children — except her own.

Danny was the first to come up with a plan.

"Ma'am?" He flashed his killer smile and leaned toward Marian, in her comfortable shoes, with a sweater draped over her narrow shoulders despite the heat. "Can you swim?"

"I could manage to splash about a bit." She put down her teacup and pursed her lips. "I daresay I wouldn't make it across the English Channel in record time, or at all. You see, as a child I had a nasty bout with rheumatic fever. Exercise was forbidden. No sports allowed. I was a far more delicate creature then than I am now."

"Good." He laughed aloud. "I might have an idea for you."

He explained. They brainstormed, argued,

311

improvised, and streamlined.

"Think you can do it?" Venturi said, turning to Keri. "More important, are you willing? It's risky."

"I can. I will," she said without hesitation. "Absolutely. I love it!"

Marian clapped her hands in appreciation. "How extraordinary! You people are a combination of *Extreme Makeover, Mission: Impossible,* and *CSI* — in reverse."

She added, "Now you're probably convinced that I watch too much TV."

Time was crucial. Marian immediately left each of her children a telephone message. Without divulging her precise whereabouts, she said she planned to return to New York in a few days and was eager to see them.

The real fun followed. Giving away money gave Marian Pomeroy the rush that shopaholics experience on spending sprees. She quickly and systematically began to divest herself of her assets.

She and Keri, wearing shades and scarves, drove through the city, invisible secret Santas, slipping checks for half a million dollars under the doors of Goodwill Enterprises, the Salvation Army, Miami's Rescue Mission, Lighthouse for the Blind, and Camillus House, a downtown homeless shelter. They left cash-filled envelopes at a battered women's refuge and mailed donations to the Sierra Club, a Juilliard school of music scholarship fund, environmental causes, and organizations committed to saving premature infants, baby seals, whales, manatees, the oceans, homeless pets, and polar bears. Smaller checks went to worthy individuals named in recent news stories, such as the waiter who rushed to the rescue of a young woman attacked by a violent carjacker. The police kept the hero for some time as they completed their paperwork. He missed the lunch hour rush as a result. Finally free to return to work, he was fired instead of congratulated.

More money went to inner-city churches, struggling theater groups, and a college fund for the children of cops killed on the job. Marian laughed a lot, as she and Keri became giddy at the joy of giving.

The donations were anonymous and a condition of their acceptance was that they remain that way. Marian Pomeroy never felt so free. She needed no receipts for tax purposes. Who cared about taxes? Not her. Her beneficiaries, her children, would have to deal with the IRS.

Before leaving home in Manhattan, aware that it was most likely for the last time, she had taken out a reverse mortgage for the maximum amount allowed on her brownstone. Upon her death, her home would be sold to satisfy the mortgage — unless, of course, her children chose to buy it back.

She had left her safety-deposit box empty except for the mortgage papers.

Heirlooms she couldn't discreetly sell in New York she had shipped to South Florida, so she could dispose of them herself.

She and Keri visited the mean streets of Miami's Overtown and Liberty City, distributing crisp one-hundred-dollar bills from large shopping bags to strangers on the street. Crowds quickly assembled, but each time they did, Danny or Venturi whisked the women away before police arrived.

It reminded Venturi of the day money rained on the Bronx.

The story and cell-phone photos shot by some of the lucky Miami recipients would soon find their way into the news, along with descriptions of the anonymous benefactor described by witnesses as a kindly grandmotherly type. Eventually she would be identified as Marian Pomeroy, too late of course to use in a competency hearing, but it could serve as an explanation of where her money had gone. No way to know exactly how much she gave away on the street.

Marion was careful to point out to the others that she did not hate her children. Her fervent hope was that her last resort might save them, force them into becoming self-reliant and independent. God knows, nothing else had worked. And, if this didn't, *c'est la vie.*

Not a bit sentimental about her grand-children, she confessed that she probably wouldn't know them if she saw them, since they had neither visited nor acknowledged her gifts over the years.

She delighted in selecting her last cruise, as Keri, Danny, and Venturi pored over the plans, layouts, and accommodations of the various choices. They selected a modest seven-day voyage to Montego Bay, Grand Cayman, and Cozumel.

"The menu looks lovely," Marian said.

A typical main course: prime rib of beef with béarnaise sauce, snow peas, glazed turnips, and Dauphin potatoes, or broiled red snapper filet with red wine sauce, vegetable couscous, and pepper relish.

She and her late husband had planned to cruise the world in retirement, but he died young. She later enjoyed a few cruises with her only sister, who died a decade ago, then, took a few solo. But this would be the cruise of a lifetime.

At first Venturi worried about Marian: What if her children and the board of directors were right? If she couldn't handle her own assets, how could she manage a smooth transition into a new life, as another woman?

But he soon lost his initial reservations and became convinced that she was as competent as anyone, in fact more so than most. "She's as sharp as anybody in this room," he told the team, "although I'm not sure about everybody in this room."

"Quit ragging on me!" Danny said. "Enough is enough."

"Why do you think I meant you?"

"Stop bickering, boys," Victoria said sternly. "It does none of us any good. We have work to do."

Marian spent the night before departure writing, in her graceful Palmer penmanship, postcards to her children. Each pictured a dramatic moonrise over Miami.

Darling!
A delightful change in plans. Instead of returning home tomorrow, I'm off on a little cruise.
It should be great fun.
See you soon,

Love,
Mother

She sent others with similar messages to her attorney and several acquaintances. She dropped them in a mailbox on the way to the Port of Miami. With any luck, they'd arrive at their destinations in about a week.

Upon boarding, the ship's photographer snapped her photo, capturing her sweet expression of eager anticipation.

Another passenger, Dr. Keri Spangler, filed onboard about ten travelers behind Marian Pomeroy, bypassed the photographer, and hurried to her cabin. The two travelers never acknowledged each other, never spoke, were never seen together. Their paths never crossed, as shipboard security cameras would later reveal.

Each passenger was issued an identification card to swipe in a machine not unlike a credit-card processor each time they disembarked or reboarded the ship.

Most passengers disembarked at Montego Bay, the first port of call. Some took short cruise-sponsored tours; others elected to shop or explore on their own.

That day Marian Pomeroy wore hot pink linen slacks with an elastic waist and a matching loose blouse, walking shoes, a large straw sun hat, and oversized sunglasses.

Keri wore khaki cotton slacks with a beige

T-shirt, sandals, and a Marlins baseball cap. Each disappeared, apparently without ever seeing the other, into the nearby straw market. Each eventually hailed a cab and rode off alone.

Each was dropped off near the same small motel. Marian arrived first, tipped the driver well, and asked him to pick her up at a nearby intersection in precisely three hours.

Minutes later she knocked on the door of a corner first-floor room. Victoria let her in and they went to work. Venturi was waiting inside. Danny didn't make the trip. His original idea had him surreptitiously boarding the cruise ship, handling the scene, and then going over the side to be picked up by boat.

To his regret, the scenario had been simplified.

Keri arrived at the motel minutes later. When she was certain no one was watching, she knocked, then also vanished inside.

Marian had changed into a smock. Her hair was already being dyed a soft fawn that complemented her light complexion. As they waited for a timer's signal to wash out the dye, Keri drew blood from Marian and stored the bag in the minibar.

Then Keri undressed. Venturi helped strap padding around her hips and waist while

Victoria shampooed and set Marian's hair. When Marian was settled under the dryer, Vicki began to apply Keri's makeup.

"This reminds me of my high school play," Keri said cheerfully.

"Hold still," Victoria warned. Working quickly, she covered Keri's freckles with pancake makeup, then used a narrow brush to apply darker fine lines at the corners of her mouth, making it appear to droop. She stroked then blended more small lines between her nose and mouth. By the time she finished, Keri's cheeks seemed to sink in as her jowls puffed out, aided by wads of gum inside her cheeks. Small plastic rings inserted just inside each nostril changed the shape of her nose.

When the makeup was powdered and set in place, Keri changed into Marian's clothes.

"Yikes." She stared in the mirror. "Now I remember why I never wear this color." Hot pink did little for her red hair.

"We'll take care of that right now." Vicki braided and pinned up Keri's hair then opened a wig box. She lifted out a soft gray human hairpiece styled precisely the way Marian had worn her hair for decades.

Keri put it on and pinned it in place. She and Marian could not suppress their giggles.

"Don't forget these." Victoria inserted several foam rubber inner soles into one of the comfortable walking shoes Marion had worn off the ship.

"Let's see you walk now," she said after Keri put on the shoes.

Keri crossed the room twice. The padding in only one shoe gave her the uneven gait and uncertain balance of a senior citizen slightly unsteady on her feet.

Keri donned Marian's big straw sun hat and oversized sunglasses, and carefully concealed the blood-filled plastic bag inside a pocket sewn into the padding around her waist.

"Here are the souvenirs you two bought at the market today." Victoria handed Keri a large straw bag with two smaller bags inside.

"You look fine, dear," she said, and winked playfully, "but I'm afraid you're obviously too old for my son-in-law."

"Not so fast," Venturi said.

"Like me as an older woman?" Keri cocked her head coyly.

"Hell, yeah. You're hot. I want you to dress this way back home. The wrinkles, the padding, the wig. I love it. I'm turned on right now."

"You are a sick puppy," she said.

He gently kissed her mouth.

"No smooching!" Victoria warned. "If you mess up her face we'll have to start from scratch." She checked her watch and picked up a pair of scissors. "Time's running out. She's got to go."

Keri pulled a chair up next to Marian, who was having her hair cut. Manicure tools and nail polish were spread out on the table.

"Good-bye, Marian," she said, eyes glistening. "We can't cry. My face gets red and my nose will run and I'm not allowed to streak my makeup. So let's say a happy good-bye."

"Thank you, darling girl, for this chance," Marian said. "My time here with you has been a blast. I'll never forget it. Please be careful. Get home safely. You're like a daughter to me. I wish you were mine."

"I am," Keri whispered. "I'll think fondly of you every day for the rest of my life."

"Unlike my own children." Marian laughed wryly. "You'll always be in my prayers."

They hugged gingerly.

Keri got to her feet, picked up Marian's oversized handbag, her straw bags of souvenirs, and walked to the door in an excellent imitation of an older woman's gait.

"*Bon voyage,* baby," Venturi said. "You

know what to do. Be careful."

"I love you all," she said, eyes fixed on Venturi, then closed the door behind her.

Five minutes later, and two blocks away, she climbed into Marian's waiting taxi. The driver flipped over the meter. "Back to de ship, lady?"

"Yes," she said, in her best imitation of Marian's voice.

Back at the dock, she swiped Marian's cruise-ship identification card, paused as though it hadn't registered, then swiped her own. She reboarded among a throng of fellow passengers. A few smiled in recognition. She nodded back, then blew her nose, keeping her handkerchief in front of her face.

She went straight to Marian's cabin, unpacked the souvenirs, read the letters Marian had written on ship's stationery, then relaxed until dinnertime.

She ordered an early meal in her room. A butler brought champagne first and set it up next to a table on her stateroom's small terrace while she remained seated at her desk as though writing.

The meal, poached salmon with a salad, arrived a short time later and was served on the small outside table so she could dine while watching the sun set.

After the waiter left, she hung the Do Not Disturb sign on the door, showered, washed off the makeup, then cleaned the shower stall and changed back into her khaki slacks, T-shirt, and sandals, which had been rolled up in the straw bag. She pulled on rubber gloves then drank a champagne toast to Marian and her new life.

She sat, marveling at the sunset, surrounded by endless sky and sea, wondering in amazement what the hell she was doing here sipping champagne in someone else's cabin. This had to be the craziest thing she'd ever done, and she wondered why it felt so good. She put down the glass and went to work. She used Marian's digital camera to shoot half a dozen photos of the setting sun, then flushed half the meal and some of the champagne down the toilet, careful not to stop up the plumbing. She left a small amount of champagne and the remaining food so it would appear as though the cabin's occupant had consumed half her dinner.

Then she gently tipped over the table and chair on the terrace, spilled the food, and knocked over the champagne bottle. She dropped the camera nearby. By then it was dark. A boiling black sea filled the horizon, and she was glad that they had overruled

Danny about going over the side. She took Marian's blood from the tiny stateroom fridge and stained the railing.

One of the souvenirs in her straw bag was a coconut with a silly face painted on it. She saturated the coconut with blood, cried out, then hurled it off the terrace with all her might. She thanked God for good aim when it struck the lifeboat hull below and bounced off into the sea, leaving a bloody splotch behind.

Most passengers on that deck had already gone to dinner. Swiftly and silently, she locked the room, left the Do Not Disturb sign on the door, and went to her own cabin without seeing a soul. She quickly dressed for dinner. She wore a stunning black ensemble, lipstick, mascara, and dangly earrings to the bar.

She danced with several men during the evening and seemed to be in full vacation mode, lighthearted and enjoying herself. After retiring to her stateroom, she called Michael's home phone to leave a message.

"Wanted to say good night," she said, her voice dreamy. "It's so relaxing out here on the water. Having a wonderful time. 'Nite, Mikey. Sweet dreams."

He and Vicki heard it when they arrived back in Miami a few hours later. Elated, they called Danny with the news.

No one missed Marian Pomeroy until morning, when someone saw blood on the lifeboat hull and looked up. They knocked, then checked her stateroom. What they found was alarming.

Keri, in a two-piece mint green swimsuit, her fair skin slathered with sunscreen, was lounging near the pool with a good book when passengers first became aware that something might be wrong.

The ship was searched from top to bottom. When no sign of Marian Pomeroy was found, the ship's captain alerted the Coast Guard, the Jamaican authorities, and the FBI. The ship heaved to and retraced its course, searching the waters cruised shortly after Marian Pomeroy's last meal was served.

The evidence seemed clear. The missing passenger, an elderly woman, weary after going ashore, had dined alone in her room. She'd consumed much of her meal. The champagne bottle was nearly empty.

No foul play was suspected. Her purchases, her identification, her money and passport were all in her stateroom, along with several letters ready to mail. None appeared to be a suicide note. In one she wrote:

As you may remember, the anniversary of the day I met your dear father was this past week. I felt so swept away by nostalgia and happy memories that I sprang into action! In his honor I gave away a great deal of money to those in need. It was the best thing I have ever done! He'd be so pleased, and I have never been happier. As a result I plan to scale down my lifestyle considerably when I return to New York next week. The brownstone had grown to be way too empty, and too large for me. Until I am settled in a smaller place, perhaps on the Jersey side of the GW bridge, I thought I'd stay with each of you for a few months to get to know you and your children better. It will be great fun. I'm bringing you all souvenirs from Montego Bay and Cozumel. See you soon, my dears. Your father would be so pleased.

Love,
Mother

In a separate letter to her attorney she was more clear:

My late husband and I provided substantially for our children during our lifetime, and I have given a great deal of money to the foundation during the past three decades. Therefore I recently made the decision to use my remaining resources to help deserving recipients directly, one-on-one, rather than through the many layers of charitable organizations. It gives me such joy to see their faces! I cannot wait to tell you all of their stories.

Warmest regards, Marian

As the ships and planes called off their fruitless search at dark, Claire Waterson's flight was landing at Heathrow. Newly blond, professionally made up, and wearing a brilliant blue suit, she boarded a train to her destination.

Investigators boarded the cruise ship, examined the scene, inspected Marian Pomeroy's camera, and concluded that the avid amateur photographer had climbed up on her chair in order to focus from a wider angle. She may have suffered a dizzy spell due to a stroke, exhaustion, or champagne-induced high spirits. Whatever the reason, she tumbled over the railing. Her body glanced off the lifeboat hull then plunged into the sea.

Few passengers recalled speaking to the missing woman. One couple on the deck below recalled hearing a cry at sunset but assumed it had come from fellow passengers engaging in horseplay during happy hour by the pool.

The young doctor from Miami, taking a break from her busy practice, did not recall meeting or even seeing the wealthy widow from Manhattan.

The ship's security cameras yielded a few glimpses of the missing woman, always alone, both before she went ashore and after her return with the bag of souvenirs found in her stateroom. Marian Pomeroy's body was never found.

When her photo, shot by the ship's photographer, was released to the media, many in Miami recognized her instantly: Marian Pomeroy, the missing cruise ship passenger, was the kindly grandmother who gave away big bills to strangers, as her shipboard letter confirmed.

Psychological profilers who studied the case and the letters to her children found no signs of depression or suicidal tendencies, despite the fact that she had in recent days divested herself of most of her assets.

The conclusion, after an inquest, was that

she climbed on a chair, then lost her balance while trying to snap a more dramatic picture of the sunset. She struck her head on the lifeboat and was most likely dead or unconscious before she hit the water.

The blood on the railing and the splotch on the hull matched the missing woman's DNA.

Marian Pomeroy was declared legally dead due to a regrettable accident.

CHAPTER
TWENTY-SEVEN

Venturi's hotline rang as he broiled burgers for him and the dog.

"You watching CNN?" Danny asked.

"No."

"Homicide in Minneapolis. A guy whacked and dropped off a bridge into the river. Somebody wanted to make a statement, to tell the world, 'Look what I did!' "

"So? There've been six murders here in six days." Venturi opened the packet of cheese slices to top the burgers.

"Yeah, but my spook hotline says the Minneapolis victim didn't exist. His ID didn't check out. He was somebody else, somebody in the witness protection program."

Venturi turned off the broiler. "Did you hear a name?"

"He was initially identified as Louis Messineo, operated a trucking business in the Twin Cities."

Venturi dropped into a kitchen chair, as

though the wind had been knocked out of him.

"Thought I'd give you a jingle," Danny said casually, "in case he was one of yours."

"Christ, Danny! He is. He was. He's one of my cases! I was his contact agent. Real name, Dominic DelVecchio. He testified in a string of extortion and conspiracy cases over in Jersey. What the hell happened?"

"CNN and Fox say he was shot multiple times, then thrown off a bridge into the Mississippi. Get this: no fatal bullet wounds. Shot in the kneecaps, elbows, shoulders; alive till he hit the water."

Venturi sprang to his feet and walked the floor, running his hand through his hair. Scout plodded behind him. "How did they find him? What did he get himself into? Last time I checked, when I was still on the job, he looked like he was on the straight and narrow, though that doesn't mean a damn thing."

"Let's see WITSEC claim again that they never lost a protected witness. It'll be interesting to hear what they say when the press starts asking questions."

"I can tell you right now," Venturi said. "They'll blame DelVecchio. They claim they never lost anybody who followed the rules. What they don't say is that one of the rules is 'Don't get killed.'

"Damn! The Marshals Service will probably want to talk to me. I'm the one who relocated him to Minneapolis and had the most contact with him. Maybe I should call them. I should offer my help. But given the circumstances when I left . . ."

"Don't kick a sleeping tiger, bro. Don't ask for grief from men in suits. If they really need you, they'll find you. Look, we need to talk, ASAP, about something important. I can stop by or you can come for dinner. Bring Vicki if she's home."

She wasn't. She was out apartment hunting with a pushy realtor whom Venturi strongly disliked.

He felt comfortable in the house, decided to buy it, and was about to close on the sale. He'd improved the roof and the security gate. Vicki had planted a garden. He hoped she'd stay.

He and Scout went to Danny's. The kids were delighted. Luz seemed quiet. Her pregnancy was beginning to show. Warm and delicious aromas wafted from her kitchen.

Danny wore a DON'T TASE ME, BRO T-shirt.

They ate chicken with yellow rice, peas, and sweet plantains.

Aware that Keri was out of town, Luz had invited Mirta, the well-endowed nurse, to join them.

Danny took Venturi back to his study, leaving Luz and Mirta cleaning up and putting the kids to bed.

"Hope Luz doesn't think we're dissing her and her friend," Venturi said.

"Don't worry about it," Danny said. "Did you ask her to procure you a woman? Neither did I. She knows you're seeing Keri."

"Everything all right with you two?"

"Sure. *No problemo.*" Danny put down his beer, pulled a chair up close, and lowered his voice. "We're gonna crash a plane, bro."

"That so? And who is 'we'?"

"You and me. 'We' is us, amigo. I have us a new client. You're gonna love this guy. He needs our help and can afford to pay his own expenses."

"At least it's not a woman," Venturi said.

Danny ignored the remark. "You ever hear of Errol Flagg?"

"No."

"Man, what planet did you fall from? In what century do you live?" He picked up his beer and took an impatient swig. "Ever watch MTV?"

"Nope."

"Read *People* magazine?"

"Nope."

He gave a huge sigh and shook his head. "You've gotta move into the twenty-first century, man. Remember I said I worked private security for a while? Errol Flagg was one of my clients."

"Who the hell is he?"

"Only a rock star. You should only have his groupies," he said, rolling his eyes. "I had to beat them off him with a stick. I needed a stun gun, a cattle prod, and a baseball bat to protect his bod from hot babes who wanted it."

"And he finds that a problem?"

"He's got a shitload of problems, all basically because he's a damn nice guy, too nice for the world he's caught up in. He's got it all, and it makes him miserable."

"He could quit."

"That is the problem. The music biz is like the mob, you can't quit. When he was young, starting out, and trying to make it, he signed ironclad contracts. He's tied to a bunch of unscrupulous managers, greedy agents, and recording executives. They'd sue his ass from here to kingdom come if he tried to renege.

"He lost his wife, his childhood sweetheart, to the lifestyle. He can't quit. But she could, and she did. He's been caught up in the treadmill of touring, the drug culture, lawyers, agents, stalkers, groupies, tabloids, and hangers-on for fifteen years. He's exhausted, has had enough, but he's committed, tied up for life.

"He wants out, big time. In the beginning it was all about the music. He loved it. Now he doesn't care if he ever sees a guitar again.

"He's been busted for drugs and drunk driving, has been in and out of rehab at least twice. He's clean now, but knows he'll never stay that way if he goes back on tour, which he is contractually obligated to do."

"Did he have kids with that childhood sweetheart?" Venturi asked. "Can't he just square things with her and make it work?"

"They had no kids when she bailed. She's got several now. Married a guy who comes home at the same time every night without having to fight off a thousand different temptations, from booze to drugs, to rock 'n' roll sex."

"Does he have another lifestyle in mind?"

"You'll love this — you'll goddamn relate to it, man." Danny gestured like an orchestra conductor. "His dream is to be a deep-sea fisherman."

Venturi smiled. "He can't be all bad. But does he have enough brain cells left to pull it off? Can he stay off the drugs and alcohol?"

"Yeah, but since you seriously doubt my judgment these days, why not talk to him? See what you think."

"I don't doubt your judgment, Danny."

"Don't tell me that. It's obvious, ever since Solange. You know I could've found a way onto that cruise ship the other day. Could have done the job, and slipped off, *no problemo*. Instead, you let Keri take the risks."

"The risks were fewer. That's the point, Danny. That plan was a thing of beauty. It all came together so smoothly, no heroics, no life-threatening stunts required. She walked on, then walked off the ship, as opposed to you being retrieved at sea in the dark, with twelve hundred possible witnesses and more shit than you can think of that might go wrong. Sure, you coulda done it. But why, if you didn't have to? Save the risks for the big one, when there is no other recourse. You're just sulking 'cause you couldn't be a hero."

"You don't get it, Mike. This stateside spy-versus-spy shit can be so goddamn boring that sometimes I feel like I can't breathe."

"Tell me about it. I miss the action, too. But you're too important to Luz and the kids to take unnecessary risks. Why ask for trouble? Which, unfortunately, reminds me — you mentioned a plane?"

Danny's eyes brightened. "A jet. We can bring it down in the Atlantic where the water's too deep to retrieve the fuselage. Errol Flagg flies his own plane. You know, like John Travolta, JFK Jr., and lotsa other celebrities. Beats flying commercial. I flew his Cessna Citation a few times myself, took over while he was busy doing the mile-high thing. Lands like a dream, all you need to do is watch the horizon.

"I miss flying, Mike. Can't wait to fly the Osprey. You know the one. Is it a bird? Is it a plane? Is it a chopper? Can't wait to pilot one of those babies."

Venturi had heard about the new military aircraft that takes off and lands like a helicopter but when airborne converts to a turboprop plane after the rotor, transmission, and engine nacelles rotate ninety degrees forward.

"I thought they were still experimental," he said. "With problems. Heard they were widow makers."

"Don't believe the media, Mike. The first squadron is already in Iraq, deployed last month. The Osprey flies faster and farther. The cockpit's got night vision and missile-warning systems, and it's nuclear, biological, and chemical warfare protected. I can't wait to fly one.

"Look, just meet Flagg, decide for yourself. I'm betting it's a go. You're gonna love him."

Errol Flagg wasn't as tall as he looked in the photos Venturi found on the Internet. Probably because most were taken from below, as he spun around up on stage in the spotlight's glare, with his guitar, band members, backup singers and dancers.

Vicki was in the kitchen when Flagg arrived. Venturi had told her that Danny and a friend were coming for lunch.

Errol Flagg arrived first, driving a silver Porsche.

As he and Venturi shook hands, Vicki appeared with a salad bowl. She paused, her expression startled. "Errol Flagg," she said, matter-of-factly, without hesitation. "I'm a great fan of yours."

Her instant recognition did not surprise Flagg but did take Venturi aback. Maybe he *was* anchored in a different century.

Flagg's hair was spiky and blond tipped. He wore skintight jeans anchored by a big silver belt buckle and looked hollow-eyed, too pale, and too thin. "Where's Danny?"

he asked.

Everybody always asked him that, Venturi thought, annoyed. He wondered himself. He had hoped Danny would arrive first, with the latest on the murder in Minneapolis. According to the news, investigators suspected that DelVecchio had been abducted from outside his home. They knew where he lived! What went wrong? Where the hell was Danny?

A buzz from the gate answered his question.

Danny and the rocker greeted each other like old war buddies.

"We've been through hell together," Flagg explained gravely.

"I know the feeling," Venturi said. He offered Flagg a whiskey, impressed when the man declined.

"I'm fresh out of rehab, the third time," Flagg said candidly.

"Third time's the charm," Danny said reassuringly.

"I guess Danny's told you what it's like," Flagg said. "I'm sorry he left the business. I miss him. He was a good influence, did a lot to keep me straight." The timbre of Flagg's speaking voice and his worn expression exuded the weary resignation of a troubled Shakespearean actor.

"It's tough to explain. No one under-stands," he said earnestly. "I can't go anywhere, do anything. The paparazzi cre-ate a traffic jam if I go out for a beer and everybody, including waiters, waitresses, and the people who deliver room service, tries to sneak pictures with their cell phones to peddle to the tabloids. It's a bummer to never have a private moment."

"Wouldn't you miss playing music, being in the spotlight?" Venturi said.

"Not the spotlight, I've had my fill of that. Someday, maybe, I might pick up a guitar again, but only for my own enjoyment. No band, no amps, no screaming crowds.

"To disappear forever," he said longingly, "would be an impossible dream come true. Like finding a girl who wants sex with you because she cares, not so she can tape the deed and sell it to the highest bidder."

"*You* wouldn't disappear," Venturi said. "Errol Flagg would. He'd be legally dead and gone, with an obituary and a death certificate. He'd no longer exist."

"Dying young would be excellent," Flagg said fervently. "Traditional. Rock stars die young. Did you know they live to an aver-age age of forty-two in the USA and thirty-five in Europe?

"Buddy Holly, Elvis, Janis Joplin, Jim

Morrison, Jimi Hendrix, Kurt Cobain. Good company," he said jauntily. "Who am I to buck tradition? I've beaten the odds so far." His smile faded. "But not much longer. It's either that, or your way."

Danny explained his idea.

"The impact would be in deep water, so deep that the plane breaks up and the fuselage — where you are — can't be recovered," he concluded.

Flagg looked pained for a long moment. "*Ceci?* My Cessna Citation? But I love that bird."

"Never love anything that can't love you back," Danny said. "You're leaving it behind either way. Why not take it out with you in a blaze of glory?"

"I like it," Flagg finally said, after some thought. "Quick. Clean. Flying high into the big forever." He looked pleased. "So, who will really be flying her when she goes down? You, Danny?"

"No, no, Errol," Danny said. "It's you, it has to be you."

"Oh," the rocker said thoughtfully.

CHAPTER
TWENTY-EIGHT

Venturi had no trouble spotting her in the crowd. He couldn't miss her energetic walk and her red hair, pulled back into a bouncy ponytail, beneath a white baseball cap.

They met at the Port of Miami beneath the huge gantries and tall ships etched against a bright blue sky. Miami's silver and pastel skyline loomed behind them.

He caught her in a bear hug, kissed her forehead, and took her bag.

Fellow passengers, though happy to be home, seemed somewhat subdued about the one left behind. The tragedy gave their trip a certain mystique.

"Never found."

"Lost at sea."

"So sad."

"Sweet little old lady."

"Had to miss a port of call because of the search," one man grumbled.

"A terrible accident," a sad-eyed woman

murmured.

"Did you hear what happened?" Keri asked solemnly, as the comments of other travelers swirled around them. "The FBI interviewed everyone on our deck."

"I'm sorry," Venturi replied, "but in spite of it all, getting away did you a world of good. I swear you look younger than the last time I saw you."

He saw the smile in her eyes.

Safely in the car, windows closed, she asked. "Did it go well? Did she make her flight?"

He nodded.

"Yesss!" She erupted into happy laughter. "Yesss! What a wonderful, wonderful cruise!"

She'd had a blast, she said. The FBI agent who spoke to her had even hit on her.

"So you plan to date him?" Venturi asked.

"You mean her — and no."

He mentioned a new client, with no details, and asked if she'd help, since she was not due back at the office for two more days.

She asked who referred the client.

"Danny," he said placidly, ignoring her expression.

Keri came to his place later, after checking

her service, unpacking, and sifting through the mail.

Venturi steered her right to the war room. Errol sat at the big oval table, a bottle of Smartwater beside him, watching a video-tape with Vicki. They were discussing small fishing villages along the coast of Scotland.

Before he could introduce her, Keri, in blue jeans, sandals, and a halter top, approached the conference table slowly, as though on tiptoe, eyes wide, expression transfixed.

"Errol? Errol Flagg? I don't believe this! "Living Love" is my all-time favorite song. I play "Black and Chrome" when I drive to the hospital, so I don't speed and get pulled over. I am your biggest fan."

"No," Victoria said quickly. "I am."

All three turned expectantly to Venturi, as though he, too, would stake a claim to the title. "I was always working," he said sheepishly, "and didn't listen to much music."

They all stared at him quizzically.

When Keri left the room to let Scout out, Errol Flagg's hungry eyes followed approvingly. Venturi caught the look. "No," he said softly, firmly shaking his head.

"Okay, mate." Errol flashed both palms in instant surrender. "I've always had a thing for redheads. But understood," he swore, "absolutely understood."

CHAPTER
TWENTY-NINE

The day Errol Flagg died was gray and overcast under an indifferent sky. The forecast was for rain as a tropical depression moved in from the southeast.

Perfect. It meant fewer witnesses in the sky and on the sea.

Errol Flagg boarded his Cessna Citation at Opa Locka Airport, northwest of Miami. His flight plan listed his destination as Treasure Cay on Abaco Island. A frequent visitor in the past, he was to meet his manager, some friends, and models to party over the weekend.

He signed autographs for several airport maintenance workers and support personnel.

A recently hired, young fixed base operator fueled the Citation, checked the oil and engine, then cautiously asked the star to pose for a photo with him. Flagg, wearing his trademark stubble, spiky hair, boots, and designer jeans with a pale blue short-sleeved silk and linen shirt, cheerfully agreed.

A number of witnesses saw Flagg's Cessna taxi down runway nine left, lift into the sky and make a wide turn, east-northeast toward the Bahamas.

Danny and Venturi scanned the sky, elated, as menacing thunderclouds built on the horizon. The weather was indeed perfect.

Twenty minutes into the flight, at nineteen thousand feet, Errol Flagg began to closely monitor his latitude and longitude. He had never liked flying over open water and had said as much to a number of friends and interviewers in the past. Those unplanned remarks were now fortuitous, foreshadowing, evidence of a grim premonition. He knew it would become part of his legend.

He scanned the vast sea and prayed that the outline barely visible in heavy rain below was Danny's boat. Flagg made the sign of the cross, said his first Hail Mary in years, then keyed his radio.

"Mayday. Mayday, Citation Jet 79Juliet. I have smoke in the cockpit. I think I'm on fire. Request vectors to the nearest suitable airport."

Miami Center to Citation Jet 79Juliet. Turn right heading 270, vectors to Freeport. When able, say fuel remaining and souls onboard.

Do you read me?

Errol Flagg did not respond. Instead he depressurized the plane so he could open the door.

Citation Jet 79J, Miami Center, over. Citation Jet 79J, Miami Center how do you read?

Flagg turned off the autopilot.

Citation Jet 79J, Miami Center, over. Citation Jet 79J, Miami Center how do you read?

He donned the parachute, turned off the transponder, then banked into a sharp right turn and descent. That insured that when he jumped, the plane would be moving away from him as it spiraled downward.

We lost the transponder.

The air traffic controller's comment to his supervisor was heard on the air.

Errol Flagg released the flight controls and pushed open the left cockpit door.

Citation Jet 79Juliet. Miami Center, over.

No answer.

We only have a primary target now.

Nineteen thousand feet over the Atlantic, Errol Flagg swung open the door of *Ceci,* his beloved Cessna Citation. He kissed her cold metal skin. "Good-bye, beautiful," he said, then hit the air in a huge leap of faith. "Geronimo!" he yelled, not quite sure why. It was something he vaguely recalled from an old World War II movie he'd seen on TV.

348

But it seemed appropriate. He always had a flair for the dramatic.

His parting cry was swallowed by a rush of wind, rain, and panic that literally sucked his breath away.

He counted to three and yanked the ripcord. To his immense relief, the parachute blossomed above him like a flower. The ride was a high. Hitting the water was a bitch. He landed hard, the air knocked out of him, and became tangled in the lines. The water was colder, the waves higher than he expected. He struggled to free himself but became further entangled, unable to swim or escape the chute. Beaten, battered, and buffeted about by natural forces that pushed, pulled, and dragged him under, he swallowed vast amounts of seawater.

The plan was for Danny to make the rescue alone. Venturi had also suited up, as a precaution — which was a good thing now that the mission seemed to be going awry.

They hit the water simultaneously, as the out-of-control Cessna tightened into a steeper and steeper spiral in a turbulent sky, accelerating past maximum operating speed.

Fighting towering waves, Danny reached Flagg first. He dragged him to the surface, held his head above water and tried to avoid becoming entangled himself as Venturi cut away the cords with his knife.

"Don't lose the chute!" Danny shouted.

A deployed parachute was the last thing they wanted found near the wreckage.

They managed to maneuver both Flagg and the parachute back to the boat.

Both were so busy they barely saw the Citation slam into the sea several miles away, but they heard the impact.

Target disappeared from radar.

Do you know who that was? said a shocked voice at Miami Center.

The Coast Guard and Bahamian authorities were notified for search and rescue.

Flagg was limp, a dead weight, as they wrestled his body into the boat.

"Shit," Danny said, as the wake from the plane's impact rocked the vessel.

Venturi, nearly knocked off his feet as he stowed the chute below, shouted, "Is Errol still breathing?"

"Goddammit," Flagg responded. Sprawled out on the deck, he spit up seawater. Gasping for breath, he croaked, "I could've been killed!"

"Right," Danny said. He turned the key in the ignition as Venturi guided the anchor line into the rope locker.

"Let's go!" Venturi shouted above the wind and a stinging horizontal rain. "This will look like rush hour in a few minutes!"

Danny turned the key again. The engine did not respond. He and Venturi exchanged tense looks through the rain. He tried again. Nothing.

"How long do we have?" Venturi yelled, dragging out the tool kit.

"A Coast Guard chopper or two will be overhead in less than twenty. The whole world will be right behind it." Danny tried the engine again. Then again. The fifth time, it kicked in with a comforting explosion of sound.

Venturi breathed again. "Get below, out of sight!" he told Errol, who staggered and half-fell down the steps.

"My life was flashing in front of my eyes," Danny said from the helm. "I saw it end with our faces plastered all over the press as the boaters accidentally in the right place at the right time to rescue rock star Errol Flagg.

"We'da had a whole lotta 'splaining to do. Or we would have had to drown Errol ourselves. This was close." Danny grinned.

"Too close," Venturi said as they turned toward home through rough seas.

CHAPTER THIRTY

Only an oil slick and thousands of bits of shattered wreckage surfaced in the area where Errol Flagg's plane fell off the radar.

The media descended on South Florida. *Entertainment Tonight,* Greta Van Susteren, and Larry King all broadcast from South Beach. Geraldo piloted his own boat out to the site south of Grand Bahama Island, halfway between Freeport and Treasure Cay, and described it live as "Errol Flagg's final resting place, a watery grave not far from Miami, his favorite personal playground.

"Is Flagg yet another victim of the infamous Bermuda Triangle?" Rivera asked. "Did his own personal demons play a role in his tragic end? Or did the luck of the high-flying rocker simply run out? The truth may never be known. The sea keeps its secrets."

Human scavengers bent on salvaging

memorabilia battled the Coast Guard, NTSB investigators, and each other over priceless bits of wreckage, as flotillas of weeping fans in bikinis flung flowers into the waves at latitude N 26 32.0, longitude W 078 00.

Many collided with Coast Guard cutters, members of the press, and each other. Charter captains, sightseeing planes, boats, blimps, and choppers sold out trips to the site, creating a seagoing traffic jam.

Rescuers initially hoped to find an intact fuselage and the pilot but quickly realized there was no hope of recovering human remains. The Cessna had been shattered, totally destroyed on impact.

The Coast Guard called off the mission after three days but was kept busier than ever with a record number of arrests, rescues, and medical emergencies as rock fans from all over the world converged for moments of silence at latitude N 26 32.0, longitude W 078 00. Their numbers continued to grow, catching the Coast Guard unaware.

Aerial shots of flowers floating as far as the eye could see were broadcast all over the world, encouraging even more fans to make the pilgrimage. Some never really had been fans, but the drama of the music star's tragic and untimely death fascinated them in a macabre fashion.

His recordings sold like hotcakes.

Sightseers and mourners dangerously over-loaded small boats. Some attempted the trip in unseaworthy craft, using anything that would float: rafts, hang gliders with pon-toons, sailboards, Jet Skis, and even a personal two-seat submarine. A growing number even tried to float to the site on in-ner tubes. If Cubans could successfully flee their homeland and float more than ninety miles to South Florida on inner tubes, fans believed they could surely make it to N 26 32 W 078 00. Coast Guard crews soon found it difficult to distinguish incoming refugees fleeing Cuba from departing Flagg fans seeking the crash site. Nearly all of the latter were inexperienced boaters, many were nonswimmers, and most were under the influence of illegal substances. They swamped and sank, or ran aground on the flats. Small boaters ran out of gas or into each other's anchor lines, entangling their propellers. A number were injured when they went into the water to cut the lines and free the props. The blood in the water resulted in frightening shark sightings. Circling news and sightseeing helicopters nearly collided on several occasions. A few fans failed to think ahead and parachuted out of small aircraft over the site. A woman on one boat went into labor and had to be airlifted to the States. Others fell overboard, nearly drowned, overdosed, threatened suicide, hallucinated, or became dangerously dehydrated and disoriented. Miraculously, no one died. Many came close.

Errol Flagg's last address, longitude N 26 32.0, latitude W 078 00 appeared on T-shirts, hats, and bumper stickers within twenty-four hours of the crash.

His final words: "Smoke in the cockpit. I think I'm on fire," were broadcast over and over. Even Errol Flagg wept copious tears upon hearing them.

Venturi yanked the plug on the TV in order to refocus Flagg on his future.

An unspoken but real fear among team members was that his fans' grief and adulation might move Flagg to launch his own resurrection and comeback tour.

The young airport employee who had fueled Flagg's Cessna sold the rocker's last photo to *People* magazine for big bucks.

The more the world loved the late Errol Flagg, the more annoying he became to team members. Excited by the prospect of life in Scotland with its medieval castles, ancient battle sites, and the Loch Ness monster, he endlessly practiced his brogue, studied his new look, and posed in front of the mirror. The spiky hair was gone, so were the blond tips.

When the women attempted to restore his hair to its natural shade, he had difficulty remembering the color and in his eagerness to assist, inadvertently exposed himself to Keri and Victoria.

"Sorry," he said.

"Don't make me kill you," Venturi warned him, not for the first time.

"Understood, Michael. No problem. I mean, one's a doctor, the other's a worldly woman of a certain age. I didn't think . . . didn't realize . . . I'm not accustomed to interacting with women who have standards. My apologies. That might be another behavioral issue we should address."

Venturi agreed.

Flagg's trademark swagger had to go. Vicki spent hours demonstrating how to walk normally, which in itself was hilarious, since she had a pronounced limp.

"That's it, that's it!" she told Flagg at one point. "You've almost got it. Now just kill the limp."

"No! That's not it. Walk like a man, like

356

this," Danny insisted, stomping about like a demented bull.

Flagg's accountants and handlers were unaware, he said, of a secret stash of cash he'd squirreled away long ago to buy drugs, or whatever. He turned it over to Venturi for expenses, with the remainder to be wired to an account in a Glasgow bank, in his new name, Andrew McCallum.

Though his dream since childhood was to be a commercial deep-sea fisherman, Errol Flagg had actually gone fishing only twice in his life. But he loved the fact that Scotland's fishermen are Europe's most environmentally friendly. Now he faced reality, the backbreaking work and dangerous life of deep-sea fishermen off the wild Scottish coast. Oddly enough, as he experienced it through virtual reality, he fell even more in love with the challenge. They warned him it was like learning to be a professional boxer before ever stepping into the ring or taking a punch.

Venturi and Danny mercilessly worked him in the gym. He became stronger and more confident. He didn't hesitate to jettison his trademark height-enhancing boots, happy to settle for his true height, five feet nine inches tall. The shrinkage helped his transformation. According to Errol Flagg's official bios and press releases, the rocker stood six feet tall.

Andrew McCallum wore a brown suit from the Men's Warehouse on the day he departed, shoes shined, laces tied. He wore blue contact lenses over his brown eyes and carried a newspaper to read on the long flight.

At the airport he crushed Keri in his arms and startled her with a passionate kiss on the lips. "Good-bye forever, beautiful," he said. "I'll be seeing you — but only in my dreams."

Victoria cautiously offered her cheek, but he swooped in to score one on her lips, as well.

He grinned at Venturi. "Can't kill me now." He chuckled. "I'm already dead."

"Go catch the damn plane," Venturi said, "or you'll die twice."

The two shook hands.

McCallum hugged Danny last. "Thanks, mate. I'll never forget you."

"Have fun, fisherman," Danny said. "Stay away from the sharks this time."

Andrew McCallum nodded briskly and marched off to catch his flight.

"Think he'll be all right?" Victoria said doubtfully.

"Sure," Danny said. "He'll be fine."

They watched his flight depart through the picture windows in the terminal and returned to Venturi's place with a sense of relief. It lasted only until Danny turned on the news.

Chapter
Thirty-One

Had the killer used a gun, a baseball bat, or his bare hands the story would not have made national news. What made the murder sensational was the weapon: a garrote, a thirty-two-inch nylon cord with wooden knobs, a commando-style tool of death not seen in the United States for more than twenty years, according to the FBI.

Danny's relentless channel surfing had paused on a Fox News exclusive, a man garroted in the stairwell of a four-star hotel.

"Don't see many of those these days," he said thoughtfully.

The camera focused for a moment on the anguished features of a middle-aged blonde described as the victim's widow. She saw it, covered her face, and turned away, but not quickly enough.

Venturi had glanced up from his desk at Danny's comment. He sprang to his feet.

"You see that?" he whispered hoarsely.

"See what?" Danny said.

"The woman. She looked a helluva lot like Angelo Conte's wife. Her name's Celia."

He joined Danny in front of the television, studying the screen, willing the woman who was being helped to a car by two young men to turn around.

She did, just enough for him to see her profile clearly for a moment.

"That *is* her!" Venturi sounded alarmed. "What the hell's happening? Is that Portland?"

Danny nodded. "It's probably not her. You could only see her for a second. You can't be sure."

"Nine and three-quarters on a scale of ten. I relocated him, his wife, and two teenage sons to Oregon almost two years ago. He testified in a major racketeering and public corruption case in Philly."

"Holy shit," Danny said. "If you're right, this ain't good news. In fact," he placed his palm to his forehead and closed his eyes, "my psychic abilities predict that you are about to hear from men in suits who work for the federal government. Time to lie low and circle the wagons, goombah."

Fox went to another story. Danny flicked to CNN, then MSNBC. Nothing more on the case. Yet.

"What the hell?" Venturi looked bewildered. "I don't get it. What went wrong?"

"What was that on the television, boys?" Victoria asked affably.

"Nothing important," Danny said without making eye contact.

The two men retired to the war room without further comment as she and Keri stared.

"That was rude," Keri murmured.

"Something's up," Victoria said. "If so, we'll know soon enough."

Danny slumped in a chair at the oval conference table. "Think this hit is related to the Minneapolis homicide? Were Conte and DelVecchio both on the same mobsters' hit parade?"

"Their cases were totally unrelated," Venturi said, shaking his head. "DelVecchio and Conte weren't associates. I doubt they even knew each other. They only had one common denominator: me. I worked with them both."

They stared at each other.

"How many in the Marshals Service had access to their new identities and locations?" Danny asked.

"Three — four tops. But I worked with different agents and prosecutors on each of those cases. That narrows it down to me."

Danny's expression grew increasingly serious.

"They were my cases," Venturi said. "I probably know more about them than anybody in the Marshals Service and more than their immediate families. DelVecchio's wife, for instance, didn't know that WITSEC also relocated his mistress to Minneapolis. I should call the office, find out what's going on, and offer to help."

"Don't do it, man," Danny warned. "Don't poke a rattlesnake with a stick or kick a sleeping tiger."

"But I need to find out what the hell's happening. A preemptive strike is better than sticking my head in the sand and hoping it all goes away. Doesn't a lack of interest make me look more suspect?"

"Damned if you do and damned if you don't," Danny said. "If you do talk to them, they won't tell you a damn thing. And they'll twist whatever you say to use against you."

"But . . ."

"*Omertà*, man. Silence is golden."

"If I offer to unload everything I know about the victims, it might help the investigation."

"You have an inflated opinion of your own

importance. What do you know? *Nada,* zilch, zero. You've had no contact with either of them lately. Who knows what worlds of crap they got into? Not you. Let's hope the local cops identify the killers as unrelated badass robbers or trigger-happy hometown hoods who had no clue who they were whacking."

"How likely is that?" Venturi said derisively.

Danny shrugged. "Until we hear different, we can hope."

"Hope is disappointment delayed," Venturi said. "If the press learns that two protected witnesses were hit, the program will be in chaos."

"Witnesses sure won't run to join it. It'll be a front-page scandal, bro." Danny shook his head somberly. "News like that can't stay secret long. The feds are scrambling for a scapegoat as we speak. And man, if no better target pops up on the horizon — tag, you're it."

"Jesus, Danny."

"Maybe you should talk to a lawyer."

"Oh, sure." Venturi rubbed his forehead with his palm. "Nothing like lawyering up to make you look innocent."

"Sometimes a little legal advice will clarify

a situation. Listen to me, man. You know
—"

They stopped abruptly as Keri popped her
head into the room. "Gotta go," she said
cheerfully, her smile fading at their expressions. "I'm heading to the hospital."

"Okay, I'll call you later," Venturi said. He
didn't get up. Danny was preoccupied, pacing.

"Something wrong?" she asked.

"I'll call you later," Venturi repeated
shortly.

She closed the door quietly without another word.

Danny stopped pacing, sat on the corner
of Venturi's desk, and lowered his voice.
"So, where were you, man, when somebody
used DelVecchio for target practice then
dropped him off a high bridge? What's your
alibi, bro? Isn't that about the time you took
a little day trip to Jamaica? What do you say
when they start asking questions about that?
And now Conte. Your alibi is that you were
driving *who* to the airport?"

"You're right," Venturi said. "I'd jeopar-
dize us all."

"Only use prepaid cells to call anybody,
especially me, from now on."

"Right."

"And watch your back."

Danny rumbled out of the driveway on his Harley a short time later.

That evening, for the first time, Venturi encouraged Victoria in her hunt for an apartment. She responded calmly, but he saw the hurt in her eyes. He had nearly persuaded her to stay on. They were like family. They *were* family.

Her son, Sidney, had somehow posted bond and was now harassing her with angry calls. He was demanding that she return to New York, that she drop charges, that he speak to Venturi. "He's irrational and furious," she said.

Venturi had more important problems than Sidney to think about and simply suggested she stop answering his calls.

It was midnight when Scout began to bark. The buzzer at the gate sounded moments later.

"It's me," Keri said over the intercom. "I'm sorry it's so late. But I have someone I want you, Vicki, and Danny to meet."

"Danny's been gone for hours. Can it wait until tomorrow?"

There was a painful pause. "No," she finally replied. "There may not be one."

None of this is her fault, he told himself, and what she said made him curious. "I'll make coffee. Drive on up."

At the sound of voices, Vicki stepped out of her bedroom wearing a bathrobe. Her eyes looked puffy.

"Sorry," he said. "Keri's back. Someone's with her."

"I wasn't asleep, dear."

"Can you join us? I'm making coffee."

"Make mine decaf. I think there's some pie left, and a banana loaf in the freezer."

The woman with Keri was slightly built, young and dark-haired, with huge, frightened eyes and a silk scarf wrapped around her throat, almost to her chin.

Keri introduced her as Maheen. As they settled around the kitchen table, Keri explained that a hospital administrator had helped bring Maheen to Miami from New York and had arranged a job for her in the records department. But now she was unable to go to work.

"Maheen's family is Iranian," Keri said. "And her parents still cling to the old ways, the traditions of their homeland. Many of those traditions are against the law here, but they practice them nonetheless."

The girl took a single sip of coffee but did not touch the pie Vicki offered. Eyes downcast as Keri spoke, she bit her oddly puckered lower lip, her hands folded in her lap.

"Maheen is American," Keri continued, "the only member of her family born here. She went to high school in Paramus, New Jersey. Her parents didn't allow her to attend dances, proms, pajama parties, or football games. She was forbidden to date or learn to drive. They insisted she quit school at age sixteen. She rebelled at that. She wanted to graduate with her class and hoped for a college scholarship. She didn't want to wear a head scarf like her mother and older sister. Her family situation became more tense when she took a job at a department store, at the cosmetics counter. When she was eighteen she met a boy, an American boy, and began seeing him, despite her parents' often violent objections.

"They demanded she quit the job and forbade her to see the boy again. She said she was American and wanted to live like an American girl. The clash of cultures was inevitable." Keri sighed and reached for the girl's hand.

"On a freezing night last January, her boyfriend drove her home from work so she wouldn't have to take a bus. Her parents and older brothers were waiting. The boy, a premed student, was beaten so severely that he was comatose for three weeks."

Tears flooded Maheen's eyes and began

368

to spill over.

"The young man survived," Keri said, "but he's severely brain damaged. Maheen's family dragged her into the house. Her mother and oldest brother held her down while her father tried to disfigure her with acid."

Victoria gasped.

"He tried to throw it into her face and eyes, but she struggled so violently that it splashed onto her throat and breasts instead," Keri continued.

She gently murmured something in the girl's ear. Maheen nodded, then sat motionless, without lifting her eyes, as Keri unwrapped the scarf from her throat.

Venturi's gut tightened. Vicki began to cry.

The burn scars were horrendous. Although only her throat was exposed, it was clear that the burns extended down the front of her body. Miraculously, just a tiny drop of acid had struck her face, puckering her lower lip, Keri explained.

Neighbors called the police. Maheen was still struggling, screaming in fear and pain when they kicked in the front door. Her father was attacking her with a ball-peen hammer, as the rest of the family helped him.

"Had the police not intervened, she would

have been killed," Keri said. "Had the acid struck her face and eyes as intended, she would have been permanently blinded and brutally disfigured.

"The father, the family patriarch, devoutly believes that all he did wrong was fail to finish the job." Yet the prosecution hit a snag when the brain-damaged boy was unable to testify and Maheen's family was released on bond.

She was hospitalized and terrified. Once released, she went into hiding.

The girl picked up her scarf and covered her scars as Keri continued to speak. That was when Venturi saw that her right hand, which she'd kept concealed in her lap, was also shriveled and scarred, burned by the acid as she fought her attackers.

Her father and brothers were convicted of reduced assault charges and served brief sentences.

The parents were indignant that anyone, including the police, had interfered in a family matter. They believed they had every right to do what they did.

"They feel disgraced, that her disobedience has stained the family honor. In their eyes there is only one way to restore it: they have to kill her."

Keri studied their faces, lingering the

longest on Venturi's, before continuing.

"A victim's advocate, a social worker at the hospital where she was treated, helped her. She came to Miami, worked at the hospital, shared an apartment with another girl, and was doing beautifully" — Keri put a protective arm around the girl's narrow shoulders — "until last week. That was when she saw her father and her oldest brother watching the building where she lives.

"They will kill her if they can, then claim it was their duty to do so. She needs our help."

They both knew exactly what Keri meant. She eagerly watched their faces, eyes expectant.

Venturi was furious that anyone could turn such savagery on their own child or sibling. He hated himself for what he said next.

"Has she filed a police report? Did she apply for a restraining order?"

Keri blinked in disbelief, tears welling. "Yes, to both." She sat taller in her chair. "But as you are aware, they are paper. Nothing more."

She gave him a baleful look. They all knew that women with restraining orders die violent deaths every day.

"Too bad Danny isn't here," Keri whispered wistfully.

Is she implying that Danny has a bigger heart? Venturi wondered. *That he's man enough to right a wrong without hesitating?*

Even Victoria watched him with troubled eyes, her brow furrowed.

"I'll give this some thought and call you later," he said, getting to his feet.

"Thank you for listening," Keri said coldly.

For the first time Maheen looked up and made eye contact with Venturi and then Victoria.

"I am an American," she said, her voice a whisper. "I love America. All I ask is to live and work like an American. To live . . ." She chewed her puckered lip and averted her eyes again.

Before leaving, Keri turned and stared at Venturi in bewilderment. Then the two women disappeared into the dark. He let them go, watching the car's taillights vanish into the night.

"Do you think they're safe?" Victoria asked in alarm. "How can we let that girl go back to her apartment?"

He knew she believed the girl would be safe there with them.

"So scarred, so young, with no one," she

372

said. She cocked her head, trying to read his expression. "What's wrong, Mikey?"

"I've got a lot on my mind."

She waited for him to explain. He didn't.

He spent a long and sleepless night, trying to block the image of the girl's scars, imagining what the acid had done to her breasts. He didn't call Keri later, though he wanted to. He wondered how much Dr. Gordon Howard could help Maheen and whether he'd accept the challenge. He knew this was no time to even entertain such thoughts. How could he? If he went down, his troubles could take them all down with him. He had to distance himself from the people he cared for the most.

He thought about former colleagues in the Marshals Service who hated him for wanting to do the right thing. About Gino Salvi behind bars, where he belonged. And the angry, anguished faces of parents whose little girls lay in grass-covered graves, where they did not belong.

How did the program fail? Again? If old enemies hunted down the newly murdered witnesses, how? Did the victims or their family members break the rules by contacting friends or relatives? Was the fatal factor the dead mens' reversion to criminal behavior? And what were the odds that both would screw up and pay for it so swiftly?

In the process of making amends he had endangered those he loved along with the people they'd helped. He cursed his life. He cursed his luck.

He checked the clock again and again. Time dragged by in excruciating slow motion. By 5:45 a.m. he could wait no longer. He heated the coffee from the night before, drank a cup of the bitter brew so hot that it burned his throat, walked barefoot to the war room, and picked up the phone. He sat alone in the dark listening to the dial tone, wondering if he was doing the right thing, then closed his eyes and punched in the numbers.

CHAPTER
THIRTY-TWO

She answered on the third ring.

"Hey, Ruthie. You awake?"

"I was up. Is it really you?" she whispered, shocked to hear his voice. "Where are you?"

"Still out of town. You alone?"

"What do you think? My life hasn't changed that much, unfortunately. I almost didn't pick up the phone. Caller ID said 'No Info.' I figured it was a wrong number."

"Glad you answered. It's good to hear your voice."

"Likewise. I've missed you a lot. You've obviously heard the news," she said. "What a mess. The office is in complete turmoil."

She sounded like the old Ruth Ann, the only real friend he had back in the office.

"Has my name come up?"

Her laugh was sardonic. "I'm surprised your ears haven't burst into flames."

"Do they have any idea what the hell happened? How could DelVecchio and Conte be hit so close together?"

There was a long pause.

"Omigod. Then you *haven't* heard."

He froze, dreading what was to come, praying to be wrong.

But he was right.

"You don't know what happened last night?"

"No." His voice sounded thin, like that of a newly orphaned child about to receive more bad news.

"Another witness was murdered."

"Not one of mine?" His prayer went unanswered.

"Carmine Cuccinelli. In Mobile, Alabama."

"I know where he was," Venturi snapped in frustration. "I put him there three years ago. What the hell happened?"

"It was savage, Michael. Unspeakable."

"Good God! Who's killing them?"

"Nobody knows, but they really want to talk to you. Since DelVecchio was killed, thrown off that bridge in Minneapolis, Salvi's been writing and calling from jail in New Hampshire. He insists he was framed by the same person who hit DelVecchio. Somehow he heard about the murder right away. Apparently they grew up in the same neighborhood. He called with another awful tirade yesterday. Unfortunately, I picked up the phone. Nobody else in the office will talk to him. Salvi hates you, Michael. He blames you for his nephew's death and his own arrest. His defense lawyer has put you on the witness list for his trial. He's pleading not guilty."

"Sure, he'll probably claim I killed the little girls and planted their bodies to frame him."

"It's all so crazy," she said. "You think he still might still have enough clout to orchestrate these hits from jail?"

"No way," he said. "Given his reputation as a rat and now as a child predator, he probably doesn't know anybody who wouldn't like to kill him. And how would he know their new names and locations? One, maybe. But all three? Does anybody up there have a credible theory, or even a clue?"

"No, but they sure want to talk to you. Their world is about to implode. I'll be surprised if any of us have jobs by the time it's over. Brian Ross, that investigative TV news reporter, found out that DelVecchio was in WITSEC and is about to air a story. To make matters worse, Conte's widow is mad as hell. She's agreed to a television interview condemning WITSEC for failing to keep its promises and protect her husband."

"Damn. Anybody try to talk her out of it?"

"Are you kidding? An entire team, agents and prosecutors, including Archbold, were practically on their knees, promised her a new location, a new identity, the goddamn moon. But she wants none of it. She's totally pissed off. Right after her husband's murder she gave the local homicide detectives his real name and the contact number of his control person in the Marshals Service. They were told that no one in the U.S. Marshals Service had ever heard of her or her husband. They went round and round. She asked for you first, by the way. Said you were the only federal agent her husband trusted."

"What did they tell her?"

"That you were no longer with the service. By the way, her interview is with *Sixty Minutes.*"

"Holy shit."

"The boss urgently wants his people to have face time with you, Michael. If I were you, I'd make the first move. If you reach out to them, you can keep a little control over the situation. If you don't, it's just a matter of time before they come a'knocking.

378

They know you went to Florida."

He sighed. "Thanks for the heads-up."

"I know you tried to do the right thing, Michael. I've always thought a lot of you. Still do. You were the best they had. If I need to, is there a way to reach you?"

"I'll call you," he said.

"Take care. This is more serious than I can tell you. Be careful what you say. And watch your back."

The echo of those words resonated as he watched the news at seven a.m.

By ten a.m., he'd booked a flight to Atlanta and reserved a room at a hotel on Peachtree Drive. Then he called the U.S. Marshals office in New York City and asked for the chief.

"Michael Venturi here," he said crisply.

His response was a brief silence. The chief was obviously signaling someone else that he was on the line.

"Venturi! Good to hear from you," he boomed too heartily. "Bet I know what prompted this call."

"Right, I've been out of the loop. Fishing, boating, taking it easy. Just heard the news."

"I'm surprised it escaped you, the way you study newspapers so carefully."

Venturi ignored the comment. "It's all

hard to believe. Any idea who's responsible?"

"We thought we might ask you."

"Haven't heard a thing since you took my
badge. Last I knew, when I was still on the
job, those guys showed no signs of problems. Obviously a lot has gone down since.
Because I knew them and their families, I
thought I'd offer to help if you think there's
anything I can do."

"Your name did come up because, as you
say, you knew them so well. Nice of you to
call, Venturi. Frankly, I'm surprised you did.
You seemed so disillusioned with the job,
even bitter, the last time we spoke."

Venturi wondered who else was listening,
how many had gathered around the chief's
desk.

"Nothing that a good vacation and some
R and R couldn't cure," he said evenly.

"We can send some people down to meet
with you tomorrow. If you can just give me
your —"

"Sure," Venturi said affably. "But I'm
about to leave town on business. Maybe,"
he added brightly, almost as an after-
thought, "I can meet your guys halfway, in
Atlanta."

It had to be on neutral turf, far from

home, his personal life, and those close to him.

The chief was hot for it. "Let's say tomorrow, late morning, at the U.S. Attorney's office in Atlanta."

"Whoops, that interferes with my business meetings," Venturi lied, as though consulting his calendar. "How about my hotel? I can call your guys when I see a break in my schedule."

Had to be neutral turf.

"The U.S. Attorney's office is more convenient," the chief replied brusquely.

He'd be crazy to walk into that lion's den alone.

"Well, maybe it's better to wait until next week." Venturi sounded disappointed. "Hey, by then it may not be necessary. They must be working around the clock, running down leads, checking out suspects. They might wrap it up by then."

"What hotel? Where are you staying in Atlanta?" the chief demanded. Obviously there was little chance that the murders would be swiftly solved.

Venturi gave the chief his hotel information. "Have you tightened security and reached out to other witnesses?" he asked.

He heard the smile in his former boss's words.

"Sorry, Michael. You, of all people, know we don't divulge sensitive information to the public."

So now I'm the public, he thought after hanging up. He quickly punched in another number.

"Clay? I know it's short notice, but I need a polygraph done ASAP. Strictly confidential. An emergency. You available?"

"I'll make the time."

"I'm on the way."

"Is Danny coming?"

"No."

"So it's just you and the subject?"

"No. Just me."

After the lie detector test in Clay's office, Venturi went home to pack. He plugged a TravelDrive into his computer and backed everything up. He locked the laptop into the war room's floor safe, secured the hurricane shutters, checked the alarm system, and left a note for Victoria. He said he'd be away for a few days.

He carried his bag out to the car and cursed softly under his breath. A car had pulled up to his gate.

CHAPTER
THIRTY-THREE

Keri stopped her car halfway up the driveway, stepped out, and stood watching him. Hugging her elbows, face solemn, she looked small and forlorn in sneakers and green scrubs, a breeze lifting her hair. He bit his lip, stowed his bag, slammed the trunk lid too vigorously, and turned to face her.

She hadn't moved. He sighed and tried to smile as he walked toward her, regretting bitterly that he had not moved faster. Had he made his getaway five minutes ago, he'd be gone with no questions, awkward explanations, or recriminations.

He couldn't tell her the truth. Her life focused on her job. He didn't want her distracted by fears that her career, or he, might be in jeopardy. He hated lying.

He hated the look in her eyes even more.

They held a gaze for several beats. He looked busted. She looked hurt.

"You're leaving town?" she said, speaking first. "Without saying good-bye. How long? Is it for good?" Her lower lip quivered.

"No, it's not for good."

"Going to the airport? Taking a tour? Embarking on a cruise?" she asked lightly. "What about Maheen?"

"I have something to take care of first."

"What?"

"It's personal, and complicated."

"Whatever happened to no secrets? Or is it that I am not smart enough to understand something complicated? Or that I'm not a big girl who can handle it?"

He sighed. "You are the smartest, coolest, and most beautiful woman I know. I wanted to call you last night," he said earnestly. "I needed to . . . but couldn't. I can't expose you, or anyone else, to problems you shouldn't be involved in."

"I'm already involved." She raised her stubborn chin. "I volunteered."

He worried about the time but avoided checking his watch. Doing so wouldn't score him any points. In his head, he could hear the relentless *tick, tick, tick* of the *60 Minutes* clock. Traffic would be a bitch. Detours and major construction stood between him and the airport.

"Let's sit down," he said, and stroked her

384

hair lightly. They sat on a decorative stone bench Victoria had installed between the flower and the vegetable gardens she had planted. He tried to behave with Keri as though he had all the time in a world that revolved around her.

"I've got baggage. Some of it involves the reason I left the Marshals Service."

She frowned, her eyes curious. "What sort of baggage?"

He sighed, as though the story was too long, too complex, and too painful to tell.

"I'm the reason two little girls were murdered by a sexual predator. They were eight and nine years old."

She recoiled, then stared as he told her about Salvi.

"How could you?" she muttered eventually. "When you knew who and what he was?"

His explanations sounded lame even to him.

Though they sat beside each other, it was as though they were a thousand miles apart.

"I'm afraid for you," he concluded, head down, elbows on his knees. "And for Vicki, for Danny, for everybody who helped us, and for the people we took to the airport. This mess is mine. I own it. It's all my fault. Now I have to figure out what broke and

385

how to fix it."

He looked up and was startled. He saw no sympathy in her eyes.

"How can you live with yourself?" she demanded. She didn't wait for an answer. He heard her ragged sob as she sprang to her feet and nearly ran to her car. He realized she'd heard nothing beyond two little girls murdered. Nothing else he said mattered.

He did not go after her.

She threw her convertible into reverse and backed out at a high rate of speed. He wondered where Maheen was, if she was safe, as Keri's car fishtailed in the dust. She veered onto the main road and burned rubber.

He watched her speed away and wondered if it was for good.

He called Victoria from the airport to say he'd left a note, without indicating its brevity. He dodged her questions with a lie, saying his plane was boarding.

It wasn't.

He took a taxi from Atlanta's airport to his hotel. The young desk clerk scrutinized him surreptitiously as he registered. Moments later, when he glanced back from the lobby elevator, the clerk was on the telephone.

From his room Venturi ordered dinner. While waiting for the meal, he swept the room for a camera or a listening device. He found it in a fire alarm sprinkler head in the ceiling. He didn't tamper with it or ask to change rooms.

He knew the three phones, on the bedside table and the desk, and in the bathroom, would be monitored from the hotel's telephone room.

He turned to the business pages of the Atlanta newspapers he'd picked up at the airport and began to make local calls on his prepaid cell phone using the names and titles of people whose names appeared in articles. He spoke to them about various business deals and haggled over investments, franchises, options, and real estate. He confirmed meetings, dropped first names, last names, full names, and various interchangeable combinations. He wheeled and dealed, energized and animated, doing business, making money, having fun.

The conversations were all one-sided. There was never a voice at the other end. His cell phone was turned off. But he improvised enough fascinating dialogue to keep investigators busy for days checking it out.

"I'd like my participation kept strictly confidential," he'd say during each call. "As you know, I prefer to stay low-profile when it comes to business."

He didn't care whom the FBI annoyed, interviewed, called, or questioned as long as they didn't approach anyone near and dear to him.

After tipping the server well, he ate prime rib and a caesar salad, and drank half a carafe of excellent wine.

Later he stretched out on the soft bed, sipped scotch from the minibar, and "called" an imaginary lady friend in Atlanta. He announced his arrival and arranged a romantic rendezvous for the following evening. He chatted with her about mutual acquaintances, dropped more names, a few fictional, others straight out of the newspaper, and mentioned a number of events he'd recently attended. None of it was true. But it gave the FBI lots of people, places, and facts to sift through. Enough, he hoped, to keep them too busy to focus on the real people in his life.

His "conversation" with the lady evolved into playful sex talk. He grinned, imagining the investigators, who could only hear his side of their intimate discussion, creatively filling in the gaps as he reacted to the woman's propositions and racy remarks.

He ended the marathon phone session at one a.m., leaving hours of conversations to transcribe, dozens of people to interview.

He double-locked the door and retired. He hadn't slept the night before and needed to be alert for what was to come. Still, he stared sleepless at the ceiling, acutely aware of what failure would bring. The FBI would probe his bank records, personal life, close associates, and recent activities. That scrutiny would prompt questions he dared not answer. Images from the lonely graveyard of his past filled the night around him. The little girls. Dead. Salvi's nephew in camouflage. Dead. Every man he killed in the military, faces he thought he'd forgotten. They all materialized like an angry mob.

He replaced their faces with the people he had to protect. Danny asleep beside his wife, their baby in her belly, their young children dreaming nearby. At least he imagined Danny asleep beside his wife. No one was ever sure where Danny really was or what he was doing. The only certainty was that Danny would always cover his back.

He thought of Keri curled up in her bed, beeper nearby, or masked in a sterile environment as she delivered a small and helpless new life into a dangerous and unpredictable world. And Victoria, safe and asleep in her room at his home, her metal and plastic prosthesis resting against the headboard. And Scout, on his dog bed, legs jerking as he ran free through some canine field of dreams.

Alone in his strange bed, in a strange room, Venturi endured the night terrors that slither into guilty minds like snakes in the dark. He knew, to his infinite regret, that they would all be safer had he never intruded into their lives.

Madison appeared as always, along with those recent brief acquaintances, the legally dead, still alive and breathing out there in the world.

He wished Keri was beside him, his thoughts strictly carnal. Time in her arms would bring him the peace he needed for sleep.

Exhausted at dawn, he made an effort to sound cheerful when he called room service. He ordered a hearty breakfast despite his lack of appetite. He projected the image of an innocent and successful, happy man with a healthy lust for food, drink, and sex, not necessarily in that order, a man at the top of his game in both life and business. He put on a good act.

The bright eyes of the young woman who

delivered breakfast roved his room as she arranged the meal on his desk. Hotel employee? he wondered. Or rookie agent on her first undercover mission? Hoping she was FBI, he tipped her lavishly in cash, asked her first name, then called her sweetheart instead. He did everything but pinch her backside, hoping she'd walk out of his room with serious questions about her career choice.

Later, whenever the food service cart rumbled down the hall, he'd peer through the peephole. Someone else was always pushing it. He didn't see her again.

He picked at the food: three eggs over easy, bacon, sausage, hash browns, a side of grits, a tall orange juice, a pot of fresh coffee, and a small wicker basket piled high with fragrant sweet rolls and miniature Danish. He wished Scout, whose appetite never flagged, was there to enjoy it.

Without activating his cell phone he continued to make fake business calls. He even used a second cell, brought for that purpose, to call the first so that his phone rang constantly.

"No way!" he informed one caller. "I want no part of that. Not on your life."

He paused, as though listening.

"Screw profits!" he boomed indignantly.

"It's a goddamn federal offense. Run it by your lawyer. He'll tell you. Way too risky. Count me out."

He canceled their fictional meeting, then used the hotel room phone to call the number the chief had given him. He was not surprised to hear Archbold, the prosecutor, answer. The lawyer tried without success to persuade him to meet them at the U.S. Attorney's office.

When Archbold reluctantly agreed to come to the hotel, Venturi said his room was much too uncomfortable, too small, and hadn't been made up yet. He offered to meet instead in the hotel's main dining room in an hour.

The more public the better.

Not sure what the FBI could set up in an hour, he hung the Do Not Disturb sign on his door and went downstairs to explore.

He found a conversation pit with potted palms, hanging plants, and big comfortable armchairs around a coffee table in a secluded atrium off the lobby.

He rearranged the chairs, then returned to his room. Aware that the FBI would examine whatever he'd left there, he selected random numbers from the Atlanta phone book and scribbled them on a pad next to the bedside phone. He took his mostly uneaten breakfast and left the tray outside a suite down the hall around the corner and past the ice machine. They didn't need to know that their imminent arrival had killed his appetite. He left a laptop he'd brought with him, snatched up his briefcase, and took the elevator down to the dining room, stopping only once, to dispose of his newspapers in a receptacle two floors below.

The dining room staff was busy setting up long banquet tables, a microphone, and a podium during the lull before lunch. When Venturi said he expected some colleagues shortly, the maître d' quickly pointed out "a quiet table" near a bay window visible from the street. Asked about the banquet tables, he said they were for today's Chamber of Commerce luncheon.

Perfect.

Venturi ordered coffee, took a few sips, then saw Archbold arrive with two strangers. He went to greet them, pumped Archbold's hand, and was introduced to Snow, a boyish-looking FBI agent in his thirties, and Harrington, a veteran in his fifties.

"Sorry." Venturi frowned as though annoyed. "We can't stay here. The Chamber of Commerce is about to descend. But I have a place where we can talk in private."

Archbold and the agents exchanged

glances, then all three trailed him across the lobby, past the elevator bank, to the secluded nook near the atrium. Venturi slid into the only chair shaded by greenery from the sun streaming through a skylight.

"We can have coffee brought out," he said, taking secret pleasure in the way they sank into the soft cushy armchairs that made it impossible to maintain their posture and authoritative demeanor. They declined coffee. They wanted answers.

Archbold kicked it off, mildly asking how and what Venturi was doing these days. The older agent fumbled for his shades. The other squinted into the blazing sun.

The money made Venturi's answers easier. His former colleagues were aware of Madison's death along with their unborn child and the cash settlement that eventually followed. They were also aware of his spartan lifestyle. He never lived above the income his paycheck provided.

They'd even wondered aloud why he worked at all. They compared him to a lottery winner who reports to work as usual the day after his big win. At least they did until Ruth Ann coldly pointed out that what happened to him "wasn't like winning the lottery, it was like losing it."

"After my wife and baby were killed,"

Venturi candidly told Archbold and the two agents, "I received a substantial financial settlement." He paused. "But I could never bring myself to touch it. It felt too much like blood money. But after I turned in my badge, I took time off to decide how to spend the rest of my life. That's when it finally seemed right to use those assets to make the transition easier."

Archbold listened, the agents took notes. Their questions made it clear he was suspected of passing confidential information to the victims' enemies. Or that he killed them himself.

Unanswered questions about the armored-car robbery and Salvi's arrest had created enormous hostility among his embarrassed superiors who were now under fire. The Salvi case created a storm in the press, public outrage, and, worst of all, the high-profile scrutiny of a Congressional oversight committee whose members were scheduling hearings, asking questions, and compiling reports.

Losing the Schoenberg case was unforgivable.

No one could prove what role, if any, Venturi had played in the entire debacle. But speculation flourished, private conclusions were reached. Certain people, powerful people, would never forgive him. They *wanted* him to be guilty.

Pinning everything, including murder, on him would be justifiable payback in their eyes.

He saw their side, and it dismayed him.

They could build a case based on his state of mind after his wife's death. He had taken little time off, received no counseling, started drinking. Their lost infant was a girl.

Prosecutors could forge a believable argument that when the little girls disappeared, Venturi focused on Salvi and lost it. That he was a disgruntled former employee bent on undermining the program.

He'd sound like a madman.

His lawyer, he thought, could build a defense based on temporary insanity or diminished capacity. How outlandish to be thinking about a defense. How ludicrous to think he'd need one. The killers were out there somewhere. The three men carefully scrutinizing his demeanor and noting every word should get off their fat federal asses and go find them.

Pressed for his whereabouts at the time of each murder, he was deliberately vague. "All I know," he said, frowning, "is that I was in the South Florida area. I'm not sure of precise dates, but this trip is the farthest north I've been since I left the Marshals Service."

They asked what he thought had happened to the three murdered witnesses.

"Hard to say. It's been a long time. Conte's wife was always a concern because of her family ties. Their sons were relocated with them, but her parents insisted on staying in New Jersey. She cried a lot, and I knew she'd be tempted to contact them. You know how family members gossip and leak secrets to friends.

"The other two seemed to be doing fine. I don't know what they got into." He shook his head. "We all know that one in four, that we know of, reverts to old criminal behavior, or picks up new, nasty habits. Like Sammy the Bull.

"Wouldn't it be ironic," he speculated, thinking aloud, "if their deaths had nothing to do with their pasts?"

They didn't buy that; he saw it in their eyes.

He cocked his head, as though thinking it through. "Of course, the time frame tells us they must be related. They took place in such quick succession." He frowned. "That can't be coincidence.

"What's your theory?" He looked from one to the other. "Have you got ballistics, or forensics linking them? Witnesses? Descriptions? Tag numbers?"

No one responded. "You know we can't discuss an open investigation," Archbold finally said.

Then what the hell am I doing here? he thought.

The dumb fucks were too stupid to trust the one person who might help them. They intended to pick his brain without revealing anything in return. It was what he expected, what Danny had predicted, but it still pissed him off.

"Are you willing to undergo a polygraph test?" Archbold asked casually.

"Absolutely not! No way," he said, properly indignant. "Why should I?" He raised his voice. "I've done nothing wrong. Not a damn thing. I've spent my whole adult life in service to my country. And you'd accuse me?" He rose to his feet as though to leave in a huff.

"Calm down," Harrington said soothingly. He gestured toward Venturi's chair. "Take a seat. Don't fly off the handle. We're not accusing you. But if anyone raised the question, it would be convenient to say you've been eliminated. It would save us all time and trouble."

Reluctantly, still scowling, Venturi sat down.

"I resent the implication," he said, his voice tight. "I thought I might assist in your investigation. That's why I'm here, because I know them. *Knew* them."

"That's the hell of it," Snow said. "You knew them and their locations. Obviously people will look at you."

Venturi thought for a moment, drummed his fingers on the coffee table, his anger appearing to subside. "If I agreed, it would have to be a highly regarded and experienced private polygraph operator, not someone from your office."

The three men exchanged glances. "That can be arranged," Archbold said. "There are good people in Atlanta. I'll get some names."

"Do that," Venturi said. "But no fishing expeditions. Only questions relevant to the three cases."

They agreed.

Snow could not hide his elation.

Archbold made some calls and came up with three names. One was Joe Harper, the man Clay had said was the best in Atlanta.

"I don't know any of them." Venturi scanned the names. He shrugged. "How about number three, Harper?"

Three hours later he was seated in an office near the courthouse. They agreed to four relevant questions.

There were also two control queries: "Do you believe I'm going to ask you any questions other than the ones we have discussed?" and: "In the past five years, did you lie to someone who trusted you?"

"Yes," he said to the latter, thinking of Victoria, just the day before.

"Did you kill, or do you know who killed, Dominic DelVecchio, also known as Louis Messineo?"

"No."

"Did you kill, or do you know who killed, Angelo Conte, also known as William Rubino?"

"No."

"Did you kill, or do you know who killed, Carmine Cuccinelli, also known as Joseph Mannozzi?"

"No."

"Did you ever give, sell, or provide to anyone the new identities and/or locations of any protected witnesses?"

"No."

They told him he'd passed.

I know, he thought, *because I passed the same test yesterday in Miami.*

Archbold and the two FBI agents were

crestfallen.

"What do you think?" Archbold asked him candidly, over a drink later. "Where would you start? What's your gut reaction?"

"I'd look where the files are," Venturi said. "Ask people with access to submit to polygraphs. I'd focus on finding what the three victims had in common — aside from me. They didn't know each other to my recollection, but they must be linked somehow. A mutual friend, enemy, or lover. Check ex-wives and childhood sweethearts. The neighborhoods where they grew up. The schools they attended. Find their juvenile records. See who they ran with back in the day. Maybe they did know each other once. Maybe . . ." He shrugged.

"Maybe, maybe, maybe." Archbold sighed. "Unless we get lucky, or a local cop stumbles onto something, it won't be easy."

"I really wish you good luck, man," Venturi said. He meant it.

Back in his room he found, as he expected, that the contents of the laptop he'd left had been accessed and copied. He'd filled the hard drive with endless files full of Sudokus. None of the numerical puzzles had been solved. With a playful smirk, he wondered what the super-serious FBI analysts and cryptologists would make of that.

Although he was eager to fly back to Miami, he stayed until the next day, still pretending to conduct business.

He didn't want them to realize that they were the only reason he had come to Atlanta.

Spirits lifted, Venturi relaxed on the flight home the next afternoon. He even began to think about how to help Maheen, the disfigured girl still in peril. He landed in Miami far more at ease than when he'd left, picked up his car at the airport, and drove home.

He used his remote to open the front gate but it stood motionless; the system failed. When he stepped out of the car to punch the code in manually, he saw why. The box containing the motor had been smashed, the gate forced.

He backed across the road and stopped behind some trees, took his gun from under the seat, locked the car, and returned to the house on foot. He vaulted the fence to avoid touching the gate, keeping out of view from the front windows, and ran to the front door. It hung open, kicked in, the wooden frame broken.

He entered cautiously, gun in hand. There had been no finesse used here, just brute force. The house was quiet. Too quiet.

Where was Victoria? Scout? What happened to the alarm? The control panel for the security system was dark, dead, dismantled.

He sidestepped down the hallway, light on his feet, back to the wall, stomach churning. Where were they?

He wanted to call their names but didn't dare.

The faucets were on in the guest bath, the one clients used. Water running out from under the door. No one inside. He let the water run and kept moving.

Scout's bed lay on the floor just inside Victoria's room. There were bloodstains and a bullet hole in the hallway wall. No one in her room. The mattress dragged off the bed, bureau drawers upended on the floor. He couldn't tell if the bed had been made. Did the intruder arrive in the dark? The thought chilled him to the core.

In a sudden panic, he headed for the war room. It, too, had been ransacked, savagely ripped apart, papers and files scattered everywhere. The floor safe had been forced open. His laptop was gone.

In it were the confidential files of the six people he'd relocated since coming to Florida. It would take work to decipher; the clients' original names were not included, but their new ones and their destinations were.

Why hadn't he erased them?

Rage overwhelmed him. Was it the government? No search warrant was posted. Who else knew he was out of town?

His mind raced. Were the recent killings an attempt to flush him out? If so, who was hunting him?

He turned off the faucets in the guest bath, then punched in Victoria's cell number. It went directly to voice mail. He heard something as he hung up. A stealthy footfall outside, or perhaps the wind in the melaleuca trees, or maybe the dog. The quiet house was full of shadows.

He positioned himself next to the front door. He would kill an intruder. He would be within the law but hated to have to explain it to the police.

He sensed rather than heard something. The door burst open an instant later. All he saw was the muzzle of a .45-caliber automatic inches from his face. He dropped, rolled for cover, took aim. His finger tightened on the trigger. Then he saw the face behind the .45 and gasped.

CHAPTER
THIRTY-FOUR

"Goddammit! I almost killed you!" Danny said.

"No you didn't!" Venturi stuck his gun in the back of his belt and punched at the wall. "I almost killed you!"

"Son of a bitch! You nearly bought it!"

"Like hell!"

Danny collapsed in a chair and inhaled a deep breath, his head between his knees, still clutching his gun. "Christ, we almost shot each other!" He glanced up, his eyes roving the shadows. "Is the place clear?"

"I've been through the whole house. Nothing. What the hell are you doing here?"

"Heard you left town, tried to call you, then came by to check things out." Danny squinted impatiently at the caller ID on the vibrating cell phone clipped to his belt, then ignored it.

"Vicki isn't here. I'll kill anybody who hurts her, I swear it, Danny. They took my

405

computer with the personal info on our clients," he said wearily, his voice thin, "and I think they killed my dog."

"Scout? Son of a bitch! My kids loved that dog."

"He's gone, too. And there's blood and a bullet hole in the hall near his bed."

"Did you call the cops?"

"Would you?"

"Hell, no. They don't investigate, they complicate. They'd try to justify their existence by writing reports we probably don't want to see on public record."

"We might have to call them if Vicki doesn't turn up fast. If she's been abducted or . . ." His voice trailed off.

"Where the hell were you?" Danny asked. "I hate hearing the news by eavesdropping on my wife. Keri was boo-hooing to Luz. Said you took off."

Venturi told him.

"I figured you'd take a preemptive strike. Shoulda told me, though. Did you forget everything you learned in the Marines? Teamwork, that's how you win." Danny surveyed the room. "Think they did this?" He checked his vibrating cell again, scowled, and didn't answer.

"Doubt it, but I hope it was the feds."

"Why?"

" 'Cuz if it wasn't them or a random junkie burglar, it's whoever killed those protected witnesses."

"Shit." Danny whistled between his teeth. "We're in trouble then. A random junkie burglar would have beat feet with the TV, the microwave, and the whiskey. They're still here. Damn, I hate when things get complicated."

"The only plus about the cops," Venturi said thoughtfully, "is their dandy toys, like high-tech forensics, which they would never use in a burglary investigation. Think we can get a crime-scene workup done here?"

"Sure," Danny said. "I know a guy. Used to run the crime lab at Miami-Dade. Former Navy submariner. Retired now. Lectures, teaches, writes scientific papers. I'll try to get him down here. Meanwhile, don't let anybody touch anything inside or out by the gate. Where the hell's your car?"

"I wanted to surprise anybody inside, so I left the car behind the trees on the other side of the road."

"That's why I almost killed you."

"No. I almost killed you."

Danny hand went again to his cell phone.

"Christ, Danny. Who keeps calling you?"

"My wife." He looked beleaguered. "I just saw her half an hour ago. We're busy, right?"

"She's pregnant, for God's sake. What if something happened to her or one of the kids? Find out what the hell she wants so she quits calling."

"Did you answer your cell when I called?"

"I was on a goddamn plane!"

"So I'll tell Luz I was on a goddamn plane!"

Danny rocked back and forth on his heels, edgy and restless. He didn't want to contaminate the crime scene, so he couldn't pace. "Look, I'll get Bill down here. Let's bail now, secure the place, and make sure nobody else walks in."

"Call your wife!"

Danny rolled his eyes, but when his cell vibrated again seconds later, he checked the caller ID, then answered.

"Wuzup, babe?"

He listened, then raised a significant eyebrow at Venturi. "Good, hon. Shoulda called me right away. Oh. I didn't hear it. He's with me. We're on the way."

"You were right, amigo." He snapped his phone shut. "Shoulda answered. Good news. Vicki's at my place with Luz. She's upset, but okay. Says somebody broke into your house. Wants to talk to you. Let's go."

Danny called Bill on the way. More good news. He agreed to meet them at the house in an hour.

"Can he be trusted?" Venturi asked. "Once a cop, always a cop. He must still have ties to the department."

"Don't worry about him," Danny said confidently.

Luz met them at the door. "Have you talked to Keri?" she asked Venturi.

"No, I just got back in town."

"I can't reach her." She gazed balefully at him, one hand resting on her belly.

"Where's Vicki?" Venturi said anxiously. "Is she all right?"

"In the Florida room, resting. Did somebody really break in?"

He nodded.

"I'm sorry," she murmured earnestly, her soulful dark eyes brimmed in compassion and something else that he couldn't quite place, as though she knew something he didn't.

He didn't pause to pursue it.

Victoria was already on her feet, using her cane. Her usually impeccable hair was tousled, her clothes disheveled. "I heard your voice," she said. "Thank God you're all right."

"Ditto. I was worried as hell about you."

Danny strode into the room, his face serious. "Hey, bro, something you should see."

409

He went to the window and rolled up the rattan shade.

Danny's kids were at play in the backyard. Then Venturi saw what they were chasing.

"Damn!" he said with relief.

Danny called the children to come wash their hands before dinner. They resisted, balked, and begged for more time. But Scout flew like a bullet, bolted through the door, and jumped all over Venturi.

"Is he happy to see you, or to escape from my kids?" Danny grinned.

The dog panted and grinned as Venturi scratched his head, rubbed his belly, and checked him for injuries. Other than a bruised nose, he appeared unscathed. "What happened?" he asked, turning to Vicki.

"I'm so sorry, sweetheart, so sorry," she said contritely. She wrung her hands. "I didn't know where you were, or how to reach you. I wanted to call the police but was afraid it might be a mistake. I tried and tried to call you. I didn't know what to do."

"Start from the top."

"I went out for groceries and gas at about eleven this morning. When I came back just before two, the gate was broken, and Scout was loose outside, standing by the side of the road. I'd left him in the house. The front door was open and there was a terrible mess inside. Water running, overflowing, every-where. The faucets were all on, full blast. I ran from room to room, turning them off, until Scout started barking out by my car. I panicked. I thought he'd come back." She hiccupped a sob. "I was afraid to face him alone. I think the water was still running in the guest room.

"I couldn't see what Scout was barking at. I think a car had pulled up to the gate. It was gone by the time I got out there. I didn't know what to do, so I took the dog and left. I didn't know when you'd be back, so I came here.

"I'm so sorry he did this to you." Tears streaked her face.

"Who?" Danny asked.

"Sidney, of course." She fumbled for a handkerchief. "Who else would do such a thing?"

Danny turned to Venturi. "Your brother-in-law?"

Venturi nodded, sat next to Vicki, and took her hand.

"He's furious at me," she whispered. "I told him he's wrong, but he blames you for everything. For having me here, for persuad-ing me to prosecute, and refusing to post his bond."

"Think he'd come here while free on bond

in New York? How would he find my place?"

"He's been calling even more than I've said," she admitted. "He wants me to drop the charges, goes into rants, accuses me of abandoning him."

"And how would he find my place?" Venturi repeated, fearing the answer.

"He's my son. I am his next of kin." She averted her eyes. "I know now it was stupid, but he called weeping one night, said it wasn't right that he didn't know where his own mother lived. I gave him the address. I'm so sorry."

"That was a mistake," he said. "But I'd be very happy if Sidney is responsible."

"But why, Michael?"

"Because it would rule out more dangerous people."

"I wish it wasn't him," she said. "Then I wouldn't feel it's my fault. But it's his style, his MO. He's done it before."

Danny checked his watch. "Let's go find out, amigo. Bill will be at your place in twenty."

CHAPTER
THIRTY-FIVE

Bill wore a gray-streaked ponytail, boots, blue jeans, and a T-shirt with a submarine on the front and the message: THERE ARE 2 KINDS OF BOATS — SUBMARINES AND . . .

Venturi wondered what the second was but didn't ask. He saw the answer when Bill turned his back to inspect the damaged gate: . . . TARGETS.

He and Danny greeted each other like long-lost brothers.

Vicki was still at Danny's. Convinced at first that Sidney was guilty, she now harbored hope that he was innocent. Venturi hoped as fervently that he was not.

What else, he wondered, *had Vicki told her errant son?* He kept secrets, so it troubled him when those he trusted didn't.

"It never occurred to me that she might confide our business to that junkie burglar piece of crap," he told Danny.

"Blood is thicker, my friend," Danny said. "Your mother will take you in when nobody else will."

Mike wouldn't know. His own mother fell dead on the street, killed by an aneurysm as she shopped for produce in New York's Little Italy, when he was fourteen. He fondly remembered her hugs, her smell, the fragrant herbs in her kitchen.

"A mother will mortgage the farm to bail a badass son out of jail, then lie for him in court," Danny was saying.

"Mother or not, I hope to hell it was snot-nose Sidney," Venturi said. "He's no problem. He's already a quart low and knocking."

"We'll know soon." Danny sounded confident. "The blood in that hall didn't come from your dog."

Bill lifted transfer evidence, light blue paint, from the gate where the intruder had rammed it with his own vehicle. Bill suspected he'd used a truck. Some have painted bumpers. He measured the marks so he could match their height to a specific model. The gate sprang back after being struck. Its white paint would probably be found on the suspect's vehicle.

He photographed the tire tracks from four

angles, using a tripod and a detachable strobe, painstakingly removed tiny pebbles and vegetation that had fallen into the impressions, then photographed them again. After measuring the tracks, he took impressions with Diecast, a plasterlike product mixed with water.

He obtained the vehicle's track width by measuring the distance between the tires and calculated the wheelbase by measuring from the leading edges of the front and rear tire impressions. Then he'd use the figures to search a database for vehicles that could have left the impressions.

"Bill's the best," Danny muttered, as they watched him work. "Guarantee this burglary will be better investigated than most homicides."

"I need that laptop back," Venturi said grimly, "for peace of mind. Sidney's not smart enough to do any damage with it." He shuddered at what someone smarter and more dangerous might do.

"If he did this," Danny muttered, "we should shoot Sidney's skinny ass and dump him out there." He nodded toward the Glades.

"He's not worth a murder rap," Venturi said.

"It wouldn't be murder," Danny said,

"more like retroactive birth control."

Bill worked quickly and efficiently while he still had some light and it wasn't raining. Towering storm clouds built in the west. After determining the vehicle's turning radius, he concluded that it was a pickup truck.

He studied the shoe impressions leading from the truck to the front door and collected soil samples that might match those found on the intruder's shoes or in his truck.

"Some people claim the soil's all the same in this part of the state. It's not," Bill explained. "It's often a mix of lots of things. People use compost, fertilizer, or mulch. Sometimes you can make a perfect match." He turned to Venturi. "If you find your suspect, collect his shoes ASAP. That'll minimize any changes to the tread. Package them separately and get them to me."

Impressions on the front door appeared to be made by a sneaker. The pattern could identify the brand.

Determined to finish outside before dark, Bill hadn't even checked the house. When he did carry his equipment — fingerprint powder and brushes, chemicals, swabs, a master processing kit, and a handheld UV alternate light source — into the house, he stopped for a moment and smiled.

The intruder had touched so many things, had been so active, he'd obviously worked up a sweat. Even if he wore gloves, he surely touched his head, face, or beard. Even a smudged fabric impression could yield DNA.

"You sure?" Venturi asked.

"The sample is only as good as the collector and the test as good as the examiner, but oh, yeah, sure, it's doable," Bill assured him.

The intruder had spent considerable time and had been inside all three bathrooms. Bill processed the underside of each toilet seat, the walls nearby, and all the doorjambs for fingerprints.

"You can't take a leak with socks on your hands," he said.

He studied the blood trail in the hall. "I can tell you right away if it's animal or human. A species test is simple."

"It's probably the perp's," Venturi said. "We thought it was my dog's. But he turned up uninjured after we called you."

"Definitely human," Bill affirmed in minutes. "I can give you the blood type tonight. That's the good news. The bad news is that same-day DNA results happen only on television. It takes a week to ten days, and then, if your suspect isn't in the database, you have to find somebody to match it to."

"But we can rule out or identify a suspect with mitochondrial DNA from his mother, right?" Venturi said.

"Most definitely." Bill focused on the blood. "The tails on the drops show the source's direction of travel. You can see from the edges of these drops that they fell several feet from an upper extremity. And there" — he pointed — "see where the drops look like stretched-out exclamation marks? They flew through the air and hit the wall. The end of the stain with the smallest blob reveals which way the bleeding individual was moving.

"And here we have circular blood drops that fell less than twelve inches at a forty-five-degree angle." He shot photos and stepped back to scrutinize the scene.

"That bullet hole is in the wall a foot away. Looks like he missed a shot at close range. He was using his left hand.

"What kind of dog do you have?"

They described Scout, as Bill pieced it all together.

"Up to here," Bill said, "the dog is following and probably barking. But as the intruder approaches the bedrooms, the dog becomes more aggressive.

"He bites the intruder's lower leg or ankle,

drawing blood. The man takes a swing at the dog, who latches onto his arm, tearing the flesh with his teeth.

"The man swings again or tries to throw the dog off. That motion casts his blood onto the floor and the wall.

"He moves this way," Bill said, following the intruder's path. "Trying to fight off the dog, he fumbles for his gun and tries to shoot him. He fires from his left. Surprising to miss at such close range. He must be right-handed. He's not ambidextrous. Lucky dog."

After being shot at, Scout must have retreated, bolted out the front door and ran through the gate.

"Good dog," Venturi murmured.

"So he's a biter," Danny said with a frown, "and he's home playing with my kids, one of whom is also a biter."

He called Luz and told her not to let the children play too aggressively with Scout, who was asleep on Julee's bed at the moment.

"I'm gonna buy that dog a steak," Venturi said.

"He already ate." Danny snapped his phone shut. "Arroz con pollo. He likes chicken and yellow rice."

Bill collected hairs from Scout's bed and

standards from the rugs to match to hairs and fiber found on the suspect's clothes or in his truck, then dug the bullet out of the wall.

He raised his eyebrows at the war room, then examined the floor safe. "These aren't as secure as the ones built of concrete with round steel doors," Bill said. "All he needed was a hammer and chisel to peel it back. Had to work at it, though. How'd he know it was here?"

"Good question," Venturi said. "That throw rug covered it. Maybe he found it by accident. Or was looking for my laptop and wouldn't quit till he found it."

"Maybe," Danny said, "he already knew where it was."

They swept the entire place for cameras and listening devices. None had been planted.

Before Bill finished he wanted elimination fingerprints from anyone who'd lived there recently. He took Mike's and Danny's.

"What if he runs the prints and finds Errol Flagg's or Laura's or Casey's?" Venturi told Danny privately. "They all had arrest records. There's never been a link between them and this house, or us."

"Trust Bill," Danny said.

"I don't know who to trust anymore."

"Okay, okay. Don't get paranoid. Bill knows nothing's on the record."

"But like you always say, people make mistakes," Venturi argued. "What if Bill hits the wrong computer key? Or his assistant finds the standards on his desk and decides to do him a favor by running them through the national database? If hits start coming back, questions will be raised."

"We're not dealing with the police department. Bill works alone." Danny rolled his eyes. "Mike, trust somebody, sometime. Trust me."

They secured the front door and padlocked the gate.

Despite the hour, they went to Danny's to wake Victoria.

"So this is the big bad guard dog," Bill said as Scout scrambled from Julee's room to greet them, tail wagging.

"I wish he could talk," Venturi said.

"Then you wouldn't need me," Bill said.

Venturi rapped on the guest-room door. It took Vicki several minutes to answer.

"Michael, what is it?" She squinted at him, dazed. "Is something wrong?"

"No," he said. "We just need you in the kitchen for a sec."

She borrowed a bathrobe from Luz and joined them, pulling the robe more tightly around her when she saw the stranger.

"This is Bill," Venturi said. "He needs to take your fingerprints and a DNA swab."

She blinked. "It's the first time anybody ever asked me for that in the middle of the night."

Bill took her prints on the kitchen table.

"Nice." He studied his handiwork, as though admiring her loops, whorls, and swirls. He smiled. She smiled back.

Then he took a swab from inside her mouth.

"Vicki," Venturi said, "do you know Sidney's blood type?"

She gasped, her hand flying to her throat, where it left smudgy prints. "Has something happened to him?"

Danny rolled his eyes and turned to wink seductively at Luz, who was watching from the doorway. She was wearing one of his big Marine Corps T-shirts over her maternity pajama bottoms.

"No, not at all," Venturi assured Vicki. He explained.

She gave a slight nod. "Of course I know. He's A-positive, just like his sister. Remember, dear? Madison was A-positive."

He nodded. The sudden lump in his throat caught him by surprise.

He told Vicki he'd have a cleaning crew at

the house in the morning, along with the alarm company, a locksmith, and a repairman for the gate. Hopefully, home would be livable again by day's end.

Venturi planned to spend the night at his house in case anyone came back. But the place was trashed and he was exhausted. A lot had happened since his day began in Atlanta. He'd been relieved then, thinking he'd resolved his problems. Danny persuaded him to sleep in the pool cottage and get an early start in the morning. Luz gave him the key, then walked him to the Florida-room door.

"Sidney didn't do it," Luz said softly.

"Then who did?" he asked casually, wondering how much she knew. Did Danny tell her more than he let on? Did everybody in his life suffer from diarrhea of the mouth?

Luz pursed her lips, eyes mysterious. He didn't push it. He kissed her cheek and walked through the quiet yard to the cottage, Scout plodding behind him.

Exhausted, he went right to asleep. His cell phone woke him at precisely 4:22 a.m.

"His blood type is A-positive," Bill said. "I'll be back in touch." He hung up before Mike could respond.

CHAPTER
THIRTY-SIX

Danny responded to the news with a thumbs-up.

"Too soon to celebrate," Venturi warned. "It's a common blood type."

Vicki was sunny and smiling at breakfast. "I think I was wrong," she announced. "I believed it was Sidney. It looked like his work. But now I don't think so."

Sidney himself had changed her mind. He had called during the night with another rant. When accused, he swore he was in New York and had been since his release from jail. He also swore that he'd suffered no recent dog bites.

"What else would he say?" Venturi asked mildly.

"To prove it," she said, "he put total strangers on the phone to tell me where they were. They all said New York City, except for a man who was quarreling with his wife. He said he was in hell."

"Same thing," Venturi said. "Maybe he was in New York. There are jet planes. Let's ask his bondsman, his lawyer, and the prosecutor if he's been around lately, and whether he's sporting teeth marks on his right arm and ankle."

She agreed to make the calls while he dealt with the repairmen at his house.

He was meeting with ADT personnel hired to upgrade his alarm system with lights, sensors, and surveillance cameras when she called. The lawyers and the bondsman said that to their knowledge, Sidney had not been out of town lately. The bondsman said he'd check for dog bites.

Danny urged them to leave word for Sidney that Scout was foaming at the mouth and had been diagnosed with rabies.

They gathered at Danny's for a special event the following night. Luz checked the wall clock and pushed back her chair. "It's time! It's time!"

Danny clutched his heart. You know how I panic when you say that.

"TV time!" She laughed. "Okay?"

"Thank God." He sighed in fake relief.

The tension-building *tick, tick, tick* of the *60 Minutes* clock was already opening the show.

"You taping this?" Venturi said.

"Sure thing, it's rolling," Danny said.

The blonde wore black and was televised with her face in shadow for her protection.

"Guys with guns and badges knocked on my door in the middle of the night," she said. *"They scared the hell out of us, got us out of bed at two a.m. It was cold and pouring rain. My oldest boy wasn't home, he was spending the night at a friend's house in Clifton.*

"The marshal's name was Venturi, Michael Venturi."

Venturi looked pained. It was worse than he thought. "I didn't think they'd use my name."

"Nice work, bro," Danny said, from the sofa beside Luz. "Prime time, national TV. Nothing like keeping a low profile."

"He said we had to leave immediately and could never come back to Jersey. I thought he was joking. I said, 'What do you mean, never come back?' He told me to pack some clothes and sent one of the others to pick up my boy. He said my husband, Angelo, had agreed to testify against Niccolo Sabbatino and his crew.

"Angelo had just been sentenced to fifteen years for extortion. But the marshal said my husband was outta prison and in protective custody. Word was already on the street that

he'd made a deal, and Nico had put a hit out on him and his family. Another marshal with a gun was standing on my front porch watching the street like they thought guys with guns would be there any minute. Venturi said we had to get out. He said everything would be all right. And that's how it all started. He promised they'd take care of us. He said nothing would go wrong."

She fingered the crucifix on a chain around her neck. *"But it did. Eventually, everything went wrong."*

The reporter asked Celia Conte if she'd known her husband was considering an offer to testify against his longtime cohorts and join WITSEC, the federal witness protection program.

"Never." She shook her head vigorously. *"I visited him the weekend before. He was depressed about going to prison but never said nothing about that. I was shocked when they came to my door. Nobody asked us.*

"Venturi said they'd give us new names and we'd be relocated. I was born in Passaic, New Jersey, lived there my whole life. My family, my friends all live there. He said we couldn't even say good-bye.

"They sent us to Portland. We were all homesick. My sons were upset about leaving the old neighborhood and changing their

names. They didn't know who they were anymore. The marshals said they'd put my furniture in storage and send it to us. It didn't come for four months.

"Angelo joined us after a while, but he had to keep flying back and forth to testify at the trials. He'd be away for weeks, sometimes months. One time he came back really scared and pissed off. He flew into Newark as usual and somebody sent to pick him up at the airport missed him at baggage claim and had him paged, under his real name!

"He coulda got kilt right then and there. Everybody in that whole damn airport knew where he was."

"I had nothing to do with that," Venturi muttered, shaking his head. "It was really stupid."

"They warned me not to call my mother. Or my brothers. Nobody was supposed to know where we were. Everybody called Angelo a rat, but he lived up to his end of the deal, did a good job. They convicted them all, and Nico got a life sentence. Angelo came back feeling proud. They got him a job and things were going good. But after a while a man named Dominic DelVecchio got murdered. It was on the news. Somehow Angelo knew he was in the Witness Protection Program, too. He called the marshals, a little worried, and

428

asked, like what's going on? He wanted to talk to Venturi. He was the only one Angelo trusted. They would speak in Italian, like old friends or family. But nobody would put him through to Venturi, they kept giving him the runaround. Kept saying don't worry, don't worry."

Her voice trembled and she began to weep.

"Two days later, my Angelo was killed. Garrotted. I'll never get over it. He was worried, he called the program for help, but nobody did nothing. I told the Portland homicide detective my husband was in WITSEC and gave him the contact number. But when the detectives trying to solve my husband's murder called it, they were told nobody at WITSEC had ever heard of us. The detectives thought I was lying to them. I kept telling 'em to get ahold of Venturi. Finally somebody at WITSEC admitted he wasn't there no more. When they finally did talk to the detectives they admitted Venturi was also the contact for DelVecchio.

"What's going on? Where is Venturi?" Her voice rose. *"Is everybody he protected getting kilt? What is this? In the beginning they said we were safe, that they never lost a witness. In forty years nobody ever got kilt."*

The interviewer gently guided Celia Conte

through the last day of her husband's life. It was their twentieth wedding anniversary. They planned a night out and had invited another couple, new neighbors, to join them. Celia had just stepped out of the shower, about to dress for the evening, when there was a knock at the door.

She thought one of her boys had forgotten his key and answered the door without makeup, in a bathrobe, her hair in curlers.

It was déjà vu. Men with badges and bad news.

Crime-scene footage followed, then a brief interview with the lead homicide detective who described the case as "unique and very complex." He appeared offended that this problem had been visited on his city and his department by a federal agency.

"This case had nothing to do with Portland," he complained. "Everything that led up to this homicide happened elsewhere, outside our jurisdiction. We didn't even know the victim was in our city." He did not sound optimistic about solving the case.

Celia Conte said she and her sons were given a second set of new names and relocated to a strange city where, again, they know no one.

"It's easier for little kids to handle change," she said. *"They don't know no better, but my*

boys are young men, with schools, sports teams, and girlfriends. It's not fair.

"That's what the program did to us, how it took care of us." She dabbed frequently at her eyes with a handkerchief.

"If my husband had refused to testify and done his time in prison, at least he'd be alive. He'da come home in a few years. We'd still be a family. The way they treated us . . ." She broke down.

The interviewer went on to say that WITSEC's budget could be in jeopardy. After relocating more than twenty thousand people, federal witnesses and their families, over more than thirty-five years, politicians were now questioning the program's $55 million annual budget.

Those in command at WITSEC had declined on-air comment because of the continuing investigation, she said in conclusion, but they did confirm that U.S. Marshal Michael Venturi had been fired. Venturi, she said, could not be reached for comment.

"Ouch. She is *not* your friend," Danny said.

"Can't blame her," Venturi said. "Wish I could talk to her."

"That reporter?" Danny asked. "Wouldn't mind talking to her, myself." Luz jabbed him with her elbow.

"No," Venturi said. "Celia Conte. She met Angelo when she was a teenager. Was eighteen when they got married. None of this is her fault. What did she know?"

"She knew at some point what he did for a living," Vicki commented from her armchair.

"This can't be good," Danny said grimly.

Luz stood on tiptoe to kiss Venturi's cheek as he left. Her dark eyes shimmered liquid in the dim light, as she whispered, "Have you talked to Keri?"

"Left a message, she hasn't called me back."

"I can't reach her, either," Luz murmured. "Her phone goes straight to service and another doctor on call returns her messages. I'm not due for a while, but it makes me nervous." She patted her belly.

"I'll call you right away if I hear from her," he said.

Her expression was unsettling.

Brian Ross went on the air with his own report the next night. He fit yet another piece into the puzzle — the third protected witness, Carmine Cuccinelli, killed in Mobile, Alabama. As in the other two cases, his contact in WITSEC had been Michael Venturi.

Venturi, he said, was reportedly living in Miami, Florida.

"Eh, goombah." Danny pressed his palm to his forehead, eyes closed. "I now foresee . . . sound trucks rolling up to your gate."

When Venturi pulled up to the newly repaired gate an hour later, he saw a strange car, a late-model Audi, parked in his driveway, next to Vicki's. Had it already begun?

CHAPTER
THIRTY-SEVEN

He tucked his gun into the back of his belt and approached the front door cautiously.

He heard laughter inside. Bill and Victoria, drinking wine.

Bill wore a suit this time.

"Oh, here he is now," Victoria said, looking up as Venturi opened the door. "I'm glad you're home, dear."

"Thought I'd stop by," Bill told him. An eight-by-ten manila envelope lay on the coffee table beside his wineglass. "Probably should have called first."

The two men shook hands and retired to the war room.

"Gotcha some results," Bill said, after closing the door.

"Did you tell her?" Venturi asked, ready to fly off the handle if he had.

"Hell, no." Bill took a seat. "We were just talking." He looked around the room. "You didn't waste any time putting this place back together. You'd never know anything happened."

His eyes focused on Venturi. "Sorry to hear your name on *Sixty Minutes.* The press can be a bitch. Saw that and decided to deliver the results in person instead of by phone." Bill used a small Swiss Army knife on his key chain to slit open the still-sealed manila envelope. "The truck is a Ford. About forty-one thousand left the factory with those tires. Twelve thousand were blue. Eight hundred of 'em registered in South Florida. Of course, the truck could've been driven here from anywhere.

"I knew your first priority was to either eliminate or identify a particular individual. So I called in a favor to get a hurry-up on the DNA.

"Bottom line, the man who broke in here is in no way related to that fine woman out there."

The news hit Venturi like a sledgehammer. "You sure?"

"DNA doesn't lie."

"Damn." He rocked back in his chair, mind racing. "I was counting on it being that rotten little punk."

"Sorry," Bill said. "We got some good prints." He frowned. "None from the punk. A few still unidentified. Two hits."

"Who?"

"One," Bill said, his face screwing into a puzzled expression, "came back to an ex-convict from Massachusetts. Sex offender who did time for abusing children. The man and his wife both died here in South Florida recently, an apparent suicide pact."

Venturi feigned surprise. "Where'd you find that?"

"In that room you use for a gym."

"This place used to be a fishing camp," Venturi said. "I guess that explains it. What about the other?"

"A Russian punk last arrested in New York for attempted murder. Jumped bond last October, has outstanding arrest warrants. Ivan Kazakov, white male, age thirty-nine." He pushed the Russian's mug shot across the table.

Venturi stared. A blue-eyed, pockmarked, and bloated stranger with straggly, too-long dirty blond hair stared back arrogantly. He looked ten to fifteen years older than his stated age. "Never saw him before. I wouldn't forget that face."

"Seems to know you."

"Where were his prints?"

"The bottom of the toilet seat in the master bath, on the floor safe in this room, and on the hallway wall about a foot and half from the bullet hole, where he was tussling with your dog."

"Bingo!" Venturi said. "So he's the guy with Scout's teeth marks in his arm and ankle."

Bill nodded. "Dog did a good job — spilled the guy's blood and gave us his ID. Neither the dead ex-con nor the Russian has or had a blue Ford pickup registered. But the one he used mighta been rented, borrowed, or stolen." He got to his feet. "One other thing . . ."

Venturi tore his eyes off the Russian's picture and looked up expectantly.

"Do you mind if I take that lovely lady out there to dinner?"

"Now?"

Bill nodded.

That's why the man arrived better dressed and driving a flashy car instead of his work truck, Venturi thought. He had a dual purpose.

He felt protective, as though he were Vicki's father, but decided against trying to set a curfew.

"No, not at all," he said.

"Good," Bill said, "because I already asked and she said yes."

"Have a nice evening," Venturi said. "You do know she's the closest family I have."

"She'll be treated like royalty."

"Nothing less," Venturi said.

They joined Vicki in the living room.

"You were right," Venturi told her. "It wasn't Sidney."

"I'm elated," she said heartily. "But realistic enough to know that given the chance, he'd do as much, or worse." She smiled ruefully.

He showed her the Russian's picture.

"Ever see him here, or in New York? Drives a blue Ford pickup."

She studied the face and shook her head. "Can't say that I have. He doesn't look familiar."

Watching them leave in Bill's Audi ten minutes later, he picked up the phone.

"It wasn't Sidney," he said, his voice brittle.

"Crap," Danny said. "He was so right for it."

"DNA rules him out. Fingerprints rule in a Russian mobster out of New York, along with a certain late, lamented fire victim, whose prints are still on the chin-up bar in the gym."

"Whoops. What does that say about your housekeeping? What else?"

"Vicki just took off in a sports car — with Bill."

"Saw them hit it off the other night."

"Thanks for the heads-up," Venturi snapped. "Didn't see it at the time. You sure Bill can be trusted?"

"With your mother-in-law or our little secrets?"

"Both."

"I vouch for him, positutely."

"Good enough. I don't know where the Russian fits in, but our clients are compromised. The only thing he took out of this house is the laptop with their information. What if it's not about WITSEC but one of them that the killers want?"

"How do you figure?"

"What if somebody was trying to flush me out to find one of them?"

"And whacked three federal witnesses to do it?" Danny said skeptically.

"I don't know what to think." Venturi stared out a window into the twilight. "Why would anybody be hunting one of our people? Think one of them lied to us and was really on the run from something or somebody that ruthless?"

"Jesus," Danny said. "Which one?"

"No clue. I'll recheck their backgrounds. We're running out of time. Your vibes were right on, the news story is building. The press is bound to show up here. When they do it'll be impossible to accomplish anything. I might have to break the rules."

"And do what?"

"Call them. Reach out, warn them that their information is in the hands of a stranger with a violent past."

"We swore no contact."

"Who knew their new identities would be stolen?"

"I can reach out to Micheline."

"No so fast, Danny. Let me see what I can find out first."

He gave Danny the Russian's date of birth, a former address in the Bronx, and his lengthy rap sheet. "He's five foot eleven, weighs one ninety, dirty blond, blue eyes. Been around the block. Looks old for his age, with a face like mashed potatoes, you know, all bumpy, bloated, and scarred."

"Sounds charming. Can't wait to meet 'im. Hope it's soon."

Venturi went to work. Fast. The killers' trails were growing colder as the story grew hotter.

He used his new laptop to search the Internet for posthumous fallout in the lives of the legally dead. He had checked them thoroughly at the start. Had something new surfaced since their deaths?

Since Errol Flagg's fatal plane crash, three women — a leggy New York model, a buxom Atlanta cocktail waitress, and a blond aspiring LA actress — had filed paternity suits against his estate. All three sold their stories to the tabloids, claiming the rock star had fathered their illegitimate children, who ranged in age from an infant girl to a boy of four.

Flagg's publicist had issued a statement dismissing their actions as "opportunistic attempts to cash in on his tragic death by women who probably never even met the man."

Venturi wasn't so sure when he read that two of the plaintiffs were redheads.

Their lawyers all demanded DNA tests to determine paternity, but since no body had been recovered, there was nothing to match. Flagg had no siblings, his mother was dead, and his father had abandoned the family when Flagg was a toddler.

The three women had already agreed to appear together on Larry King's show.

Venturi wondered if samples of the children's DNA would be compared to each other to determine whether they shared the same father. If none matched, that would prove that at least two of three claims were false, but which two?

No wonder Flagg wanted to disappear and go fishing. Venturi remembered reading that after singer James Brown's death, more than a dozen people stepped forward claiming to be his illegitimate children.

A number of those who had worked with and for Flagg, his agent, manager, and musicians, had made claims against his estate for money owed. Nothing sinister there.

Lots of hits on Lyle Gates, nothing new.

Solange Dupree came up in troubling stories out of Louisiana. The name of the judge who lost her family and nearly her own life because she refused to be compromised had, since her demise, surfaced in a corruption scandal.

Two judges, a prosecutor, and several defense attorneys had been indicted. Others were being investigated. Several were trying to negotiate deals by ratting out others. One of the names dropped was Judge Dupree's.

But the probe had been under way for some time. Her name never came up before her fatal sailing accident. Now accusations were suddenly being made against someone unable to defend herself.

A familiar scenario. Criminals love having a convenient dead guy to blame.

If Solange was dirty, why didn't she take a

bribe and acquit instead of convicting the drug kingpin who sent hit men in revenge?

He was still at the computer when Victoria came home. He heard laughter and conversation in the kitchen, the refrigerator door closing, and smelled fresh coffee brewing. He ignored it, shushed the dog, and gave them their privacy. He wondered when Bill would leave, or if he would.

After thirty minutes or so he heard the front door close, the deadbolt click, and Bill's car leave. He heard Victoria's bedroom door gently close. Soon the house fell quiet. He was alone in the glow of the computer screen, except for the dog who watched him soberly instead of sleeping. Did he sense the tension?

It would be two p.m. tomorrow in Australia.

Audra answered the phone. Despite his concern, he couldn't help savoring the cheerful lilt in her clear voice. It *is* working, he thought. She's happy. They're happy. He hated to spoil the illusion with doubts and dark warnings.

"You never expected to hear from me again. This is Michael Venturi."

"Wrong number," she said, and hung up.

Exactly what she'd been instructed to do.

He hit redial. "This is important," he said tersely.

"What's your problem, mate? You've got the wrong exchange."

She hung up again.

She didn't answer the third call.

The fourth time the number rang busy, as though the phone had been deliberately left off the hook.

He sighed. He could find no newly established telephone number, or any trace of Andrew McCallum, the former Errol Flagg. He wondered why the man did not have a telephone number? Was he in Scotland pursuing his lifelong dream, or was that story a lie?

He called Richard Lynch in Ireland.

"Richard, this is Michael Venturi. I need to . . ."

"Sorry, you've got the wrong party."

"I'm calling Richard Lynch."

"No one here by that name." His voice sounded odd.

"Something's come up. I need to talk to you."

"Wrong number." He hung up.

He found no number for Micheline Lacroix. A French-speaking operator informed him it was on *la liste rouge,* the red list. Unlisted.

He called Claire Waterson, the former Marian Pomeroy, in a village near Bath in the south of England. Startled when a man answered, he checked to see if he had dialed correctly. He had.

He asked for her.

"Are you a relative?" the man asked officiously.

A leak sprang in Venturi's heart and it slowly sank.

"Yes," he lied. "I'm Claire's nephew, calling from Canada. Can I speak to her?"

"Your name, please."

"What's going on?" he demanded irritably. "Is she there?"

"I'm afraid I have bad news," the man said. "Very bad news."

"Is she all right?"

"I'm afraid not. There's been a regrettable incident. She's been killed. I'm the local constable. We're waiting for a team from Scotland Yard."

"I don't believe it," Venturi said truthfully. "You're sure it's her?"

"I'm afraid so."

"What happened?"

"Where did you say were calling from?"

"Ottawa, Canada."

"Well, sir, I'm afraid I can't go into detail until Scotland Yard arrives, but she appears to have died of gunshot wounds, multiple wounds. We've never seen anything of the sort here before. Terrible, just terrible. And your name is?"

"Robert Waterson," Venturi lied, hand over his eyes.

"And the number where I can ring you back?"

"Of course." He glanced up at the detailed map on the war room wall, gave the area code for Ottawa, then stopped speaking, as though the phone had gone dead.

"Hullo?" the constable said. "Sir?"

A lump in his throat, Venturi heard the man say hullo a few more times, then hung up.

He thought of Marian Pomeroy, so small in stature, so large in life. She found such joy in giving, had sat in this very room not so long ago. He could still hear her laughter during her transformation in that motel room in Jamaica.

His first impulse was call Keri. *Where is she?* he wondered. With Maheen? Were they safe?

The news would devastate Keri. She'd ask questions, lots of questions. He needed answers first. Out of friendship, gratitude, and her own basic decency she had taken huge risks for Marian Pomeroy. She'd achieved something amazing. Why spread the misery? He massaged his temples and tried to think. Perhaps she should never know.

Were the others safe? Was Marian Pomeroy the sole target? If so, why? If her greedy children had learned she was alive, which seemed unlikely, they could commit her. Why kill her? It made no sense.

Unless someone was hunting, stalking them all.

CHAPTER
THIRTY-EIGHT

He worked until daylight; his sense of
urgency increased with every hour. He
listened to the BBC and read on the Internet English newspaper accounts of the Bar-
rington Fields homicide.

The victim, Claire Waterson, had set up
an easel, a palette, and brushes in her flower
garden on the morning she died. He smiled
with sad irony. She had followed up on her
lifelong wish to paint. But she'd been interrupted, her easel knocked over, paints
overturned, a flower bed trampled. She had
been dragged into the house. A Scotland
Yard spokesman called what happened unspeakable.

Claire Waterson was a new resident, from
Cardiff, said authorities, who had succeeded
in retracing her steps during the last twenty-
four hours of her life. It wasn't difficult.
There were numerous witnesses. The day
before her death she had perched on a stool,

in front of a crowded classroom at a village school where she had recently volunteered, and read from Robert Louis Stevenson's *Treasure Island.* She lunched alone later at a department-store tearoom. That evening she and an acquaintance, a female teacher at the school, attended a concert at the local bandshell. Afterward they stopped at a local pub for a drink, at which time she mentioned that if the light and the weather cooperated, she intended to work on a landscape in the morning. She returned home without incident shortly after eleven o'clock.

She appeared fine the next morning, waved to passing children on their way to school, and exchanged pleasantries with a neighbor for whom she cut a bouquet from her garden.

Thirty minutes later a postman on his rounds spotted the overturned easel and scattered paints. Her front door stood ajar. He knocked, called out, then found her on the floor.

Her wounds were all at close range, but only one was fatal.

Venturi knew what that meant. The killer had been exacting information, asking questions. Authorities suspected she had been forced to divulge the whereabouts of money, jewelry, or other valuables. That made little sense since the victim's neat, modest cottage was small enough to be easily searched.

No one heard the shots.

A silencer, he thought. *All the earmarks of a professional.*

There were no immediate suspects. Tensions were running high in the once-peaceful village as shocked residents locked doors and looked over their shoulders for a killer among them.

Scotland Yard was attempting to locate the dead woman's relatives. A constable had spoken briefly to an overseas nephew but had lost the connection. They hoped he would ring them again.

Only a matter of time before they discovered she was unknown at her former address in Cardiff. Murder was not one of the endless projections and possible scenarios they had covered in depth. They had been planning a new life, not sudden death.

He drove to Danny's, where they huddled in his study.

"Christ almighty!" Danny exploded in shock and anger. "What sadistic son of a bitch would hurt that woman?"

Venturi shook his head. His attempts to warn the others had failed. All he knew was that the two who'd hung up on him were alive — for the time being.

"We did our jobs too well," he said ruefully. "They wouldn't listen or acknowledge knowing me."

"Next time," Danny said, "we need to arrange a code word."

"What next time? Are you crazy? No next time's gonna happen."

Danny's cell rang. He checked the number. "Sorry, I need to take this, bro. You look like hell. Go pour yourself some coffee."

Venturi wandered numbly into the kitchen.

Luz was feeding baby Michael, a happy cherub smiling in his wooden high chair, food on his face, his bib, and both fists.

"I told you it wasn't Sidney," Luz said softly. She looked up placidly, put down the spoon, and wiped the tot's mouth with a soft washcloth. "You look terrible, Michael. I warned you."

"What?" He rubbed the stubble on his chin. He should have shaved.

"Keri was not for you."

He blinked, confused.

"The first time I saw you look at her, I said, she is not for you. Remember? I introduced you to some wonderful women, my friends."

"What does that have to with . . . ?"

451

"Keri is the best doctor, best friend, best godmother, but she has problems, Michael. We're like sisters. She told me everything, her secrets."

"Such as?" Venturi's head began to ache.

"They wouldn't be secrets if I told you." She turned back to the toddler in the high chair.

"Does Danny know?"

She shook her head, the tiny spoon in her hand.

"What kind of problems? Keri's fine." Except for the last time he'd seen her. He pulled a chair up close and sat facing Luz. "Stop dropping hints and playing games. Level with me. It's important."

She stared at the floor, then raised her eyes. "When Keri was a little girl in Pennsylvania, something happened to her and her baby sister." Luz sighed and paused. The spoon stopped halfway to little Michael's mouth.

The child waited, mouth open in anticipation.

"Her mother left them with a boyfriend, a heavy drinker and drug user. He was also a pedophile. Keri was eight years old, her sister was four."

Tears flooded Luz's eyes as the words rushed out. "The mother's boyfriend assaulted Keri, but when he started to touch her little sister, too, she tried to stop him, fought back. He was drunk. Crazy. She was only in the third grade. Her sister died. Keri needed surgery. The mother visited the man in jail and testified in his defense that it was all a mistake."

"How could she?" Venturi said, his expression pained.

The patient toddler, his empty mouth open like a baby bird's, began to whimper. Luz cooed and steered the spoon into his mouth.

Keri's grandmother raised her, Luz said.

"She has issues. Psychological problems. A college romance ended badly. She trashed his place, burned his clothes, destroyed his stuff.

"She was so ashamed. Said she couldn't help herself and realized then that she was too damaged to ever sustain a successful long-term relationship. That was when she made a major decision — to focus all her energy and creativity on what she can do well, her work. I give her credit. It makes sense."

He frowned. "So when you said it wasn't Sidney, you thought Keri broke into my house," he said. "She didn't. I wish I'd known . . ."

"I didn't want either of you hurt, Michael. I tried." She gazed at him accusingly. "Now," she said sadly, "I can't even reach her."

"I'm sure that's temporary," he said, then entertained a dark thought. "Does Keri have any Russian friends?"

"She doesn't have many friends. Only her patients." Luz paused. "There is a Russian girl. She has a heavy accent. I see her in the office sometimes. She's due next month. She's from Russia and works as a waitress at a Cuban-owned Italian pizzeria in Little Haiti." She smiled. "That's Miami."

"Is the Russian girl married?"

She shrugged. "I never saw her baby's father. She's young, teens, I think. Keri has a soft spot for young mothers. She helps them all she can."

He took a bitter swallow of strong Cuban coffee. "How did you hear that Sidney was cleared?" Was Danny talking too much?

"Victoria called, she was so happy."

"She *is* relieved," he acknowledged. "When did she call?"

"Yesterday afternoon, after *Oprah*." She aimed another spoonful at her drooling target.

The baby pounded his high-chair tray with chubby fists. Venturi envied him. He, too, wanted to vent, to pound something with his fists.

Vicki had called Luz while he and Bill were still discussing his report in the war room. Bill had leaked the results to her first, hoping to hit on her.

Did anybody tell the truth? Was everybody thinking with their genitals?

"No bombs, no bullets, no problems," Danny said tersely. An interesting end to his phone conversation as Venturi rejoined him.

He didn't even ask. Instead he filled Danny in on the Louisiana corruption probe and the fact that Solange's name had surfaced.

Danny was incensed. "Every criminal caught red-handed starts pointing fingers! It's the old SOD defense: Some Other Dude did it."

"I didn't believe it, either," Venturi said. "What happened to Marian is my fault, Danny. I only meant to do it once — I thought we could pull it off. A good launch for a frustrated astronaut, a man who deserved a second chance. It felt so good that it got away from me. I played God. I must be crazy."

"If so, you're not alone, bro."

"What were we thinking?"

"Don't beat yourself up, Mike. Our intentions were good. What's done is done."

"The only decent thing I can do now is protect those people out there all alone and unaware."

Vicki met him at the door, eyes wide.

"Mikey, someone came looking for you about twenty minutes ago. He had an envelope addressed to you and I signed for it. Did I do the wrong thing?"

He tore the envelope open. Legal papers and a copy of a lawsuit.

He was shocked but not surprised.

"What is it, Mikey? Who was he?"

"A process server," he said wearily. "The parents of the little girls murdered in New Hampshire are suing the Marshals Service, WITSEC, and me, personally, for the wrongful deaths of their daughters."

His cell phone rang.

"Michael?"

He recognized the voice instantly. Lyle Gates aka Richard Lynch.

"Sorry for breaking the rules." Lynch sounded confused. "I don't know what's going on, but I've got a bad feeling. When you called, I thought it was a test and I passed. But something's happened."

"Tell me." Venturi took out a notebook and picked up a pen.

"A few hours after you called, I took the trash out to the alley beside the apartment house. I heard a car door close, thought nothing of it, until two men tried to push me back into the building. I knocked over a coat tree in the lobby and tried to force them out. One pulled a gun. I threw an umbrella stand at them and took the stairs trying to outrun them. A neighbor opened her door, saw them run across the lobby, saw the gun, and started screaming. Somebody called the police. An officer on foot patrol heard the screams and came running. They got away, but they shot at my neighbor and grazed the officer. I locked myself in my apartment. Nobody knows it was me they were after. But I'm sure it was. Did your call have anything to do with this?"

"I'm afraid it did. I wanted to warn you. Thank God you're okay, Richard. You did everything right. Good job. Any doubt at all that it was you they were after?"

"No. One said, 'There he is. Get him.' "

"I'm not sure who's behind it. But you *are* in danger. I want you to get out of there. Now. Make sure you're not followed. Did you get a good look at them?"

"Fair-skinned, thirties or forties. One

medium height, the other a little taller. Spoke English with an accent, could've been Russian. One had really bad skin and a tattoo on his arm, looked like a cross, some sort of religious symbol."

Venturi told him about the stolen records.

"But who? Why?" he pleaded. "People hated Lyle Gates, but nobody ever tried to kill him. I landed a great job here with a straight shot at the top. Everybody likes me. I think."

"Tell your boss you have a family emergency and need a few days off."

"But —"

"No buts. Take your cell phone. You have my number. We'll stay in touch. Be careful. They will kill you if they can. Hide out. Lie low. Keep moving till I get back to you."

"What did I do wrong, Michael?"

"Nothing. It's me. It's my fault."

He heard the front-gate buzzer but ignored it, until Vicki appeared in the doorway signaling frantically. He hung up the phone.

"Mikey?" She looked distressed. "There are people outside."

"Who?"

"The one who pushed the buzzer said her name is Judy Grimes."

Why did that sound familiar? Then he remembered: the reporter who called him just before he left New York.

"She says she's from the *Washington Post.* She's not alone." Vicki was wringing her hands.

"Who else?" he asked, moving toward the front door.

"A woman from the *Miami News.* And a van from Channel 7."

"Oh, no." As he peered from behind a curtain, a sound truck bearing the call letters of the local CBS affiliate lumbered off the main road and stopped.

He turned calmly to Victoria. "Will you take care of Scout and the house until I get back?"

"Of course, Mikey."

"I need your help. Here's what I want you to do. Open the door and casually walk out, let them think you're coming to them. Instead, go to my car." He pressed the remote key into her hand.

"There's a leather folder taped under the glove box. Take it out, don't let them see it. Signal them that you'll be right back and bring the folder to me."

"What are you going to do?"

"Bail out, but I can't let them follow me." She nodded.

"Take your cane," he said. "Use it, and move slowly."

She went to the intercom and told the reporters she'd be right out.

The aggressive pack of cameramen jockeyed for position and crowded closer to the gate. Why do they do that, he wondered, even when someone is willing to talk to them?

Vicki did as he asked, smiled reassuringly at the reporters, signaled them to give her a minute, and brought the folder back to the house.

By then he'd thrown some things into a duffel bag.

He heard the reporters' aggrieved shouts from the gate as she reentered the house and closed the door. Somebody put a finger on the buzzer again and didn't take it off. He took the folder from her, checked through it: his passport, a bank book, ID, and credit cards were all there. He snatched up the duffel bag and the computer's Travel-Drive.

"I'm out of here," he said. "But don't let them know that. When I close the back door, you step out the front and move down the driveway as slowly as you can.

"Smile as if you can't wait to meet them. Ignore the cameras. When they ask for me, answer with questions. 'Who is it that you're looking for? How do you spell that? You sure you have the right address?' Look confused. Be vague but charming. When they ask your name, act coy. Be shy. Say you're visiting. That you're the caretaker, or the real estate agent, or a tourist who rented the place for a week. Say whatever you like. Use your fertile imagination. Just speak slowly and keep them occupied long enough for me to split.

"If they realize I'm making a run for it, they may call in a news chopper. That could be a problem.

"Once I'm gone, leave your car where it's parked. They can't see the tag number from there without trespassing. If they do, call the police. Say you're alone, frightened, and strangers are breaking in. Use my car. The gas tank is full."

"I know, dear. It's always full."

"Love you, lady." He kissed her cheek. "Hold down the fort till I get back."

"I will," she promised. "Don't worry about a thing. Love you, too, Mikey. No problem. Be careful."

"Take care of her," he told the dog, who panted and wagged his tail.

Venturi looked back. Vicki stood poised, one hand on the doorknob.

"I'm ready for my close-up," she said, and blew him a kiss.

He closed the back door behind him as she swung open the front. The reporters began to shout.

CHAPTER
THIRTY-NINE

"Danny, where are you?"

"Douglas Road, on my way to the house of death for more fun and frolic."

"Can you pick me up? I need your help."

"I'm on the way. Where you at, bro?"

"In my boat, headed west in the canal toward the levee. You know the one. Meet me there."

Venturi did his best to conceal the boat, which he left tied up in the mangroves, and waited by the road.

"Thought you were going to Europe," Danny said, as Venturi yanked open the car door and threw his bag into the back.

"Had to go over the wall at the house. It's surrounded — a three-ring media circus."

"I heard."

Venturi did a double take.

"Luz just saw Vicki live on the noon news and called me. Said she had a half dozen microphones stuck in her face. Looked like one of America's most wanted, or a politician. Oops, I'm being redundant."

"Hated to leave her there, but I didn't have a choice."

"No sweat. Luz said she looked like she was having fun. Misinterpreting their questions, acting confused and hard of hearing. Made them scream and shout, which made Scout bark his brains out. When the TV people asked her to shut him up because he kept ruining their takes, she slooowly turned and started to limp after him. The reporters all screamed, 'Never mind! Never mind.' Nice work."

They bumped off the rutted dirt road onto solid pavement.

"Where to, boss?" Danny flashed his trademark grin.

"MIA."

"Gotcha."

At the airport, Danny drove into the long-term parking garage and snatched a ticket from the machine.

"What are you doing?" Venturi demanded. "Don't park. Just drop me off."

"And do what with the car?" Danny looked puzzled.

Venturi blinked. "You don't . . . ?"

"Think I'd miss this? Let you have all the fun?"

Their eyes locked.

"You don't have to come, Danny."

"No way I'm not."

"Got a passport and ID handy?"

"Always." He ticked them off on his fingers. "I've got American, Canadian, and Colombian, among others."

"What about Luz?"

"She and the kids have 'em, too. The world's closing in on us, bro. Never know when the big shit bomb hits the fan and we all have to make a run for it."

"No, no. I meant does she know you're leaving the country, for Christ's sake."

"I'll give her a call from there."

Venturi rolled his eyes. "I'm glad I'm not married to you."

"The feeling is mutual. Hate to have to tell you this, but you were never my type."

"Thank God for small favors."

Danny hoisted his duffel bag from behind the backseat. "It's always packed," he said. "What's our first stop?"

"France, the closest as the crow flies."

"Hoped you'd say that." He flashed his wicked grin.

Mike frowned.

"We going as strangers, amigo?" Danny asked.

"Yep. We should travel alone."

"Makes sense."

Danny strode straight through security. Venturi was wanded, groped, and had his bag searched twice. They boarded separately, assigned to different sections of the next flight to Paris. Venturi slept, or tried to, during the flight. Several times he heard Danny's hearty laughter from somewhere behind him. On a trip to the restroom he saw him seated next to the emergency exit, chatting with the young couple beside him. Danny saw him, too. Neither gave any sign of recognition.

They disembarked at Orly Airport and met at a taxi stand outside the terminal. Danny gave the driver a Paris address, to "pick up some things for the party," he said.

Venturi waited in the taxi while Danny disappeared into the side door of a costume and party supply store. He returned in minutes with a large shopping bag and a wooden box, which he stowed in the trunk. Then they took off for Tours, more than an hour's drive into wine country.

There they rented a car. Danny filled out the forms. Venturi drove while Danny called home.

"*Bonjour,* sweet face. Yeah. I know I'm late. Won't be home for a while. Paris. No, not Texas. Yeah, Paris. As in France and that

466

skinny Hilton broad. Duty calls. Be back quick as I can. . . . Not sure. Kiss the kids for me and tell 'em Daddy loves 'em. . . . I'm always careful. . . . Love you, too. *Au revoir,* baby."

He turned to Venturi. "Happy now?"

"Look for Rue Vendome, number 414," Venturi said.

"How did you get her address?" Danny asked.

"Her *nom de guerre* is Micheline La-croix . . ."

"Yeah, but she's on *la liste rouge.*"

"And you know that because?"

He scowled. "Did an operator give you her damn address?"

"Nope. Read the news from Tours last night on the Internet."

"Hell, tell me she didn't make the news. Did she?" Danny furrowed his brow. "What happened to low profile? If you could find her that way, so could somebody else."

"Probably not her fault. Online in a business column. Micheline Lacroix was named as the new manager of a specialty wine and food shop in Tours. But you're right, which is why this is our first stop. We can make short hops to cover the 'hood north of here later, if we have to. Lyle Gates is on the run.

Hopefully he can take care of himself for a while.

"Shoulda heard him, Danny," Venturi said earnestly. "In spite of all the shit raining down, he made me proud. He's not the man I first met, ready to lie down and die in a swamp. He handled himself like a champ. Fought for his life. Loves his new job. Excited about the future. How can I regret what we did? He's a goddamn success story. Which is why this is so damn unfair to him, and to Marian Pomeroy. I hope Audra is savvy enough to have a heads-up after my call. She and Aiden are the farthest away. Hopefully that makes them safer, at least for a while.

"I'm not sure where the hell father-of-the-year Andrew McCallum is, or if he's even in Scotland. If we don't find him fast, we may have to forget him and go to Australia."

"I'm up for that." Danny sounded enthusiastic. "It's one place I've never been. Slow down! Here's rue Vendome." Danny stared through the windshield.

They had little trouble finding the specialty shop called Epicure.

They parked nearby and Venturi called the telephone number on the sign outside.

Micheline Lacroix was expected in thirty minutes, he was told.

Danny took the party supplies from the trunk. They opened the packages behind the tinted windows of the car. In the box were two high-powered .45-caliber, fifteen-shot automatic handguns and boxes of ammunition. In the shopping bag were two military-grade protective vests. Body armor.

They loaded the weapons.

"Nice," Venturi said. "How'd you line this up?"

"Made a few calls from the airport, before we left the States."

Venturi, who still hadn't shaved, wandered into the shop, browsed the gourmet foods, and bought pastries and coffee to go.

They drank the coffee in the car.

Danny, restlessly scanning the street, didn't touch the food.

"There she is!" he finally said. "Incoming, at three o'clock. On foot." He whistled appreciatively. "Oh, man." He moaned. "Look at her."

Micheline Lacroix owned the street, a head turner in a white silk shirt, tight black skirt, and stiletto heels, the epitome of French womanhood; clothes fashionable, hair sleek, exuding a kick-ass attitude of sultry self-confidence.

Danny reached for the door handle.

"Not on the street," Venturi warned.

"Remember, you were on the outs, persona non grata, when she left. Let's approach her inside where she's less likely to make a scene."

"Makes sense." Danny's eyes never left her. "Oh, catch that hip action! It's killing me."

She walked by, no more than a few feet from their tinted windows, and entered the shop.

"At least we know she's alive," Venturi said, worried about Lyle Gates.

They gave her a few moments, then walked into the shop. Micheline was at the back, donning a silky black bib apron. She tied it at her narrow waist, glanced up, and saw Danny.

For a moment she looked stunned. They both stared.

"Bonjour, cherie."

"*Oh, mon Dieu! Qu' est ce que sont vous faisant ici?* Oh my God! What are you doing here?"

Venturi watched the familiar heat sizzle between them.

"You couldn't stay away. I knew it." She smiled triumphantly, then turned her back. *"Laissez moi tranquille. Je ne veux pas vous parler,"* she murmured. "Leave me alone. I don't want to talk to you."

She walked away, chin up, all business, speaking rapidly to an employee she called Emile. They couldn't hear the conversation, but Emile didn't seem to notice them.

"We should have snatched her off the street," Danny muttered, as they took seats at the counter.

They ate sandwiches and sampled gourmet salads. She kept her distance, overseeing the kitchen, the bakery, the front, and the cash registers.

Danny finally asked an employee to pass her a folded handwritten note. *Micheline, it is urgent that we speak,* scrawled in French on a napkin. Discreetly, so that only they could see, she tore it into tiny shreds and flung them into an ashtray.

Eventually they left, drove off, then circled, and parked down the block.

"I don't get the big attraction," Venturi said, perplexed. "That is one damn difficult woman. It's like she has chronic PMS."

"I like taming the wild ones. You have to break them, like horses," Danny said.

"You're not having much luck with this one. If she gets the chance, she'll stomp you to death."

Customers and employees began to straggle out shortly after 9 p.m. An hour later, the place went dark and she emerged,

471

accompanied by Emile, who stood by as she locked the door.

"Crap, who the hell is he?" Danny said. "If he goes home with her . . ."

The two chatted for a moment, then walked to their separate cars.

She paused at hers for a moment, glancing up and down the street, her expression disappointed. As she unlocked her car, a BMW screeched to the curb beside it.

"Who the hell's that? Go! Move it! Go! Go! Go!" Danny yelled.

Before the words were out of his mouth, a man burst out of the passenger side and caught Micheline around the waist and by the hair. Muffling her screams with his hand, he dragged her, kicking and struggling, into the BMW's backseat.

Venturi pulled away from the curb without lights as the BMW peeled out and wheeled around the corner.

"Don't lose 'em! Damn! We shoulda seen that coming! Don't lose 'em!" Danny pounded the dashboard.

The BMW now moved sedately at the speed limit from a less-traveled street onto a main thoroughfare. They were three cars behind as it merged into traffic. Only the driver was visible.

"She could be dead already. We have to

stop them."

"Right," Venturi said, as the car made a sharp turn into the parking garage of a multistory shopping mall. They followed, several cars behind. The first level was full. There were a few open spaces on the second, but the BMW kept ascending through the nearly empty third level and the vacant fourth and fifth.

"Where the hell are they going?" Danny pulled the body armor over his shirt. He tossed a vest to Venturi, pulled on a pair of latex gloves, picked up a gun and racked one into the chamber.

The car emerged on the empty rooftop level and stopped in the center, stars overhead, the glow of city lights below.

Venturi, still without headlights, crept to the entrance.

"Didn't know the party would start so soon." He pulled on the vest, hoping that the men who snatched Micheline off the street were the same two who attacked Lyle in Ireland and that one was the man who had invaded his home.

"Put the gloves on, man," Danny reminded him.

Venturi did so. "Stay low," he warned.

"That son of a bitch in the backseat is mine," Danny said. "You take the driver."

On his count of three, they slipped out of the car, leaving the doors ajar. As they approached, guns in hand, the back door on the driver's side burst open. They heard Micheline scream and saw her legs flailing as she tried to escape but was dragged back into the car.

Before her abductor could close the door, Danny wrenched it out of his hand. He reached in, caught the man by the throat, yanked him from the car, kicked his feet out from under him, and slammed him facedown on the pavement. He still clutched a gun in his right hand but let go when Danny stomped his wrist.

Venturi had smashed the driver's window and jammed his gun to the forehead of the man behind the wheel. "Don't move! Don't move! Don't move!"

The man replied in Russian and lifted his weapon.

Venturi fired once, then reached in to snatch the man's blood-spattered automatic weapon.

He turned back to Danny, who had his knee jammed into the back of the man on the pavement, as Micheline kicked at her assailant.

She scrambled back into the car for her shoes and purse.

"Don't kill him." Venturi gestured toward the prone man on the pavement. "He's all we've got. We lost the driver." He searched the car's bloody interior, took the keys from the ignition, and unlocked the glove box. No personal effects. Nothing but a rental agreement two days old.

He checked the dead man's arms. No tattoos. He removed a cell phone from the body and the ID from a wallet in his pocket.

"Let's go, let's go!" Danny said impatiently. He handcuffed the surviving Russian and forced him into the backseat. As Venturi and Micheline piled into the front, lights swept up the entrance ramp behind them.

"Crap. The cops!" Danny said. "Let's roll."

Venturi gunned it toward the exit ramp on the far side of the roof as Danny peered out the back window.

"Uh-oh, these ain't no gendarmes."

A big black Mercedes rolled slowly onto the roof. The doors to the BMW hung open, exposing the dead driver and empty backseat.

Moments later the Mercedes' tinted windows lowered and two assault rifles emerged.

"Shit! Long guns! Get down! Stay down!"

Danny dove across the seat and pushed Micheline to the floorboard.

The handcuffed Russian opened his bloodied mouth and laughed. The ugly sound stopped abruptly when Danny bashed the side of his head with his gun.

One of the assault rifles let loose a fiery burst of ten rounds.

Venturi floored it, racing down the winding exit ramp at high speed, the Mercedes in hot pursuit, both cars careening over speed bumps.

Another burst of gunfire pockmarked the concrete columns and walls, sending debris bouncing off the windshield.

"Looks like four of them," Danny said calmly. He opened a window and returned fire as they took a curve. Sparks flew as a slug hit the Mercedes' grille. Another shattered a side mirror.

Micheline crouched on the front floor, hands over her ears, as Danny fired.

"Uh-oh," Venturi said. Traffic had picked up as they speeded around the fourth level, then the third.

Some event had apparently ended, and a long line of traffic ahead of them crept slowly toward the open-air single-lane exit ramp.

Venturi ignored a yield sign and cut off

476

several motorists. Drivers blew their horns in protest. Several cars were now between them and their pursuers.

The driver of the Mercedes leaned on his horn, as though warning other drivers to clear the way. They were not impressed.

On the last two floors, the one-lane exit ramp consisted of a solid wall on the inside and a six-foot wall on the outside, which slowly dwindled to about four feet in height during the descent.

The Mercedes was five cars behind as they inched downward.

Something hit the rear window of their car, spiderwebbed the glass, leaving a hole, then crashed through the windshield and kept going.

The gunman stood in the Mercedes' open sunroof, his head and shoulders exposed as he aimed the AK-47.

The panicked motorists in front of him had nowhere to go. Wildly swerving, braking, blowing their horns, they collided with the wall and the cars in front of them.

The captured Russian in the backseat kept trying to struggle free and reach the door handle. Each time Danny pounded him again with the gun or his fists.

"Don't kill him!" Venturi said. "We need his intel."

"Time to expedite," Danny announced calmly. "At the next curve, shut it off, and hit the emergency brake. We'll lock it, leave it, and go over the side. I take him. You bring her."

Micheline gasped. Venturi didn't like it, but he knew Danny was right.

In agonizing slow motion, they crawled down and around the next curve, briefly out of sight of their pursuers.

"Now!" Danny said.

"No!" Micheline cried.

"Shut up," Venturi said. He put the car in park, turned off the key, put it in his pocket, stomped the emergency brake, and hit the trunk release.

The wall was now down to about three and a half feet high. Danny dragged the still-struggling Russian out of the car, swung, and landed a haymaker square on his jaw. He caught the Russian before he crumpled to the ground, picked him up, flung him over the side to a grassy swale six feet below, then vaulted over the wall after him. The terrified elderly couple in a Citroën behind them began to scream.

Baseball cap pulled down over his eyes, Venturi darted to the trunk, snatched their duffel bags, and tossed them over the side. He grasped Micheline's arm. "Take off your shoes. Don't look behind us. I don't want people to see your face."

She resisted.

"Don't be afraid."

She stared into his eyes, more defiant than afraid, as he picked her up and dropped her over the ledge. He saw Danny half-catch her, breaking her fall onto the grassy area below.

He jumped, landed on his feet, and staggered several steps. He almost stumbled over the Russian seated on the ground, still handcuffed and bleeding profusely from the nose. A cacophony of car horns blared behind them.

Hand raised like a traffic cop, Danny stepped directly in front of the final car to exit, a late-model Volvo that had been in front of them. All the other traffic stood still behind the roadblock they had created.

"Police business," he said in French. "Step out please."

The driver, a plump, round-faced, middle-aged nanny, studied the gun in his hand, bit her lip, and gestured to her passenger, a dark-haired girl about eleven years old. They exited the car without argument.

"Wait! Your handbags." Danny politely handed them their purses. "My supervisor will return the vehicle to you in excellent condition tomorrow. Do not call the police now," he warned, as he slid behind the wheel and popped the trunk. "We are too busy with grave matters of national security. Foreign terrorists," he said softly. *"Merci."*

The nanny's uncertain eyes focused on Micheline, bruised and disheveled, her right eye swollen.

"He is helping to save France," Micheline said. "He is a patriot. What he says is true."

The woman looked back at Danny and smiled shyly.

Venturi wrestled the surprisingly strong Russian into the trunk and slammed it shut. Danny gunned the engine and they took off, Micheline beside him, the sounds of car horns and the sporadic *pop, pop, pop* of rapid gunfire fading behind them.

"Hope they're only firing into the air to scare drivers out of their way," Venturi said.

"They won't kill innocent bystanders," Danny said confidently. "Not when they're trapped and know the *gendarmes* are on the way."

"How the hell many are there?" Venturi asked. "I wanted it to be just two. But I didn't see Ivan Kazakov, who broke into my house. One of two who went after Richard in Ireland had a religious tattoo on his right forearm. No tattoos on the two we got."

"We had at least four in the Mercedes," Danny said. "The two we got, two more in Ireland, somebody in England. Your friend, Ivan. Ten minimum, most likely more. With assault rifles, automatic handguns, and silencers."

Venturi frowned.

"We need bigger guns, and more of them," Danny concluded.

"Who the hell were those guys?" Micheline asked in English. "They weren't Colombian."

"What did they sound like to you?" Venturi asked.

"Russian?" She shrugged. "What's that all about? And who's Richard?"

"You don't want to know." Venturi sighed. "It's a long story."

"Where to?" Danny turned a corner.

"My place isn't far," Micheline said.

"Too risky," Danny said.

"What do you mean?" she said, suddenly realizing the enormity of her situation. "I can't go home?" She paused. "For the last two days I felt like I was being watched. Didn't see anyone but sensed it. Was it you?"

"No," Venturi said. "We just got here."

He saw the fear in her eyes.

"We need a quiet place to debrief him." Danny jerked his head toward the trunk.

"First we better get rid of this car and pick up another one." Venturi scanned traffic behind them as sirens yelped in the distance.

"The driver who gave it to us believed me," Danny said. "She won't report it till tomorrow. You see the nice little smile she gave me?"

"Your charm has its limitations," Venturi said.

"It's very overrated," Micheline agreed coldly.

"What about your car?" Danny asked her. "It's probably still parked outside the shop. The place is empty, neighboring shops are closed now. It's as good a place as any for a while. The boys in the Mercedes are probably still busy."

"Do you have a security guard who checks the premises?" Venturi asked her.

"We had no need for one," she said frostily, "before you arrived. Why is this happening? Why are you here?"

"We don't know who's behind it." Venturi explained about the burglar and the stolen data. "We came to warn you that your security might be compromised."

"A little late, aren't you? We were not to make contact again, ever," she said bitterly, "so why did you carelessly keep records that could be stolen?"

"My mistake," he said. "They don't know everything. Only your new name and destination."

"They know who I was," she insisted. "Why else would they try to kill me? Your thief probably sold my information to the Colombians who hired them to finish the job." She buried her face in her hands. "I thought that hell was over forever."

Danny drew her close, his arms around her. She did not resist.

"We'll figure it out and make it right," he promised. "That's why we're here."

"But I *like* Micheline," she said wearily, her bruised cheek resting against his bulletproof vest. "I *love* being her. Don't make me change again."

The street appeared quiet, her car parked in the same spot. They drove to an alley behind the shop and marched the Russian in the back door. "We need running water," Danny said. "A sink, a tub, or toilet."

Danny duct-taped the man's eyes and mouth, handcuffed him to a pipe in a windowless restroom, then stayed with him while Micheline drove the Volvo to a wooded area several miles away. Venturi followed in her car, wiped the Volvo free of fingerprints, and backed it deep into the trees.

Danny was alone in the darkened gourmet

shop, eating a croissant when they got back.

"Excellent," he told Micheline, and held up the croissant. "You bake this yourself?"

She stared at him and went to check the bathroom.

"What did he tell you?" Venturi asked.

"Name's Viktor. The driver was Sergey. Both from New York. Foot soldiers for the Russian mob. They were in England for Claire Waterson. Then the boss sent them for Micheline. He wasn't sure why. They were told to kill her, but only after she answered questions about how and why she got here and what she had to do with you.

"They were supposed to get the questions from the big boss by phone after they had her. That's why they took her to the roof. The immediate boss and his people in the Mercedes planned to do the interrogation there. When they got their answers, these two were going to throw her off the roof.

"Another team went to Ireland. Ivan, your burglar, is one of them. Viktor didn't know about any others."

"Jesus."

"Had condoms in his pocket," Danny offered, almost as an aside. "Didn't want to leave DNA. They were going to rape her before she went off the roof."

Micheline appeared in the doorway.

"Where is he? The Russian? He's gone."

"Yeah," Danny said. "He's gone."

She stared at him. "You'd never know he was there. The room is clean, except for the water on the floor."

"Sorry, I meant to take care of that before you came back. You made good time. I'll do it now." He got to his feet. "Where do you keep the mop?"

Micheline gingerly opened a closet not far from the restroom.

"You're sure he's gone?"

"Absolutely, *cherie.* He learned his lesson and won't be back."

Venturi followed Danny down the hall.

"She's back there checking the freezer, and the big oven," Venturi said. "He isn't here somewhere, is he?"

"Of course not." He looked offended at the suggestion. "Think I'd do that to her?"

"So, where is he?"

"A storage warehouse, three doors down. In a locked unit that looks like it hasn't been opened in years."

"Will he be talking to anybody?"

"Not anymore."

"Did he tell you everything?"

"Everything he knew, which wasn't much.

"He took orders from Vasily, the big boss in New York. They're into extortion, drugs, white slavery, prostitution, stolen auto parts, weapons, money laundering, and gambling between New York and Florida. Our situation stems from another phase of the business he didn't know much about. He was just following orders.

"Once they had Claire Waterson, he waited in the car while two of the guys in the Mercedes dragged her inside. He said they weren't happy. Apparently she didn't cooperate, kept insisting she was who she was, and had no idea what they were talking about.

"She was a brave woman," Venturi said sadly.

"A stand-up broad," Danny said.

"We have the driver's cell phone," Venturi said. "Let's use it."

"Okay. Soon as I mop up."

CHAPTER FORTY

They sat in the darkened shop watching reports of the parking garage shooting on a small TV in the office, while Micheline made coffee and sandwiches.

One motorist had suffered a heart attack and there were a number of minor injuries, but no one was dead except the BMW driver on the roof and one of the men in the Mercedes, killed in an exchange of gunfire with police.

The police were asking that the driver who abandoned his rental car on the exit ramp contact them. The car had been rented to a Canadian named Raoul Truffant. They assumed he fled on foot after being caught in the line of fire.

Danny shrugged in response to Venturi's questioning glance. "Just call me Raoul."

Police suspected that the occupants of the Mercedes murdered the BMW driver, then panicked when trapped in traffic as they tried to flee. A small arsenal of weapons had been seized from their car. The investigation was still in its preliminary stage. All the witnesses had not yet given statements, and no ballistics tests had been completed.

Another passenger in the Mercedes suffered head injuries during his capture.

The other two carjacked another driver and crashed through the wooden gate at the garage entrance. They narrowly missed a head-on collision with arriving police but escaped after a brief chase.

"Damn. Can't believe they let them get away," Danny said. "Time to relocate. Now."

Micheline ran for the keys to lock the shop as Venturi hit redial to the last number the dead driver had called. He had probably called to tell his boss that they had Micheline.

A man answered in Russian.

"Speak English," Venturi said sharply. "I have a message for Vasily, your boss, the man in New York."

The Russian demanded to know who he was.

"I'm the man with Sergey's phone and your friend Viktor. Call New York and tell your boss to call this number. Now. Before it's too late."

Half an hour later as they drove toward

the City of Light in the dark before dawn, the dead man's cell phone rang. Danny stopped the car as Venturi answered.

"You wish to speak to me?" a gruff voice said.

"Yes. Call off your people, now," Venturi said.

"Some things cannot be called off, Michael Venturi."

"What do you want, Vasily? Who do you want?"

The man did not answer but Venturi could hear him breathing. "Let's meet," he said, "talk man-to-man, and negotiate."

"I will consider it," the caller said, and hung up.

"He didn't call anything off," Venturi tersely told the others.

"If I die here," Micheline said softly as Danny swung back into traffic, "I want to go home. I want to lie next to my children, my husband, and my mother. My name is already on the monument. Only the date of death is blank. I want to go there."

"You can't," Venturi said. "The date of Solange Dupree's death isn't blank anymore. The day of her sailboat accident is engraved there. Solange died, remember? She and her family are together."

"And Micheline Lacroix is alive and well,"

Danny said, "except for an extremely sexy black eye. Micheline will live a long, long time, if we have anything to say about it. Her name won't appear on that Big Blackboard in the Sky for fifty years. So don't talk like a loser. You won't win if you don't believe you will."

She nodded slowly.

Venturi called Richard Lynch, relieved to hear his sleepy voice. "You okay, buddy?"

"So far. Can I go home and back to work?"

"Not yet, but we're working on it. Danny and I are outside Paris right now. Just wanted to check in. Are you all right?"

"Having the time of my life," he said drolly. "On a tourist bus trip. We're visiting ancient castles along the coast of Ireland."

"Good idea. Get lost in the crowd and enjoy the tour. But if you see anything, or anybody, suspicious, follow your gut. Do whatever you have to do to protect yourself, then get the hell out. Hopefully this will be over soon."

"Yes, sir," he said without humor. "I'll enlist the little people and we'll take our shillelaghs to 'em."

"Atta boy. How'd it go with your boss?"

"I couldn't believe it." He sounded amazed. "Said to take as much time as I need. Made me swear to come back. They like my work, Michael."

"They ain't seen nothing yet. Stay safe. We may see you soon."

Danny turned down a winding country road. "Here we are," he muttered.

The sign at the wrought-iron gate said Les Soeurs de la Charité.

"What's this?" Micheline asked.

"Cherie." Danny gently touched her cheek. "This is where you'll stay for a while. Until this blows over."

He glanced back at Venturi. "She'll be safe here."

"Oh, no." Micheline looked alarmed. "A convent! You are not leaving me here. No. No," she said firmly.

"It's the perfect place for you," Danny said seriously.

"What about my car?"

"We have to borrow it for a while, *cherie.*"

"The only way you leave me in a convent and drive away in my car is over my dead body." She turned to Venturi, eyes pleading. "Without you two I would be dead. Until this is finished I'm only safe with you. What if they find me here? Do you think nuns can protect me?"

"They have friends in high places." Danny raised a meaningful eyebrow toward the heavens.

Her look was scathing. "You will not abandon me here. I won't let you. You'll have to drag me in there kicking and screaming and I'll call the police before you're out the gate."

She refused to listen or relent.

"You can't travel with us. We're leaving the country. You have no papers, no passport, no ID," Venturi pointed out.

"Are you crazy?" She reached for a leather folder in the glove box. "Of course I do. You think I learned nothing from Danny?"

"She *would* be safer with us," Danny conceded.

Despite his misgivings about how they looked at each other, Venturi shrugged and left the decision to them. He thought of Keri. Was she protecting Maheen? Would she ever look at him again with anything but contempt? He wished he'd known she was as badly scarred as that girl. The only difference was that her scars didn't show.

On the way to the airport, Micheline bought a hat and makeup to mask her bruises. She frequently examined her spectacular black eye in the car's mirror.

"If I'd put ice on it at the start, it wouldn't look this bad," she said woefully.

"It's hardly noticeable," Venturi lied. "This your first shiner?"

"Of course not." She shrugged. "I think my first was when I was five and jumped out a window. I blackened both eyes water-skiing when I was eleven. I had another one when the boom knocked me off a sailboat. When I was sixteen, my horse stumbled during a jump and I fell over his head into a fence. That, of course, was all before I totaled my first Porsche."

Danny listened, his expression lovesick.

She left a phone message at the shop that she had been called away due to a sudden family emergency.

"Lots of that going around lately," Danny said.

He and Micheline flew together.

Venturi traveled solo on the same flight after tangling with airport security, who clearly considered him suspicious.

Eventually they arrived in Scotland and drove a rented car along narrow roads to the quaint coastal fishing village they sought.

"How do we find him?" Danny asked as they passed a stone windmill and rows of whitewashed cottages.

"We don't even know he's here. He's supposed to be, but who knows? We'll give it our best shot, then move on."

"He who?" Micheline demanded.

"Nobody you know," Danny said.

It was late afternoon. The boats had returned with their catch. A few fishermen nodded when they heard Andrew McCallum's name, but were less than forthcoming.

As Danny drove slowly along the windy docks, Venturi thought he saw a familiar face. "Wait! There! Hold on. Slow down."

Out of the car before it came to a complete stop, he overtook a man walking along the side of the road.

"Andrew?" Close-up, he still wasn't sure.

"What the hell?" The grizzled, bearded fisherman glanced about to be sure no one was watching. "How do you happen to be in this part of the world?"

"Trying to find you, buddy. Warn you. Something's happened."

The fisherman's expression turned grave.

Danny left Micheline standing near the car and joined them. He pumped Andrew's hand, then caught him in a bear hug.

"Never thought I'd see your faces again in this life," the fisherman said.

"Why the hell don't you have a telephone?" Venturi demanded. "It would have saved us time and trouble."

"Telephone?" Andrew looked startled, then offended. "Why would a simple fisherman without a family need a telephone? Who would I call? I don't know anybody. Remember? Every moron on the street is using a cell phone, even here. They only lead to trouble.

"I said I wanted a simple life. Uncomplicated. Battling the elements. The sea. The camaraderie of teamwork. Things that mean something. That's what I found here. Only one comfort missing." He sneaked a glance at Micheline, inhaling the salt breeze, looking out over the North Sea.

"Now, there's a very attractive woman. The black eye is exciting. Enhances her appeal. Works for me. One of you two boys into rough sex?" His eyes sparked and lit up. "Or is it both of you?"

He grinned slyly at Venturi. "How's Vicki and the redheaded doctor?"

"They send their regards," he lied, aware that he was lying a lot lately. "We needed to be sure you're all right."

"Couldn't be better."

They filled him in on what had happened.

"You should get lost for a while until we straighten it all out," Venturi concluded.

He nodded. "I'm about to do that. I'm off in a few hours for three weeks of fishing up toward Iceland. We stay at sea until early next month."

"Check before you sail that no new strangers have joined the crew, especially Russians."

"I'm the new man on board. The rest grew up here."

"How do we contact you if we need to?"

He scribbled the name and number of the boat's owner.

"Have you seen any unfamiliar faces, maybe Russian, asking questions?"

He shook his head.

"Didn't want to alarm you but we had to give you a heads-up. Be careful," Venturi said. "Sorry to intrude."

"No intrusion. It gives me a chance to thank you. Again. Occasionally I see a newspaper. But not too often. Don't want it to become a habit." His blue eyes crinkled in a face already weathered by cold sea winds and salt air. "Errol Flagg became a legend in his own time. That's the way to leave the world. Still young and strong. You're never a has-been. They never see you grow old. But they don't ever forget you. I must say, I've become a fan of the man, the myth, and the legend myself. Good-bye." He smiled again, flashed an approving glance at Micheline and winked at her, then turned and walked away. He did not look back.

"Who was he?" Micheline asked, when they rejoined her. "How strange. I'm sure I don't know him but somehow I think I did. I think I knew him."

"You never met him," Danny said. "He's nobody."

"That's right," Venturi added. "Most of the fishermen who grew up here are related and look alike."

Inside the car, a cell phone rang. Sergey's phone.

CHAPTER
FORTY-ONE

"I'll be there," Michael said. "But only if you call off your operations until after we meet."

"Agreed," the gruff voice said.

"Where? Paris? London?"

"No," Vasily said. "Panama."

"Why Panama?"

"Why not? It is closer to the U.S. and my pressing business commitments. In thirty-six hours?"

"You've got it, if I can make connections."

"And Viktor?"

"We'll discuss him then. I'm in constant contact with my colleagues abroad. If any further hostile action is taken against any one of them, our meet is canceled, and Viktor will be turned over to the authorities to tell his story about the murder in Great Britain and the attempts in Ireland and Tours."

"Understood."

"Where in Panama?"

"The Canopy Tower. It's in the Gamboa area of the former Canal Zone. Somewhat remote, which will give us privacy, but only forty minutes from downtown Panama City. I look forward to our meeting, Mr. Venturi."

"So do I. Leave your soldiers behind," Venturi said. "This is a peaceful negotiation, not a war."

"Of course, and I expect as much from you. You are alone?"

"I may have a driver, but that's all."

"I know the place," Danny said. "It's an old U.S. radar installation transferred to Panama as part of the handover of the Canal in 2000. You can see it from the canal, like a big golf ball up above the tree canopy. I heard it's been converted to a tourist stop for bird-watchers from all over the world."

Micheline argued to accompany them.

"You can't," Danny said. "You don't belong on that side of the pond. It's too damn risky. You ever been to the Panama Canal Zone? It's a jungle over there."

She shrugged. "I can shoot a weapon. And I'm not afraid of heat, hardship, snakes, or mosquitoes."

"In case it doesn't work out," Venturi said,

"we want you safe, on this side of the world. And we need you here. There's no one else we can rely on. Only you. Drop us at the airport, then go back to France, and wait at the convent until you hear from us."

"No," she said vehemently. "If I can't go with you, I can stay here with your friend, the fisherman."

"Not possible," Venturi said quickly.

"No way." Danny looked alarmed at the possibility. "*Cherie,* you didn't win the argument last time. We could have drugged you, left you at the convent. Don't think it didn't cross my mind. We didn't give in out of weakness; we brought you with us because we care for you. But there's no way you can win this one. Marines don't lose the big ones. We go. You stay. Next stop, the airport."

She nodded solemnly.

"We'll pick up more disposable cell phones," Venturi said, "and then, depending on how it goes, we'll either call you with an all-clear or a duck-and-run. Forget the fisherman. He's in more danger then you are, so don't go there. He's not trained to protect you."

"And he's already sailed," Danny said, checking his watch.

"I'll go back to Paris," she said grudgingly,

"but not the convent. I saw bed and break-fasts in that area. Is it all right if I stay at one of those?"

"I like the big iron gate around the convent but if you feel so strongly, do as you damn well please," Venturi said impatiently. "It's your life."

She was quiet — pouting, he thought — as they neared the airport.

Danny kissed her good-bye in the car, then did it again. Then she kissed him. He kissed her back, and they began all over again. Venturi feared he'd need a fire hose to end the farewells. When Micheline tear-fully murmured, "I may never see you again," he rolled his eyes.

"You're torturing me," Danny moaned breathlessly, finding her lips again.

"That's right," she retorted, also breath-less. "You deserve it. I want you to remember everything you'll never have again."

"I know, I know."

"We have to go, now," Venturi interrupted from the front seat. They did.

Danny painfully extricated himself from the backseat. She followed and leaned provocatively against the car, watching them.

When Danny looked back, she was still watching. He walked backward, eyes on her face for as long as he could.

They were getting out just in the nick of time, Venturi thought.

Danny breezed through security unmolested, as usual.

Venturi drew special scrutiny. Again. He knew it was because he fit the profile, traveling alone, paying cash at the last minute for a one-way ticket. But so did Danny, he groused to himself.

Strangers again, they sat in different sections. Venturi was glad they didn't sit together. Danny's mood was dark after the painful parting. Venturi didn't hear his laugh ring out at all during the flight.

With little rest for forty-eight hours, Venturi tried to sleep.

Tocumen International Airport in Panama City was not as busy or bustling as the others. They stayed alert but didn't spot a tail.

"No Russians on the radar," Danny muttered as they connected at a car-rental counter. They stopped for party supplies again, this time from the back room of a downtown flower shop. They included military-grade night binoculars, night-vision goggles, military-issue knives, guns, and flash suppressors.

Then they took the main road south.

The Canopy Tower rises well above the thick jungle surrounding it. Hundreds of species of bright-winged birds, toucans, red summer tanagers, and eight different varieties of woodpeckers, flock to the forest, which is also the habitat of monkeys and sloths, according to the tourist brochures at the airport.

The lodge nestled close to the top of a steep hillside; half a mile higher was the observation platform, with a rest area below.

They encountered a gaggle of bird-watchers upon arrival. Three middle-aged couples in comfortable shoes hiking down the hill from the observation tower, binoculars around their necks, bird books in hand.

"Look!" cried one of the women, giddy with excitement at a rare sighting. "There it is again!"

A huge white-bodied bird circled, riding wind drafts high above the forest.

Cameras clicked, binoculars were raised. They were jubilant.

"It's a rare scavenger," one of the men explained. "Never seen in North America and rarely here."

"What is it?" Danny asked.

"A King vulture!" they chorused.

They watched the bird vanish into the clouds, then went on their way.

"I don't like it," Danny said. "A bad omen."

The accommodations were far from four-star. Small rooms, no air-conditioning, simple meals, few luxuries. They checked into rooms across the hall from each other on the same floor. No messages. No one called. "I guess we wait," Danny said.

They did a recon of the lodge and its outbuildings, then climbed the half mile uphill to the deserted observation tower, took in the view, and memorized the narrow paths through the dense forest. Few vehicles. Other than their own, most seemed to belong to the hotel.

Back at the lodge, they ate dinner in the dining room and found themselves the only guests. The bird-watchers they had seen must have departed. The meal was simple, served with red wine.

As night fell, the jungle outside their open windows came alive with exotic sounds and smells.

Keri would love the place, Venturi thought, wondering if she'd found the rare white ghost orchid she had hunted in the Everglades.

Danny ranted against Jimmy Carter, lamenting the loss of the Canal Zone's strategic advantage. "Worst president we ever had. Should've stuck to growing peanuts."

"He's a better ex-president than he was in office," Venturi said.

"Nah, he runs around shooting off his mouth like a nasty little old lady with no clue what he's talking about. Guess he's senile and forgot the mess he made with Cuba and Iran. Remember the hostages?"

"Looks like no action tonight," Venturi said.

Even the hotel staff seemed to have vanished, leaving them alone in the deserted dining room.

"Think they wanted us out of the way," Danny said, "so they could go after Micheline and the others without us interfering?"

"Nothing would surprise me," Venturi said. "We should stay in the same room tonight."

"Bro, I'm a married man. You need to find yourself a woman."

"I'm serious. We'll take turns standing watch."

"Actually, I was about to suggest that myself. Toss you for first watch."

Danny crossed the hall and rolled up some towels and a bath mat to make his bed look occupied as Venturi checked on the others by phone. Andrew's fishing boat had sailed on schedule. Richard was at an Irish dance festival with his tourist group.

Micheline surprised him. She was at the convent. "They were expecting me," she whispered. "The nuns are wonderful. I feel so safe here in my little room, a crucifix over my bed and a Bible beside me. I'm glad I followed Danny's advice. He has my best interests at heart. Is he all right? Can I talk to him?"

"Briefly," he said, as Danny walked in and locked the door behind him.

"It's spooky out there," he reported. "Dark as a coal mine. The power's out. Not a light in the place, bro. Not a sound. I don't like it."

Venturi offered him the phone. "Micheline wants to say hello. Guess where she is?"

"Better not be on a fishing boat," he muttered. "I'll take first watch."

He sat on the floor, his back to the wall between the door and a large window, his gun in one hand, the phone in the other.

"*Bonjour,* baby." His soft murmurs into the phone lulled Venturi into an uneasy sleep. He had taken his mattress off the bed and shoved it into a corner away from the windows. Lying there, a .45-caliber handgun and an assault rifle beside him, he dreamed

506

of Miami. He awoke still feeling the city's hypnotic pull on his psyche.

He blinked. Danny was still on the phone. How long had they been talking? He listened, drowsy, wondering what time it was.

"Love you, love your body, darlin'. If I could be there I'd rub your back and kiss you all over. What are you wearing? . . . I can't wait to lie down beside my warrior woman again. I can never find the words to say how much I love you. Kiss the kids, and tell them Daddy loves them." His words faded as Venturi relaxed and dozed again.

Sergey's cell rang, like an electric shock in the dark, just after 2 a.m. It seemed even later. Danny silently handed him the phone. Venturi cleared his throat and shook his head before he answered, hoping to sound wide awake and alert.

"Mister Venturi? Vasily here." The slick, oily voice sounded energized and in control. "I hope you and your friend find your rooms comfortable."

"They'll do. I've been wondering where you were. Let's meet at last. Are you here? On the premises?" Silently, he rolled off the mattress and crouched in the dark near the window, the gun in his hand.

"In a manner of speaking. On the observation deck, half a mile up the hill."

"Come down, we can meet in the dining room."

"Come up. Someone else is here, an interested party eager to meet with you in private."

"When?" he asked, aware he'd be crazy to go.

"Now. What better time?"

"It's private down here, and easier. I'm unfamiliar with the grounds. There are no lights. It's the dead of night in a jungle."

"I'm from New York myself and in the same position."

"You picked the place," Venturi said shortly.

Vasily sighed deeply. "I thought it was of utmost importance to you to meet as soon as possible."

"How about dawn?"

"Our interested party has pressing commitments. Time is fleeting. Does the dark disturb you?"

"No. Do you fear the light of day?"

The Russian laughed unpleasantly. "This meeting was arranged to accommodate you. If you're no longer interested, we can revert to our prior status and see what transpires."

"I wouldn't have come if I wasn't interested. But it's foolhardy to climb up there on strange turf in the dark."

"What strange turf? Birds are most active at dawn. Every day tourists hike to the observation deck through the dark before dawn. The trail is well marked, used by bird aficionados, tourists, even senior citizens. It's easy to find, even in the dark. Pretend to be a tourist," Vasily wheedled.

Venturi sighed, weary of cat-and-mouse. Danny, his face in shadow across the room, gave a thumbs-up and whispered, "Go. Go."

"All right. Where are you exactly?"

"Up on the deck, of course, where the view is most excellent. I will watch for your approach."

"I don't like it," Venturi said.

Danny smeared camo paint on his face and the backs of his hands, then passed it to Venturi.

"Didn't think I'd be using this stuff again."

"It's the new one. Repels insects, too." Danny picked up a pair of night-vision binoculars. "I'll see how many are out there."

Venturi was still donning his gear.

From a room above them Danny looked down on the jungle paths between the lodge and the observation deck.

"I'm seeing six armed between here and the deck," he said softly into his radio. "Two moving around on either side of the main path halfway up, at that huge ficus. One stationary at the front foot of the tower, two others at three and eleven o'clock along the path, another at five o'clock about a hundred yards up. I'll take him first."

"Roger that," Venturi said. "What about the tower?"

"I only make out two up on the deck, one overweight, the other about our size."

Danny ran down the stairs taking two at a time. "I always knew we'd be shooting at Russians someday," he said as they met in the hall. Locked and loaded, they slipped out into the night.

CHAPTER FORTY-TWO

"Like old times, bro," Danny whispered. He drew his knife from the scabbard. "You and me against the world."

"Watch yourself," Venturi said. He adjusted his night-vision goggles, looked up, and realized he was talking to the dark. Danny had already disappeared into the steamy night like a ghost.

Venturi moved stealthily up the hill, listening for sounds and movement in the jungle, most alert for what he didn't hear, insects and native wildlife reacting to intruders with sudden silence.

Danny's quiet voice spoke in his earpiece. "One down."

Danny was the best. He hadn't heard a thing.

He didn't see the man who should have been on his side of the path halfway up the hillside. He stopped to listen, then heard whispers in the dark and smelled cigarette smoke. The two were together on the far side.

Before he could take action, he heard the *thup thup* of gunfire from a silencer-equipped weapon.

He heard Danny's whisper in his earpiece. "Three down."

Three to go. Venturi accelerated his pace toward the deck.

A brief, low cry in the night stopped him in his tracks, unsure if it came from man, bird, or beast.

Someone else heard it, too.

He heard a murmured exclamation. He didn't know much Russian but believed it to be "What was that?"

As if in answer, the whisper in his earpiece said, "Four down." That had to be the man at eleven o'clock. The exclamation had to have come from the one at three o'clock. He moved toward the sound and saw him holding an assault rifle, staying low.

He fired once, and the man fell. He moved up, crouched beside him, took his gun, and checked his pulse. Weak, erratic, going, going, gone. He couldn't be sure, couldn't risk a light, but the dead man appeared to fit the description of Ivan Kazakov, the burglar who had triggered all of this.

"Five down," he whispered into his radio.

"Roger that. About time. Can't see six. Go see the Russian."

Venturi circled through the undergrowth to the rear of the tower and threw his rope up to one of the metal supports. The hook caught, with a metallic *click* that resounded like an echo. He froze for a moment, then heard muffled words less than fifty yards away, a one-sided conversation as though on a cell phone.

From sixty feet above, someone on the observation deck must have called the lookout down below.

He began to rappel, hand over hand, up to the deck, hoping that Danny had his back if he was spotted from below.

He pulled himself up onto the wooden platform and lay still, listening for a moment, then began to inch forward, toward the small, slightly elevated screened-in room at the center.

When he and Danny had checked it out earlier that day there was only a rough, round wooden table and a few chairs inside.

Now a Coleman lantern, its light turned down low, and a pistol — it looked like a Russian-made GSh-18 — were on the table, along with a bottle of whiskey and paper cups. An AK-47 rested against one of the chairs. Two men inside spoke in low voices as they peered down into the darkness through binoculars. Both wore suits, strangely out of place in the wilderness setting. The Russian — a bald, shorter, mustachioed man — was overweight and looked rumpled. The taller man's attire was expensive and well tailored. His voice sounded sickeningly, gut-wrenchingly familiar, but in that moment more than two thousand miles out of context, Venturi couldn't instantly place it. Then he did.

He kicked the door open easily and burst into the room, gun in hand.

Both men looked astonished, as though he'd dropped from the sky.

"Surprised?" he asked. "I thought you expected me."

The paunchy Russian dropped his binoculars and lunged for the pistol. Venturi upended the table. The lantern hit the floor and went out. The whiskey bottle and the weapon spun across the wooden planks just out of the Russian's reach. Venturi snatched up the rifle.

The other man never moved.

He and Venturi stared, their eyes locked for a long moment.

"Why?" Venturi finally asked, outwardly calm, reeling inside. It all made sense now. How could he be so wrong about someone he trusted?

He remembered Keri saying: "If it involves sex or money, trust no one."

"Don't move," he said.

"As you can see, Michael, I haven't. I know you too well."

At gunpoint, Venturi ordered the two men to right the table, pick up the lantern, and sit down.

The Russian sat quietly, still breathing hard from his recent exertion.

"We're here to talk," Venturi said, his heart weary. "Tell me, Jim. You owe me that much."

"I owe you a helluva lot more," said his former FBI colleague, friend, and financial adviser. Jim Dance smiled ironically, lowered his head, and massaged both temples. "I wish you hadn't spilled that good whiskey. I could use a drink right now."

"Talk to me, Jim."

"Obviously, you're now aware that my career path, from the bureau into business, failed miserably.

"My wife is young and likes to live large. She wants . . . wants, wants bigger, better everything. Her lust for life, her enthusiasm, her acquisitiveness was contagious. She knew how to make me feel successful, as though I could work miracles. So I quit

515

government work to do so, for her. Unfortunately, I was a better FBI agent than a financial adviser."

"But you were successful," Venturi said. "The big office, the assistant, the new house in Connecticut."

"All for show. If you want to be a millionaire, live like one, look like one, act as though you are one, and it will happen. That's the theory. That's what the book said. Unfortunately, I gave bad advice and made worse investments.

"When I had nowhere else to turn, I laundered money for the Russian mob — our friend, Vasily, here. When things got worse I was forced to use a great deal of their money. Soon they wanted their cash or my head."

Vasily nodded in agreement.

"Tiffany liked going to Vegas. I tried to win the money back. Remember what a good poker player I was?

"A losing streak coincided with my attempts to recoup. The cards can sense desperation. I couldn't do anything right and lost more. Now I owed money to the casinos, the Russian mob, my creditors, and the IRS. Only one way to stay afloat. I dipped into your portfolio, over and over.

Based on your prior disinterest, it seemed safe."

"So, all those positive financial statements . . ."

"Bogus. Faked." He sighed. "Right about that time Tiffany decided she wanted a baby and we got pregnant. She also wanted a lake house for weekends. I was out of my league, under pressure, with an expensive lifestyle to maintain. Remember, I still pay alimony and child support to my first wife. My oldest is starting college.

"Your money saved me, Michael. I thought I could replace it eventually. My luck had to change. But it got worse. Suddenly, out of left field, you began to draw on the money. Again and again. Spending like a drunken sailor. A house, a boat, God knows what else. I couldn't let you keep it up. I needed that cushion. Only one way to stop you — destroy your reputation, send you to jail, frame you for the murdered witnesses."

"Now I remember," Venturi said. "We did work on two of those relocations together before you left the bureau. But what about the third witness, Cuccinelli?"

"Not difficult to find. My ex-brother-in-law, still with the bureau, worked with you on it. He has the proverbial loose lips after a few drinks."

"You killed them?"

"Of course not, Michael. I'm not that off track, wouldn't have the stomach. That's where Vasily and his organization stepped in."

Vasily nodded modestly, as though proud of his role.

"They agreed to assist if it meant complete restitution with interest of their laundered money and future use of my services in their various enterprises. When I heard from a friend in the Marshals office that you'd apparently weathered the storm, Vasily sent one of his people to take your computer. We had to learn precisely what you were doing, where the money was going, in order to stop the bleeding." He frowned. "I'm still puzzled. My best guess is that you were relocating individuals at your own expense for reasons that totally escape me. I was sure you'd stop if they were killed. It worked, temporarily.

"I didn't expect you to react so aggressively, or swiftly. Frankly, Michael, I liked you better when you were drinking — numb, grieving, and somewhat ineffective. We were friends," he conceded, "but things change." He shrugged, his pale eyes suddenly wet. "Love happens. My God, Michael," he said passionately. "You know what love is! You had it and lost it. I didn't want to lose my wife. You of all people should understand that."

Venturi noted Dance's use of the past tense. "How is she?"

"The financial pressures severely strained our relationship." His sigh was ragged. "She changed the locks and hired a lawyer. She's seeing someone. But I'm hoping everything will settle down after this, and I'll be able to go home."

It was all about the blood money, Venturi thought, the settlement he'd refused to touch for so long. Sex and money.

"How can you believe that now," he asked Dance, "with blood on your hands? You think Tiffany will visit you in prison?"

Vasily smugly raised an eyebrow.

"No," Dance said. "Because I won't be there. Sorry, Michael."

Vasily smiled, eyes moving to the face of his watch.

The truth hit Venturi with sudden clarity. *Jim Dance isn't quietly confessing because it's good for the soul. He's buying time.*

Reinforcements. They were killing time until the reinforcements arrived.

He tried without success to raise Danny on the radio and saw the knowing glance the two men exchanged.

"Concerned about your driver?" Vasily inquired, his pudgy hands folded on the table in front of him.

"He's not my driver. He's a U.S. Marine who is neutralizing your people as we speak."

"I'm sorry, Michael," Dance repeated, his expression maudlin.

Several bursts of automatic-weapons fire erupted below. Venturi could tell they came from a number of weapons fired from different distances.

Dance and Vasily perked up and exchanged smiles.

"Surrender, Michael," Dance said. "You have no way out."

"Call them off," Venturi told the Russian. "Pick up that phone and call them off right now or I'll kill you."

Vasily's mouth opened and closed like that of a fish yanked from the sea. He stared at the phone and considered his options.

Several sniper shots cracked down below.

"He won't do it," Dance told the Russian confidently. "He can't. I know him."

Venturi slammed Vasily on the side of the head. Hard, with the gun. "Call them. Now! Now! Now!" He struck another blow with each word. Blood trickled down the Russian's pale forehead as he tried to shield himself. The final blow knocked him off his chair. Venturi towered over him, menacing in his face paint and camouflage gear, jerked him to his feet, and sat him back down.

"Now!"

Rapid gunfire rattled the jungle below.

Vasily clutched the phone, hands shaking.

"Tell them to cease fire!"

He did. They heard shouts below. Within seconds, the gunfire stopped. The jungle was quiet.

Dance began to look uncomfortable.

"And you," Venturi told him. "Use your phone, call your partner in New York. Call him at home. I don't care what time it is. Instruct him to wire the entire balance left in my account to my Miami bank at once."

He raised the gun as if to bludgeon him, as well.

Dance quickly snapped the phone open. "I'm disappointed in you, Michael. You were more likable when you considered it blood money and refused to touch it."

He licked his dry lips and punched in the number. Venturi took the phone to verify to whom he was speaking. "I have Mr. Dance on the line," he said. "Hold please."

Venturi handed Dance the phone with one hand while the other nestled the barrel of his .45 automatic against his forehead, his finger on the trigger.

Dance followed orders. "That's right," he concluded. "To the same account as the prior dispersals. ASAP. I'll explain when I get back."

As Venturi dismantled both phones, Dance lunged for the gun.

As they struggled for the weapon, Vasily hit Venturi with a sloppy tackle that threw him off balance. He and Dance fell over a chair as they fought. The Coleman lantern toppled off the table and went out again.

"Get the other gun," Dance shouted to Vasily. "Get that gun! Shoot him! Shoot him!"

His bald head reflecting faint light from the moon and stars overhead, the Russian began an unsteady creep like a giant baby, huffing and puffing, reaching out, groping blindly in the shadows for the gun on the floor.

Dance, though twenty years older than Venturi, was fit and surprisingly strong. He'd almost succeeded in wrenching the weapon away when Venturi pulled a smaller .32-caliber handgun from his boot and shot him in the chest.

Vasily's groping fingers clutched something eagerly as Venturi wheeled to face him, his finger tightening on the trigger. He blinked. It looked at first as though the Russian had found the gun in the dark and was pressing the barrel to his own chin in a suicidal gesture. But it was no gun; it was the whiskey bottle.

The Russian closed his eyes to block out the gun pointed at his head and sucked the dregs from the bottle.

Venturi found the pistol, left the man huddled on the floor licking the empty bottle's rim, snatched up the rifle, and, with fear in his heart, went to find Danny.

CHAPTER
FORTY-THREE

He left the observation deck the way he'd come, only faster, and hit the ground running toward the last place he'd seen Danny.

The air smelled like blood and gunpowder.

From the deck he'd seen six or seven Russians regrouping on the central path, awaiting new orders.

He ignored them and tried again to raise Danny on the radio. Nothing. Then he stumbled over something. A corpse, eyes open, skin still warm, still clutching a rifle. A stranger.

He spun around to draw down on a small movement in a thicket several feet away, then heard a ragged gasp.

"Danny?" He dropped to the ground, pulled away the palm fronds Danny had used as cover, and found him in a sitting position, his back against the trunk of a banana tree, his rifle across his knees, his head fallen forward. His knife glinted beside him; the automatic was still in his hand. Empty casings were scattered on the jungle floor. He'd been trying to reload.

Venturi felt for a heartbeat, then searched frantically for the source of all the blood.

"Stop groping me, you perv," Danny mumbled. "I'm hit."

"I know," Venturi said, relieved to hear his voice. "Where?"

"My right thigh, nicked the femoral artery. Took one in the left shoulder, another in my side. Can't feel my legs."

Danny had tied a tourniquet built into the new combat uniforms above the wound in his right leg. Blood still bubbled from a gaping hole in his side.

"Crap," he said, as Venturi cut away his clothes. "Hell of a place to die, bro. This ain't no blaze of glory. Shit. This ain't nothing, not even a damn war." He gasped in pain. "Tell Luz I love her. Tell my kids I was a Marine."

"Tell 'em yourself." Venturi applied pressure to the bleeding wound in Danny's side with his hand, ripped open a QuikClot pack with his teeth, and pressed it over the wound. Danny cried out in pain as he tore open a second pack, loosened the tourniquet, and applied it to stop the bleeding.

" 'Member the night you decked me at your place because of Micheline?"

"Yeah, Danny."

"I never got hit harder. You nearly knocked me out, man."

"I'm sorry."

"Micheline." Danny swallowed, in severe pain. "Don't tell her," he gasped. "I don't want her to know. She's been through enough."

Mike paused to stare into the starry sky above the tree canopy. "Relax, Danny. It isn't there. It's not there."

"What?"

"I just saw your goddamn Blackboard in the Sky. Your name ain't on it. I see a lot of Russian names. Jim Dance's name. But not yours."

"Get the hell outta here, Mike, while you still can."

"You're right. It's time to go." He hoisted Danny over his shoulder in a fireman's carry.

Danny groaned. "Leave me here!"

"Don't talk like a loser. You only win when you believe you will, and all that shit," Venturi said. Staggering beneath the weight, slipping down the hillside, eyes searching the darkness, he moved as quickly as he could toward the lodge.

A gunman loomed just off the path, shouted a warning, and raised his rifle. Venturi held his fire. If he started shooting, everybody would. He shouted back, "Vasily ordered cease-fire," and kept moving.

Danny stopped moaning and lost consciousness. But as Venturi stumbled toward the lodge, his hand found Danny's wrist, found his pulse. Though weak and thready, it did not stop.

Then he heard shouts and looked back. He saw what he feared most. Someone, it had to be Vasily, was out on the observation deck swinging the lantern, yelling commands.

He should have shot that son of a bitch when he had the chance.

He ran all out as the gunfire began.

A round buzzed past his head like an angry wasp and slammed into a nearby tree trunk.

He hit the porch sprinting, stumbled and fell, then dragged Danny through the door and behind the front desk for cover.

They charged the lodge, shooting as they came. He hit the floor as bullets splintered the woodwork overhead. He fired back. One fell. The others scattered.

Danny mumbled something unintelligible in the noise and the panic. He said it again.

"Mike, I have a number."

He's delirious, Venturi thought. "Take it easy, Danny."

"Call, give 'em the number, tell 'em what's happening. They'll get us out."

"Who?" Venturi shoved the barrel of his rifle through a torn window screen and returned fire.

"Here." Danny reached painfully toward him, trying to hand him a blood-soaked cell phone. "It's programmed. Just call. Give 'em my ID number." He muttered a six-digit number interspersed with letters.

"Damn!" Something wet splashed across the screen. Gasoline. The smell was overwhelming. It reminded Venturi of the day they burned human bones and a car in the Everglades. He could see the flames.

He managed to get Danny to his feet but his legs were useless. Venturi dragged him toward the back door. "They're about to burn us out, buddy. Time to get outta Dodge. Let's hit the road."

He thought five or six shooters were left. At least half would be waiting out back.

As he dragged Danny out the back door, he heard the *whoosh,* saw the fireball behind them, and felt the heat.

Two gunmen dashed full tilt around the side of the building. He shot them both.

"Gimme my gun, bro. Gimme a gun." Danny was spitting up blood but still talking.

Venturi slapped the gun from his boot into Danny's hand and closed his fingers around it, as he half-carried him toward the car. "Can you hold onto it? Can you fire?"

His answer was a shot fired past his ear and a scream from the man it hit. "One shot, one kill. That's Marine training, bro."

He got Danny into the car, slid into the driver's seat, fired a barrage from the rifle, then floored it. The car kicked up dust along the dirt road as Danny fired two more shots out the window.

Danny looked puzzled. Blood and mucus dripped from his mouth and nose. "Is this what we used to call fun, bro?"

"It is, if we live through it."

As they careened toward Panama City more than forty minutes away, Venturi knew in his heart that Danny wouldn't make it. He wasn't even sure where the damn hospital was, or if it was any good.

"Call, give 'em the number," Danny mumbled before passing out again. The gun dropped from his hand and thudded onto the floorboard.

Venturi glanced down to see where it had fallen and saw a gleaming, dark, fast-growing puddle. Danny was bleeding again.

Flames filled the sky behind them and darkness lay ahead. He made the call.

The man who answered had a Southern accent and sounded bored.

"I was told to give you this ID number." Venturi repeated it slowly, hoping to hell he had it right.

"Where is he?" The voice suddenly became interested.

"With me. He's badly injured, unconscious, shot several times. I applied Quick-Clot patches, but he's bleeding again. I'm on the Gamboa Road headed for Panama City. It's forty minutes out. He won't make it. I need help. Is there anything you can do? Is there a doctor, a clinic, a closer place to take him?"

"And who are you?"

He identified himself. "We served in the U.S. Marine Corps together, Force Recon."

"Where are you exactly?"

He said they had just left the lodge.

"Can you return to that location?"

"No, hostiles are in control. The place is on fire. They shot him."

"Who are they?"

"Russians."

"Did you say Russians?"

"That's affirmative."

The pause was so long he thought he'd lost the connection. A second voice came on the line. "Turn off at a dry riverbed approximately five miles ahead on your right. Somebody will pick you up there soonest. Where is he hit?"

Venturi told him. "He's lost a lot of blood, can't use his legs."

"Damn. Do what you can to keep him going till we get there."

"How will I know you?"

"You can't miss us."

He reached the turnoff, stopped, took Danny out of the car, and did what he could to make him comfortable. Still unconscious, he was bleeding from the thigh again. Venturi applied direct pressure, then used the tourniquet.

Did he make a mistake, he wondered, admitting they'd been at the lodge? The scene back there would be hard to explain. But keeping Danny alive took priority.

He saw headlights. A car sped by up on the road. His first instinct was to flag it down. But what if it was the Russians?

He didn't like the way Danny was breathing.

"It's okay," he told him over and over. "I gave them the number. I made the call."

He hoped Danny heard. He didn't seem

to. What if no one came? He fought the urge to give up waiting and race toward Panama City. How could he let Danny just slip away? He had to do something. He couldn't wait. He opened the car door to move him into the backseat, then heard something in the distance. Was it his imagination? No. An aircraft. A chopper? Could it be what they were waiting for?

It hovered overhead. He blinked as it trained a blinding spotlight on the car, circled, and landed nearby. The powerful blades pounded the air into a miniature hurricane.

Two medics scrambled out and ran toward them, keeping low.

"Lt. Venturi?" one shouted.

"Yes, sir. He's over here."

They took over, cut away the rest of his clothes, and checked his wounds. He saw the looks they exchanged.

"You can save him," he said, as they inserted an IV with 500ml of Hextend. "He's strong. Had to be to make it this far."

"We'll take it from here," the taller one said as they lifted Danny onto a gurney.

"I'm coming with him."

He was given a curt nod.

"Where are we headed?" he asked as they ascended into a dark sky. "Panama City?"

"Hell, no," the pilot said.

"What the hell is this thing?" Venturi asked as the chopper shifted and sprouted wings.

"An Osprey," the pilot said. "But we'll deny it."

Venturi didn't know who else to call as they prepared to land in Miami, where medics train to fight panic and chaos on the battlefield. She answered on the first ring.

"It's me," he said. "Sorry to wake you. Sorry about everything. I need you, Keri."

"What's wrong?"

"I've got bad news."

CHAPTER
FORTY-FOUR

Danny's heart stopped twice on the flight to Miami. The medics brought him back and kept him clinging to life until they landed at the hospital's helipad. The medics waiting on the roof ignored the Osprey, focusing only on the patient who was rushed to surgery.

Venturi felt numb, sick, and dreaded being debriefed. How could he attempt to justify what now had to be an international incident?

He had washed up and donned a set of scrubs during the flight and now waited, head in hands, outside the operating room. Doctors told him nothing, but he heard the call for more blood, closed his eyes, and prayed.

Keri appeared. Calm, cool, and compassionate, as always. "He's with the best," she assured him.

"He looked gray," he told her. The image

still shocked him. "His lips were blue. He's like my brother, Keri. He *is* my brother. He's all I've got."

"No, he isn't," she said matter-of-factly. She sat beside him, her arm around him. "You have Victoria and, like it or not, you have me. What happened? How was he shot? Who shot him?"

"Russians. We were in a firefight. In Panama."

"Panama?" Her brow crinkled.

Hospital types appeared with clipboards, admittance forms, and questions. The aircraft had long since gone, but a crew member, a man Venturi had assumed was the copilot, intervened.

He told hospital officials that Danny was shot by heavily armed seagoing pirates who tried to hijack his sports-fishing boat in international waters off Bimini.

Local authorities had no jurisdiction. Federal agents were handling the case, he said, and showed his identification. He instructed that information be released only to Danny's immediate family.

Keri held Venturi's hand, listened, and said nothing.

A hospital employee asked for Danny's next of kin.

"She hasn't been notified yet," Keri said.

"His wife is my patient, the mother of three small children, and more than eight months into a difficult pregnancy. I wanted to assess the situation before telling her in person."

When they left, Venturi buried his face in her neck.

For days he monitored the news for information out of Panama. The lodge had burned to the ground, stories said, apparently torched by vandals. No injuries were reported.

Who cleaned up the mess, disposed of the dead and injured? He didn't ask.

An old friend in NYPD intelligence reached out to ask if he had a beef with Vasily. The Russian was back at the same old stand in Brooklyn, peddling drugs, porn, and prostitution, though his crew seemed smaller. A number of hoodlums were out of the loop. Some had been reported missing by worried families.

Police intelligence heard that Vasily had been mentioning Venturi's name in anger. They wanted him to have a heads-up that the Russian mobster may have put a hit out on him. They wondered why.

Venturi thanked his contact and said he had no idea why the man would do such a thing. It had to be a mistake.

Danny walked out of the hospital, using a cane, ten days later. He refused to sit in a wheelchair despite strict hospital policy. By the time he left, the nurses, aides, and doctors were all in love with him, his wife, and his children.

That was the good news.

The bad news was that Venturi had been subpoenaed to appear in front of a Washington, D.C., grand jury to answer questions about WITSEC, the Salvi case, the armored-car robbery, the murdered witnesses, his activities in Florida, and trips made out of the country. They wanted to see his passport, his financial records, and his income tax returns. They also asked for the names of witnesses who could corroborate his testimony. Vicki was mentioned by name, among others.

He also needed to prepare a defense in the wrongful-death action filed by the parents of the two little girls murdered by Gino Salvi.

He discussed his complicated future in Danny's study one night after dinner.

"The FBI, the Justice Department, federal prosecutors, the IRS, and the Russian mob are on my case," he concluded. He had already consulted a Miami lawyer and hired another to represent him in Washington.

"You know how our justice system works," Danny said. "It may not be perfect, but it's the best in the world. You know what you have to do, bro. You have no choice."

"I hate the idea, but you're right," Michael said. "I have to respond to the subpoena and answer their questions. Vicki's coming with me. She's willing to testify."

"So am I," Danny offered. "Luz and the kids will have to come along. She's close to her due date. After all that's happened, I have to be there when the baby arrives."

Venturi explained it all to Keri. She also volunteered.

"I won't let Luz travel without me in her condition. She's been under so much stress. I didn't see her through this pregnancy so a total stranger could deliver this baby. And I want to be there for you, Mikey."

"You don't have to," he said. "It's high profile, a big deal, a huge sacrifice."

She was adamant. "Do you mind if Maheen comes along? I've been in contact with a reconstructive surgeon in Baltimore. I'd like him to see her while we're there."

Venturi had no objection.

Keri notified the hospital that she'd be away for at least a week.

Danny chartered a plane to fly them from Miami to Dulles Airport.

No one was left to care for Scout and Venturi hated to board him, so he booked a pet-friendly hotel and the dog went with them.

They left Miami in what pilots call severe clear, a brittle cobalt blue sky with not a cloud in sight. Perfect flying weather.

They took off early, with Danny at the controls. Venturi had a 4 p.m. briefing set with his lawyers and was scheduled to testify at 11 a.m. the following day.

The event was highly anticipated in the press. Several columnists and TV pundits predicted that the future of the Witness Protection Program might hang on the revelations to come.

A *Miami News* reporter showed up at the airport to interview the departing witnesses. Resigned to what lay ahead, they were friendly; they smiled, waved, and boarded the plane.

The flight, skirting the East Coast, took slightly more than an hour.

A number of Venturi's former colleagues at the U.S. Marshals Service were also on the witness list.

Ruth Ann, the office manager, answered a phone call shortly after noon.

Coworkers heard her cry out and saw her rush into the chief's office, her expression stricken.

"What's wrong?" he demanded.

"Something terrible happened! Michael Venturi, his friend's family, a doctor, all of them . . ." She burst into tears.

It took several moments before she could catch her breath and speak. "Their flight exploded in midair," she gasped, "off the Georgia coast east of Savannah. The passengers and pilot of a Delta jet and witnesses on the ground saw the fireball. The plane went down in pieces."

The chief stared at her in disbelief. "Survivors?"

She clutched her arms, as though in pain, and shook her head.

"All the Coast Guard and rescue ships found was an oil slick, wreckage, and scattered luggage.

"They're gone. All of them."

ACKNOWLEDGMENTS

I am grateful to pilot Tim Boyens, that high flying-captain of the sky, to the ever cool Daniel Eydt of the Miami-Dade Police Bomb Squad, to Susan Fleming, whose resourceful and dedicated work always inspires me, to the adventurous globetrotting journalist Sibohan Morrissey, and to artist Carol Garvin, who captures Miami's true essence.

Former Miami Shores Police Chief Dick Masten, the world's greatest cop, generously shared his expertise, as did former NASA assistant specialist Larry Painter, and Gary Alan Ruse.

I owe special thanks to the friendship and fertile imaginations of Rodney Toth, Mitzi Major, Char Eberly, Dr. Larry Baretta, Lynn Fitzpatrick, and super tenor, Dale Kitchell.

The brave and beautiful redhead with a gun, Lt. Joy Gellatly of the Savannah

Chatham Metropolitan Police Department, never lets me down. Neither do the three other glamorous redheads, Mimi Gadinsky, Teresa Lane, and Marilyn Lane: my chief accomplice, coconspirator, and getaway driver.

Thank you to Pauline Winick, Howard Kleinberg, Mort and Sybil Lucoff, and to all my other brilliant and eloquent Sesquipedalian friends, including my steadfast and accomplished buddies: Patricia Fussell Keen and Dr. Howard Gordon: surgeon, pilot, and raconteur extraordinaire.

Terry Bauer and U.S. Marine Sgt. Scott Jones didn't hesitate to share with a stranger.

My mouthpiece, Florida's foremost criminal defense attorney Joel Hirschhorn; my pastor, the Reverend Dr. Garth Thompson; and my friend Leonard Wolfson do their best to keep me out of trouble. Not an easy job.

Dr. Stephen J. Nelson, Chairman of the Florida Medical Examiners Commission and Chief Medical Examiner for the 10th District of Florida, and William C. Cagney III are always there when I need them, along with Shane Willens, his girls Crystal and Angel, Renee Turolla, David M. Thornburgh, Ann Hughes, Mary Finn, Kay

Spitzer, Norry Lynch, Edward Gadinsky, and my friend Juan Pujol, who can open any door — without a key.

My heartfelt thanks go to Karen Sampson and her late husband and partner, forensic genius William Sampson. He will always be alive in our hearts.

Dr. Mel Yoken, *Miami Herald* reporter Andrea Torres, and retired *Herald* veteran Arnold Markowitz all helped with this book. As did the famous Ruth Regina, Simon & Schuster's meticulous and creative Mara Lurie, ace private investigator Ralph N. Garcia, and the astonishing Glenn Lane. They all have more great stories than any newspaper, and they are willing to share.

Thanks as always to my agent, Michael Congdon; to my editor, Mitchell Ivers; and to Katie Grimm, Katie Grinch, and Cristina Concepcion.

And a big, long-distance smack on the lips to the tough and savvy Daniel P. Hughes.

Friends are the family you choose.

ABOUT THE AUTHOR

Edna Buchanan commanded *The Miami Herald* police beat for eighteen years, during which she reported the stories of three thousand homicides and won scores of awards, including the Pulitzer Prize in 1986 and the 2001 George Polk Award for Career Achievement in Journalism. She attracted international acclaim for her classic true crime memoirs, *The Corpse Had a Familiar Face,* reissued by Pocket Books in 2004, and *Never Let Them See You Cry.* Her first novel of suspense, *Nobody Lives Forever,* was nominated for an Edgar Award. In 1992, Buchanan introduced Britt Montero, a Cuban-American reporter, in *Contents Under Pressure.* Montero's adventures in crime continued through eight novels; the most recent was *Love Kills,* in 2007. Her first entry in the Cold Case Squad series was *Cold Case Squad,* published in 2004, followed by *Shadows*. In addition to seventeen books, Buchanan has written numerous short stories, articles, essays, and book reviews. She lives in Miami.